A TOM MARL[illegible]

SNIPER ALLEY

NEW YORK TIMES #1 BESTSELLER **TONY LEE** WRITING AS

JACK GATLAND

Hooded Man MEDIA
INSPIRATION • PRODUCTION • PUBLICATION

Published by Hooded Man Media.

Cover design by L1graphics

First Edition: February 2025

PRAISE FOR JACK GATLAND

'Fast-paced and action packed, Jack Gatland's thrillers always deliver a punch.'

'This is one of those books that will keep you up past your bedtime, as each chapter lures you into reading just one more.'

'This book was excellent! A great plot which kept you guessing until the end.'

'Couldn't put it down, fast paced with twists and turns.'

'The story was captivating, good plot, twists you never saw and really likeable characters. Can't wait for the next one!'

'Totally addictive. Thoroughly recommend.'

'Moves at a fast pace and carries you along with it.'

'Just couldn't put this book down, from the first page to the last one it kept you wondering what would happen next.'

Also by Jack Gatland

DI DECLAN WALSH BOOKS

LETTER FROM THE DEAD

MURDER OF ANGELS

HUNTER HUNTED

WHISPER FOR THE REAPER

TO HUNT A MAGPIE

A RITUAL FOR THE DYING

KILLING THE MUSIC

A DINNER TO DIE FOR

BEHIND THE WIRE

HEAVY IS THE CROWN

STALKING THE RIPPER

A QUIVER OF SORROWS

MURDER BY MISTLETOE

BENEATH THE BODIES

KILL YOUR DARLINGS

KISSING A KILLER

PRETEND TO BE DEAD

HARVEST FOR THE REAPER

CROOKED WAS HIS CANE

A POCKET FULL OF POSIES

CHEATING MY DESTINY

STAND AND DELIVER

TOM MARLOWE BOOKS

SLEEPING SOLDIERS

TARGET LOCKED

COVERT ACTION

COUNTER ATTACK

STEALTH STRIKE

BROAD SWORD

ROGUE SIGNAL

SNIPER ALLEY

SHADOW THREAT

ELLIE RECKLESS BOOKS

PAINT THE DEAD

STEAL THE GOLD

HUNT THE PREY

FIND THE LADY

BURN THE DEBT

LIAM HARPER BOOKS

FINAL STRIKE

BLOOD RIDGE

DAMIAN LUCAS BOOKS

THE LIONHEART CURSE

STANDALONE BOOKS

THE BOARDROOM

As Tony Lee

STANDALONE

TWELVE TASKS

THE PLAYING CARD WAR

KNAVE OF SPADES

QUEEN OF BLADES

For Mum, who inspired me to write.

For Tracy, who inspires me to write.

For Alan, who read these until the end.

CONTENTS

1

CLEANING ROTA

TWILIGHT CREPT ACROSS LONDON'S FINANCIAL DISTRICT, casting long shadows between the glass and steel monoliths of Canary Wharf, as the last traces of sunlight caught the windows of One Canada Square, transforming the pyramid-topped tower into a glittering beacon against the darkening sky.

Forty-six floors up in the offices of *Durrant Capital,* Tom Marlowe guided an industrial buffer across the trading floor's polished wood and marble surfaces, its steady hum almost a counterpoint to the distant thunder of the last DLR trains of the night below, most likely travelling back towards the east of London. The floor itself was a testament to modern excess; three hundred metres of prime real estate filled with curved trading desks, multi-monitor setups, and ergonomic chairs that probably cost more than Marlowe's monthly salary back in his MI5 days.

Bloomberg terminals blinked in standby mode, their screens reflecting across the half-lit offices, and to Marlowe, the place stank of money, ambition – and something else.

Fear, maybe? The kind of fear that came with knowing too much about what you were doing, which was one reason why Marlowe was there in the first place, smiling politely at other cleaners as he continued his work.

'You know,' Trix Preston's voice crackled through his earpiece, breaking his concentration, 'for someone who made such a dramatic exit from the intelligence community, throwing his toys out of the pram and stomping off in Germany, you sure spend an awful lot of time doing their dirty work.'

Carefully, Marlowe adjusted the buffer's path, maintaining the slightly stooped posture he'd cultivated over the past three nights.

'This isn't really intelligence work,' he muttered, keeping his head down as a late-working analyst hurried past, tablet in hand, not even registering the cleaner's existence. 'This is a favour for Katherine, while following our own remit.'

'Same thing, different letterhead,' Trix replied, her tone amused. 'Although, I suppose taking two bullets for someone does earn them a get-out-of-jail-free card.'

Marlowe hadn't wanted to think about Hong Kong, after all, it was back in his MI5 days, but the memory surfaced unbidden –Katherine Saito's blood on his hands, the crack of sniper fire, the way she'd smiled through the pain and told him *he owed her one.* And now, four years later, he was paying that debt by investigating suspicious patterns in her asset's data.

The fact it involved breaking into one of London's most secure trading houses was just an unfortunate detail if you really thought about it. Of course, the fact it involved breaking into one of St John Steele's biggest allies' buildings, with a chance of finding out exactly what he was up to, was more a *fortunate* one.

'Camera sweep in thirty,' Trix said, her keyboard clicking in the background. 'These trading patterns I'm seeing ... they're not random. Someone's built a perfect prediction engine, then weaponised it.'

'Katherine's asset figured that out, I'm guessing.'

'If they did, look where it got them?'

'Yeah, well, maybe the asset didn't know.'

'I'd say that's pretty likely. These algorithms? They've got intelligence agency fingerprints all over them. CIA, MI6, FSB – everyone's using Durrant's system to manipulate their enemies' markets. Crash an economy here, trigger inflation there ...'

She stopped. A clicking of the keyboard.

'You've got movement in the east stairwell. Looks like the cleaning supervisor doing his rounds.'

Marlowe guided the buffer in a careful arc, using its bulk to shield his movements from the cameras he assumed were concealed in the light fixtures above. Three nights of building this cover – Trevor Orloff, mild-mannered janitor, had taught him the patterns: the guards who actually paid attention, the cameras with blind spots, the areas of the floor deemed too important or, rather, too *unimportant*, to monitor closely.

'I'll try not to look too competent with the buffer then,' he whispered.

'That won't be too difficult for you,' Trix added, with what sounded to be a smirk in her voice. 'I've seen your house-keeping skills. Remember Barcelona last year?'

'That was one time,' Marlowe replied, bending to change the buffer pad – a movement that allowed him to plant another analogue keystroke device under a desk. Old-school tech, but definitely the kind that wouldn't show up on digital sweeps or emit signals that modern security systems might catch. 'And, in my defence, the safe was behind the washing machine.'

'You flooded the entire apartment.'

'It still worked, didn't it?'

He could practically hear Trix's eyeroll down the line. Looking up, he saw the cleaning supervisor had appeared at the far end of the trading floor, clipboard in hand, performing his nightly checks with the methodical precision of someone who took floor maintenance a bit too seriously. Marlowe adjusted his path again, making sure to stay in character – NHS glasses, slight stoop, the practised invisibility that came with wearing a hi-vis jacket in a place where everybody else wore bespoke suits – as he moved aside, merging into the office itself.

'You're two minutes behind, Trevor,' the cleaning supervisor said, but it was more a case of speaking for speaking's sake than an actual reprimand; the supervisor had to look busy, after all. Marlowe simply gave a thumbs up and moved a little quicker down the path.

'Tell me about the hardware again,' he whispered once the supervisor had moved on, using the buffer's noise to cover his voice.

'You know, you really should write these things down,' Trix sighed, though there was affection in her exasperation, an understanding that Marlowe's asking her to repeat herself meant he trusted her implicitly to hold the details.

Rather than couldn't be bothered to learn, Marlowe grinned.

'Durrant's mainframe is isolated and air-gapped, but the trading terminals need real-time data for the algorithms to work, so that's our way in. The devices you're planting will pick up keystroke vibrations and electromagnetic emissions from the monitors.'

'This is old MI5 tech?' Marlowe asked. 'It's not something I recognise, but Marshall Kirk always used to blather on about tech from "the good old days" and all that.'

'Marshall Kirk's a drunk who blathers on about anything,' Trix replied sarcastically. 'This is old KGB tech, updated for the digital age.'

'And how the hell are you getting hold of old KGB tech?'

'I was given it as a present,' Trix admitted, a slight tinge of embarrassment in her voice.

'Who gave you old KGB tech as a gift?'

'It's not important right now.'

Marlowe chuckled. *Sounded like Trix had a new admirer, and someone who knew exactly how to get to her heart.*

'So, go on then,' he said, deciding to change the subject. 'Katherine thinks this'll prove her asset's been set up, yeah?'

'That's the theory. Although ... hang on ...' The typing stopped. 'Movement on the executive floor. Martin Voss just stepped out of his office.'

Marlowe kept buffing, maintaining his rhythm, though his mind raced through the data he had here. Martin Voss, head of security, was an ex-Royal Marines Commandos Colonel, with a reputation for thoroughness that bordered on obsession. Over the last year, he'd vetted every employee in the building, except, ironically, the cleaning staff. They were contracted out, changed regularly, and considered too low to pose a threat.

The perfect cover, assuming you could maintain it.

The problem, though, was that Martin Voss was known for his uncanny memory for faces, and would likely recognise Marlowe – a onetime Corporal in the Royal Marines who'd been dragged in front of him on more than one occasion, and worked under him when he first joined the Corps – on sight.

'He's got company,' Trix added. 'Two more signatures heading down from the executive level. Probably muscle, probably armed.'

'Wonderful.'

'Stay cool. They're doing a regular sweep. You've got about three minutes before they reach the trading floor. Just keep—'

She broke off abruptly.

'No, wait. New problem. David Kelly just entered through the north stairwell.'

Marlowe's hands tightened on the buffer's handle.

'Kelly? *MI6* Kelly? What the hell is he doing here? This wasn't a sanctioned op – that's why Katherine came to us.'

'Yeah, sorry about that. Didn't come up on the system. Looks like he's quit the service, working private sector now. Want to guess which firm?'

'Shouldn't you have known about this before I went in?' Marlowe muttered, irritation creeping into his voice.

'He wasn't on any of the employee files I accessed,' Trix apologised. 'He must be very new.'

'Again, wonderful.' Marlowe kept buffing, his mind racing through scenarios. He'd worried about Voss recognising him, but David Kelly had been close protection during his MI5 days. They'd worked together on joint ops in Berlin, a mess with an arms dealer and a banker's wife he'd had to fix with him ...

Martin Voss be damned. If *anyone* could spot him through his disguise, it would be Kelly.

The quiet of the trading floor was suddenly broken by approaching footsteps. Marlowe hunched further over his buffer, angling away from the sound, but he could hear the footsteps slowing, pausing. In a reflection on a nearby monitor, he caught Kelly's familiar outline – shorter than he remembered, but still moving with that predatory grace that marked him as ex-services.

'Excuse me?' Kelly's voice carried across. 'Should you be here right now?'

'Sorry, running late,' Marlowe continued buffing, hoping the noise would mask any tremor in his voice.

'Name?'

'Orloff. Trevor.'

A pause. Marlowe didn't look up, hoping Kelly had moved on.

'Hey, could you look at me, please?'

Marlowe winced. He knew the moment he turned to face Kelly he'd be exposed, but there was no other option. If he didn't, Kelly would likely pull a gun.

'Go loud?' Trix asked, tension in her voice. In the background, he could hear her fingers flying across keys, probably already working on an exit strategy.

'Not yet,' sighing, Marlowe straightened and turned to face his old colleague.

'Marlowe!' Kelly's eyes widened in surprise, then a grin split his face. 'I bloody thought it was you. Your costumes are as shit as ever. Only Clark Kent can rock the glasses disguise.'

The years hadn't changed Kelly much – same close-cropped hair, same watchful eyes, same way of standing that suggested he was ready for anything.

'Hello, David,' Marlowe greeted him with a calm smile. 'You're looking well. Private sector agrees with you.'

He noted that Kelly's hand was already moving towards his jacket.

'What are you doing here, Tom?' he asked, looking around nervously.

'Would you believe I'm now an expert in basic sanitation?' Marlowe gestured with the buffer. 'Pay's not great, but the hours are flexible.'

The joke fell flat on the empty trading floor. Somewhere in the distance, a printer whirred to life, the sound unnaturally loud in the tension.

'Martin Voss is going to be here in about ninety seconds,' Kelly said, his hand hovering near his jacket. 'And he won't be as understanding as I am. What's the play here, Tom? Because if it's what I think it is ...'

'David, don't.'

'After what happened with your father, the sleeper agents, Rubicon and bloody Orchid, I figured you'd lie low,' Kelly's voice hardened. 'But here you are, in my building, wearing that ridiculous outfit. Either you tell me what's going on, and why Wintergreen sent you, or I raise the alarm.'

'I don't work for Wintergreen anymore,' Marlowe said, his tone darkening.

'I can trigger the fire suppression system, give you some cover, but if I do that, we'll lose any chance of getting what Katherine needs.' In his ear, Trix was back, her voice tight.

Marlowe didn't reply, keeping his eyes on Kelly, measuring distances, options – anything that might help. The buffer sat between them, a half-ton of industrial cleaning equipment that could serve as a weapon if necessary, though it would be a slow, loud one. And Kelly would expect it; they'd likely trained with the same people, if at different times. Kelly would know his moves.

'You know, I vouched for you,' Kelly continued, taking a step closer. 'All that mess with the President's visit, when you almost blew up Westminster and were forced out of MI5, there were ... questions ... about your loyalty. I stood up for you, told McKellan you were one of the good ones.'

'I am one of the good ones,' Marlowe said, releasing the buffer's handle, letting his arms hang loosely at his sides. 'That's why I'm here.'

'Voss and his team are on the move,' Trix warned in his ear. 'Forty seconds.'

Kelly's eyes narrowed.

'You're wearing an earpiece,' he noted. 'Who's running you? Orchid?'

'Nobody runs me anymore, David. You know that.'

'Is it Trix Preston? Is she still in your circle?' Kelly's smile faded. Marlowe stayed silent, and in the pause, Kelly's face shifted, realisation dawning. 'Oh no. Don't tell me this is about Katherine Saito.'

A slight shift in Kelly's stance told Marlowe everything.

He knew something about why Marlowe was here. But nobody should have known.

'Martin Voss incoming,' Trix's voice urged. 'North corridor. Move now.'

But Marlowe held his ground, watching his old friend's face.

'What do you know, David?'

'Enough to know you shouldn't be here, and you're being set up as a patsy,' Kelly exhaled slowly, as his hand finally moved away from his jacket. 'There are things happening at Durrant ... things that ...'

He glanced over his shoulder.

'You need to leave before this gets messy. You were Royal Marines; Voss'll recognise you, and he won't hesitate.'

'It's already messy,' Marlowe replied, stepping forward.

'Katherine's asset's going to disappear if we don't get proof. You know how this works.'

'Someone always disappears, but it helps if they exist in the first place.'

The distant sound of voices grew louder, Martin Voss and his security team approaching from the north corridor as David Kelly stepped back, his enigmatic comment now between the two men. Their footsteps echoed off the marble floors, a steady rhythm matching Marlowe's racing heartbeat.

What did Kelly mean? Was Katherine being played as well? Or was Katherine playing Marlowe?

'Twenty seconds,' Trix urged in his ear, her voice tight. 'Please tell me you have a plan.'

'Are you here with Voss, or did McKellan send you?' Marlowe asked, suspicious. Kelly was too nervous right now; as if he wasn't really supposed to be here, either. Had McKellan sent him in for something similar? Saito was known to both MI5 and MI6, after all.

Kelly seemed to wrestle with something – perhaps loyalty to his new employers, or maybe memories of old friendships. Finally, he reached into his jacket, pulling out a key card and sliding it across a nearby desk.

'Executive elevator,' he whispered, ignoring the question. 'It'll take you to the basement. There's a service exit that's not on the main security grid. I'm going to raise the alarm in ninety seconds. Make it count.'

Marlowe grabbed the card. 'David, don't—'

'Whatever Katherine's got you looking for, be careful. Some stories have a basis in truth, and some are fantasy. And I'll guarantee your name isn't what they know you as here,' Kelly cut him off, his tone sharp.

The voices were nearly upon them now; Marlowe could hear Voss's distinctive Austrian accent, gained from his teen years living with his mother in Styria, giving instructions to his team.

In seconds, they'd be around the corner, and everything would be over.

'Marlowe,' Trix's voice had an edge of panic. 'Remember that thing I said about the fire suppression system? Well, funny story ...'

As she spoke, the trading floor sprinklers burst into life with a hiss, drenching the expensive equipment.

Immediately, alarms blared out.

'That wasn't me,' Trix protested. 'Someone else is in the system. We're being pushed out.'

Kelly spun towards Marlowe, water streaming down his face.

'You bastard—'

'This wasn't us,' Marlowe said quickly, raising his hands, the key card visible.

'Go!' Kelly shouted over the noise. 'Now!'

Marlowe didn't need telling twice. As Voss and his team burst onto the trading floor, he was already moving, the buffer abandoned, Kelly's key card clutched tightly in his hand. Behind him, he could hear Kelly shouting about *an intruder,* directing the security team in the wrong direction.

'Executive elevator, behind you, twenty metres,' Trix guided him. 'And, Marlowe, we've got another problem.'

'Just one?' he muttered.

'Yes, because the car's already moving. Someone's using it and they're heading up to you.'

'Of course they are,' Marlowe muttered, water streaming down his face. The NHS glasses were already becoming a liability, blurring his vision, but he couldn't risk removing them just yet. 'Can you stop it?'

'That's what I'm trying to tell you,' Trix's fingers clattered across her keyboard. 'Someone's locked me out. The entire system's gone dark. Whoever's up there, they ... Tom, they were waiting for me.'

Marlowe reached the elevator, slapping Kelly's keycard against the reader. The display stayed stubbornly dark. Behind him, voices echoed through the deluge – Voss organising search patterns, the heavy tread of security boots on marble.

'Options?' he asked, trying the card again. *Had Kelly given him a dud, hoping he'd be caught, or had they already revoked clearance for Kelly?*

'Working on it. But you should know, the cameras caught your face when the sprinklers hit. In about thirty seconds, facial recognition's going to ping, and then ...'

'Helpful, Trix. Really helpful.' Marlowe looked around, mind racing. The executive elevator was set into an alcove, flanked by wood-panelled walls that probably cost more than his altered church apartment. Above it, a service hatch for maintenance led to ...

'The shaft,' he said. 'If I can get up there ...'

'You're not seriously—' Trix paused. 'No. Absolutely not. The counterweights alone could—'

But Marlowe was already moving, pulling a slim multi-tool from his jacket. The service hatch was secured with standard screws – no security there because *who'd be mad enough to try this?* Twenty seconds of work, and the panel came loose.

'Marlowe, the elevator's stopping. Two floors above. Forty-eighth floor.'

'Executive offices?'

'Penthouse. Technically doesn't exist on any plans I can access.' A pause. 'You're going up there, aren't you?'

Marlowe pulled himself into the service shaft, trying not to think about the drop below.

'If we can't get the information the usual way, the proof's going to be in Durrant's private servers. Want to bet where those are?'

'I'd rather bet on whether Saito's screwing us right now.'

'We'll cross that bridge later,' Marlowe muttered as he looked upwards. The elevator shaft was a cathedral of steel and shadow, cables and counterweights forming a complex geometry in the dim emergency lighting. The elevator car itself was two floors up, stationary now.

More importantly, it blocked his view of whoever had used it.

'Security teams are spreading out,' Trix reported. 'Kelly's buying you time, but Voss isn't stupid. He's already ordered a shutdown of all exits.'

Marlowe climbed, using the maintenance ladder built into the shaft wall, but took care, as his wet shoes made each step treacherous.

'Tell me about the penthouse.'

'I can't. It's completely isolated from the major building systems. But satellite scans show some serious power usage up there. And get this – they've got their own dedicated fibre line, completely separate from the building's network.'

'A secret server farm on top of one of London's most prominent buildings.' Marlowe paused to catch his breath. 'Subtle.'

'Says the man currently climbing up an elevator shaft in soaking clothes.'

'Not my choice.'

He was a floor beneath the car now. The doors to the forty-eighth floor would be on the opposite side of the shaft – he'd have to swing across, somehow get them open, and deal with whatever security waited on the other side.

A sound echoed through the shaft – voices coming from the other side of the door.

Marlowe pressed himself against the ladder, listening.

'... complete the transfer,' a woman was saying, her voice carrying clearly in the confined space. 'Once it's done, trigger the deletion sequence. Whoever this is, I don't want them setting us up for something we didn't do, or airing dirty laundry that isn't ours.'

'You think they'd do that?' A man's voice, Austrian accent. *Voss.* It sounded echoey, as if spoken through an audio speaker. Which, if Voss was still beneath him, would fit.

'You know, for someone with such a distinguished career, you're incredibly naïve in the world of business,' the woman laughed bitterly. 'Of course they would.'

'And the cleaner?'

'Find him. Kelly's lying about which way he went, but it doesn't matter. In ten minutes, there won't be anything left to find, anyway. Get up here now.'

The woman's voice was familiar, but Marlowe couldn't place it.

'Facial recognition just hit,' Trix said suddenly. 'They know who you are. Your name's just been flagged on their security network. They're sending it to every security station in the building. Along with ...'

She stopped.

'Oh.'

'Along with what?'

'Along with orders to shoot on sight.'

The footsteps lessened, retreating deeper into the penthouse, voices stopped. In the sudden silence came a new sound – the soft whir of the elevator motors engaging.

'Tell me that's not what I think it is,' he muttered.

'The second car's been activated,' Trix's voice came through, tight with tension. 'Voss is inside. It's coming up. Fast.'

Marlowe glanced down. The elevator car was indeed rising, gathering speed as it raced towards him. In the dim shaft, he could see the heavy counterweights descending on the opposite side. If he stayed where he was ...

'There's a maintenance platform two metres above you,' Trix said quickly. 'Emergency brake system. If you can reach it ...'

He was already climbing, moving as fast as he dared on the slippery rungs as below, the elevator car accelerated upwards. The platform Trix had mentioned was a small metal grid protruding from the wall, barely wide enough to support him.

'Five seconds,' Trix warned.

Marlowe lunged for the platform, fingers gripping its edge just as the elevator rushed past upwards, stopping at the floor beside him. For a moment, he hung there, muscles straining, legs swinging in open space.

'A little warning next time,' he grunted, pulling himself up onto the grid. 'Right, I'm heading in. Anything I need to know?'

'The deletion sequence they mentioned? It's already started. I'm seeing massive data transfers from the penthouse servers, followed by systematic wiping.'

Marlowe pressed himself against the wall as counterweights thundered by.

'Can you stop it?'

'From out here? No chance. You need to get to those servers. Assuming you survive the next bit.'

'Next bit?' Marlowe looked across. The elevator had stopped, blocking most of the shaft. But there, in the gap between the car and the wall ...

'Yeah. You're going to have to jump.'

Marlowe measured the distance. The elevator's maintenance hatch – a standard requirement – was just visible. If he timed it right ...

'Heat sensors are up – now showing three figures on the floor. Likely Voss, Durrant and a third; maybe an analyst, maybe a bodyguard. But security teams are checking the shaft,' Trix reported. 'Starting from the ground up. You've got maybe five minutes before they find the service panel you opened.'

'Then I'd better make this count.' Marlowe took a breath, centring himself. 'If this goes wrong ...'

'It won't.' Trix's voice softened. 'But if it does, don't worry, I'll delete your browser history.'

Despite everything, Marlowe managed a smile.

Then he jumped.

2

HIGH JUMP

THE GAP WAS NARROWER THAN IT HAD LOOKED.

His fingers caught the edge of the maintenance hatch, his muscles screaming as he hauled himself up. The top of the elevator car was a tangled maze of machinery: motors, cables, control boxes. And there, set into one corner, was a small panel marked *Emergency Access.*

'I'm on the car,' he whispered, crawling towards the panel. 'Any idea what's waiting on the other side of these doors?'

'Not a clue. The penthouse is dark to my systems, just the three signatures. But, given that Voss is there, I'd say probably not a welcoming committee.'

Marlowe reached the panel, examining the mechanical release.

'You know what's funny?'

'Your career choices?'

'Katherine never actually told us what her asset found. What was so important it's worth killing for. I'm starting to wonder what it actually was Katherine wanted us to find.'

'Whatever it is, you've got about four minutes to find out.'

Marlowe gripped the release handle, yanking it hard. The panel clicked open, revealing the penthouse's elevator doors beneath him.

'If I don't call back in four minutes ...'

'I'll spend our war chest on tech and toys. I promise.'

The elevator doors opened into darkness, broken only by the soft blue glow of server racks. Marlowe moved in silently, immediately dropping into a crouch. The penthouse was a stark contrast to the opulent trading floors below – no marble, no wood panelling, just raw industrial space filled with the hum of machines. He knew One Canada Square had fifty floors, so there were two more floors above him; the chances were this was the hub, while the floors above were the more opulent areas of the building.

'I'm in,' he whispered.

Only static answered. The server room's shielding was clearly blocking his comms.

No more witty commentary from Trix, then. Just him and whatever waited in the shadows.

Moving between the racks, Marlowe oriented himself. The space was larger than he'd expected, stretching away into darkness. Temperature-controlled air whispered through overhead vents, carrying away the heat from countless processors. This was more than a corporate server farm – this was military grade.

At the far end of the room, a door spilled light across the polished floor. Voices drifted through it:

'I've had the order to start the final transfer, then wipe everything. Steele's getting nervous.'

'Bullshit. He doesn't care. It'll be his bloody Vegas lapdog.

They're the one that's nervous, and they're using his name to force things along.'

Steele. That had to be St John Steele, and anything involving him was top of Marlowe's priority list – although who the "Vegas lapdog" could be, was a question Marlowe also wanted to know. He edged closer, using the servers for cover, and through the doorway, he could see what looked like a control centre; multiple screens covered one wall, displaying security feeds, financial data, and what appeared to be encrypted communication channels. A dozen workstations faced them, most dark now. But at one, a figure worked frantically at a keyboard.

'Transfer at sixty percent,' the technician at the keyboard announced, a young man with a nervous energy. 'But we've got a problem. Someone's trying to breach the outer firewall again.'

'That'll be his tech,' the woman replied, her voice carrying the crisp authority of someone used to giving orders. 'The one we locked out. Ignore it. Focus on the transfer.'

Marlowe reached the doorway, staying low. The woman stood at a central console – expensively dressed, early fifties, silver hair catching the blue glow of the screens. He recognised her from the financial press: Diana Durrant herself, CEO and majority shareholder.

'What about Marlowe?' This came from a man near the main door – broad-shouldered, military bearing, the same voice Marlowe had heard through speakers in the elevator shaft. Martin Voss.

'Mister Marlowe is a complication,' Durrant replied, a flicker of irritation passing across her face. 'But not an insurmountable one.'

'I know him from the Military,' Voss again. 'He's not one to be underestimated. We should try to turn him, convince him—'

'We'll do no such bloody thing,' Durrant snapped. 'Once the transfer is complete—'

She stopped as Marlowe's borrowed keycard decided at this point to slip from his soaking pocket, clattering to the floor, skittering across the polished surface.

Every head turned towards the sound.

Bollocks.

'You know,' Marlowe said, deciding to make the best of it, stepping into the light, palming a small EMP device in his right hand, 'if you're planning to destroy evidence of corporate espionage, it's probably best not to discuss it out loud.'

Diana Durrant didn't flinch. If anything, she looked almost amused.

'Corporate espionage?' she gave a small, disdainful laugh. 'Oh, my dear Mister Marlowe, you have no idea what you're looking at. Do you really think intelligence agencies would scramble their best assets just for some trading algorithms?'

Marlowe considered this with a slight nod of acceptance.

'What Katherine's asset found, then, it's not just about market manipulation. It's about control. Absolute, untraceable control of the global financial system.'

Martin Voss glared at Marlowe, who could now see the familiar ramrod posture and bearing return now, as the older man shifted to block the main door. Marlowe heard the elevator moving again, likely going down to pick up more guards.

'Transfer's at eighty percent,' the technician said, still typing.

'Katherine Saito's asset,' Marlowe continued, staying perfectly still, calculating angles. 'What did they find?'

Durrant's amusement faded, her gaze turning cold.

'Miss Saito should have been more honest with you,' she said icily. 'She should also have known not to send a blade when a bullet's required.'

She waved around the room.

'Do you see her asset?' she asked mockingly, before shaking her head. 'Exactly. Mister Voss?'

'The building's sealed,' Voss replied, his eyes fixed on Marlowe. 'Security teams are sweeping up from the ground floor. No way out.'

'There's always a way out,' Marlowe smiled, though there was no humour in it. 'For instance, your technician there has been cycling through passwords for the past thirty seconds, trying to lock my tech backup out of systems we're not even in yet. Which means you're afraid of something bigger than a bit of market manipulation.'

'Ninety percent,' the technician announced.

'You should be proud, Marlowe,' Durrant continued. 'Very few people get this close. Perhaps we should have paid more attention to the cleaning detail.'

Marlowe wanted to ask when the Orloff identity was compromised, but before he could, there was a ding behind; two more security guards emerging from the elevator, guns in hands.

Voss stepped forward, drawing his sidearm with practised ease.

'On your knees, Marlowe, and hands where I can see them.'

Instead, Marlowe looked back at the technician. Young, nervous, probably in way over his head.

'The server behind you,' he said conversationally. 'The one with the blinking red light. That's your primary backup, isn't it?'

The technician's eyes widened, just slightly. *Enough to confirm.*

'Mister Voss,' Durrant snapped. 'If Mister Marlowe moves a muscle ...'

But Marlowe was already moving, his arm hurling the small EMP device towards the server rack. He'd used one of these before, on a superyacht, and he'd seen the chaos it caused, first hand.

He just hoped this would be equally as chaotic.

Voss' gun hand was up and firing in a heartbeat, but the shot went wild as Marlowe dove behind a console, and Marlowe heard explosions and sparks where the round hit something expensive and server-related, followed immediately by Durrant's shouted warning to 'be careful' - But it was too late for that - the EMP device triggered, flooding the servers with a massive high voltage pulse, and everything went dark.

The sudden silence was broken only by the low hum of emergency lighting as it flickered on, casting the room in a dim red glow.

Durrant's voice was the first to pierce the darkness, her tone edged with fury.

'Reboot the systems! Now!'

The technician scrambled, pressing buttons on his now-dead keyboard, but the servers remained silent. Marlowe could hear Voss and the other guards moving in the darkness, their footsteps slow, uncertain.

'They're not responding,' the technician stammered,

panic fraying the edges of his voice. 'The surge ... it's fried everything!'

'He did this,' Voss snapped.

'And you didn't bloody help, you fool!' Durrant snapped back. 'Do you *know* what you shot? No? Well neither do we!'

The room was chaos. Security personnel stumbled in the darkness, shouting commands that overlapped and contradicted one another. Someone attempted to reach the main door, only to find the electronic lock dead. They were all trapped now, sealed in by the very security systems meant to keep intruders out.

'The data!' Durrant's voice cut through the chaos. 'Get the physical drives!'

Marlowe used the confusion to his advantage, moving between servers like a ghost. The near-darkness worked in his favour – he'd memorised the layout during his entrance, while the others were still adjusting to the loss of their screens and systems.

A guard appeared suddenly in front of him. Marlowe fired a throat strike, followed by a knee to the groin – and the now limp man sagged to the floor.

He quietly toed the guard's gun under a server; guns made noise, drew attention. In this environment, silence was his ally.

'Where is he?' Voss's voice, controlled but tense. Professional. Dangerous.

'The drives are gone.' The technician again, disbelief lacing his voice. 'The surge ... it didn't just stop the transfer. It corrupted everything. Years of data, all the records ...'

'Enough whining! We have backups at Rushmore, we'll have to re-install,' Durrant's composure had cracked. 'Voss, your team should be here by now. Where are they?'

As if in answer, alarms sounded from below, distant at first, then growing louder. Fire alarms, security alerts, all cascading through the building's system.

Marlowe allowed himself a small smile.

Once the EMP fried the technician's terminal, he couldn't keep stopping Trix from getting back online.

The technician's station, now abandoned as he ran from server rack to server rack, trying to reboot them, revealed one last prize – a small external drive, likely meant for the backup. As Marlowe pocketed it, he saw data scrolling across the screen: market projections, currency manipulations, and something else; codenames.

CIA FSB MSS

Every major intelligence agency using Durrant's algorithms to quietly destabilise rival economies.

'Trix,' he whispered as he quickly connected his phone to the hub, keeping low so he couldn't be seen, 'Are you there?'

'Yeah, got back on when you blew out the floor's systems.'

'Good. I'm sending you a data packet.'

There was a moment of silence, and then.

'Got it. Jesus, Marlowe. These algorithms ... they're not just predicting market crashes. They're causing them.'

'Fractal Destiny?' The name was an algorithm from Marlowe's past that had caused similar before.

'I'll check for any of Ciaran's coding, but I don't think so.'

Marlowe was about to reply, but paused as Voss's voice rang out:

'*There!*'

Marlowe dropped, yanking his phone connection from the hub as bullets slammed into the console where he'd been standing. Rolling behind a server rack, he found himself face to face with Diana Durrant. She held no weapon, but her eyes were deadly calm.

'You have no idea what you've done,' she said quietly, fury tightly coiled beneath her words.

'Actually,' Marlowe replied, 'I think I do. You've allied with St John Steele. Perhaps with his new gang? And now those same people are going to know you screwed up here. You might have only lost a base, but it's a lot of time and money ruined here. And now they'll wonder what you told me.'

'I've told you nothing!'

'Let's revisit that after I look into "Rushmore", yeah?'

For the first time, fear flickered across Durrant's face, as more alarms joined the cacophony from below. The sprinkler system activated, sending cold water cascading into the server room; steam rose from the overheating equipment, turning the space into a technological hell. In the flickering red emergency lights, Marlowe saw Durrant's people were converging on him, with more now appearing, tired and out of breath, from the stairwell, likely having run up the floors between where Marlowe had been, and where he was now.

But Marlowe was already at the far end of the room, the hard drive in his pocket, heading towards the maintenance hatch he'd used to enter. If he could make it out of the building, he could seriously piss off Steele, clear his debt to Katherine Saito, and seriously put a crimp into Durrant's empire.

All he had to do was survive the next ten minutes.

Martin Voss appeared through the steam, his gun hand leading, and fired as soon as he saw Marlowe - but in the chaos of water and emergency lighting, the round again went wide. Marlowe used the moment to drive a vicious kick into

Voss's midsection., and as Voss doubled over, Marlowe drove him backwards and slammed his head into a bank of servers, sparks showering around them as damaged equipment shorted out.

'... can you hear me? Marlowe?'

'Bit busy, Trix.' Marlowe blocked a strike from Voss.

'Building systems are coming back online,' Trix said quickly. 'But you've got bigger problems. I'm seeing police chatter. SCO19 and Flying Squad's been mobilised.'

Marlowe broke free from Voss's grasp, using a server rack for leverage.

SCO19 was the armed response unit. That meant more guns.

'Options?'

'The maintenance shaft. East side of the building. If you can—'

Static swallowed her voice as Voss caught Marlowe with a snap kick to the ribs.

'You know, I remember you being less of a pussy when I trained you in the Royal Marines,' Voss mocked.

'And I remember you being younger, and faster,' Marlowe hissed as they circled each other, looking for an opening as steam and water made every surface treacherous.

'The building's surrounded!' Durrant's voice cut through the chaos. 'It's over, Marlowe. Whatever you think you've found ...'

Her words were drowned out by a new sound – the deep thrum of helicopter rotors. Whether this was Flying Squad, or rather an emergency exit strategy for Durrant, Marlowe wasn't sure, now distracted, as emergency lighting caught the steam in strobing red pulses, turning the room into something from a nightmare.

Marlowe broke away from Voss, using the steam for cover.

'Clear the steam!' Voss shouted. 'Get these systems powered down before—'

The explosion caught everyone by surprise. One of the damaged servers, its cooling system compromised, detonated in a shower of sparks and glass shards, and more followed as the combination of water and electrical damage began creating cascading failures.

'Marlowe!' Trix's voice cut through again. 'East shaft! Now!'

Marlowe ran. Behind him, he heard Voss organising an evacuation, Durrant shouting orders that Marlowe couldn't hear clearly in the noise. The server room was dying, taking its secrets with it.

The maintenance shaft entrance was where the one several floors below had been – a simple metal door, its electronic lock now dead. Marlowe hit it at full speed, the impact carrying him through into darkness.

'You've got about thirty seconds,' Trix said. 'After that, armed police will have the building completely contained.'

Marlowe climbed down the metal rungs set into the shaft wall. Far below, he could see emergency lights marking each floor.

Forty-eight storeys. In thirty seconds.

Marlowe looked down at the shaft's dizzying drop.

Then at the maintenance platform motor above him.

Then at a slack cable that ran its length.

'Marlowe?' Trix's voice had that tone again. 'You've stopped. You don't have time to stop, so whatever you're thinking ...'

'Can you access the building's exterior lights?'

'Yes, but ... oh no. No, no, no.'

Marlowe pulled the cable free from its mountings.

'Oh yes, yes yes,' Marlowe slid the cable between his legs, then back around the front of his torso, over one shoulder, and across his back into his strong-side hand. He ripped the hem free of his "Trevor Orloff – cleaner" jacket, and wrapped it around his braking hand. 'You said I had to go faster.'

'You're insane,' Trix said as Marlowe shook the slack out of the cable. 'You know that, right? Clinically, certifiably insane.'

Boots thundered on metal somewhere above – Voss's team, having found his exit route.

No time for second thoughts.

'When I say now,' Marlowe checked his makeshift harness, 'kill all exterior lights on the east face.'

'You're not seriously planning to—'

'Now, Trix.'

The east face of One Canada Square went dark.

Marlowe began his controlled descent, the cable burning against his overall and hi-vis jacket as he managed the friction.

Ten floors. Twenty.

Each stop at a maintenance platform giving his arms the seconds they needed to recover, letting the cable cool.

'Security teams sweeping up from ground level,' Trix reported. 'You haven't got time for careful.'

'Rather be slow than dead,' Marlowe replied, but he increased his pace, the stops becoming shorter.

Thirty floors down, now. Thirty-five.

His arms screamed protest, the cable's heat becoming almost unbearable even through his jacket, and the makeshift glove on his braking hand was starting to smoke now.

On the fifteenth floor, he heard the teams above him.

On the tenth, his arms were shaking.

On the fifth, he knew he couldn't hold on much longer.

'The loading bay basement Kelly told you about is coming up,' Trix said. 'But there's movement down there.'

The loading bay level was connected to the underground car park, and just under two floors below his position, when the cable finally ran out of length. A controlled fall from this height he could handle, he'd trained for worse in the Royal Marines. But, before the cable ended, Marlowe used it to kick off from the shaft wall, angling his descent. The elevator doors weren't closed, luckily, and he went through them feet-first, momentum carrying him into a skid and tumble that dispersed the impact across his body. It still felt like being hit by a truck, but he'd survived worse, rolling across the loading bay floor until he fetched up against a stack of crates.

Everything hurt, but nothing felt broken.

A thousand training exercises paying off in one desperate moment.

'Marlowe?' Trix's voice was barely audible through the ringing in his ears. Marlowe managed to get to his knees, his shoulder screaming in protest as he tried to free himself from the remnants of the broken cable.

'Still here,' he managed. 'How long until ...'

The sound of sirens cut him off – police vehicles rapidly approaching the building's east side. Through the loading bay's shuttered entrance, blue lights strobed against the night's darkness.

'You've got about forty seconds before they sweep this level,' Trix said.

'Outstanding.' Marlowe finally got the cable free. 'Options?'

'Maintenance tunnel. Links to the Underground service routes. If you can reach it ...'

Movement caught his eye – a shadow passing through one of the small windows set high in the loading bay walls.

SCO19, setting up a perimeter. They'd be coming in fast, working on the assumption he was armed and dangerous.

Marlowe limped quickly between the crates, keeping low, wincing with every step, his ankle complaining. He hoped it was a bruise, rather than a sprain. The maintenance tunnel access was on the far wall, partly hidden behind stacks of office supplies. Above, he could hear the tactical teams coordinating their sweep, floor by floor.

'Marlowe, twenty seconds,' Trix warned, instantly the professional again. Marlowe reached the tunnel access. The electronic lock was dead – another victim of his EMP device. But the manual release was stiff, reluctant to move after years of disuse.

Footsteps echoed from the stairwell. Voices, sharp with professional focus. Weapons being readied.

The lock finally yielded with a grinding shriek that seemed to fill the entire loading bay. Marlowe pulled the access door open just as the first SCO19 officer appeared. The tunnel exit loomed ahead, but Marlowe already knew there were too many shadows moving beyond the doorway; too many frequencies crackling on Trix's monitoring system.

'Armed police! Stay where you are!'

He didn't resist when they breached. If anything, being taken out was better than trying to escape.

'Target secured,' someone said.

'Marlowe?' Trix's voice, barely audible now. 'The algorithms—'

'We'll take that,' an SCO19 officer said as he pulled

Marlowe's earpiece out. 'Don't want you chatting with your buddies now, do we, Mister Lachlan?'

Marlowe froze. They weren't arresting Thomas Marlowe, ex-MI5 agent, or even Trevor Orloff – they were arresting *Kieran Lachlan,* Irish bomb expert and terrorist, one of Marlowe's MI5 legends.

But MI5 would have stopped this, telling them to step down ...

Wouldn't they?

3

HANDCUFFED

DAWN CREPT THROUGH THE TOP WINDOW OF THE CANARY Wharf interview room, painting stripes across the scarred metal table, battered from years of abuse, likely from angry suspects held against their will.

Marlowe studied his reflection in the one-way glass, noting how the cleaner's uniform had lost its pristine look during his arrest. The NHS glasses sat crooked on his nose, one arm bent from the enthusiastic way the police had introduced his face to their car.

Of course, the mirror could have been a simple mirror. Most police stations these days – sorry, *crime units*, as they liked to call themselves – used cameras rather than mirrors. There was indeed a camera in the corner, but it felt more natural to glare at his reflection, as if through it he could see whoever was on the other side, even if it was just a wall.

Two empty coffee cups on the table marked the passage of time. Six hours since his arrest. Six hours of the same questions, asked in different ways, while he maintained Kieran Lachlan's Belfast accent and wondered why MI5, or

Emilia Wintergreen specifically, hadn't swept in to claim him.

Probably because he'd told her to piss off in Berlin.

Wintergreen was very good at holding grudges.

At least his ankle seemed better. Sitting down for five hours meant not putting weight on it, and it'd returned to nothing more than a dull ache.

The door opened, and Detective Inspector James Morris entered. Marlowe knew the name, as Morris had informed him of this the first time they'd met, almost four hours earlier. He moved like a man who'd spent too many years playing rugby before switching to golf. Every action was methodical: the way he arranged his files as he sat, or the way he stirred his third coffee of the morning; his Essex accent had been softened by a public school education – or so Marlowe believed – but it still carried the weight of his years on the force.

'So, Mister Lachlan,' Morris began, laying out photographs of the Durrant Capital trading floor. 'Shall we try this again? You've had time to think about your situation.'

Marlowe watched Morris settle into his chair. His shirt sleeves were rolled up exactly three turns. His tie was loosened by precisely one inch, and his coffee sat exactly two feet from the case files. Everything about him was organised and calm, right down to the way he aligned his pen parallel to the folder's edge.

There was no point playing around; this guy was all about the facts.

Marlowe kept his posture slightly hunched, maintaining Kieran's working-class body language. His accent, when he spoke, was pure Belfast docks, cultivated over years of undercover work.

'Told you already,' he muttered. 'Agency sent me to clean. Simple as that.'

Morris's smile didn't reach his eyes. He turned over the first photograph, a shot of the industrial buffer Marlowe had abandoned during his escape. The machine looked lonely, out of place among the trading desks, like a prop left over from a film set.

'Cleaning equipment with what looks to be military-grade electronics hidden inside,' Morris noted. 'Interesting choice of floor polish, wouldn't you say?'

'Don't know what you mean,' Marlowe replied, his tone sullen. 'Got given the buffer when I turned up.'

Morris opened another folder, this one stuffed with technical reports and printouts. Marlowe watched as Morris's movements stayed precise, measured, each gesture calculated to highlight the weight of the evidence.

'The interesting thing about cleaning companies,' Morris continued, his Essex accent lending a contemplative quality to the words, 'is how particular they are about their staff. Background checks. References. Insurance.'

He selected a document from the pile.

'Especially for high-security buildings like Durrant. So imagine our surprise when Premium Cleaning Services said they'd never heard of a Kieran Lachlan.'

'Already said, the name's Orloff. You got the wrong fella.' Marlowe shifted in his chair, letting a hint of nerves creep in. Kieran would, after all, be worrying now, seeing his cover slowly dismantled. *Playing a character accused of playing another character.* He wondered briefly how far this could go if someone with a psychology degree were to dig in.

'So you're still claiming to be Trevor Orloff, then?' Morris spoke like a man with information on his side, information

Marlowe hadn't yet been privy to. Which meant for the moment, he had to play to the idea they had something that confirmed he was Lachlan.

As long as they didn't confirm he was Marlowe, that was okay.

'Temp agency,' he muttered, thickening the Belfast accent with a touch of stress. 'Called me in last minute, like.'

'Which agency would that be?'

Before Marlowe could respond, the door opened, and a woman entered, carrying her own stack of files. Her sharp movements contrasted with Morris's deliberate pace; everything about her radiated stress, though tempered with efficiency.

'Sorry I'm late,' she said briskly. Marlowe suspected her timing had been choreographed. 'Traffic on Westferry Road.'

Morris leaned forward, speaking into the microphone of the recorder.

'Detective Sergeant Louisa Wilcott has entered the interview room.'

He watched as she settled beside him; her files forming a wall of paper between them and Marlowe.

'Has Mister Lachlan explained the electromagnetic pulse that knocked out three floors of Durrant's systems?' Wilcott asked, fixing her gaze on Marlowe, who kept his expression blank, as unease spread through him.

There was no way the police would have identified the EMP damage so quickly.

'Electromagnetic what?' Marlowe let confusion fill Kieran's voice, his furrowed brow matching the tone.

Someone else was feeding them this. Someone who knew exactly what they were looking for. Who were the suits that'd watched his arrest? Were they connected?

Wilcott relaxed back into the chair, and Marlowe realised

she'd done this dance before, probably hundreds of times. Morris, with his methodical dismantling of alibis, and Wilcott, with her sharp insight and technical knowledge.

'The device,' Wilcott continued, selecting a photograph from her own stack, 'was quite sophisticated, Mister Lachlan. Military-grade, according to our experts.'

She laid the image on the table: a close-up of the damaged server room, the scorch patterns clearly visible.

'It's the kind of equipment more commonly found in surveillance operations than commercial burglaries.'

Morris stirred his coffee, the spoon clicking against the china in the sudden silence.

'Which makes us wonder, Mister Lachlan, what exactly you were doing there, and what exactly you were looking for in those servers.'

'Just a cleaner,' Marlowe insisted. But he could feel Kieran's persona fraying around the edges. Over four hours of questioning, and almost six hours of arrest were wearing him down, and these two were sharper than the usual Met officers he dealt with. Much sharper.

Not as sharp as Uncle Alex, Detective Superintendent of a City of London Unit, but close.

'You see,' Morris leaned forward, his voice adopting a conversational tone that somehow made him seem more intimidating, 'we've been looking into your background. Your *real* background, that is – not the Trevor Orloff cleaning company bollocks – and we've found some very interesting connections.'

As he spoke, Wilcott opened another file, this one thicker than the others. Surveillance photos and documents spilled out, and Marlowe's stomach tightened as he caught glimpses of familiar faces. There was Frank Maguire – or rather, his organisation out in Essex – and from the looks of things, the weapons deals and the money laundering arrangements Marlowe had orchestrated over the years as Kieran Lachlan were painstakingly documented.

His carefully constructed legend was becoming a trap.

'Tell me, Mister Lachlan,' Wilcott said, her tone as precise as a scalpel, 'when did you first work with Frank Maguire?'

Marlowe felt the shift in the room's atmosphere. They'd been building to this moment, he realised. Everything before – the cleaning company cover, the EMP device – had just been laying the groundwork. Now they were zeroing in on what they really wanted to know.

'I don't know who you're talking about,' Marlowe replied, letting uncertainty creep into Kieran's voice. 'Frank who?'

Morris's smile was patient, almost paternal. He selected another photograph from the stack and slid it across the table. Marlowe recognised the location immediately. It was one of Maguire's favourite "offices", a fish and chip restaurant on the northern end of Southend seafront. The image showed Kieran Lachlan sitting at a corner table with Frank and two of his lieutenants. The quality was excellent, probably taken from a surveillance team in one of the buildings nearby.

Marlowe grimaced. He knew exactly when this had been taken. He'd been arguing for the grandson of a friend to be removed from Maguire's operation. Raymond "Razor" Gibson had been a two-bit enforcer for Maguire, running the gang that Sammy Barnes, grandson of Monty Barnes had been connected to, and Marlowe had shown Maguire proof Gibson had been planning an alliance with a London gangster named Arun Nadal, Gibson's ambition outreaching his intelligence. Maguire had agreed to let Sammy free, but only if Marlowe had “solved” the Razor Gibson problem for him.

He had done his best to do this in a pub near Epping Forest, and then finished it more permanently after he discovered Razor had given Monty’s address to a hitman known as The Gravedigger, allowing him to kill the old man in order to gain Marlowe’s attention.

Razor was dead now, killed by Marlowe, using The Gravedigger’s own gun to frame him.

If that came to light, things would get even more complicated.

‘This photo,’ Wilcott said, tapping it with a manicured nail, ‘was the first time we positively identified you in Maguire’s inner circle. An ex-Real IRA arms dealer and money launderer from Belfast, specialising in Eastern European operations. Isn’t that right?'

She paused, letting her words hang in the air like a noose. More photos followed, stretching back five or six years. Meetings in pub car parks, exchanges in industrial estates, all meticulously documented, all showing Kieran Lachlan doing exactly what he’d been created to do, while building credibility in the criminal underworld of Essex, London, and beyond.

The irony wasn’t lost on Marlowe. His cover had been too good, too convincing, and now it was becoming his prison. Usually, by this point, someone from MI5 would have turned up waving a Special Branch badge, getting him out before the harder questions appeared.

This time, however, he was alone.

One picture paused him. It was a funeral; Monty Barnes' one. But the image wasn’t of Marlowe, instead it was of Maguire, watching from the side of the car park, at a distance. Marlowe had seen him there, and had tried to keep his identity secret – after all, he'd been there as Tom Marlowe, not Lachlan – but it was who was in the photo next to him that surprised Marlowe.

Peter Jericho, otherwise known as The Gravedigger, stood beside Maguire, chatting like friends.

Did Maguire know Marlowe had spent years lying to him? Had he sent The Gravedigger after Monty?

'Of course, that was just the start, wasn't it?' Morris stretched back, his hands folded over his stomach in a strangely casual pose as he brought Marlowe's attention back to the moment. 'We've tracked at least sixteen major shipments, some with very interesting customers. The kind that makes Special Branch nervous.'

Marlowe stayed silent, his mind racing. They'd done their homework. Months, possibly years, of investigation had led them here. But something wasn't right; the timing was too perfect, the intelligence too precise. Someone had handed this to them, gift-wrapped, complete with a suspect. But the question remained ... *who knew Marlowe well enough to pull this off?*

Another thought came to mind; before she'd been reassigned to Hong Kong eighteen months earlier, Katherine Saito had run the counter-terrorism ops in Thames House and Marlowe knew she'd been on ops duty while there.

She'd been the one who created Kieran Lachlan.

That couldn't be a coincidence.

Morris pulled out another photo, this one showing a warehouse near the Thames. Even in the grainy surveillance shot, Marlowe recognised last summer's operation. Eight crates of modified AK-47s, supposedly destined for Belfast. In reality, they'd been carefully tracked by MI5's counter-terrorism unit, leading to the dismantling of a long-believed dead cell operating out of a dairy. Katherine wasn't involved by then, but there was every chance she could have still gained updates.

Was he really considering this? That Katherine Saito, a woman who took bullets meant for him, who'd worked beside him since he started in MI5, who claimed to be one of his mother's proteges, was setting him up for a fall?

Two remembered comments came back to Marlowe as he considered this; the first was from David Kelly, the other from Durrant.

'Someone always disappears, but it helps if they exist in the first place.'

'Miss Saito should have been more honest with you. She should also have known not to send a blade when a bullet's required.'

'Twenty-third of July,' Wilcott brought Marlowe back to the present, as if reading his thoughts. 'Really interesting cargo. And do you know what? Even more interesting buyers.'

She pulled out a document – financial records, account transfers.

'You're quite sophisticated for an arms dealer, Mister Lachlan. The way you move money around through shell companies and offshore accounts, it's almost like you had professional training in money laundering.'

Marlowe stifled a laugh. He had no such training. It was MI5's financial experts who moved the money, creating the illusion of a criminal mastermind while likely siphoning funds for their own purposes.

'The thing is,' Morris continued, his tone deceptively mild, 'we've been watching Frank Maguire for a long time. Surveillance, wiretaps, financial tracking. Over the years, we've built a case piece by piece.'

He gestured at the evidence on the table.

'And your name keeps popping up, like a thread we can pull to unravel the entire operation.'

As Morris leant back, Wilcott picked up the narrative smoothly.

'But then something interesting happened. Last night, you showed up at Durrant Capital with military-grade electronics and sophisticated hacking equipment, having spent days pretending to be Trevor Orloff, working eight-hour shifts to get to know the layout. That's a long way from gun running or financial discrepancies.'

Marlowe recognised the technique. He'd used it himself countless times. They were boxing him in, showing him how much they knew while hinting at what they suspected. The question was, though, *how much did they really know?*

'So here's where we are, Mister Lachlan,' Morris said, his voice dropping. 'We've got you on breaking and entering, possession of restricted technology, criminal damage. That's just from last night. Add arms dealing to the mix ...'

He spread his hands.

'You're looking at serious time. Of course, there are other options.'

The room fell silent. Faintly, Marlowe heard a car pass outside. He listened to it fade, buying time, considering angles. His earpiece – his lifeline to Trix – was gone, logged as evidence. He wondered if Trix was tracking him through the official systems or if she'd gone dark, waiting to see how things played out.

Morris opened a thinner file and spoke again.

'Frank Maguire's been untouchable for years. Friends in high places, connections we can't touch. But you?' he tapped the surveillance photos. 'You've been inside the organisation.

Seen how it works, who he deals with, where the bodies are buried ... literally.'

'We can help each other,' Wilcott added, her tone softer, almost persuasive. 'A deal can be arranged. Something unofficial to start with. You help us understand Maguire's operation. We help you with your current situation.'

Marlowe, still playing Kieran Lachlan, shifted in his chair, feigning the posture of a man weighing his options. Inside, his mind was racing. The real Kieran Lachlan had been dead for six years, killed in a botched police raid in Northern Ireland. MI5 – or rather, Saito, with Wintergreen's help – had buried the truth so deep even Special Branch hadn't found it. And now here he was, trapped in a false identity, being offered a deal to betray a crime boss who thought he was someone else entirely.

Or maybe he didn't.

'Frank Maguire,' Marlowe said carefully, letting uncertainty creep into Kieran's accent, 'isn't the kind of man you walk away from.'

'No, he isn't,' Morris agreed. 'But he's also not the kind of man who can protect you from where you're heading. Think about it, Mister Lachlan. Really think about your position here.'

Another silence fell, broken only by the distant rumble of an early morning DLR train. Morris shuffled his papers with those same precise, methodical movements, a man who could wait hours for a suspect to make the wrong move. Marlowe needed to get out, before people realised he wasn't Kieran Lachlan ... but instead was a far more interesting target.

'Okay,' he said slowly, testing the waters. 'We could discuss specifics on the deal.'

Before anyone could reply, though, a knock at the door interrupted them, and a uniformed officer poked his head in, looking apologetic.

'Sorry, sir, but there's someone here with bail for Mister Lachlan.'

'We haven't finished here yet,' Morris frowned.

'Sorry, sir, it's been arranged,' the officer hesitated. 'Call came from above.'

Marlowe's stomach tightened. This wasn't MI5, they wouldn't have bothered with bureaucracy. This was someone else, moving pieces on the board.

Wilcott was already checking her phone, her expression darkening.

'Guv, you want to see this,' she said, passing her phone to Morris.

Morris studied the screen for a long moment, his face unreadable. Finally, he looked back up at Marlowe, and there was something new in his expression, not quite defeat, but the resignation of a man who had just had a major case pulled from under him.

'Well, Mister Lachlan,' he said quietly, 'seems you've got friends in interesting places.'

He leaned forward and turned off the recorder, reciting the time and date of the interview's end as he did so.

The door opened once more. Marlowe didn't need to turn to see who it was; he could tell by the way the air in the room shifted, the subtle change in pressure, that a predator had now entered its territory.

'Hello, Kieran,' Frank Maguire's voice carried its usual hint of amusement. 'Looks like you could use a lift home.'

4

CAR SHARE

MARLOWE WASN'T SURE WHAT GAME WAS BEING PLAYED HERE. The one thing he was sure of was that there was a very good chance he was being led into a trap, one possibly of his own making over many years. As they walked through the station – Kieran Lachlan and Frank Maguire, old workmates – with Maguire's solicitor walking ahead of them, Marlowe decided to see if he could work out the lay of the land.

Morris and Wilcott had shadowed them all the way to the front desk, where more paperwork awaited. Frank's solicitor – a sharp-suited woman who hadn't been there moments ago – handled it all with practised efficiency.

Nobody mentioned the fact that bail proceedings normally took hours, if not days.

Nobody questioned how Frank had known his "associate" was even here.

And now they were leaving.

'Thank you for getting me out,' Marlowe said, still trying to keep to the Kieran Lachlan legend. 'Now I owe you one.'

'Oh, don't think like that.' Maguire smiled. 'You don't owe

me one. The amount of money you've made me over the years – I'm sure we can call this evens. Don't you think, *Tom?*'

Marlowe stopped in the corridor. They were alone; the solicitor having moved ahead to give them a moment of quiet.

Maguire turned to face Marlowe, smiling.

'Yes,' he said. 'I know who you are, *Tom*. And it wasn't the police that tipped me off. It was your dead mate.'

'What do you mean?'

'The old guy. The one whose grandson had been with Razor Gibson, and who got killed.' Maguire shrugged. 'Felt guilty, didn't I? Knew it was all part of whatever had happened with my team. Thought I'd go along, pay my respects, like ... poor bugger didn't need to be attacked like that, you know. When I heard he was dead, I knew Razor was involved somehow.'

'He was,' Marlowe nodded, the accent now forgotten. 'He gave away the address. Sent an assassin to kill him. Goes by the name of The Gravedigger.'

At that, Maguire grinned wider.

'Yeah, I met him,' he said. 'At the funeral. Nice guy. Never have believed he was ... well, *him*, you know? He was watching from the side. I didn't go in; I didn't know Mister Barnes that well, but there I was, by the side of the car park, dressed in black, being all respectful-like. Then this guy comes over and stands next to me. I ask if he's part of the funeral. He tells me he's The Gravedigger.'

Marlowe kept his expression blank, forcing his anger down.

The Gravedigger had turned up at Barnes's funeral to look for Marlowe.

He'd killed Barnes deliberately to send a message to

Marlowe. Maguire hadn't been part of it, just caught on the edges through Razor Gibson – a man who'd been involved in Barnes's beating and eventually gave him up to the hitman.

'I appreciate you giving your time,' Marlowe said, unsure where this was going.

Maguire nodded.

'It's the least a man can do, you know.'

Neither of them moved, both standing still in the corridor.

'But then I see you there, don't I?' Maguire continued. 'I mean, you were hiding your face and pretending you weren't there, but I saw who you were. And when I mentioned to a couple of people, you know, did they know if Kieran Lachlan was still around, they looked a bit confused, didn't they?'

Marlowe knew where this was going. He'd been at the funeral as Tom Marlowe so if Maguire had asked around for Kieran, describing him as a *tall man, brown hair, beard,* they would have said *"Oh no, that's Tom Marlowe."*

Maguire, watching Marlowe's expression, smiled.

'Yeah, I see you've worked it out now,' he said. 'I don't know who gave me your name, but somebody explained who you were. Civil servant or something. I think it might even have been Sammy himself. Either way, once I knew you were actually someone else, I started looking into you, didn't I?'

'And what did you find when you looked into me?' Marlowe asked.

Maguire smiled, his tone almost mocking.

'I found everything, Tom,' he said, repeatedly using Marlowe's name for emphasis. 'I found out how you were not who you said you were, in more ways than one. I mean, MI5? I should have seen that coming. How does a bog-trotting Paddy soldier who once worked for the Real IRA suddenly find himself able to launder money into the millions, eh? That one's on me.'

Marlowe went to respond, but the door to their side opened, and a woman stepped through. She looked to be in her forties, with dark-red curly hair and a stocky build like a rugby player. She glanced at the two of them, then carried on walking, uninterested. As far as she was concerned, they weren't her problem.

Maguire smiled, however, as he watched her leave.

'See that woman there? That's Detective Superintendent Warren,' he said. 'She used to work with your uncle. Yeah, I know who he is, too. Not your uncle by blood, though, right? We've had a run in or two. From what I hear, she don't like him. From what I hear, she don't like you either. Or, rather, whatever shite fakery you've thrown everyone today.'

Marlowe was rapidly realising that Maguire knew way more about him than he'd thought. If Maguire knew he was MI5 and the effective nephew of Alex Monroe, there wasn't much more to hide.

'My lads even had a look at your fancy church,' Maguire said. 'We didn't go in or anything, we're not that stupid. You might have some James Bond spy toys in there, you know, blow us all up. We've seen movies.'

By now, they'd started moving again, Maguire leading him through the corridors of the police unit out into the car park at the back, where the solicitor was walking towards her own car. Still unnamed, she turned and nodded to Maguire.

'If you need anything else—'

'I'll give you a call,' Maguire replied. 'Thanks for this.'

He looked back at Marlowe.

'We're going for a drive,' he said. 'Wouldn't that be exciting?'

It sounded as far from exciting as Marlowe could imagine, especially after the events of the previous night and with no sleep. Outside, weak autumn sunlight painted the station's modern glass facade in patterns that reminded Marlowe of the trading floor he'd escaped from several hours ago.

A black Range Rover idled by the kerb, windows tinted dark enough to be illegal. Two men Marlowe recognised from Frank's security detail stood nearby, trying to look casual and failing miserably.

'Your cleaning gear's been impounded as evidence,' Morris, now having returned to allow them out of the premises, said from behind them, his tone professional but carrying an edge. 'Along with any electronics.'

'Send the bill to my office,' Frank replied without turning around. 'I'm sure we can sort something out.'

The unspoken message was clear – money solved most problems, and Frank had plenty of it. But Marlowe caught the slight tightening around Morris's eyes. The detective didn't like being outmanoeuvred, especially not on his own patch, and definitely not by his own superiors. Marlowe actually felt sorry for him here, but wondered if this was something he could actually use to his advantage, if the necessity came up.

'This isn't over, Mister Lachlan,' Morris said quietly.

'It never is with cops, is it?' Frank's smile didn't reach his eyes. 'Now, if you'll excuse us, me and my boy here need to have a chat about his extra-curricular activities.'

Marlowe suddenly wanted to stay; this wasn't the Maguire he knew. The Maguire he knew as Kieran Lachlan was an Essex gangland boss, used to small fights with interlopers on his "manor" and the occasional football riot. Sure, he dealt in guns here and there, and Marlowe had witnessed him in shootouts – at least one had been created by Marlowe himself to cause a distraction while rescuing someone – but Maguire wasn't big time. He wasn't big enough to walk into a place like this and pull out a suspected terrorist without a fuss.

Maguire had big friends now.

But who? Was he working with MI5 or MI6? Was he an asset, and using favours to get Marlowe out? Or was he an asset being *used* to get Marlowe out?

Marlowe wished he could speak to Trix and check on this, but he hadn't been given his belongings back at the station entrance, probably a pettiness that Marlowe was happy to waive purely to get out. The earpiece and the hard drive were still waiting in a plastic baggie, something Marlowe would have to sort out later.

Maguire waited for Marlowe to get into the car; Marlowe considered arguing or fighting his way out, but he knew he needed to get away from the crime unit before someone bigger and badder came looking for him ... or worse.

Frank opened the Range Rover's rear door himself, a gesture that might have seemed courteous if it wasn't so clearly an order. Marlowe climbed in, the leather seats creaking beneath him, still wearing his crumpled cleaner's uniform, his bent NHS glasses still on, steaming up slightly in the vehicle's warmth. Maguire climbed in beside him, pulling his seatbelt across with a smile. The mundane action seemed almost absurd for someone like him – a gangland boss who casually threatened lives, yet still adhered to basic road safety.

Through the tinted windows, Marlowe watched Morris and Wilcott standing on the steps of the station. They were already in discussion, probably planning their next move.

This wasn't a defeat for them, he realised, just a tactical retreat. They'd be watching, waiting, gathering more evidence, and now they thought they had leverage over one of Frank Maguire's trusted lieutenants.

The Range Rover pulled away from the kerb, joining the steady flow of traffic heading east. One of Frank's security detail was driving, the other riding shotgun, both silent as graves. Frank sat beside Marlowe, close enough that the scent of expensive cologne mixed with the faint trace of whisky on his breath.

For two minutes that felt like hours, nobody spoke. They passed beneath the DLR tracks, the same ones whose shadow had marked time in the interview room, and Marlowe kept his body language careful, uncertain.

'I don't hold it against you,' Maguire said, breaking the silence. 'Just so you know. You've made me money. You've got my arse out of the fire a couple of times, though I've helped you just as much. And judging from the way those two pricks looked in the interrogation room, you weren't giving them anything. I appreciate that. But the fact of the matter is, Tom, you've been lying to me for almost five years.'

Marlowe leaned back, exhaling slowly.

'It's part of the job, Frank,' he said. 'I'm not going to explain myself or apologise. If it makes you feel better, we were never taking you down. We were using you to take down other people and building you as an asset.'

'And what would have happened if the people *you* were taking down, decided to take it out on me?' Maguire asked, his tone sharp.

Marlowe let out a soft laugh.

'Frank, the reason we used you was because we knew you

could take down anyone who tried that. Probably take their territory at the same time.'

Maguire considered this, then chuckled to himself.

'Yeah, probably could have,' he admitted. 'You're not wrong there. So go on then – as I saved your arse – why the hell were you hanging around in a bloody skyscraper in Canary Wharf?'

'Do you really want to know?'

'I got you out of pokey, didn't I? You don't think they'd have let you go without me stepping in? You weren't seeing daylight, mate,' Maguire snapped. 'And I noticed none of your fancy friends came to get you out. So I think you're shit out of luck and shit out of friends. How about you tell me what's going on?'

Marlowe sighed, running a hand through his hair.

'Gravedigger,' he said. 'The guy you met at the funeral? He's an assassin. He was sent by a man named St John Steele.'

Maguire frowned slightly at the name, the St John pronunciation of "Sinjen" not registering.

'Never heard of him.'

'Steele's an ex-spook. Spy. He works for the highest bidder now,' Marlowe explained. 'We've had a few run-ins. Let's just say he's not my best friend. A few weeks ago, I managed to piss him off in Germany after screwing up a deal he'd made in Vegas. Oh, and something on the West Coast after that. I've been a thorn in his side, and he's not happy about it.'

'So what?' Maguire asked. 'He wants to take you out? Shoot you in the back of the head like they do in the films?'

'Unfortunately, Frank, you've been reading too many spy books.' Marlowe allowed himself a faint smile, the first genuine one all day. 'Steele wants me gone, though. Sent a couple of assassins after me. From what I can work out, there's a hit on me.'

Maguire grinned, but his eyes were sharp.

'Oh, there's a hit on you,' he said. 'I was going to get to that in a minute, but I wanted to hear your story first.'

Marlowe nodded slowly.

'Thanks for the confirmation. A couple of people have already tried. Someone tried to take me out in Central London last week. Another tried to blow up my car.'

'You should move,' Maguire suggested dryly.

'I've spent too much time doing that place up,' Marlowe replied with a faint smirk. 'I'll stay for now. It's secure. Anyway, after two or three attempts, I started piecing it together. They were all coming from the same source, but I can't find the name yet. I decided to dig a little. One of my old MI5 colleagues, Katherine Saito, owed me a favour from an op that went wrong in Hong Kong. She claimed to have an asset, an analyst working at Durrant Finance. I'd already found a direct communication from Durrant to Steele's new little organisation, and I needed to know more about it. Saito needed whatever her analyst had before they disappeared. It was a quid pro quo deal.'

'So you went into a Canary Wharf building, dressed as a cleaner, to get information for some woman who already owed you one?' Maguire asked incredulously.

'With hindsight, I think she was playing me as much as I was playing her.'

'How come?'

'They knew I was coming. And Durrant as good as stated it,' Marlowe settled into the car seat. 'Added to the fact I found nothing on this "asset" she mentioned.'

'Why didn't you go to your fancy MI5 friends?'

'We … had a breakup,' Marlowe replied. 'Wasn't the nicest of partings. Let's just say we're not on speaking terms. And judging by the fact that you were my knight in shining armour today …'

Maguire nodded slowly, understanding.

'Yeah, I see that,' he said.

'How did you manage it?' Marlowe asked. 'No offence, Frank, but I always knew you were blessed when it came to never being arrested, but even you shouldn't have had the clout to get me out.'

'I have friends in high places.'

'They'd have to be bloody high.'

'Oh, they are, Tom,' Maguire grinned. 'Higher than you'd ever work out. And, in a way, it's thanks to you.'

'And you're not telling me who?'

'Nope.'

Marlowe studied Maguire's face.

'How much is the hit?' he asked, his voice calm. 'You said there's definitely one on me, so you must know.'

'One million dollars,' Maguire shrugged casually. 'Untraceable crypto. Stablecoin – not one of those daft ones that drops to fifty quid before you can cash out. The payment's sitting in a wallet, ready to go. Completely untraceable.'

Marlowe bit the inside of his cheek, weighing his next move.

'Do you know who took the contract?'

'A man by the name of The Broker.'

Marlowe's eyes narrowed at this. He'd only ever met The Broker once, for it was likely the same man, at an auction in Punta Cana, where billionaires bid in the first round of the Broad Sword AI's sale. He hadn't continued to the US, his job done, but even from that one meeting, Marlowe had realised The Broker was a man who was an enigma, as unknown out there as The Gravedigger, and likely one of the few people best suited for high-cost hits.

But then he'd found The Gravedigger's true identity. He could do it again.

Maguire laughed, a genuine belly laugh that echoed through the car, bringing Marlowe back to the moment.

'You know what? I thought you were really interesting as Kieran Lachlan,' he said. 'The kind of guy I could have a chat with, hear some good stories. But you, Tom Marlowe? I think you're going to be way more fun.'

His laughter faded, and he leant closer.

'You know, before I claim that million dollars and shoot you in the back of the head.'

There you are.

Marlowe had been waiting for it. As they'd left Canary Wharf, he'd grabbed a pen from a desk as they passed, and holding it in his fist, he spun quickly, the tip now pressing against Maguire's jugular.

Before he could say anything, though, Maguire started laughing again.

'You really *are* a spy, aren't you? All this James Bond shite,' he chuckled, gently knocking Marlowe's hand away. 'Relax. I'm not here to kill you. I need your help.'

'What do you mean?' Marlowe lowered the pen.

'I mean exactly what I said.' Maguire leant back, still grinning. 'The reason I came for you wasn't because I was looking for Kieran Lachlan. The reason I came is that I've been having chats about Durrant Capital myself. Diana Durrant is a grade-A bitch. Crooked as hell. She's been trying to take over a chunk of London through subsidiaries and shell companies. There's a lot of money to be made, and she's taken something of mine, some "proprietary information", so to speak – to make it happen. I want it back, or at least stopped from helping her succeed.'

Marlowe watched him carefully.

'When you say you want your "proprietary information" back,' he asked, 'is that all? Or do you want more?'

'Oh, I always want more,' Maguire said as they drove down the A13 towards London. 'But I've got a problem, and you can solve it. The person I want removed sounds like a thorn in your side, too. Here's the deal – you do what I need, and I'll see what I can do about removing your hit. At the very least, I can provide some interference.'

'And why would you do that?'

Maguire finally unclicked his seatbelt, turning to face Marlowe directly, as his grin widened.

'Because you and me, mate,' he said, 'we're partners now. Whether you like it or not.'

5

FOLLOWED

Marlowe hadn't been sure where they were going, but by the time they started heading towards West London, he had realised that Frank Maguire was proving a point, most likely driving him to his actual apartment, as proof that he knew exactly who Marlowe was. However, although Frank was an established gangster and world-wise in certain matters, Marlowe wasn't sure just how good he was at spycraft. Also, now knowing that he had a million-dollar hit on his head, Marlowe wasn't sure either whether Maguire's goon-turned-driver would understand how to shake a tail. For all he knew, there were a dozen cars following them, hunting their elusive golden target.

Eventually, Marlowe had suggested to Frank to drop him off, and after a few minutes of negotiating this down the A1203, Maguire eventually arranged to drop Marlowe at a corner near Tower Bridge. He claimed it would save Maguire the time to go through London, and if he was being honest, Marlowe really needed some time on his own. Maguire had already, by this point, made his offer – a job for his secrecy –

and Marlowe knew he wouldn't be able to do anything about this until he either fulfilled the task, or worked out who was truly controlling Maguire, and *removed* them.

It was early in the morning, around eight, when Marlowe found himself dropped off in the City of London. It was smack bang in rush hour, and he was still wearing his grotty overalls over his clothing and his NHS glasses; he'd not considered asking Maguire for any kind of a loan while his "personal" items were still locked down at Canary Wharf, and therefore he didn't have any of his credit cards on his person. All he had was fifty pounds in ten-pound notes, hidden in his trainers.

He'd been pissed off that the police had dumped him, still in soaking overalls, into the cell; but then if they thought they were dealing with ex-Real IRA, they might have been a little less bothered about his comforts. He understood this; London had received its fair share of IRA attacks over the years. And the clothes were dry now, anyway.

What was interesting for Marlowe was that Durrant's facial recognition had named him as Tom Marlowe, while the police had kept the more permanent, more notorious legend of Kieran Lachlan. What was even weirder was that Tom Marlowe, as a private civilian, had assisted the police in the past frequently and was definitely in their records. Several of his recent activities, in particular an infamous "caught on phones" moment on the A40 while stopping Kate Maybury kidnapping the Home Secretary had thrust Marlowe into the news, although more as a face than a name.

Marlowe wasn't sure what to do about this. As far as he knew, the Lachlan identity was now burned, the police looking into it. The Orloff identity was likely burned as well, although that wasn't as much a loss. Marlowe was just glad he used an older, throwaway one, rather than the more recent IDs he'd gained from Helen Bonneville. They'd cost a small fortune.

He'd bought a travel-card on entering the station and had whistled at the cost. It was peak rush hour, which meant the price of a travel-card was around double what it would usually be, and Marlowe had bought an "all zone" one, just in case he needed to escape a tail; it was always easier to spot them in the suburbs than in the city, but it did mean his supply of notes had dwindled down to almost nothing, as he'd started travelling before the "off peak" time.

Rookie mistake. Should have kept walking.

Yeah, because that was going so well for you.

The money had been hidden in his trainers, under the removable sole, a last-resort case, although, if he was being honest, he hadn't expected to be caught in the first place. He'd left his Jaguar parked in West London outside his renovated church apartment, and had used the train to get to where he needed to go the previous night, intending to catch a couple of night buses back to his home. This way he could monitor whether he was being followed, while keeping up the legend of the cash-strapped night cleaner.

It'd worked for three previous nights, after all.

Although maybe that was why he'd been caught so easily.

On the subject of being followed, however; while walking down the steps towards Tower Hill Station, Marlowe noted he wasn't alone. A man, middle-aged, balding, slim, with glasses on, dressed in a suit and tie like half of the other people around was paying a little too much attention to him. Now, this could have been his strange workwear and torn hi-vis jacket, but Marlowe wasn't sure. Picking up his pace, instead of going into the station, he carried on around, up past the London Wall, and headed north, along Cooper's Row towards Fenchurch Street Station.

The man had followed, however, pulled back a little, as if worried that he might have been spooking Marlowe.

Marlowe glanced back and caught the man's eyes. He hadn't meant to, and he cursed himself inwardly because the moment he turned around again and carried on, he knew the man would veer off. True to form, as Marlowe glanced back a couple of seconds later, the man had turned off, heading towards Savage Gardens, leaving Marlowe alone once more.

Although he *still* wasn't alone.

Walking quickly around Trinity Square, a young blonde woman came out, earpods in her ears, eyes down at the ground. As far as anyone was concerned, she was another commuter heading to work. The problem was that when she walked out onto the street, she had followed Marlowe but had glanced after the suited man, almost to check where the man had gone.

Marlowe almost smiled at this but didn't dare give away that he knew. One of the best ways to tail somebody was to have a rotating team; you'd follow someone, then disappear for a while, letting someone else take over, until eventually they too would be replaced. Your target would never realise they were being followed by the same unit unless they saw you again, and wondered how somebody who'd wandered off in the other direction suddenly turned up near them.

Most of the time, the other trailers would be down a parallel road, ready to leap in at a moment's notice, or, if you knew roughly where the target was going, they would already be set up ahead at certain points.

This route, however, didn't allow that. The closest parallel was Seething's Lane, down Pepy's Street, and to go that way risked losing Marlowe if he continued to the right. They probably guessed he was trying to go home, but more importantly, Marlowe wanted to know how they knew he'd be at Tower Hill. Frank Maguire had dropped him *after* Marlowe had asked to be dropped, not because he'd *intended* to drop him there. The only other people in the car who would have known were the driver and the other guard – there had been a few minutes spent arguing the drop location, so a message passed on to whoever these people were could have been arranged in time. Marlowe didn't know the two men in the car, but he wondered whether Frank Maguire's crew were as loyal as he thought. After all, they would have gained a nice finder's fee – easily five figures, if not six – for landing Marlowe in a hitman's lap.

Or, this was MI5, maybe even MI6, checking on a stray dog that had wandered away from the pack.

Marlowe had been tailed before by MI5, and they had been just as blatant, so there was every chance it was them. He couldn't be sure, though. The one thing he needed to do, however, was lose them.

On his right was the Leonardo Royal Hotel. It was a middle-grade hotel, used mainly for its closeness to the city's main landmarks, but on a Jack the Ripper walk almost two decades earlier, Marlowe, there on a date had learnt it was also known because the remains of the London Wall ran along the back.

He walked into the reception, but before anyone could speak to him, he nodded to the receptionist as if he knew them and turned left, down the side corridor. He'd been in this hotel before, many times; not in his current guise, of course, but he knew the layout, and he knew the bar had a toilet to the side, and nobody questioned a man in a hi-vis jacket who looked as if he was supposed to be there.

In the men's toilets, he entered one cubicle, shutting the door behind him and pulling off the overalls as fast as he could.

Underneath, he wore a sweater, T-shirt, and lightweight jogging bottoms. Quickly, he bundled the overalls and the glasses together, dumping them in the waste bin beside the urinals as he placed the remnants of his cash and his travel-card into his joggers' pockets. He looked like a different person, although couldn't do anything about his hair and his beard. They weren't as shaggy as they usually were, however, the beard was still visible to anyone who looked closely.

Marlowe exited the washrooms and headed east, walking past reception again, who didn't pay this "likely hotel guest" a second glance.

A man waiting by the elevators with a suitcase caught his attention. He'd obviously just landed from a flight and was arguing with someone on his phone, and Marlowe noticed that on the suitcase handle hung a baseball cap. As he passed, he niftily snatched it. He hoped it wasn't sentimental as he placed it on his head, already out of the man's line of view. At least *now* he looked different. The jeans and sweater were a different colour from the utilitarian overalls, and the cap would hide most of his hair. He couldn't do anything about the beard, but the lack of glasses might help alter the silhouette of his face.

Instead of exiting through the main entrance, however, Marlowe slipped out through a side door leading towards the rear courtyard and patio, where the remains of the London Wall were. Without looking back to Cooper's Row, he walked towards the London Wall, where to the left was a small walkway that led eastwards, out towards a half circle of houses at the end of the street known simply as Crescent, and from there he could head down Hammet Street towards the Minories, and Tower Gateway DLR station.

He paused, though, as he walked towards the walkway. There, waiting, watching for any movement was the first man who'd followed him, staring off the other way.

Bollocks. They were covering all entrances.

Luckily, Marlowe had seen the man before the man had seen him, so he could step back out of sight in time, looking around for a new suggestion, but as he looked desperately for an option, all he saw were three tired-looking men in their own jogging bottoms and running tops. They were doing stretches, warming up, and Marlowe realised there must have been some kind of morning running group.

Bingo.

Wearing the cap and sweater didn't make him look like a runner, but it was close enough. Pulling the sweater off, wrapping it around his waist, he approaching them.

'Hey, are you about to start?'

The leader, a very thin man with ginger hair, looked up at Marlowe and gave a smile.

'We've been "about to start" for twenty minutes,' he said. 'It's bloody cold. We can't get ourselves going.'

'Come on,' Marlowe grinned. 'I've been trying to get myself to do it as well. How about we just do round the block? You do it, I'll do it.'

The runners laughed, and as they carried on warming up, Marlowe joined in. They informed him they were actually there on business, staying at the hotel, and had made a deal to run every morning, although so far this had failed dismally. But now, together, the four men started running back towards Coopers Row and the main entrance. It wasn't ideal for Marlowe, but walking out the main entrance differed from running out in a group.

As the four of them exited and turned right, Marlowe kept a weather eye on the blonde woman across the road. She glanced up briefly at the four runners, paid them no notice, and pretended to read a book as she stared at the hotel, likely waiting for her target to return. Marlowe wondered how long she and her companion would stake out the hotel and then wondered if more of them had already entered the building.

If they checked the toilets, it wouldn't take long to find the overalls.

After a couple of streets, Marlowe feigned a stitch, and bid the other men farewell. He wasn't completely lying; the ankle injury he'd picked up was throbbing, and he really didn't want to cause any damage to it in case he really needed to run for his life. Instead, he cautiously carried on northwards, bypassing Fenchurch Street and eventually arriving at Aldgate, throwing his sweater back on and leaping onto a train at the last moment.

If anyone was still tailing him, they deserved to find him.

IT TOOK HIM ANOTHER HOUR TO GET BACK TO HIS APARTMENT, mainly because he wanted to make sure all tails were gone, doubling back on himself several times just in case, utilising the travel-card's "as many trips as you want" status to its fullest advantage. In fact, when he reached Kensington, he got off the train and popped into a coffee shop, explaining he'd left his phone and jacket on a carriage, and asking if he could make a quick call to tell his wife to cancel all his cards. The barista, sympathetic, passed him the phone, and he dialled a familiar number.

Trix answered.

'Jesus,' she said after he confirmed his identity. 'I thought you were dead.'

'Not quite,' Marlowe replied, smiling faintly. 'I'm walking. I'm in Kensington. I've got no money, no coat, and I think I'm being followed.'

There was the sound of tapping on a keyboard. Trix was already working. She'd probably been on the keyboard all night. Marlowe felt sorry for doing this to her, but he waited patiently.

'Where are you?' she asked.

'I'm in a coffee shop on Kensington High Street,' Marlowe said.

A few more taps.

'Make your way to the Design Museum,' she said. 'It's closed, but it'll be fine. Then go north through Holland Park. Meet me at the station in twenty minutes.'

Marlowe nodded, though he didn't need to.

'Thanks, Trix.'

He hung up and offered his last remaining fiver to the barista as thanks for the call, but they waved it away. Instead, Marlowe spent it on a flat white. After all, if anybody was watching the coffee shop, a man walking in and leaving without a coffee would have looked suspicious, especially if he'd only been inside for a few minutes, plus the heat was very welcome right now.

The Design Museum was about half a mile to the west, and Marlowe made his way there quickly, heading northwards past the playing fields and into Holland Park itself. Once the grounds of Cope Castle, a grand 17th-century Jacobean mansion later renamed "Holland House" after it became the residence of Henry Rich, first Earl of Holland, it was revised and rebuilt several times over the centuries, mainly in the 19th-century Romantic landscaping trends, which favoured naturalistic and eclectic styles in an almost patchwork style. Severely damaged during the Blitz in World War II, the estate's remnants became a focal point of the park, which now featured landscaped gardens, including the Kyoto Garden, gifted by Japan when opened to the public.

The park was also a great place to lose a tail. Narrow pathways and overgrown passages made it easy to disappear if you wanted. In fact, it was a rumoured location for spy meetings during the Cold War, mainly because of its closeness to embassies, but also because, if someone saw you with another person, you could easily split up and disappear.

Marlowe spent a good ten minutes randomly doubling back and weaving through the lanes, checking to see if anyone was still following him. Finally, satisfied, he stepped out onto the street and continued northwards to Holland Park Avenue, and the underground station of the same name.

There, parked to the side with hazard lights flashing, was a Mini Cooper.

Marlowe smiled. *A bright yellow Mini flashing its lights was the most conspicuous thing Trix could have possibly done.*

Clambering into the passenger seat, he looked across at her.

'Thanks,' he said.

'Some bloody spy you are,' Trix grinned. 'Dropped off in

London and you can't even walk yourself home. Do we need to stick you on some kind of training course or something?'

'I had to make sure I wasn't being followed.'

Trix raised an eyebrow.

'By who? The police?'

'I don't know,' Marlowe replied, and before Trix could make another comment, he quickly explained about the potential million-dollar hit on his head. When Trix heard who he'd found out from, she whistled, and Marlowe had to recount the rest of the story, including how Kieran Lachlan was now a dead legend, and how Frank Maguire was now suddenly Marlowe's new best friend.

At the end, she shook her head.

'I warned you he'd find out eventually,' she muttered. 'Well, what a bloody way to do it. And chatting to The Gravedigger as well. Do you think he knows who he was?'

'There's a chance he might've worked with him,' Marlowe said. 'But the impression I got from Maguire was that he didn't know who the man was at the time and worked it out later, so probably not.'

'Probably for the best,' Trix said.

Marlowe noted that while they were driving, she was taking random turnings. It was the kind of evasive driving you'd expect from someone following a sat-nav giving short-cuts or from a black cab driver with "The Knowledge".

Trix had neither.

When she saw him watching, she smiled.

'Evasion techniques,' she said. 'You know, counter-what-ever-you-call-it. Like you did for an hour on bloody trains.'

Marlowe said nothing and waited until she pulled up two streets away from his address.

'You think we can drive up safely?' she asked.

'I think so,' Marlowe replied, going to pass her his key before pausing – he didn't actually have his key. It was still with his items at Canary Wharf.

'Bollocks.'

'It's okay,' Trix grinned. 'I've got my own, remember?'

'I wasn't annoyed about that,' Marlowe said. 'I'm going to have to go back and get them.'

'Don't worry about it,' Trix replied matter-of-factly. 'We both know someone who can pick it up.'

'Yeah,' Marlowe grumbled. 'But then I'll have to explain everything to him, and I always feel about ten years old when Monroe scolds me.'

'Then lie,' Trix grinned as she got out of the Mini. 'I always do with Monroe and his buddies.'

Marlowe considered it.

'Could work,' he muttered.

6

PLANNING TEAM

Marlowe stayed in the car while Trix went to find out what was going on in the renovated church apartment. He knew a blonde woman walking up to the door would draw interest, but Trix was also aware of the more secluded entrances to his church-turned-living-space, including ones that led directly to the crypt. *These* were the keys Trix had talked about owning, although she probably had the key to the front door by now as well. One of her current hobbies, other than collecting 3D scans of people's eyes and creating acrylic eyeballs of them, was to make superb wax impressions of every physical key she ever found.

Anyone watching the church would see nothing more than a woman coming to pay her respects in the churchyard. It was deconsecrated now, but Marlowe was still convinced people came there to mourn. He'd seen several bunches of flowers left where graves once were, almost as if the people who visited couldn't accept that when the church closed and the ground was deconsecrated, their loved ones would be gone.

Marlowe didn't actually know if they were gone – he'd never asked. For all he knew, there could be dozens of coffins just outside his crypt-bunker walls. This was concerning, especially if he ever pursued his idea of digging out a larger underground base. The thought of drilling through stone and finding himself face to face with a skull wasn't something he wanted to deal with.

Trix had left her phone with him to stay in contact, muttering again about him being "a 'bloody rookie spy' who didn't understand spycraft". After ten minutes, the phone rang; Trix calling from the line he'd had placed in the crypt.

'All clear,' she said. 'You might as well stay parked up there, lock up, and come over.'

Marlowe did so, sneaking down the side entrance at the back of the churchyard. A couple of minutes later, he was in his underground crypt base – his "Batcave" of sorts. Trix was already at the computer, tapping away; she'd arranged the system to be set up in the crypt shortly after they started working together, and following the war-chest windfall they'd made after the Vegas heist, she'd ensured it was a top-of-the-line system. It had been updated recently, after she discovered the guy she'd been dating was not only cheating on her, but betraying them all by working for the enemy, upgrading everything using hardware and software that the guy, Ciaran Wilson, had never touched. This way, she could be certain he wasn't hacking her.

Marlowe felt it was just an excuse to buy expensive toys.

As Marlowe pulled off his baseball cap and ran a hand through his hair, Trix looked up at him.

'Go take a shower,' she said. 'Sort yourself out – you'll feel better.'

'Is that you telling me I need to relax and get back on track, or that I smell?' Marlowe asked.

Trix said nothing, simply smiled, and continued typing.

Taking her advice, Marlowe headed up the stairs through the fake doorway, hidden in a cupboard beneath the actual stairs in the church, continuing into the kitchen and turning on the coffee machine. Waiting for it to brew, he went upstairs and took a shower. Once cleaned, dressed in fresh clothing, with a coffee in hand – since he wasn't likely to sleep anytime soon – and one for Trix, he returned to the crypt bunker that was his true base, equipped with living quarters, top-tier computer systems that would put most cyber hackers to shame, and an extensive arsenal placed on a pin board armoury to the side.

As he entered, to the left was a safe that contained his valuables, next to a small collection of metal boxes which had been "borrowed" from various MI5 store rooms at some point in the past, and were now filled with his own stores, plus a makeshift armoury of purloined weaponry, gained over the years. To the right was Trix's little den, monitors and keyboards all sending glowing neon lights across the walls, and next to that was the security system, real-time camera feeds from around the church. If intruders approached, Marlowe could retreat to the crypt and hide out behind a two-inch-thick steel door, and if this became untenable, there was the small, hidden exit to the rear of the churchyard, half covered with foliage and forgotten which Trix, and then Marlowe had entered through.

If they hadn't entered via that way, there was another two-inch steel door at the back. While investigating the tunnel that led to the exit, Marlowe had found a bricked-up hole leading to an adjacent tunnel, one leading to one of London

Transport's Central Line's many service tunnels. Now secured and covered with a black tarpaulin to blend it into the darkness of the tunnel, it provided a clandestine route into London's underground network.

'So, what do we have?' he asked, settling into an armchair he'd brought down for his own comfort. He knew Trix, despite her worry for him, would've spent the night going through the data they'd found.

'We've got names,' she said. 'Companies, units ...'

She gratefully accepted the second coffee Marlowe had made, wrapping both hands around it for warmth as she studied the data on the screen. It could've been a screensaver from The Matrix as far as Marlowe was concerned; he didn't understand a bloody word. To Trix, it was as simple as reading a children's book.

'So, you were right,' she said. 'When Katherine came to you talking about an asset, she was talking bollocks. What she probably wanted was this – the information Durrant was trying to remove. Somehow Saito's stumbled onto something Orchid – *new* Orchid – is up to.'

Marlowe grimaced. Over the last few weeks, he'd been learning in real time that Orchid – a secret organisation created over a century ago and filled with some of the most dangerous people in the world – was now embroiled in a civil war, largely because of him. As a member of the High Council, a role given to him by his late father, partly as a joke and partly to force him to clean up the organisation's sins, he'd somehow split it into two factions: one wanting to return to Orchid's traditional ways, and another, filled with oligarchs and ambitious financiers, intent on world domination. Marlowe was part of the traditionalist faction, while St John Steele seemed to lead the latter.

Trix was already pointing at the screen, going through the data, but Marlowe realised he'd drifted off.

'Sorry, could you start that again?' he asked.

'Look, I know your level of intelligence isn't up here,' Trix replied with a smirk and a level hand, 'but try to keep up, yeah? Orchid—'

She paused.

'Look, what do we call this new group? Do we stick with Orchid for the originals and give the splinter group a nickname? More-kid? Bad-kid?'

'It doesn't matter,' Marlowe said. 'They won't be around long enough to need a logo or slogan.'

'So you say,' Trix replied, tapping the screen. 'But they've got money. Checking through the data we gained, Diana Durrant's name came up as old Orchid, and now she's funding this splinter group. In fact, looking at this, at least fifty percent of the funding that used to go to the original High Council is now going through St John Steele and his merry band of miscreants. The data they were hiding shows less than forty percent of the original funders have stayed loyal, but the newer additions have probably switched sides. Mainly new blood and billionaires, but it's a telling situation, and half the war chest is up for grabs, it seems.'

'Steele's promised them the world, I bet,' Marlowe said, his tone grim.

'Just like he always does,' Trix muttered before turning to face him, leaning back in her chair and sipping her coffee. 'You could've taken Steele out by now. You've had the chance more than once, but you've kept him alive.'

'I'm aware,' Marlowe said quietly.

Trix glanced around the crypt.

'They've got billions in their war chest. They live in penthouses and have fancy offices. We've got this – a crypt. A bloody crypt.'

'Only here,' Marlowe replied. 'Eve Gonzalez and Ingrid Falkenberg still have their swanky apartments and lives.'

'Only because they've been around so long the "New Kid" doesn't want to bother them,' Trix replied thoughtfully. 'New Kid, I like it. Orchid and New Kid. We'll stick with that for now.'

Marlowe shrugged. He didn't care what the splinter group was called. What mattered was what they were using the money for. Orchid had always operated in the shadows, toppling governments and accumulating wealth, but this new faction, this "New Kid", was reckless and fast. They were making mistakes. They were more visible than they had realised. That Marlowe had learned about Durrant's activities from an MI5 agent who wasn't even part of the project showed how careless they were.

Or were they? Was Saito playing her own game? Was she part of the new breed here?

'What have you found?' Marlowe asked.

'The money's being funnelled to a hub,' Trix explained. 'In America.'

'What can you tell me about the hub?'

'It's bouncing through several places,' she replied. 'But it's mostly heading to Vegas, which makes sense. Vegas has always been a central hub for Orchid. From there, it's sent to several locations: New York, Los Angeles, Texas, Washington. Probably to pay friendly senators and congressional representatives.'

She shook her head as she studied the screen.

'But there's also a significant data flow to Black Hills, South Dakota. What's there?'

Marlowe shrugged. 'I don't know. Isn't that where Mount Rushmore is?'

Trix turned to him, her expression thoughtful.

'You think they're diverting money to rebuild Mount Rushmore?'

'Maybe,' Marlowe said. 'Add St John Steele's face to the side while they're at it.'

He paused.

'Durrant mentioned Rushmore last night,' he said. 'When they lost the data, she said they could reinstall from the backups at Rushmore. Sounds like there's some dodgy shit going on there. Some kind of data archive, perhaps?'

'Well, the one thing I know about Mount Rushmore is that there's dodgy shit going on with it,' Trix said.

'How do you mean?' Marlowe frowned; this didn't sound like mission-specific information here.

As a response, Trix smiled, lowering her voice conspiratorially.

'Well, the guy building it was supposed to create a massive secret room behind it. He didn't finish, but the room's still there. Officially, it's nothing, just an empty space, but you can't visit it. Even if you go off track, rangers will stop you. You can only see it if you convince a friendly ranger to take you, and even then, you're not allowed to enter or take photos.'

'How do you know this?' Marlowe asked, suspicious.

'YouTube,' Trix grinned. 'I watch all the conspiracy videos. Also, *National Treasure 2* – awful movie, but cool facts. Apart from the end where they go over the mountain and suddenly find a massive lake.'

Marlowe shook his head.

'I doubt Steele's planning to excavate an ancient gold temple.'

'Maybe not,' Trix said, her eyes sparkling with mischief. 'But it's fun to think about.'

'Focus,' Marlowe said. 'This could help us.'

'How?'

'Frank Maguire needs me to go to Vegas,' Marlowe replied.

'And why would Maguire want you to do that?' Trix asked. Then, realising he wasn't answering, she began muttering to herself, her pen tapping against her lip. 'He knows you're MI5 now, right? He knows you're more than you used to be. You're an asset to him. But why Vegas?'

'He needs something sorted,' Marlowe said simply. 'In return, he's promised to lift the hit that's been put on me.'

'Good luck with that,' Trix said, laughing bitterly. 'How's wannabe Z-Lister Maguire suddenly able to promise shit like this?'

'That's what you're going to find out for me.'

'Of course I am. Do you know who put the hit out?' Trix leant back on her chair, watching Marlowe. 'And how easy is it to claim if you're killed? Asking for a friend, of course.'

'Take your pick, but if it came through The Broker, then it's probably Steele,' Marlowe replied. 'In the past, Wintergreen would always deal with halting things like that, but she's not around anymore.'

'And why's that?' Trix asked pointedly. 'Maybe it's because you told MI5 and the CIA to go fu—'

'It doesn't matter,' Marlowe cut her off. 'What matters is allies. If it is him, Steele's put this hit out because he knows I can't rely on MI5 anymore. He wants me forced into the open or buried so deep I'll never resurface. Either way, it's a win for him.'

'So what allies are we looking at?' Trix asked.

'If I can't rely on the Security Service, then I'll need to turn to the more ... outsourced type,' Marlowe replied. 'If I play my cards right, I can find a few sympathetic individuals. Once Orchid deals with this offshoot, we'll move forward again.'

He nodded over at a metal box on the weapons bench, rising from the armchair.

'Technically, I shouldn't need MI5's help,' he muttered, obviously irritated. 'I'm a High Council member of a secret organisation, with a war chest in the seven figures. For us, Trix – not Orchid. I should be out there living like Bond.'

He shook his head, frustrated.

'So why are you still scrambling around like this? That's easy. Bad life choices,' Trix replied with a grin. 'But on the bright side, I've made the bad life choice of sticking with you, so let's see what we can do about it, yeah? Do you know what Maguire needs you to do in Vegas?'

'He said he'd send someone around with an envelope tomorrow,' Marlowe replied. 'By then, everything should be sorted.'

'And while we're in Vegas?' Trix raised an eyebrow.

'We?' Marlowe asked.

'Of course,' Trix said, grinning. 'There's no way I'm letting you stay on your own. As you said, we've got a decent amount of money, and I'm not coming back to find you've blown it all on black or something.'

'I'll need to make some calls. Sasha Bordeaux isn't an option anymore, so I'll need an alternative source for equipment while over there. Do you still have Ryan Gates' details?'

'Are you sure about that?' Trix asked. 'Bringing him back in might also bring Marshall Kirk sniffing around.'

'Kirk's going to show up regardless of what I do,' Marlowe stretched, the hours spent at the police station finally catching up to him. As he did, his phone buzzed. Checking the screen, he saw a familiar name.

'Uncle Alex,' he said, answering the call. 'You must be psychic. I was going to call you.'

'Aye, laddie,' came the voice of City of London Detective Superintendent Alex Monroe, thick with his Scottish brogue. 'Then explain why a friend of mine just told me she saw you at Canary Wharf police station today, under the guise of an Irish bomb-maker.'

Marlowe winced.

'I thought you and Warren weren't on speaking terms?'

'She's been helpful on a case recently,' Monroe said. 'And because of that, she told me she saw a certain someone who looks a lot like my nephew being escorted out by an Essex gangster.'

'How did she recognise me?'

'I have a photo of you on my desk. She must have seen it.'

Marlowe chuckled. 'That's nice.'

'What, that she called me?'

'No, that you've got my photo on your desk.'

'Laddie,' Monroe's tone shifted to something sterner. 'Are you in trouble?'

'It's just a case,' Marlowe said, brushing it off. 'Nothing to worry about.'

'Right,' Monroe replied sceptically. 'Well, if Wintergreen's playing silly bastards—'

'I don't work for Wintergreen anymore,' Marlowe interrupted. 'Favour for a friend. Nothing more.'

'Hell of a favour. Still, if you say you're okay, I'll step back and wait for the bodies to mount up. I'll speak to you later—'

'Actually, one thing,' Marlowe interjected quickly. 'Next time you speak to your friend there, could you ask if she'd mind sending my items back? I left in a bit of a hurry and didn't grab them.'

He disconnected the call as Monroe started laughing.

7

ASSETS

As Frank Maguire had mentioned he wouldn't be giving any information through to Marlowe until the following morning, that gave Marlowe twenty-four hours to sort everything else out before they planned for Vegas. It wasn't just a case of turning up and moving on, gaining some weapons, and finding a place to stay; Marlowe also had to find out what was going on with Durrant Capital.

He had been correct when he realised that the data coming through was from a variety of agencies and, more importantly, that the information being provided to Durrant – especially about Marlowe – was not something you'd gain off the peg.

At first, he'd wondered if it was someone like Ciaran Wilson, working for Durrant on behalf of St John Steele, maybe providing information on people he knew. But Trix had checked the data code and stated quite authoritatively that there was nothing of Ciaran's in there; either he had changed his style completely, or he hadn't been involved.

What it meant, however, was that Diana Durrant had very high-up friends, higher than her station, even.

And this meant one thing. Or rather, one of two things.

Either Diana Durrant, CEO of Durrant Industries was more important than Marlowe realised ...

Or St John Steele was.

TRIX HAD BEEN MONITORING EVERYTHING, ESPECIALLY THE fallout after the operation in Canary Wharf the previous evening. Diana Durrant had been forced to stay behind and answer questions when the police had arrived, alongside a dozen other agencies, but had been allowed to do so from her suite in the offices rather than being brought down to the crime unit like "Kieran Lachlan" had.

Marlowe still didn't understand that. For a local crime unit to gain him was surprising – Special Branch would have wanted first strike, maybe even MI5, although their reluctance could have been because they'd realised he was one of theirs.

Or someone was playing with him.

So far, Marlowe had several things he couldn't quite understand; first, how was Frank Maguire able to remove him from police custody like he was picking his favourite toy in a shop, and second, what was Katherine Saito's connection to Durrant, and had she played Marlowe when he'd spoken to her?

It was early afternoon when the call came.

He was planning his next steps, looking into Maguire's connections, when his phone rang. It was encrypted and definitely from London, but it wasn't, however, from an MI5-related number.

'Hello? Is this Tom Marlowe?' the voice asked as he answered the call.

'Wrong number,' he replied, deciding to see just how much whoever this was wanted to speak to him.

'Wait for Sir Walter McKellan.'

Marlowe didn't disconnect, and after a moment MI6 sector-chief Sir Walter McKellan's old gruff and grumpy voice came on the phone.

'I hear you're hated by Emilia Wintergreen right now,' he grumbled. 'Well done. Maybe I can finally use you.'

'This isn't the best time, McKellan,' Marlowe muttered. 'I'm in the middle of something.'

'You're always in the bloody middle of something,' McKellan snapped irritably. 'I saw that your cover was blown. The Mick gunrunner. Bloody shame, that is. We used him a couple of times as well.'

Marlowe frowned at the comment; it sounded genuine, rather than some kind of fishing exercise.

'What do you mean you used him a couple of times?'

'Inter-agency. Nothing shady.' It was almost as if McKellan was defensive at the line.

'Are you telling me that my legend was used by another agent?' Marlowe replied down the line; McKellan now had his full attention.

'You know, for somebody who claims to be quite experienced in all this, you really are quite naïve,' McKellan chuckled. 'Of course we've used Lachlan when you've not been around. You spent six months off active duty because of being shot, remember? We had two occasions that we needed somebody with the exact skillset and contacts of Lachlan. You think we'd simply wait for you to get better? I hate to burst your bubble, but the world doesn't pause when Tom Marlowe gets a boo-boo.'

'It wasn't exactly a boo-boo,' Marlowe muttered. 'I was shot multiple times, point blank. I should have died.'

'Yes, you should have,' McKellan replied icily. 'Better to sacrifice for the Service than throw your toys out of the pram and leave.'

Marlowe went to reply, but bit back his response. *McKellan was deliberately prodding him, looking for a sore point.*

After a moment, realising Marlowe wasn't biting, McKellan continued.

'We sent in a ringer. Nice chap, Finn Devitt. Irish lad, good with a blade,' he explained. 'Don't worry, it wasn't with the people you dealt with. These were "Middle Eastern", shall we say.'

Marlowe wasn't sure whether McKellan was being generic with his rather racist statement. "Middle Eastern" could have meant a variety of things in the same way he could have said "East European" and covered half of Europe.

This did, however, change the situation.

Marlowe had thought that Kieran Lachlan had been a solid identity but now he didn't have a clue what else "Kieran" had been involved in.

'I appeared out of nowhere,' he said, 'in a police investigation. One that shouldn't have known who I was.'

There was a pause down the line and he heard an almost harumphous kind of noise from McKellan, a grumble perhaps. Marlowe didn't believe anybody *harumphed* these days, but it seemed McKellan was trying to bring it back.

'Look, Marlowe,' he said, 'I'm not going to pussyfoot

around. There's a reason we've called. We believe the Kieran Lachlan legend has been compromised.'

'No shit,' Marlowe replied, forcing back the anger. 'Did you work that out before or after Durrant Capital almost threw me out of a forty-eighth floor window knowing who I was? Do you want to explain how they know? Is MI6 as leaky as everybody else again? I thought you were cleaning this up.'

'We were. I can't admit it publicly, but ... let's just say there are secrets within secrets. You are aware of this, you've been in the offices of MI5 over at Box long enough to know it's a leaky ship.' McKellan's voice lowered as if he was trying to keep what he was saying out of wherever he was. Maybe he was in a room with other people around. Maybe he just didn't want to speak loudly. 'I'm aware you've done off-book missions for Emilia Wintergreen. I'm also aware you've done off-book missions recently for Katherine Saito. In fact, it was Katherine Saito's mission that threw you into shit, wasn't it?'

Marlowe didn't like the direction this conversation was going.

'Katherine Saito's in the Hong Kong office,' he said, seeing whether McKellan would bite. 'She's—'

'No, she's not,' McKellan interrupted, confirming Marlowe's suspicions. 'Everything official says she's in the Hong Kong office, but she's been based here for the last three months.'

There was a pause.

'And, just so you know, Marlowe, as she created the legend, she was also the one who signed off for using Kieran Lachlan in the various ops you weren't part of. Now, you need to ask yourself something. What does it mean when the woman who used your legend on previous MI5 and MI6-based ops, now brings you back in, claiming she's still in

Hong Kong, using a debt owed to make you do a bloody stupid thing to find an asset's data who doesn't exist?'

Marlowe held back his anger. 'Would you know where she is?' he asked politely.

'I thought you'd never ask,' McKellan replied cordially.

McKellan had passed the information over to Trix; Katherine Saito was currently staying in a sixteenth-century manor house in Kent. It wasn't Downton Abbey, as such, more what looked to be a onetime residential home now returned to its former glory – a developer probably picking it up for a steal and turning it back into what it once was. But either way, even for a high-up member of the intelligence community with favours owed, this was a little out of Saito's pay scale.

Saito, however, didn't own this manor house. It was apparently owned by a Dubai firm, which, when Trix looked into it, was owned by a Ukrainian firm.

Before that, it had belonged to a Russian oligarch, and before that, an Indian Bollywood starlet. The list went on. At least twenty previous companies, shell companies, public names, and figures had owned this manor house in some way or another; it was such a labyrinth of ownership that even Trix wasn't sure who actually held the title.

But one name had turned up several times during the search.

St John Steele.

With the blinkers off, Marlowe had spent the afternoon deep diving into Steele's old caseloads from his time in both

MI5 and MI6, and was unsurprised to see that several times over the years, Steele and Saito had coexisted on the same ops.

'Do you think Steele lives there?' Trix had asked as Marlowe prepared himself for an infiltration.

'I don't know,' Marlowe replied. 'But we've never had it turn up on searches before—'

'Which makes it sound like a trap.'

'True, but, if it gives us answers, it's worth a look.'

Trix nodded.

'Your funeral,' she muttered.

'It always is,' Marlowe quipped. 'But if Saito's there, we might at least get some answers.'

HARRINGTON HOUSE WAS A MANOR HOUSE RATHER THAN A mansion, and even then, you had to be generous when stating that. It had a large estate, though, and was on the edge of a lake, which gave it an almost picturesque kind of setting.

Marlowe had spent a couple of hours carefully moving around, and had realised quickly that entering through the main entrance was an absolute no-no.

The walls were high with razor wire on top, the gates sturdy and unclimbable. He hadn't tried to enter; he knew people would know what he looked like, but he'd made sure that he'd watched anybody who tried, delivery drivers and mail deliverers, to get an idea of what happened.

If Katherine Saito was in there, Marlowe could see no sign of her. What he could see were guards, however; ones that didn't look to be on MI5 or MI6's payroll.

Mercenaries.

Or were they "New Kid" operatives? Had these come with the house, courtesy of Steele?

The one place they didn't seem to consider, however, was the rear of the manor house, where, against the lake, there was no wall. All there was to see was a boathouse, seemingly the only structure, leading to a jetty, which had a small staircase that led to the back garden.

This was where Marlowe would enter.

After deciding on his direction here, he'd then spent the rest of the day planning out his upcoming mission.

Was it really a mission when it was a favour from a gangster?

Marlowe wasn't sure of the technicalities here. Frank Maguire had asked Marlowe to return to Vegas, locate a stray sheep, so to speak, and retrieve some sensitive data that had been taken from him. From what minimal information Maguire had given, the missing employee, a man named Lawrence Bassett, had been with Maguire from the start, and had recently been poached by an American firm – Durrant Capital – wanting to make movements into Essex, and most likely East London.

Which, to Maguire, seemed to equate to Diana Durrant and her current London plans.

Marlowe didn't care about any of this. Gangsters were gangsters. They came and went as the tides, and this was more a problem for the police than it was for someone like Marlowe. But a favour was a favour. And if it meant that Frank Maguire would conveniently forget that he'd ever met Thomas Marlowe, then it was an option.

As it was, Marlowe was happy to do this, if it meant he could kill two birds, chasing some money – and a missing subordinate – into a Vegas hub. But he wouldn't know until Maguire sent the full information the following day.

While waiting for the information, and working from the limited information they had, Trix had looked into Lawrence Bassett himself. Interestingly, it looked like Bassett had had time in the services, working in intelligence in the Royal Signal Corps. He'd left about thirty years earlier, and now in his early seventies, was probably looking for a way to retire.

He was fit and looked younger than his age, judging from the updated passport photo he'd sent in. His passport had lapsed fifteen years earlier, and he had travelled nowhere until nine months ago, when he applied for a new passport, and in that time had attended three different conferences in America.

For a man who didn't travel for over a decade, he was definitely making up for it.

Placing his binoculars down and returning slowly back to his Jaguar, Marlowe opened the boot, the hinges creaking faintly in the quiet. The contents were laid out exactly as he'd packed them – no wasted space, nothing out of place. Organisation like this wasn't about neatness; it was about survival. If you couldn't find what you needed in the dark with adrenaline pumping through your veins, you might as well not bother.

He pulled out the duffel bag, unzipped it halfway, and flipped the top back. First came the wetsuit; basic, nothing flashy. He'd cut it down to a short-sleeve version himself, a compromise between warmth and freedom of movement. It wasn't exactly military spec, but it would do the job. Back in his Royal Marines days, kit like this was standard, though he'd learnt early on that the right modification could mean the difference between silence and getting caught.

Pulling it on, next was the utility belt. He checked each pouch quickly, but thoroughly. Multi-tool, sharp and clean. Small torch with a red filter, the battery checked earlier that day. Gloves, standard disposable latex – cheap, quiet, and perfect for avoiding fingerprints. He clipped the belt around his waist, adjusting it so it sat snugly without getting in the way.

The breathing apparatus was last; a compact model, the kind used for quick dives. It wasn't as sophisticated as the re-breather systems he'd trained with in the Royal Marines, but it would get him across the lake with little trouble. He tested the valve briefly, listening for any hiss of escaping air.

Satisfied, he tucked it into the bag.

A coil of rope came next. Sturdy nylon, nothing special, but reliable. He gave it a quick pull to check the tension, then looped it around his hand. Rope like this had served him countless times before; scaling walls, tying off kit, even dragging bodies when things got messy. It wasn't glamorous, but it worked.

At the bottom of the bag, he found a slim waterproof case. He unlatched it and flipped it open to check the contents: another small EMP device from Trix, the only person left he trusted to provide the kind of gear that didn't come with strings attached.

He shut the case and slid it into the waterproof bag.

Everything was ready.

Marlowe glanced up, scanning the dark treeline beyond the car park. The manor was out there, hidden behind the lake and its thick perimeter of trees. He hoisted the duffel onto his shoulder, shut the boot quietly, and locked the car.

No backup, no second chances. Just him, a bag of gear,

and the same instinct that had kept him alive long after others would've fallen.

It was enough. It had to be.

And at the finish line, an old friend who had a lot of questions to answer.

8

COLD PLUNGE

THE WATER WAS BLOODY COLD.

Marlowe had expected this; it was late in the year and the sun wasn't out, so the evening's coolness had already prickled at his skin as he slipped into the lake on the other side. That he had cut the sleeves of his wetsuit had helped his maneuverability, but it hadn't stopped the fact that now the cold water was on his skin.

He had to wait for the water now within the wetsuit to use his own body heat to warm up. Wetsuits didn't really stop the cold; they just held it long enough to warm it with your body heat. Still, he wasn't intending to stay in the water that long, so with some determined strokes, he slowly made his way towards the boathouse.

He was wearing a waterproof bag on his back with his dry clothes, his CZ-75 packed within it, a suppressor, his Fairbairn-Sykes knife, and a few other toys. The re-breather he wore on his face, covering his nose and mouth allowed him to dip under the water and swim through the shallows so that anybody staring out at the lake would likely not see him, let alone his ripples. It wasn't a moon-filled night; in fact, the moon was quite low, nothing more than a sliver in the sky, and that meant that Marlowe had more of a shadowed journey as he made his way to the jetty.

He was about to climb out onto it, find his way onto land and find a more secluded area to get changed when Trix's voice spoke through the earpiece.

'Guard twenty feet away,' she said gently, so as not to make a loud noise. 'Looks like he has a thermal scope. He's scanning the water. Get back in.'

Marlowe dropped to under the jetty. If the thermal scope showed any warmth from his body, it would have been diffused, and the guard would likely just feel it was residual from the earlier day.

At least, that's what he hoped.

After a couple of minutes floating in the cold, wet, dark water, Trix's voice spoke again.

'Go, go, go,' she said.

Marlowe, shivering with the cold, clambered out of the water, rolling onto his back on the jetty. He waited a moment and then slowly slid onto land. There was a garden leading up to the manor, and it was built in a step formation; therefore, the part of the garden closest to the water was a good four feet lower than the step above it. Marlowe could use this to crouch down, pulling off the wetsuit and quickly pulling out and throwing on his combats, positioning his throat mic on as he did so. He wasn't intending to infiltrate in the same way James Bond would move into a party; there was no tuxedo to put on like spy novels of old.

What he had, however, was combat webbing and an armoury.

With the dry clothing warming him up, Marlowe clipped

his CZ to his waist, sheathed his knife and, taking a couple of weights from the garden – heavy, sharply cut stones and suchlike – and placing them into the bag, he dropped it over the side, allowing it to sink into the water. He'd kept the rebreather, but if things got bad he wouldn't have the time to put the now soaked wetsuit back on – however, even though he didn't intend to use it, he didn't want anybody *finding* it. With luck, the bag would spend years at the bottom of the lake with the various future residents unaware of its location. From this point on, it was a game of cat and mouse.

Saito had obviously brought some kind of security detail with her; Marlowe had counted at least four or five rotating guards when he'd been observing, and he'd recognised none of them. Now, this could have simply been because he didn't know all the agents working in the Security Service, but he'd have expected to recognise at least one. The fact he didn't meant it was likely that these were paid guns.

And paid guns meant off the books operations.

The coast was clear for the moment, and Marlowe slid through the garden's edge; moving silently past shrubberies and bushes, decorative plants that gave him shelter from the guards who, not expecting someone to come from the lake entrance, were idly staring out into the night. He worked almost automatically, finding his way through the various obstacles in front and, as he did so, he couldn't help but consider what McKellan had said earlier that day.

Had Katherine Saito used him? Was it a setup purely to remove Marlowe from the game board?

Marlowe hoped it wasn't, but tonight would be a conversation that could hopefully answer this.

There was an entrance beside the manor house, old and padlocked, leading down into what looked to be some kind of cellar area. Marlowe had seen these on Tudor barns and houses before; this was often where ice or coal would have been thrown down. Many renovated houses would use this as a wine cellar of sorts, maybe even a gym. The lock was easy to pick, and again, Marlowe couldn't help but wonder whether he was being set up here. If there was any kind of motion detector or silent alarm on the door, he was about to trip it.

'Trix,' he whispered softly, his throat mic picking up the faintest of vibrations. 'You about? I need to know if this is live or not.'

'Scanning,' she said. 'Looks like it has something so you could use the localised EMP I left you.'

'Won't that take out the entire building?'

'Two taps,' she said. 'You'll take out everything within a ten-yard area. With luck, you won't have anything important there.'

Marlowe grimaced, pulling out the small EMP device. As well as in Durrant Capital, he'd used similar to this a couple of weeks earlier. That time, however, he'd shorted out an entire yacht, causing chaos in the process, and of course the previous night he'd started blowing up servers with one.

His belief this would go smoothly was not high.

'You're sure this'll work?'

'Ish.'

'What the hell do you mean, *ish*?'

'Well, I'm not there, you are,' Trix's voice gave the impression she was enjoying this. 'Just remember though, it's one use only, so make it count.'

'If I do this,' Marlowe muttered before tapping, 'wouldn't they notice if the systems went down?'

'You're in and out,' Trix replied. 'By the time they look to see what's going on, you'll be somewhere else in the house.'

Marlowe reluctantly agreed with the response and tapped the EMP device twice, after switching off his own devices first. After five seconds, the EMP flashed blue ... and nothing else happened. No lights flickered, no sounds stopped, and when Marlowe turned his items back on, everything worked fine. There was no way to know if the device had even worked, but then such was the way of things like EMP devices, and Marlowe had to take a leap of faith as he opened the hatch door and slipped into the cellar, closing it behind him.

He'd been correct. There had been a motion detector attached to the door, as well as a couple of other systems, which now seemed to go through a reboot loop. By the time they turned back on, Marlowe would be long gone, and anyone sitting in a room watching this would assume it was a firmware update or something; a glitch, nothing more.

The cellar had been turned into what looked to be some kind of wine and cigars vault; he'd hoped that this didn't mean there was a vault door on the other side, although why anyone would place a vault door on a room that could be opened by a cellar hatch meant that this was more unlikely by the second. Sidling through the cellar corridors, he also saw a batch of servers to the side.

This might save him a lot of hassle.

Quickly pulling out a USB device transmitter of some kind – he never asked when Trix gave him these toys – he slotted it in.

'Trix?'

'Got it.'

The device flashed blue and green, and Marlowe assumed it was connecting through to something that Trix was doing on the other end.

'It's going to take a while. You can wait there, or you can carry on through.'

'Will people find it?'

'They will, but they won't know where it came from,' Trix replied, and Marlowe could almost imagine the smile on her face. 'The moment it finishes its job, I'll flash send a reboot. It'll be back to factory settings by the time they pull it out. No idea of where it came from, who used it, or what it was even doing.'

Marlowe didn't like leaving items behind, especially expensive ones. But he wasn't sure if he'd be returning this way, especially if the shit hit the fan. So, trusting Trix's judgement, he carried on towards the main door.

It was wooden, heavy, but unlocked, and as Marlowe slowly opened it he could see that there was nobody on the other side. There was a set of stairs, old and stone, leading up into the main manor itself. Marlowe quietly drew his suppressed CZ and, with the pistol leading the way, slowly started up the stairs. He didn't want to shoot anybody, but he sure as hell wasn't gonna find himself caught on the back foot like he'd been back in Canary Wharf the previous day.

Strangely, the guards seemed to be more focused on the outside of the building than on the inside. Katherine Saito had been left on her own.

Moving slowly and carefully, Marlowe found himself in the kitchens. Opening a fridge, he could see bread, cheese, meats ... all the usual basics were there, enough for a few days for one person, maybe less for two. Marlowe opened the freezer, checking at the back of it. Freezers were a known location for spies to hide things; you'd never know what could be found behind the back of a bag of frozen peas.

Again, though, nothing.

Sighing, Marlowe moved further into the manor house, listening carefully as he walked.

'Thermals show somebody in the library,' Trix said.

'Which room's the library?' Marlowe whispered through the throat mic.

'Second door on your right,' Trix's voice came through. 'I'm using old records of the house, so it might not be a library anymore, but that's what it's named as here.'

'You're using a Cluedo map, aren't you?'

'For the good it's doing me, it might as well be.'

Marlowe nodded, even though Trix couldn't see it, and slowed as he made his way to the door. He'd considered bringing a thermal monocular, which might have allowed him a fair idea of where the person in the library was, or maybe even whether or not there was more than one occupant waiting. He hoped to God it wasn't more than two; he hated gatecrashing parties of armed guards – it never ended well. But in the end he'd decided against the thermal gear, so it was a moot point - He'd have to rely once more on his own abilities. So, with the suppressed CZ leading the way once again, he gently opened the door.

In the library was a desk, an ornate mahogany one, the type that had a green leather top-piece. Marlowe almost expected a banker's lamp to be on it. The walls were half paneled, sideboards with bookshelves above. There was a globe bar in the corner which added a slight seventies kitsch to the established style, and a window looked out onto the garden, the heavy yellow curtains now pulled. The room was half-lit and on the desk was a MacBook, open. Facing away, checking through the books on the far wall, was Katherine Saito.

'I said I didn't want to be disturbed,' she said without looking, 'unless you've—'

She'd turned to admonish whichever guard had entered the room, and her eyes widened as she realised that the combat-suited Marlowe wasn't exactly somebody on her side. She was in her mid-forties, her black hair cut into an asymmetrical bob, giving her a slightly roguish look to such an organised person. She was wearing jeans and a jumper, a chunky cable-knit one that hid her figure. The last few times Marlowe had seen her, she'd been on covert diplomatic ops, and it felt strange to see Katherine Saito in anything but a cocktail dress.

If she was surprised to see Marlowe, she didn't show it, which impressed him. The chances were she must have been expecting a visit at some time, but had hoped that something would have altered that before it occurred.

'Tom,' she murmured, her face giving the slightest of nervous smiles. 'I'm glad you got my message about the debrief.'

'You sent me a message about a debrief?' Marlowe asked, almost mocking as he spoke. 'So you *told* me to come here, yeah?'

'Well, I hadn't given the address yet, but ... I was aware you're quite resourceful, and Trix Preston is worth her weight in gold,' Saito walked over to the desk, Marlowe watching her hands, checking to see if she'd pressed any buttons, calling for help. 'You know, when she stepped away from MI5, it was an enormous loss to the security services.'

'She's young. It was reckless. Trix will likely come back,' Marlowe smiled. 'She'll get bored with working with me.'

'From what I hear, you give her what we could never do.'

'Oh? And what would that be?'

Saito's smile widened, warming up a little, as if the conversation gave her hope that this wasn't an assassination attempt.

'An unlimited bank balance to buy all the toys she wants,' she shrugged. 'Let's be honest, a civil servant's position doesn't exactly buy the toys that she would have liked. We're not even up to date on the latest operating systems half the time.'

Marlowe ignored the deprecating comment. He knew it was said purely to try to put him off guard. Saito also knew that this wasn't going the way she'd expected.

'Look, I don't know what you've been told—' she started, but Marlowe held up his hand to stop her.

'Katherine, don't,' he said, his voice calm but authoritative. 'I know what you've done. I just need to know why.'

He looked around the room as he spoke.

'This doesn't feel like Hong Kong,' he continued, gesturing around the library. 'Not in how you're acting, not in the location we're in.'

He paused, the CZ now in a low ready position.

'Tell me, Katherine,' he asked sadly, 'when did you start working for St John Steele?'

9

GUNSHOT

KATHERINE STARED AT MARLOWE FOR A LONG MINUTE, AND HE couldn't work out if she'd been expecting the question or not.

'It's not as clear-cut as that,' she eventually replied, and Marlowe thought for a second that she'd glanced around the room as well, as if checking to see if anybody else was in there, listening. He wondered if there were bugs and raised an eyebrow.

Katherine shook her head, realising what he was thinking.

'We can speak clearly here,' she said. 'I swept before I came in, but ... I didn't think you'd want to have the conversation.'

'How about you tell me what's going on, and *then* we'll decide if I want to have the conversation?' Marlowe replied. 'Tell me about your asset, your analyst, the one who apparently died.'

Katherine said nothing, and her expression didn't change, but Marlowe could tell there was a slight wince at his statement. She knew Marlowe had figured it out, and as far as she was concerned, the game was up. But Marlowe knew Katherine Saito well. She would keep arguing to the very end, to find a way out of whatever problem this was about to become.

'I owed you my life,' he said to her, taking away her option to respond. 'You took bullets for me you didn't need to.'

'And in return, you made sure I didn't die from those wounds, and it was my mistake that got us there in the first place,' Katherine replied. 'So, as far as I'm concerned, we're kind of equal.'

'We were allies,' Marlowe continued, trying not to sound hurt at the statement. 'You had my back on countless ops. Why would you screw me over?'

He held up a hand to pause her from replying.

'And please don't tell me more about how "it's complicated". Everything we do is complicated. That's the whole point of spycraft.'

Katherine nodded, accepting the comment.

'When I last saw you,' she said, 'it was what? Two years ago? Maybe two and a half?'

'About that,' Marlowe nodded.

'Before you were shot,' Katherine continued. 'Before you were taken off active duty.'

'Okay ...' Marlowe nodded again, unsure where this was going.

'A lot's happened between then and now, hasn't it?' Katherine carried on, and from her tone Marlowe sensed she believed she was somehow the wounded party here, even though she was the one who had set him up.

'What are you trying to get at?' Marlowe asked, noticing

that Katherine had moved behind the desk now, in front of the window. The curtain was closed; if she was trying to gain an advantage, he needed to figure it out quickly.

'You never spoke about your father,' she continued, 'never mentioned he was a High Councillor of Orchid—'

'Now wait a second,' Marlowe interrupted. 'I didn't know about my father being part of Orchid, or its bloody High Council. As far as I was concerned, my father pissed off when I was a kid, and the last time I saw him was when I was eighteen. I only learned about what was going on when I met him in New York less than a year ago. He told me he was dying, and then I was given his Orchid coin.'

'I wish I could believe you,' Katherine stared at him. 'But I've been given certain information—'

'Let me guess. St John Steele?' Marlowe snapped. 'I've read that you'd worked with him back in the day.'

'I did more than work with him,' Katherine replied angrily, reddening as she straightened up. 'He was my mentor ... my, well—'

'He was your lover?' Marlowe asked, surprised.

Katherine didn't reply, just glaring across the table at him, before sighing, her shoulders loosening a little as she pulled out, and then slumped, into the leather desk chair in front of her.

'Steele told me what happened,' she explained. 'How he'd been forced out of MI5 and MI6 after Emilia Wintergreen had gone for him. How he'd been forced to go undercover with Orchid and—'

'Oh, don't give me this crap,' Marlowe interrupted. 'I didn't come here for "story time with St John Steele", because that's all this is. You might know the Steele of old, Katherine, but I know the Steele of right now. The Steele who has been working with billionaires to destabilise the world. Who's been trying to take an organisation that was created over a century ago to do good, and now fill it with oligarchs and corporations—'

He realised he was pacing and forced himself to halt.

'Every time he's tried to take over the world, I've stopped him so far. And I believe we're currently at something like zero for three on his side. So, forgive me if I'm not keen to hear the most complimentary story about myself from him,' Marlowe shook his head. 'Did you know he was still part of Orchid?'

'He was never part of Orchid,' Katherine's eyes flashed with anger. 'It was always an op—'

'An op? I'm sorry, Katherine, but if you believed him, then you're not the spy I thought you were.' Marlowe almost laughed at the naivete being shown here. 'Whatever happened to the woman who did due diligence as the Hong Kong Section Chief? Who knew better than anybody how to reverse an op? How to switch an asset?'

'Is that what you're doing here? Trying to switch an asset?'

'I'm trying to work out why somebody I class as a friend would aim me at a situation that would get me killed,' Marlowe said. 'Besides that, I want to know why my so-called friend would aim me at a location that's connected to the guy who owns this house, apparently, and who we've already discovered was a previous bedroom partner.'

Katherine went to respond, but Marlowe was on a roll.

'I'd like to know why you sent me into a death trap. I'd like to know why Kieran Lachlan, a legend you knew was mine, was used without my consent. I'd also like to know what else Kieran Lachlan, or rather Finn Devitt – that's the name of the guy playing me when I wasn't around, right? – did in my name, and why it's now starting to turn up and bite me on the arse. I'd like to know why I'm suddenly being investigated by bloody local cops as well.'

He stopped, staring at Katherine with a piercing gaze.

'It feels to me like you threw me into a place purely to start me on a hunt. But I can't work out why you would do both.'

'Do both?'

'I can't figure out why you threw me at Diana Durrant, knowing she was working with Steele, to gain information that you knew didn't exist, while setting me up for a fall.'

Katherine Saito rose in anger, but then paused herself, turning the movement into a stretch, as she placed the chair in front of her, almost like a shield.

Marlowe observed Katherine for a good few seconds as she stared balefully at him.

'You make your decisions and your deductions so quickly,' she said. 'You decide in a heartbeat whether someone is guilty, whether or not they're a traitor. But the world doesn't work like that, Marlowe. It might have been black and white for you, but for me, it's always been shades of grey.'

Marlowe said nothing, allowing her to continue.

'I told you it's complicated,' she replied. 'Do I know Steele? Yes. Do I owe him my life like I owe you mine? Yes. And his debt came before yours. Do I trust him? I can't answer that.'

'Let me guess,' Marlowe said. 'You thought you could, but now you don't know?'

Katherine sighed.

'All I know,' she said reluctantly, 'was he came to me out of the blue, said that you'd gone rogue. You'd kicked off against your paymasters, now you were hunting for him, believing that he'd killed your brother. You were exacting some kind of insane revenge against him … he asked me to keep you away from whatever he was doing, find a way to distract you.'

'Durrant Capital.'

'There was a backdoor ploy I'd put together a while back—and yeah, I should have done my due diligence, but he never actually told me to move that way, he was just really good at suggesting—however, while planning it for this revised op, I checked more into Steele. I learned he was working a lot with Diana Durrant and, whether or not you trust me, Marlowe, you know she is *definitely* not trustworthy. I saw that David Kelly had gone to work for the Durrants. Kelly, by the way, had worked with Steele when he was at MI6. I'd seen messages between Kelly and McKellan, so I'm guessing he was sent in undercover, to see what he could find. There were others in MI5 and MI6 that I found, ones who'd moved away silently and quickly when you outed a ton of Orchid agents.'

'Go on.'

'I didn't know if you were being a white hat or a black hat, but I realised the story wasn't exactly what I was being told,' she said as she waved around the library. 'I came here because I knew you'd find me eventually. I'd hoped I could convince you to back off, but it looks like it won't happen. The information I sent you to get was fake, but I knew Trix would get in through some back door, and I knew she'd find something. I hoped you would come back to me confused, show me the data, and that would give me the proof that I wanted, whether or not Steele was playing me.'

She held out a hand.

'Do you have that?'

'We have information,' Marlowe replied cautiously. 'There are international hubs where money is being funded. Durrant is doing this with Steele and his new offshoot of Orchid. I'm guessing he didn't tell you about that?'

Katherine seemed to relax now, as if thinking, as if believing that her life wasn't in danger at the moment.

'And my arrest as Lachlan? Was that you?'

'I guessed you'd need an exit strategy,' Katherine nodded. 'I thought aiming people at Kieran Lachlan would mean more police and less dodgy spy types. And once you were in custody, I sent Frank Maguire to get you.'

'You outed me?'

'No, I told him to go pick up Lachlan,' Katherine shook her head. 'It'd been suggested by an associate of Steele's.'

'Durrant?'

'No, it was—' Katherine paused, as if worried about giving more away than she wanted to.

'What do you know about Operation Quicksilver?' she asked.

'Nothing,' Marlowe replied. 'I mean, I think I remember seeing it. It was around the time I was looking into Rubicon suspects, so maybe it was a nineties op or something.'

Katherine nodded.

'Mid-nineties, Conservative government closed it down shortly before Tony Blair came through with a massive landslide for New Labour. Didn't want their dirty laundry exposed. Before my time, before your time, but it still existed, Tom.'

'Okay,' Marlowe replied, confused at where this was going. 'And how does this relate to what's going on?'

'Back in the nineties, Orchid was making another pass at global power,' Katherine's knuckles whitened as she leaned against the back of the chair, still standing. 'They were stopped mainly because of the General Election going the wrong way for them, but there was a lot of money being passed around, funding into slush funds, areas in America that were gaining hundreds upon hundreds of millions out of nowhere, all part of the "special arrangement" we had back then. Even though Margaret Thatcher and Ronnie Reagan were gone, their dreams and plans were still in action.'

'We never had money back then,' Marlowe frowned. 'What were we giving in response?'

'Unfettered access to GCHQ,' Katherine replied. 'Among other things. We whored ourselves out and said "thank you sir can I have another" every time they pretended to love us.'

She shifted against the chair, uncomfortably. Marlowe knew this was a conversation she didn't really want to have.

'It's been resurrected,' she continued, 'but not as Quicksilver. In fact, if you were to check your files, you'd find that Quicksilver no longer exists. Quietly piled away into mothballs.'

'The money?'

'Disappeared, no one knows where it went. Some believe the CIA funneled about half into a dodgy off-books section—it was mostly US-given, after all. Which explains when the Conservatives came back into power, they made a point of making sure that nobody could gain information on it and realise they'd funded the CIA with UK Government money at a time when they claimed they didn't *have* any UK Government money.'

'But, let me guess, someone did know where it went,' Marlowe shook his head. 'And why do I think that someone is St John Bloody Steele?'

'Because it *was* St John Steele,' Katherine nodded. 'He

started an operation named Stone Blind shortly before he left MI6. It was created as a Black Ops mission title, but it had nothing added to it. If you check any records, you'll see it's nothing more than an information gathering op, but he used it to gain assets and links. Through them, he found the location of the missing money, still nothing more than data streams by now, and was able to divert it.'

'Are you telling me that St John Steele's new brand of Orchid has now found himself hundreds of millions of pounds' worth of taxpayers' money from the nineties – or at least the money the CIA didn't steal – to play with?'

Katherine said nothing.

'Answer me!'

'Look,' she said, 'he told me he was one of the good guys, and I thought, well, Bruce Wayne was a billionaire and *he* was a good guy.'

'Wayne is fictional,' Marlowe snapped.

'I *am* aware.' Katherine straightened now, angry. 'I'm trying to point out that I was hoping he was on the side of angels, but the more I looked into it, the more I realised he wasn't. His plan was simple, and still moving. He doesn't have the money yet, as he needed to find a way to get it without aiming everyone at him. It was a shell game. Durrant was a cog in the gears, part of the plan to move it to Vegas, where he'd be able to launder it, legitimise it with his contacts there.'

'But what, you didn't believe him?'

'Things seemed a little off, with these unknown names and faces, so I decided if I was distracting you, I could at least use you,' Katherine explained. 'You were supposed to go to Durrant Capital and find nothing. The police were tipped off that Kieran Lachlan was there – that was on me and I apologise for that – but it was to arrest you and bring you out safely. At no point were you supposed to be shot at or have anyone try to kill you. But then I'd forgotten that "Kieran Lachlan" was a little hotter than usual.'

'How so?'

'Finn, the man who had taken your role, he died two months ago. A bombing in Prague.'

She rubbed her face with her hands as if trying to wash away what she was about to say next.

'It was an unsanctioned op, Marlowe. I was doing it for Steele.'

'What were you doing?'

'It was an arms deal, but one that went wrong.'

'Let me guess,' Marlowe finished the sentence for her. 'Kieran Lachlan turned up to do an arms deal, it went wrong, there was an explosion linked back to him. Therefore, he caused an act of terrorism on European soil.'

Katherine nodded silently.

'And the moment you got the local police in to arrest Kieran Lachlan, it banged a ton of alarms everywhere.'

Katherine nodded again.

'I'm sorry, Marlowe, I hadn't considered that.'

But I bloody well bet Steele had.

Marlowe wanted to shout at her, but knew if he started raising his voice even more, he was just calling on problems.

'Who told you to use Kieran's identity last night?' he asked. 'You knew he was dead, if he died a couple of months back.'

'Steele did. But the body of Kieran Lachlan was never found, mainly because the moment we heard Finn had died, we changed his records. When the body was discovered, it was nothing more than a random bystander caught in the bombing.'

'So Finn, or whatever you called him was dead, but "Kieran Lachlan" escaped?' Marlowe was furious now. 'You've literally turned me into FBI public enemy number one! No wonder everybody wanted a shot! If I haven't got people trying to kill me because of Steele's bloody hit, I've got them trying to arrest me for international terrorism. Great work.'

'I was trying to keep you safe,' Katherine snapped back angrily. 'I was hoping you'd find out something that I could use against Steele. Force him to tell me the truth.'

'Steele doesn't understand the truth,' Marlowe shook his head. 'And where is he, anyway? I thought he'd be here.'

'He's in Vegas,' Katherine sighed. 'Finishing the next stage of the money transfer, working with contacts he made when he was last there, working as the Arbitrator ... when you murdered your brother.'

'I didn't murder my *half*-brother,' Marlowe could hear movement outside – it sounded like security was finally waking up. 'He *framed me* for murdering my half-brother. There was no love lost there, and I'd only recently learned who he was. Of course, Steele didn't exactly make my life easy with that ...'

Another thought came to mind.

'Why did Maguire get me out?'

'I'd used him a few times as an unknowing asset, mainly after we'd sent you in to work with him,' Katherine looked uncomfortable now. 'I was far enough away to keep my hands clean, and when I realised I needed somebody to get you out, Maguire's name came up as someone who'd have the connections to do it.'

'Did you know he knew who I really was?'

'No, I'm sorry. I told him to let me know if you wanted out, too. I had a team converge on Tower Hill to make sure you got home safe, but you lost them.'

Well, that explained the people following him, at least. It wasn't Maguire or his men, after all.

There was a moment of silence, and Marlowe could hear people congregating outside. They were likely waiting for a shouted command from Katherine, but currently she seemed happy to talk.

'What's going on,' he breathed. 'Like, really? Why are you holed up here rather than in Hong Kong, even wherever you've been staying the last couple of months, and why do you have mercenaries rather than operatives guarding you?'

Katherine Saito shook her head.

'It's complicated,' she repeated. 'I did what I did, sure, but I hadn't realised how wrong I've been. After you were almost killed, I went to Steele to argue this, but he was furious I'd done that. I even pointed out it hadn't been my idea to start with, and when I checked with him and his people—'

Katherine Saito's head snapped forward as the simultaneous sounds of glass breaking and the supersonic whip-crack of a high powered rifle round filled the room. Her dead body collapsed instantly, her head a mess of gore where the bullet had struck her.

Marlowe dived for cover – the curtain had been closed; there was no way someone made that shot without a thermal scope, and even then it was a hell of a shot.

'Marlowe!' Trix shouted down the earpiece.

'I'm okay,' Marlowe said as he ran to Katherine's body, quickly checking through the pockets. 'Sniper. Outside, direction of the lake.'

'You need to get out—'

'I need to find what Saito had,' Marlowe muttered as, in the distance he could hear the pounding of footsteps; the security guards, having been waiting outside, were now preparing to breach into the room.

And Marlowe was trapped by a sniper, hiding in a room with the body of their dead boss.

10

TUNNEL RAT

MARLOWE HAD BEEN IN WORSE SITUATIONS, BUT NOT *THAT* many worse situations than this. With the heavy curtains still down, the only evidence of an assassin's bullet coming from outside was a small circle of torn cloth, barely larger than a pound coin. The window behind would likely have a shattered pane, but security guards coming in the middle of the night and seeing Marlowe, gun in hand, beside the body of their boss with her head pretty much exploded all over the place, would likely shoot first and ask questions later.

Before anybody could enter, Marlowe ran to the door, locking it from the inside, wincing as a sniper round smacked into the wood, inches beside him. Luckily, it was an old Tudor door with a solid metal key, which Marlowe twisted in the lock and removed, placing it in his pocket as he did so. As he dived to the floor of the library, another round slammed into the wall, sending the curtain fluttering once more, the hammering on the door became louder as the guards, still unsure what exactly was going on, shouted through the door.

'Miss Saito!' one shouted. 'Miss Saito, are you okay?'

Marlowe didn't even want to pretend to be Katherine Saito. A high-pitched falsetto 'I'm okay' wouldn't solve anything here. Looking around, he realised that the only other option he had for escape, other than the main door, which was locked and surrounded by guards, was a window that a sniper was obviously aiming at.

'Trix,' he muttered. 'Help.'

There was a momentary delay, likely Trix checking through the systems, looking at the antiquated map she had, to try to work out what else there could be for an escape route. While she did this, Marlowe started going through the desk drawers, looking for anything that could have been left; there was nothing. He closed the MacBook, sliding it into his webbing, under his vest – it might have had nothing on it, but there was a chance that it could have information or an email that Trix could use to work out what to do next – before, finally, he turned to the bookcase. The leather-bound book she'd been pulling out when he first entered was still there.

Was she pulling it out or placing it back? Marlowe wasn't sure. So, as the hammering got louder on the door, he pulled the book out, opening it.

It was a fake book, made to look like a novel, but with the pages cut out inside to give a hidey hole for secret items. Inside it was what looked to be some kind of flash drive, although when he took it from the book, it flashed green, a sliding scanner-style light that made Marlowe wonder if he'd just accidentally given away his identity as it scanned his thumbprint.

This wasn't MI5 tech – that, he was sure about. As he placed the drive next to the key in his pocket, he tossed the book to the side, looking around to find a way of getting out,

Trix's voice came back through his earpiece.

'I've got an exit,' she said, 'but you're not going to like it.'

'Go for it.'

'Wall to the left of the door as you enter. Bookcase above, sideboard beneath.'

'I'm standing there right now.' Marlowe looked down at it. 'There's no drawers, though, it's just wood panelling.'

'No, that's what you're supposed to believe,' Trix said. 'The layout I've got is an old one, as I said, and it actually shows there's some kind of priest hole built into this.'

Marlowe had a sudden hope. A priest hole was a hidden space in English homes during the Elizabethan era, used to hide Catholic priests when they were hunted under anti-Catholic laws. These small, concealed rooms were built into walls, under floors, or behind fireplaces, often by skilled craftsmen. They were cramped, airless, and invisible to casual inspection, designed to protect priests from capture and execution. Many saved lives; some failed, leading to torture and death.

Some even led outside, and that was something Marlowe was very invested in finding right now.

'They'll see it,' Marlowe replied, 'the moment they come in.'

'Then you'd better close it up after you, so they don't think you've gone in there. You need to set up another escape route for them to follow.'

'That involves the window, and the guy shooting at me.'

The door was shaking now, as more people were slamming against it, and bullets could be heard slamming into the frame. They were either trying to shoot the lock out or destroy the hinges. Either way, the door wouldn't last under whatever they were going to do.

Sighing, Marlowe knew there was no other option. He ran

to the window and, keeping as low as he could, pulled the curtain open.

There was no gunshot.

'Hold,' Trix said. 'I'm giving you cover.'

Suddenly, the garden outside was lit up as, accessing the house's system, Trix turned on the floodlights. It was only for a moment, but the blinding light would have affected the sniper for a second. Marlowe opened one of the windows, ducking back as he heard the supersonic crack of a bullet passing far too close to his ear, before slapping into the wall behind him - he'd literally felt the round scream past his head.

Bollocks. The sniper was shooting blind now.

On his hands and knees, Marlowe made his way over to the priest's hole.

'There's a cherub in the mounting,' Trix said through his earpiece. 'Twist it anti-clockwise; it unlocks the latch.'

Marlowe did so, and the door opened.

'How long do I have to stay here for do you think?'

'It's not a room,' Trix replied. 'It leads you into the crawl-spaces between the internal and external walls. Old houses have loads of them. You should be able to get down into the cellar from there. And, well, we already know what to do once there.'

Marlowe grimaced, but knew he had little time. The door was now shuddering; the hinges were obviously about to give way.

He saw beside the door there was a large red fire extinguisher, a good thing to have in an old Tudor house where there were loads of flammable books, and he grabbed it quickly, pulling it back out of sight of the window, before he could be shot at once more. Aiming the nozzle of the fire extinguisher at the door, he pressed down on the handle, filling the room with the fire extinguisher's smoke. It wasn't exactly a smoke bomb, but it would do enough to cause confusion as they made their way through. As soon as it emptied, he tossed it aside, diving in through the door, slamming it shut behind him, already crawling on hands and knees down into the crawlspaces between the walls.

There wasn't much space, a foot or two in width at best, just enough room to slide along the wall. The crawlspaces weren't inside the building; it was more between the building itself and the external wall, but Marlowe was able to start moving away as he heard the door shatter to the library and shouts entering. He almost wished he could have stayed to see as the guards ran in, finding themselves in a room full of smoke.

There were more shouts and the slightest faint crack of glass. The sniper, it seemed, had found new targets.

'Trix,' he whispered.

'I'm already on it,' Trix said. 'I'm working out a trajectory. If she was in front of the desk when she was shot, they would have to be firing from across the lake. There's only two places they could do it.'

'Find it. I want them.'

Eventually, Marlowe found a ladder in the crawlspace. Crude and old, it was easily as ancient as the timbers the house was made from, which meant it was probably rickety as hell and likely to be filled with termites. Still, Marlowe had no choice, so placed his foot on one of the rungs. It held, and he slowly made his way down. Three rungs from the bottom, the wood gave way, and he slammed down onto the ground into the basement below – or rather the wall between the basement and the wall outside, clutching at his chest to make sure the stolen laptop wasn't struck in the impact.

It was colder down here. The other side of the wall, Marlowe knew was nothing more than foundations – no exit there. He didn't have time to think about this, so turning in the almost darkness, he moved along the wall. He knew that in the cellar, some of the server racks were placed against these walls, but when he'd placed the USB stick in, he'd seen there were spaces in between, likely for ventilation and heat dispersal, and he was sure he'd seen a grate in one of the gaps. Proving his theory correct, he could see a small amount of light feeding in from something square, around ten yards down the passage. Quickly, he moved along to it, and slid down the wall, feeling for anything he could use—

There. A ventilation grating, likely for more heat dispersal.

Metal, and two feet square, it was a tight fit, but doable. Sitting with his back against the external wall, and his boots against the grating, Marlowe took a breath, pre-emptively winced at the noise this was about to make, and slammed the soles of his boots hard against it.

Clang.

Nothing. The grating still held. Taking another breath, Marlowe tried again.

Clang.

This time, there was movement, as the screws holding the grating were forced from the softer plaster. Knowing it'd need one more, Marlowe struck once more, wincing again as the metal grate detached from the wall and clattered across the stone floor.

No turning back now. If anyone was in the cellar, he'd be walking out to a gun in the face. Sliding through the grating, Marlowe emerged into the cellar to find it currently empty.

However, he was still a good way from the hatch – a hatch, which now worked again, complete with motion-detecting sensors, the EMP's damage now gone.

A motion detector that had picked up Marlowe the moment he'd kicked a metal grating across the bloody room.

'Alarms are ringing,' Trix said. 'Get out now.'

Marlowe turned for the hatch, but stopped short as the door to the cellar opened, and a young, suited guard entered, leading with a Glock 17.

Marlowe froze for a moment, his eyes locking onto the guard. The weapon in the young man's hand was steady, but the hesitation in his posture betrayed a lack of experience.

It's not over yet.

The guard froze, so Marlowe took advantage, his left hand reaching for the suppressed CZ strapped to his thigh in a drop-leg holster.

'Don't do it,' the guard barked, his voice trying for authority but cracking slightly.

Marlowe smiled thinly.

'Do what?' he replied, his tone mocking as his fingers gripped the gun, but didn't draw it yet.

Come on. Watch the birdie.

The guard's eyes flicked down for a fraction of a second – just enough. Marlowe surged forward, but the guard reacted quicker than Marlowe expected, stumbling back and raising the Glock. As the guard started to squeeze off a round, Marlowe stepped to the side, his strong-side hand grabbing the slide of the Glock. The gun fired, but missed Marlowe, who's grip kept the weapon from cycling. Now with his right hand cupping the back of the slide, Marlowe twisted the gun up and out of the guards grip, and then drove him into one of the wine racks. Bottles shattered around them, spilling rich, likely very expensive aged reds across the floor.

Marlowe didn't want to kill the guard; it wasn't his fault he was working for the wrong people. And Katherine, for all her recent sneakiness, had been a solid MI6 Section Head. The last thing Marlowe wanted to do was kill another potential operative – he'd pissed off enough people in Whitehall already.

The guard, however, had other ideas. Frantic over being disarmed, he grabbed a bottle of wine from the rack they'd fallen against, and spun with a wild swing aiming for Marlowe's head. Marlowe dodged the bottle and retaliated with a snap kick that sent the guard stumbling hard into the rack again, shattering yet more precious bottles in a spray of red wine, which strangely brought back the moment when Katherine Saito was killed to Marlowe's mind.

Marlowe's didn't slow. He hefted a broken wine bottle, its jagged edge gleaming in the dim cellar light, and slashed upward. The guard yelped as the glass tore through his sleeve, drawing a thin line of blood along his forearm.

Scrambling, the guard reached blindly behind him and found a crowbar leaning against a crate of wines that were yet to be placed into the racks. Likely there to open the lid of the crate, it had a new purpose as, with a desperate swing, the guard aimed again for Marlowe's head. Marlowe ducked, the iron bar whooshing past, and countered with a vicious kick to the guard's solar plexus, slamming him back into another rack.

Don't hit the laptop. Don't hit the laptop.

More bottles crashed, and the floor became a slippery mess of wine and glass shards. The guard now swung the crowbar desperately in front of him, this time lower, aiming for Marlowe's knees. Marlowe jumped back, then lunged forward with the bottle. The jagged edge caught the guard's wrist, and he dropped the crowbar with a howl of pain.

Sliding behind the incapacitated guard, Marlowe wrapped his arm around the front of the man's neck, grabbing his own wrist with his off hand and applying a carotid sleeper hold.

You're done,' Marlowe growled, breathing heavily.

The guard, already winded from the fight, quickly lost consciousness as the blood supply to his brain was cut off, slumped in a heap onto the wine and glass soaked basement floor.

Quickly, Marlowe checked the guard for anything useful, but apart from a Kevlar vest, there was nothing of note on him. After checking the laptop, seeing it was unscathed, Marlowe ran for the hatch, slamming it open and leaping out into the garden, but when he was met by rounds buzzing past him, he jumped back to the cellar.

One of the guards who had fired on him outside came barreling through the doorway and made the mistake of not using all his senses to pinpoint his opponents location. Marlowe's CZ double tapped him, centre of mass, and the man crumpled to the floor instantly. He hoped the man had a vest on - if so, then those were likely non-lethal hits, maybe breaking a rib or two - if he wasn't, he was definitely out of luck. Like the other guard, it wasn't his fault he was guarding Katherine Saito. Marlowe didn't think that any of the guards here were zealots. If they were, they'd have been shooting first, asking questions after.

He heard gunshots from the near side of the manor house, and realised this was likely the guards now firing through the window at the mysterious sniper, unsure where the shots were coming from, but trying their best to regroup.

Whatever their motivations, Marlowe didn't care. He needed to get across the lake as quickly as possible. But the moment he ran out towards it, he knew a sniper's bullet would take him in the head – an alternate route was badly needed.

He recalled a track that circled the lake, and quietly headed towards that, alert for guards and other surprises. He saw a dirt bike resting against a barn wall, likely transportation used by the guards for perimeter checks and such. As he quietly straddled the bike, Marlowe hoped it was an easy starter, and luck was on his side, He kick-started the bike into life, keeping the headlight off as he sped down the lane, away from the manor house and rounding towards the assassin on the other side of the lake.

THE PATH THAT CIRCLED THE LAKE WAS NARROW BUT FIRM AS HE followed it anti-clockwise around. He had a fair idea of where the sniper would have been firing from; there were only two or three spots that afforded the shooter the hide they'd need to have made the shot that killed Saito. As Marlowe neared the far side of the lake, he saw a Land Rover driving off at speed.

The assassin, it seemed, had heard the bike and was spooked.

Or the job was done.

With no need to hide his location anymore, Marlowe flicked the headlight on, revved the bike's engine, and jumped a ditch, landing on the narrow B road that lead away from the assassin's hide. The Land Rover's rear lights were nothing more than red specks in the distance. Marlowe quickly realised that a 125cc bike with a top speed around forty miles an hour wasn't going to cut it.

Swearing to himself, he spun the bike, returning off-road, moving through the forest, heading back to the small dirt track where he'd parked his own car.

Arriving back, he saw the burgundy Jaguar had been untouched. Either the assassin hadn't realised he'd parked there, or the assassin *wanted* him to escape. Discarding the bike, Marlowe ran to his car, grabbing the keys from underneath the back wheel. But, as he went to open the door, he paused as he saw the new piece of paper on the windscreen.

Pulling it off, he saw it was a torn page from what looked to be a *field notes* book, a slim notebook that many in the services used. On it, scrawled in what looked to be a biro, were four words:

see you in Vegas

Folding it carefully and sliding it into his combat webbing, Marlowe climbed into the Jaguar, carefully placing Katherine's laptop on the seat next to him. He wanted nothing more than to crumple the page into a small ball and toss it into the lake, but he knew Trix would pretty much tear him a new one if he did that; there was a chance something left on the paper would be lost forever. As it was, he had a strange hard drive for Trix to break in to, a laptop to check, and there was also whatever she'd found from the server farm downstairs.

Katherine Saito was dead, but maybe something could be saved from this.

Reversing out of the clearing, heading back up the track towards the road, Marlowe finally reviewed the last few moments with Katherine Saito. She'd been starting to tell him the truth that her suspicions of Steele were more than expected, and that Durrant was playing her own game, explaining about someone in Vegas who looked to be doing the same ... and then someone had shot her, either to frame him once more or to stop her from saying anything else. Marlowe wasn't sure, and for the timing, the location was either bugged or targeted by a powerful directional microphone. But one thing he *did* know was that all of this could now be linked back to St John Steele and Diana Durrant.

Who, if the conversation had been heard, now knew Marlowe was gunning for them.

11

ENCRYPTION

MARLOWE HAD TAKEN A COUPLE OF HOURS TO GET BACK TO HIS church-turned-house, making sure that there was nobody following him. Even though there was every chance that he was safe, he knew still that there would be assassins out there trying to kill him, looking for their million dollar bounties. There was every chance that the man who killed Katherine Saito was one of these. Perhaps Saito had been a mistake? Thermal imaging wouldn't allow a shooter to pick specific people out. Maybe the assassin had been trying to kill Marlowe, and Katherine was an unfortunate bystander.

No, the assassin had been waiting, watching the library.

Trix had been waiting back in the crypt. She didn't look concerned anymore, and Marlowe knew the chances were she'd been following his car. She had an annoying habit of sticking small trackers onto it that only she could use. It was endearing in a weird, twisted kind of way, but Marlowe wished that sometimes she'd find someone else to worry about.

As he'd gone to have a shower to wash the remnants of

the lake, and Katherine Saito, off his skin and hair, Trix had started on the laptop. When he emerged, dressed once more in jogging bottoms and a sweater, she looked up from the computer system.

'You were lucky to get the key,' she said.

Marlowe looked at the large iron key that he'd taken from the door. As he did so, Trix shook her head.

'Not that bloody thing,' she said. 'I have no idea why you took that apart from some kind of twisted keepsake.'

'I thought you could wax imprint it.'

'Oh, you remembered my hobbies!' Trix grinned. 'No, I meant this.'

She held up the item that Marlowe had believed was a flash drive.

'So, it's not some kind of hard drive?'

'No,' Trix shook her head. 'This MacBook's got some serious tech inside it, way past shop-created, and links to an air-gapped forum through tech that even I don't understand. This stops the files from being encrypted way past my pay grade.'

'So, what did we get?'

'Operation files,' Trix said, staring at the screen of one monitor, watching scrolling data go past. 'From what it looks like, the laptop recently downloaded every single op Katherine had ever been involved in while at MI5 and MI6 from some kind of online resource folder, kept somewhere deep in Whitehall. There's a ton of Hong Kong operations here. There's a few UK ones that she wasn't even connected to, so God knows how she found those, or why she wanted them.'

'Let me guess – they're connected to Steele somehow,' Marlowe muttered as he walked over to the weapons area to field strip and clean his CZ. It was a nervous action more than anything else, something for his hands to do while he waited for the bad news to be given.

It was always bad news when Trix turned to face him, and she'd just done that.

'The last document opened was a government one,' she explained carefully. 'But it wasn't one about St John Steele. It was on *behalf* of St John Steele.'

'How do you mean?'

'He claimed that he'd been set up, that an organisation within MI5 and MI6 had targeted him.'

'Let me guess,' Marlowe said. 'Orchid?'

Surprisingly, Trix shook her head.

'No,' she said. 'The organisation was never named. But some people inside it were.'

She tapped at the screen.

'Walter McKellan. Emilia Wintergreen. Joanna Karolides.'

'Karolides? The Home Secretary? How the hell is she involved?' Marlowe muttered. 'She's not even part of the services. She's a government Minister.'

'They needed somebody to fund them,' Trix shrugged. 'Honestly? It looks like Steele was aiming at Caliburn.'

Marlowe nodded. He'd already come to that decision when he heard the names. Caliburn was a longstanding think tank in the espionage industry, although it'd been positioned by Kate Maybury as a potential threat to UK stability. He remembered Emilia angrily grilling him after the shootout on the A4 overpass.

'McKellan has been a mainstay of MI6 for decades. You think Caliburn is some sort of Masonic order for spies? For God's sake, it's a research caucus! Nothing more! I'm a member of Caliburn, Tom. Your mum was a member of Caliburn. It's been around for

decades. Technically, if you wanted, you could have been a member of Caliburn.'

Marlowe's actions that day had likely removed his chances of membership.

'He needed a target for people. Something he could unite his troops behind,' Trix mused. 'And, as we know Kate Maybury worked for the same people who paid Steele, there's a chance this has always been the plan.'

'So, let me get this right,' Marlowe said. 'Katherine Saito has history with St John Steele. Possibly romantic, definitely professional. They worked together on several ops—'

'Was more than that,' Trix interjected. 'I checked the records. He literally mentored her through the ranks. She wouldn't have had a career if it wasn't for Steele.'

'Owing a career is enough to do anything,' Marlowe replied. 'Okay, so Steele is Katherine Saito's fairy godfather. He works with her in the services and then one day disappears. He claims to her he's the victim of some kind of black ops mission, people trying to remove him, throws a few names around: Caliburn, Orchid, Wintergreen, McKellan ... it's enough for Saito to believe.'

'I didn't think she was that naïve,' Trix replied.

Marlowe shook his head.

'You don't need to be naïve to believe it,' he replied. 'You just need to look at the facts. Walter McKellan and Emilia Wintergreen were connected to Caliburn. They were doing a lot of secret squirrel shit back in the day, and Wintergreen had me go off books to look into Orchid. Then add Joanna Karolides almost being killed by "Caliburn", before sending me up to Scotland to check into Broad Sword, off books and non-sanctioned. There's enough shadow in there to aim Saito away from the light; every single one of them has worked with me at various points. There's enough smoke to make you think there's a fire happening.'

He shook his head, mainly to himself, rather than to Trix.

'But she wasn't believing it completely,' he replied to himself. 'There was obviously part of her that didn't trust the story.'

'I think that part was you,' Trix replied. 'Steele would have played you up as a villain, the person trying to frame him for murder, trying to take him out for God knows why. He would have told her about your father and how you'd been accepted into the High Council of this traitorous organisation ... but to Saito, you were the guy who saved her life in Hong Kong, a person who she'd worked with on other missions, who she'd used as Kieran Lachlan in the past, and that probably didn't sit right with her. How could you have been this person, the one that Steele talked about? It was enough to make her suspicious, or at least suspicious enough to investigate.'

'Fat lot of good it did for her as well, though,' Marlowe muttered.

'Kept you alive,' Trix returned to the computer now. 'Steele was using you as a pawn. He placed a hit on you, and when no one was killing you, he put you into a kill zone at Durrant Capital, and got his own people to do it. Or, Durrant herself suggested it, maybe for leverage, and maybe because of Katherine Saito.'

'I can see that,' Marlowe nodded.

'Once he had you there, it was simply a case of getting the right people to come and kill you,' Trix returned to the monitor screen. 'What he didn't know was that Saito had raised the alarm about "Lachlan" being there; she probably didn't mention that part to him. This was why Durrant knew you as Tom Marlowe, but the police arrested you as Kieran

Lachlan. She had you picked up by Morris and Wilcox, knowing they'd been working with Special Branch. She'd probably given them the information for the case that they were working on herself; enough to bring you in, but still have you as somebody they could "turn", to work with them against Frank Maguire.'

She laughed a dark, humourless chuckle.

'She probably genuinely thought she'd covered all bases. Bringing Frank Maguire to pull out Kieran would keep your identity safe; Frank would get you out, and Kieran Lachlan would disappear. Sure, Kieran Lachlan was wanted for terrorism, but you were no longer part of MI5. All she had to do was never use the legend again.'

'But she didn't know that Maguire knew who I really was,' 'Marlowe sighed. 'Okay, so does anything that you found help with the information we got from Durrant?'

'Actually, it does,' Trix nodded. 'For a start, it tells us Steele's in Vegas as he tries to regain the first of the Operation Quicksilver money. Or, as I should call it now, Operation Stone Blind.'

She looked back at Marlowe.

'Be aware, however, that no matter what Saito claimed, Stone Blind isn't a sanctioned MI5 or MI6 op and, from what I can see, although he took credit for it when telling her, Steele isn't connected to Stone Blind in any way.'

'Then who's running it?'

'CIA,' Trix said, and from her tone, she was unhappy about this, 'However, no one can seem to claim credit for it, almost as if the person who's truly in charge—'

'Keeps changing their bloody name,' Marlowe finished. *Bloody Sasha Bordeaux.* It had to be. However, he couldn't call and ask her like he could before, not since he'd told her to piss off back in Germany. 'So, Steele is stealing money from the CIA that they gained in part from us? That sounds about right.'

'Looks like it. So, what now?' Trix leant back from the computer.

'Keep checking the laptop,' Marlowe suggested. 'I'm going to have a nap, book a couple of flights to Vegas for the day after tomorrow, and wait for Maguire's messenger to arrive.'

MARLOWE HAD EXPECTED A MESSENGER TO TURN UP THE following morning, but around ten o'clock, it was Frank Maguire who knocked on the church's ornate entrance. Marlowe had managed four or five hours of sleep – not enough to be anywhere near peak fitness, but he hoped he'd be able to catch some more on the plane to Vegas the following day. He was rubbing at his unshaven face as he opened the door, half-yawning.

'Morning, Tom,' Maguire said, smiling. 'Gonna let me in?'

'Do I have a choice?'

'Not really,' Maguire pushed past Marlowe, walking into the room. 'You know what? I'd envisioned what this place would look like, but I expected more spy shit, you know?'

He glanced back at Marlowe, a slight grin on his face.

'Let me guess,' he said, 'you got it hidden away in fake walls. If I stamp on one of the tiles, three wall sections spin around and show me all your weapons.'

'I think you've been reading too many James Bond novels,' Marlowe smiled, walking over to the kitchen. 'Coffee? I'm afraid it doesn't come from any secret compartment.'

'Actually, if you've got a tea bag, I'll have a builder's tea,'

Maguire smiled, and Marlowe found the forced "jolliness" was grating on him. 'It's too early in the day for me to have coffee.'

'Too early?' Marlowe raised an eyebrow. 'Usually I hear people saying it's too late in the day for coffee.'

'Yeah, but I have different hours, don't I?' Maguire shrugged, almost apologetically. 'Got to keep myself awake until the early hours of the morning with my lifestyle. This? Well, you know, this is "morning glory" time for me. Looks like it is for you as well.'

He nodded at the unshaven appearance, and Marlowe shrugged.

'Just getting everything ready for my trip to Vegas tomorrow,' he said. 'Have you got the information you need me to take?'

'Oh, I'm guessing you already know what I have,' Maguire looked around. 'Is she here? The woman who tells you what to do?'

'I told you, Maguire. I don't work for MI5 anymore.'

'Oh, I don't mean her,' Maguire laughed. 'I mean the blonde woman that you work with. Saw her once, you know. Pretty girl. Bit young for you though, so I hope it's purely a work relationship.'

Marlowe didn't know whether to laugh or take offence at the comment, considering Trix was in her early twenties, and he was in his mid-thirties. Instead, he just ignored it.

'She'll be here later,' he said. 'After you've gone.'

'Sure she will,' Maguire nodded, reaching into his inside pocket and pulling out an A4 brown envelope. 'Here's everything you need.'

'Paper? Old school,' Marlowe said. 'Usually it's flash drives these days.'

'Best way to be when you're not as legitimate as some people want you to be,' Maguire replied. 'I learned that, when MI5 started using a fake gangster, arms-stealing Mick bomber, to make me their patsy.'

Marlowe said nothing. He understood why Maguire would be angry and chanced something.

'Katherine Saito's dead,' he said matter-of-factly. 'In case that changes anything you need me to do.'

Maguire's eyes widened.

'You?' he asked.

'No, but I was there when it happened,' Marlowe replied. 'Sniper took her out. She was looking into something. We're yet to find out what it is. We think it was something to do with old MI5 and MI6 operations.'

He cocked his head slightly.

'I was hoping you might answer some of those.'

Maguire slowly nodded.

'You want to know whether she was working me?' he asked. 'I see no problem with that. Yeah, it was Saito. When they sent you in as Lachlan and we started getting cosy, it didn't take long for the men in suits to turn up. They never said it was you that had brought them to me. In a way, they made me think I had to keep using you, because they were going to take you down.'

Marlowe smiled.

'So, all that shit you gave me about not being truthful to you, and there you were trying to take me down.'

'Now, you were apparently a Real IRA bomb maker, weren't you?' Maguire grinned. 'I was doing my civic duty and all that.'

He rubbed at his chin.

'Of course, if Saito's dead, that changes things a little.'

'Why?'

'Because she was the one who told me I had to get Bassett back,' Maguire turned his attention back to Marlowe. 'Fact of the matter is, I haven't seen Bassett in a while. I can't explain why.'

'Why not?'

'Official Secrets Act,' Maguire shrugged. 'And don't tell me you're a signatory too, and we can talk to each other about it, because we both know it's not some kind of member's club, and I ain't going to find myself dumped in some MI5 black site because of you blabbing. At the moment, I'll keep quiet until somebody above you tells me I can tell you.'

Marlowe laughed.

'I never thought that the mighty Frank Maguire would be the one to talk to me about rules.'

'No offence, Tom. But Saito told me I needed to get you after Bassett in Vegas. I was to say that he was proprietary information. Which, in a way, he was. But he's not what you think he is. You get me? In a way, the accountant I knew for decades isn't the same guy that you're hunting. I can't explain it right now, but ...'

Marlowe nodded.

'I get it. I've been in your position. Don't worry, if Saito wanted you to get me to go to Vegas ... even if Saito's dead, then I'm going to follow Bassett.'

'Why?' Now it was Maguire's turn to frown. 'You just said she's dead. She's not controlling either of us anymore.'

'I got the impression she realised she was being played,' Marlowe said. 'And if that's the case, then her sending me to Vegas wasn't her following rules. It was her trying to circumnavigate them.'

He passed the mug across to Maguire.

'I think I'm going to be planning for an op, but it isn't the one I thought I'd be doing,' he continued. 'Anything you have is good but, to be honest, I'm not sure if anything you can provide me right now is worth it.'

Maguire shrugged.

'Take it, use it, whatever you can do,' he said. 'But do me a favour, yeah? When you find Bassett? Tell him he owes me.'

'And how does that work?' Marlowe smiled.

'I didn't give away his secret for a start,' Maguire grinned.

12

VEGAS STRIPPED

'WELCOME TO VEGAS!' TANNED AND STOCKY, WITH SHORT, almost-shaved hair and a whitening beard, Ryan Gates exclaimed, arms out wide as Marlowe and Trix emerged from Harry Reid International Airport. Marlowe carried only hand luggage; Trix, however, had a suitcase, likely filled with a variety of technological devices essential for whatever was coming next.

On seeing Ryan, Marlowe frowned.

'How did you know we were on this flight?' he asked.

Gates pointed back at the airport.

'There's only one flight a day to Vegas from London,' he replied. 'If you're flying British Airways, anyway. And I know you'd choose British Airways, business class. Some kind of hang-up from your days as a spy, most likely.'

He took Trix's suitcase, wheeling it for her as they walked towards the car park.

'I didn't need to figure out who you were flying under,' he continued. 'I just waited until a pretty blonde girl and a scruffy-looking guy with a beard showed up. Surprisingly, there weren't many of them on your flight.'

'We could have come yesterday.'

'You would have been rushed if you did that.'

'We didn't need a driver,' Marlowe muttered.

'You didn't, that's true,' Gates replied. 'But you did need someone to give you what you wanted. Let's be honest, Marlowe, if I wasn't here, I'd have to come to your suite.'

He winked.

'It will be a suite, won't it? You do so hate the normal rooms us ordinary folk stay in.'

Marlowe allowed the jibe. Ryan Gates had earned it. He'd also earned the fifty thousand dollars in bearer bonds he'd made the last time they worked together. Back then, Gates had played the role of The Gravedigger, convincing Vegas wannabe gangster and casino owner Gabriel Rizzo he was a hitman while Marlowe used him as a spy in an organisation. Unfortunately, this had put Marlowe on The Gravedigger's radar, starting a chain of events that led to Monty Barnes' death, a confrontation on the ground floor of a Cupertino tech firm, and Razor Gibson's murder with The Gravedigger's own weapon.

Marlowe was amused to see Ryan Gates still driving the same car – a Red Corvette, with tinted windows – that he'd been in when they first met. As he helped Trix load her suitcase into the boot; or trunk, as they called it in America, Gates turned and passed across a small box.

'My friend in Arizona made you another,' he said.

Marlowe quickly checked inside. It was a CZ 75BD, likely unregistered, and with a trigger as smooth as butter. He placed it into his rucksack as Gates rummaged in his pocket, pulling out a steel chain.

'You left this behind the last time as well,' he continued, passing it across. 'I thought you'd want it back.'

Marlowe looked down at the length of steel chain in his hand. It was known in the trade as a self-defence bracelet, almost a metre long and with a dragon's head clasp. To the untrained eye, it might have passed for an unusual piece of jewellery, a bold fashion statement. But Marlowe knew better. The chain was a tool, simple but deadly in the right hands, and in the past he'd used it as a whip, a garrotte, or even a restraint when needed. The dragon's head, more than mere decoration, was sharp enough to leave a mark, its design as functional as it was ornate. It was the kind of weapon you carried when subtlety mattered more than brute force, and Marlowe suspected he'd need both before he left Vegas.

'Thanks, I thought I'd lost this,' he smiled, already wrapping it around his wrist while Gates climbed into the driver's seat.

'It was found by a cleaner at your suite the day you checked out,' Gates said, as he started the engine. 'I'd checked in to make sure everything went smoothly and they passed it to me. They thought it was some kind of BDSM thing. I didn't have the heart to break their dreams.'

He laughed at Marlowe's stricken expression.

'When I first got hold of it, I thought it was a one-of-a-kind special edition. Now you've had, what, three of them? It's not that exclusive if someone keeps getting the same thing.'

'If they mass-produced it in every country in the world, somewhere I could pick it up, I'd be more than happy,' Marlowe said. 'It's saved my life on more than one occasion, as has the gun. Thanks.'

Marlowe was a recent convert to the CZ-75, having spent most of his career using the better-known SIG Sauer P228.

While heavier than a Glock, it had better balance for him. The CZ, however, felt like a revelation.

As he climbed into the car, Marlowe glanced at Gates.

'Horseshoe Casino,' he said. 'It's central, cheap, and I'll be able to keep an eye on things.'

He looked back at Trix sitting in the rear seat.

'This time, I've booked a suite for myself and my daughter.'

The last time they'd been in Vegas, Marlowe had come alone, but Trix had followed, knowing he'd need her help. On arrival, she'd claimed to be his daughter to get a room key; Marlowe had been mildly insulted she hadn't pretended to be his wife – after all, there was only about ten years between them – but, of course, Trix looked younger than her age, while Marlowe looked older than his thirty-three or so years.

Trix chuckled darkly. She didn't contradict.

THE JOURNEY FROM HARRY REID TO THE HORSESHOE CASINO was usually quick, but this time traffic was unusually heavy. Marlowe frowned as they crawled through roadworks and spotted construction gantries everywhere.

'Formula One,' Gates said knowingly, pointing at one of the gantries. 'The race is here in a week and a half. They're setting up the track.'

'What, they're using Las Vegas as a racetrack?'

Gates nodded.

'Same as Monaco. Most of the roads won't be affected, but an enormous section of the Strip is being used. Logically, they want the famous shinies to be seen. So they've had to build new roads, gantries, and bridges to reroute traffic.'

Before they stopped to a crawl in the traffic, Gates pulled into the back of the MGM Grand Casino.

'Of course, if you know the service roads, it doesn't affect you,' he added, then tutted as he found more vehicles ahead. 'But these days, anyone with good sat-nav like Waze figures out the shortcuts as quickly as I do. Being a local doesn't help when everything's online.'

Marlowe studied Ryan Gates as he drove. He was shorter than Marlowe, but stockier, with grey hair shaved short and covered by a baseball cap. His white goatee beard was neatly trimmed, and he wore a polo shirt over jeans. An ex-military man, he'd been a friend of Marshall Kirk, and had moved to America the previous year, after working briefly as an actor over the decades. Yet, for most of his life he'd been a soldier in the Intelligence Corps, attached to the Director of Special Forces and working with the Special Reconnaissance Unit. Because of this, he probably still had connections to the Security Service, and Marlowe wondered how much he knew about their current mission.

Almost as if reading Marlowe's thoughts, Gates smiled.

'You're wondering if I know why you're here,' he said. 'I've got an idea.'

'Go on.'

'Your mate Steele, isn't it?' Gates grinned. 'I've heard he's popped back up around here.'

'He has?'

'Yeah, been seen talking to Gabriel Rizzo – I guessed you wouldn't be far away from that.'

'I thought Gabriel was destroyed,' Marlowe frowned. The last he'd seen of Rizzo, Sasha Bordeaux, there under the fake

"René Montoya" name, had bundled him into an ambulance, claiming she was taking him to the hospital to treat his burn wounds, and had driven off. His casino had been emptied, and the fifty million dollars he owed to various powerful billionaires within the higher echelons of Orchid, among other dangerous organisations, had vanished.

Gates shrugged.

'It's Vegas,' he said. 'The place where anyone can make millions from nothing. Seems Rizzo was bankrolled to carry on as he was. Chances are your CIA friends have him on a short leash, but—'

'But he's still free to do what he wants,' Marlowe finished the sentence. 'Great.'

'You might find him on your side, though. There's talk he's pissed at his old friends, that might include Orchid and Steele. So, what's the plan?'

Marlowe shook his head.

'There's no plan, Ryan,' he replied. 'What you've done is more than enough. If I need anything else, I'll call you. From what I can work out, I think we're just in and out.'

He paused.

'Although, if you can dig up any information on a man named Lawrence Bassett, I'd greatly appreciate it.'

'Who's he then?' Gates asked. 'Some kind of super-spy? A member of a secret organisation that needs taking out?' His voice carried an edge of amusement at the idea.

'From what I can tell, he's an accountant,' Marlowe laughed. 'Works for a gangster in Essex called Frank Maguire.'

'Maguire?' Gates frowned. 'Never heard of him.'

'Well, let's just say Maguire's got a friend, Lawrence Bassett, with a lot of information on him, his organisation, his dirty little secrets and all that … who seems to have turned tail,' Marlowe explained. 'Ostensibly, we're here to find him as a favour for Maguire. But, in reality, we're hunting Steele.'

'And Orchid, I'm guessing.'

'Not necessarily Orchid,' Trix spoke up from the back seat. 'There've been a few changes since the last time we saw you.'

'Orchid's split apart,' Marlowe continued. 'Two distinct factions.'

'We're calling the other one "New kid",' Trix added. 'It hasn't caught on yet, but I've got hopes.'

Gates chuckled at this.

'Let me guess,' he said. 'Steele's part of Orchid, and he's annoyed at the new lot?'

'More the other way round,' Marlowe replied. 'It seems the originals in Orchid want to go back to how it was before people like Steele, Donziger, Delacroix, and Rizzo turned it into their personal piggy bank. The problem is, the people trying to return it back to what it was, still have sway. Hence the split, and hence … New Kid.'

Gates nodded as he turned into the Horseshoe Casino car parking area.

'I'll ask around, but you'll probably get more information from Clarissa,' he said. 'I'm guessing you'll be chatting with her tomorrow.'

'Is the swap meet on?'

'Every morning.'

'Then I'll speak to her tomorrow,' Marlowe smiled.

The swap meet was well known, and Marlowe was certain Clarissa would be there to help. After all, the last time they'd crossed paths, he'd given her a substantial sum of money, a million dollars in fact, as thanks for her help against Gabriel

Rizzo, using Rizzo's own money. With a history of information gathering within the CIA, and a hatred of the "one percent", Clarissa and her army of eyes on the ground were Marlowe's go-to, even before Ryan Gates.

'So, this Bassett, anything else I need to know?'

'Yeah, there's more to him than we can work out,' Marlowe added.' The source who asked us to find him was told to do so by an MI6 Section head who not only worked with Steele, but we think suspected him ... before she was killed. So, "Bassett" might not be "Bassett", if you get what we mean. Tread lightly.'

'That's advice you should take too, Tom,' Gates replied softly. 'Just so you know, I've asked around, and you've got people looking for you already.'

'How do you mean?' Marlowe turned in the seat to face the stockier man, who shrugged in response.

'They're not looking for you under whatever name you flew in by – which, by the way, I don't want to know, just in case. But I've heard whispers, yeah? Clarissa will probably know more.'

'What *do* you know?'

'Well, I know for a start you've got a hefty price on your head, and if people don't know you're in Vegas already, they know it's on your itinerary,' Gates' voice had lowered now they were parked. 'Expect a few speed bumps while you're here.'

Marlowe shook Gates' hand, as Trix pulled her suitcase from the back of the car before he could help.

'Stay safe,' Gates said. 'And, if you need anything, you know where I am. Just ... can we skip the makeup and acting this time?'

'I thought you enjoyed acting?' Marlowe raised an

eyebrow. 'You do enough Comicon signings to make people think so.'

'Not when every scene could be my last,' Gates replied with a shrug. 'Genuinely, though – stay on the six, yeah? Eyes on swivel. If you're here more than a couple of days, I'd get yourself some backup. More than a gun and a bit of chain, yeah?'

'That's the problem,' Marlowe said with a rueful smile. 'I don't have backup anymore. Both Sasha Bordeaux and MI5 are pretty pissed off at me at the moment.'

'They were pissed off the last time I saw you as well,' Gates replied matter-of-factly as he walked back to the driver's side. 'That doesn't mean they won't help you if they think there's something in it for them.'

With that, Ryan Gates climbed into his little red Corvette and drove off, leaving Marlowe and Trix alone at the entrance to the Horseshoe Casino and Hotel.

'Come on,' Marlowe said, grabbing his hand luggage and cabin bag, wheeling it towards the main entrance. 'We've got a suite to book into.'

'Yes, Dad,' Trix grinned. 'Ooh, I like that. Can I call you "Daddy" on this mission?'

'Remember, I'm the one with the gun,' Marlowe growled. 'So I really suggest you don't, before your foot sprouts a bullet.'

'Yeah, but bullet wounds heal,' Trix continued grinning widely as they entered the hotel. 'What I can do to your credit records would last a lifetime ... *Daddy*.'

13

SWAP MEETING

THE CHARLESTON SWAP MEET WAS A LAS VEGAS TRADITION that Marlowe had learnt about the previous time he was around. Leaving Trix in the suite, already working on the information he'd gathered from Harrington House, Marlowe attended alone, walking down the lines of stalls, mostly bric-à-brac items set out on wallpaper tables, until he found the one he wanted.

Clarissa, surname still unknown, specialised in uranium glass. Marlowe had bought every piece that she'd had the last time he saw her, crushing it down and using it to convince Orchid members that they'd been poisoned in a massive misdirect. But, it seemed that in the intermediate months, Clarissa had replenished her supply. A variety of jugs, vases, plates and bowls decorated her table as Clarissa herself sat behind it.

In her late seventies, with leathered "Las Vegas" skin and wiry grey hair, she was in her wheelchair, thanks to a foot blown off by an IED, her leg prosthetic from the knee down, and she smiled as she saw Marlowe walking towards her.

'Heard you were in town,' she said, shifting in the chair as she turned to face him. Marlowe gave a smile in return, but wondered whether or not this statement was true. Unless Ryan Gates had spoken to her, there was no real way that Clarissa would have known that Marlowe was around. Perhaps this was her usual greeting, to make her sound like she was some kind of super spy asset.

Which, of course, in a way, she was.

'What do you need?' she asked.

'Missing person,' Marlowe replied.

'Missing from Vegas?'

'Missing from London, believed to be in Vegas.'

'Not like you to do private investigator shit.' Clarissa clicked her tongue. 'I'm guessing there's more to it.'

'I was in Vegas anyway,' Marlowe shrugged. 'Lawrence Bassett.'

At the name, Clarissa started to laugh.

'Of course, it's bloody Lawrence Bassett,' she said. 'Everybody in the world's looking for goddamn Lawrence Bassett.'

Marlowe hadn't expected the outburst.

'I'm guessing you already know him?'

'I'm aware of him,' Clarissa nodded. 'The question I've got for you, though, Mister Marlowe, is whether you're here for the same Lawrence Bassett as I know.'

'Well, I'm hoping there's only one of them,' Marlowe forced a smile. This sounded very familiar, and he wondered if Clarissa was about to tell him what Maguire couldn't.

'That's not what I mean, and you know it,' Clarissa folded her arms. Marlowe picked up one item on the table, examining it as she continued. As far as anybody watching was concerned, he was simply an interested customer.

'Why don't you tell me what you know,' he asked. 'I think I've earned some credit from the last time I saw you.'

He knew Clarissa would probably have started some kind of quid pro quo conversation, and he wanted to cut that dead.

Clarissa nodded, accepting the comment. She had indeed made money from him, enough to keep her arm of informants going for a very long time.

'Lawrence Bassett is a CIA asset,' she said. 'Has been for the last year.'

'Let me guess, informing on Frank Maguire?'

'I've got no idea who he's informing on,' Clarissa replied, examining her nails disinterestedly as she did so. 'All I know is that he's a Brit, spent some time in the US, and was poached by our side mainly to look into your side, years ago. I think they were interested in him as a numbers man. Eidetic memory, you see.'

Marlowe started to understand why Bassett was important now. Someone with an eidetic memory, otherwise known as a photographic memory, could be very useful when you wanted to keep things out of books. Being able to turn the man, ask Bassett a question, and get an immediate answer was nothing to be ignored.

But that information could be used by anybody else.

'Is he over here on his own cognisance?' Marlowe asked.

'You mean has some beefy guy kidnapped him and dragged him over here against his will? Not that I've heard of.' Clarissa watched Marlowe carefully. 'This about Durrant Capital?'

'And why would you think that?'

'Because they're the ones paying for his hotel room, they're the ones who brought him across on a swanky jet,' she grinned. 'And they're the ones who had their entire forty-eighth floor destroyed a few days back by a guy in a beard. Internet chatter says it was you.'

'Internet chatter?' Marlowe raised an eyebrow.

'Well, the forums I attend anyway,' Clarissa grinned. 'You give your girl some time, and she'll find them as well.'

Marlowe wasn't liking the way this conversation was going. From the sounds of things, people already knew that he was aiming at Durrant, and if Clarissa knew he was in Vegas – if it really wasn't some kind of mocking guess – then there was every chance that others would know as well.

'Do you know who came on the plane with him?'

'Diana Durrant, and some guy named Voss?' Clarissa shrugged. 'I can get the information in more detail if I want it, but until now I didn't really need to. Unless you're telling me it's *worth* looking into?'

'Very much so,' Marlowe replied. 'I would appreciate it if you could.'

Clarissa wrote a note on a piece of paper and then whistled with two fingers. A young blonde girl across the walkway, late teens at best, currently standing beside another craft table filled with figurines, looked up, ran over, and took the paper.

'Mason,' Clarissa said. It was one word, but Marlowe assumed this was the person who the note was meant for.

The girl nodded and left. Clarissa returned her attention to Marlowe.

'Now,' she asked matter-of-factly, 'I hear it's a million.'

'I'm hoping the million I gave you would mean you weren't looking to gain a second million right now.'

'I'm always looking to gain another million, Tom,' Clarissa waved at her table of wares, or at her prosthetic leg, he wasn't sure. 'After all, as you can see, I'm a woman of high tastes.'

Marlowe smiled at this.

'How well known is it?' he asked. 'The hit?'

'If you're asking if people are going to come for you once they know you're here?' Clarissa cocked her head as she considered this. 'Honestly, I'm surprised they haven't already tried.'

'Damn.' Marlowe looked back up and down the swap meet walkway, almost as if expecting someone to already be there.

'Don't you worry,' Clarissa said. 'They wouldn't dare try here. The car park, however, that's a different matter.'

She tidied the table.

'One thing I can tell you about Bassett,' Clarissa said, leaning closer, placing her elbows on the table. 'If Durrant brought him across, it's because she needs him for something.'

She cocked her head to the side as she spoke, considering what she said, and Marlowe fought the urge to think of her as some kind of Collie waiting for a command. He understood what Clarissa was saying. If Maguire had been correct about Durrant wanting to take over areas of London, using her legitimate business to create financial opportunities for herself off-books, opportunities that would go against Maguire himself, then utilising Bassett would indeed be something worth doing. If Bassett was ever what he claimed he was, Saito surely wouldn't have cared about such small-time issues.

But why would Durrant bring him to Vegas?

'Anything you can find out,' he said, 'I'll pay good money.'

'You've got a line of credit with me already,' Clarissa said, 'so don't you worry about that just yet. I have a feeling, however, we're going to see a lot of you, Mister Marlowe, before you go back to England, and *that's* when the tallies will build.'

Marlowe gave a nod, threw down ten dollars for one of the items, a heavy, slim vase, and Clarissa dutifully wrapped it in some paper. Marlowe picked it up, taking it with him, for all intents and purposes just another customer but, as he walked out of the swap meet, he stared at the surrounding people a lot more cautiously. If it was well known in Vegas that he was around and a target, then anyone could look to gain a payday.

Walking out into the car park, he wondered whether he should have hired a car rather than called for cabs, but he needn't have worried as waiting outside was a black SUV. As Marlowe exited the building, the driver door opened and a suited man climbed out. Marlowe didn't recognise him, but he recognised the type. Off-the-rack suit, shirt, tie, and a bulge where his gun was. He could have been private security or something similar, but he held himself with the mannerisms of someone who believed himself to be an authority.

That left FBI, NSA or CIA.

'Mister Marlowe,' he said, all attempts at small talk thrown out of the window. 'Get in the car.'

'Thanks for the lift, but I'm really busy today,' Marlowe started, but the driver patted his chest.

'You really don't want to make a scene,' he said. 'Get in the goddamn car. We'll drive you back to your hotel.'

Sighing, Marlowe walked to the rear passenger door and opened it, looking in as he did so. The man sitting waiting for him was an actual surprise. Stocky, but not fat, square headed, with short hair at the sides, a tuft of brown or dirty ginger curly hair on top, the man was strangely pale for the Las Vegas climate, and his rimless glasses gave him the appearance of a "bookish librarian". He wore a charcoal-grey suit made from what looked to be some kind of wool blend, definitely not the thing to wear in the Las Vegas heat unless you were some kind of masochist; a thick white shirt, and a dark-blue striped tie which looked very much as if it was some kind of group or university colours, especially as it was the same one he'd worn the last time they'd met.

'Oh, hello, Agent Massey,' Marlowe said. 'I thought you'd have been fired by now.'

THE LAST TIME MARLOWE HAD MET REYNARD MASSEY – NOT HIS real name, as he'd once told Marlowe the surname was his mother's, and the first name was based on "Reynard the fox", a fictional character that Marlowe hadn't had the heart to mention was likely more intelligent than the man taking the name for himself – had been in a diner, back when Marlowe was about to cause a visible and highly dangerous heist at the aptly named Gold Strike Casino. Reynard had been a CIA operative who had his own personal issues with Sasha Bordeaux, or whatever name she called herself back then. And the conversation hadn't gone well; Reynard wanted Clarissa, Orchid and Marlowe working for him. He also wanted Gabriel Rizzo, if only to get one over on his boss. Marlowe had watched Massey's fall from grace; siding with corrupt Interpol agent Sandra Reilly had been his biggest mistake. Last he'd heard, Massey had been demoted and transferred, which made it interesting to see the man back here, and back in what looked to be a semblance of power.

As the car started towards the Horseshoe Casino, Marlowe looked over at Massey, staring out of the window, almost as if he didn't want to have eye contact with the man in the car next to him.

'I understand you've pissed off Sasha,' Massey remarked as a matter of conversation. 'That was careless of you. Someone like that, she can make sure the vultures don't strike.'

'Let's just say I wasn't happy with her choices,' Marlowe replied. 'And if I recall correctly, I don't think you were that happy with them either, back when we last spoke.'

'Back when we last spoke, things were a completely different situation,' Massey muttered.

'Were they,' Marlowe smiled. 'How did you get back?'

'A senator owed my daddy a favour,' Massey shrugged, as if it was the most obvious thing in the world. 'Why are *you* in Vegas?'

'Don't worry, I'm not performing another heist.'

'Then why *are* you here?' Massey pressed again.

'I'm looking for an old friend, and while I'm at it, I'm trying to sort a few old issues.'

Massey leant back in the car seat, examining Marlowe.

'The problem you've got, Brit,' he said, 'is I simply don't believe you. You screwed me around badly last time you were here.'

'If I remember correctly, Mister Massey, you were just as guilty of screwing around as I was,' Marlowe snapped, tiring of the pretend friendly back-and-forth banter they were currently engaged in. 'You wanted Rizzo for your own reasons. You allowed yourself to be catfished by a rogue Interpol agent, and almost went to prison, let alone a demotion. You wanted Sasha Bordeaux gone and, from the looks of things, she's gone.'

He made a pantomime of looking around the car as if she were secretly there, as he said the last line. Massey shrugged.

'From what I can work out, she's gone up the ladder a little more,' he said. 'Means we see less of her, which is fine by me. Bitch tried to end my career, so I'm happy to see her gone.'

Massey grinned as he watched Marlowe now, staying silent for so long it actually felt uncomfortable.

'I have new friends,' he said. 'High up ones who think Bordeaux needs to stop playing her own game. I understand it's due to you she's got shiny new toys to play with, too. You're rapidly becoming the CIA's greatest asset.'

Marlowe forced himself not to react to the comment, though inside, he wanted to wince. The asset they were referring to, the "shiny toy" that Sasha Bordeaux was likely playing with, was a satellite system that she and Emilia Wintergreen had stolen from Germany following the battle with Viktor Lazarev and St John Steele. Marlowe still had unfinished business with the third in Steele's little group, Max Schen, but he'd been clever enough to get the hell out before the shit hit the fan.

Next time, then.

Massey, however, had veered the conversation elsewhere and now stared out of the window as he continued.

'There's talk of a man,' he said. 'Some Brit being used by Diana Durrant. Brought across to use his "Rain Man" skills to show her how to break apart London, make money. Some kind of algorithm that he's made, but all up here.'

He tapped the side of his head as he looked back at Marlowe.

'You know, the businessman version of counting cards.'

'Really?' Marlowe kept his face impassive.

'Don't give me that shit.' Massey laughed. 'I know damn well that you're here because of this.'

'I couldn't possibly confirm or deny,' Marlowe shrugged. 'I'm here as a private citizen, having a holiday, doing a bit of gambling.'

'Well, let's make sure your vacation money's the only thing you're gambling with, shall we?' Massey snapped. 'I would so hate to find you dragged away and dumped in an off-site gulag for something that wasn't that important.'

There was a long, awkward tension in the air. Marlowe knew Massey was, in a way, offering his services, but Marlowe didn't really want to owe the CIA any more than he already did.

'I thought you'd know more than me,' he suggested, 'considering he's a CIA asset.'

Massey said nothing, but his eyes glittered at the comment.

'If anything happens,' Marlowe continued, 'I'll let you know. But I'll be honest, I'm in and out this time. No heists, no big fights. I'm hunting the guy for a friend, and when I find him, I'll take him home.'

It was a lie, and both Marlowe and Massey knew it. But until Massey could prove it to be so, Marlowe had a little time and wriggle room. He looked out of the window and saw they were approaching the side entrance of the Horseshoe Casino. Massey nodded to the driver, and they pulled in.

As the car pulled to a stop, Massey pulled out a business card and passed it over.

'In case you threw away my last one,' he said. 'Seriously, Marlowe, you've got a lot of people looking for you right now. Your dance card is already punched and ready to go. I'd rather not see any locals get caught in a crossfire.'

'I'd rather not see any crossfire, full stop,' Marlowe smiled. 'But, do me a favour, Massey. If Sasha Bordeaux does decide she wants to come to Vegas for a visit, let me know.'

'Why? So you can send her a gift?'

Marlowe stared hard at Massey.

'No,' he replied. 'Because if she is playing with the toy I think she is, I want to shoot her in the head.'

'Thatta boy.' Massey laughed, slapping Marlowe on the back as he climbed out of the car. '*Now* you're getting it. *Now* you're playing for the right team.'

14

HITMAN

After watching the car drive off, Marlowe turned and walked away from the kerbside. The Horseshoe Casino's entrance beckoned, its late morning quiet a stark contrast to the usual Vegas chaos. Marlowe paused at the doors, letting his eyes adjust as he moved from morning light into the artificial day of the gaming floor.

He didn't know why, but it was here that he suddenly felt a desire to confirm he had weapons on him; the talk of assassins had spooked him a little. The vase in the paper bag was in his left hand still as he cautiously rubbed at his right wrist. The thin steel chain wrapped around it felt cool against his skin, hidden beneath his shirt cuff.

Good. But why the nerves?

Something had obviously alerted his subconscious brain, but what was it? Carefully, he took a slow rotation, taking in his surroundings, the bored look of a man deciding where to go next. He spotted the blond man immediately; late twenties, expensive suit, trying too hard to look like just another tourist. The scar running down the left side of his face caught the light from the slot machines, however, the tissue was still pink and new, maybe a year, possibly less.

Something about him nagged at Marlowe's memory, but the connection stayed frustratingly out of reach as he tried to act as if he now wasn't painfully aware of the suited man watching him from the slot machines.

If it was paranoia, then fine. But if it was a case of someone waiting for him, then he needed a new place to stay – and fast.

The casino floor was caught in that peculiar limbo between late night and mid-morning. A few hardcore gamblers hunched over slot machines, day-gamblers now inserting themselves between them, while cleaning staff worked around the empty blackjack tables. Security cameras swept the space in regular patterns, their blind spots mapped out in Marlowe's mind like a second language.

The blond man had backup. He saw two others were trying to blend in near the craps tables. Professional posture, eyes constantly moving – hitmen, not tourists. The bounty on Marlowe's head must have finally attracted serious attention. One of them, a fat man with a shaved head, had gained a little luck, and it'd been the shout of the crowd around as he'd rolled a winning number that had pulled Marlowe's eyes over to him, seeing the man visibly wince as he was spied.

If it's close to a million? Stay there, Marlowe mentally willed the man, but noticed out of the corner of his eye that the bald man was now gathering his winnings quickly, while motioning for his companion to move on. They were good, he'd give them that. Positioned to herd him towards the back exits, away from cameras and witnesses. The construction work for next week's Grand Prix had turned that part of the Strip into a maze of temporary walls and barriers.

Perfect for making someone disappear.

But Marlowe had other ideas.

Casually, as if not aware the three men were now following him, he moved deeper into the casino, forcing them to adjust their positions. The blond man peeled away from his spot at the bar, trying to parallel Marlowe's path while his companions moved to cut off alternate routes.

A server appeared with a fresh tray of drinks, temporarily blocking the blond man's line of sight. Seeing this, Marlowe used the moment, slipping between slot machines towards the high-limit room. Now unclipped, the steel defence chain began uncoiling down into his palm, still hidden but ready.

The high-limit room was only just beginning to gather fresh interest, with the new dealers starting their day-shifts. Plush carpet absorbed footsteps as Marlowe moved past green-felted tables, forcing his hunters to split up to cover the room's multiple exits. In the mirrored walls, he caught glimpses of their movements – professionals spreading out, trying to avoid crossing each other's lines of fire.

Shit.

The blond man had drawn closer, hand resting casually near his jacket. That scar – Marlowe knew he'd seen it before, fresher perhaps, in a different context. But there wasn't time to chase memories.

The high-limit room opened onto a discreet service entrance, the kind used by staff to deliver high-roller drinks without disturbing the flow of games. Marlowe pushed through into the corridor beyond, hearing his pursuers adjust their positions. The passageway curved left into the heart of the casino's back-of-house operations.

Unlike the plush gaming areas, however, these corridors were purely functional: plain walls, exposed pipes overhead, floor marked with coloured lines guiding staff to different areas. The yellow line led towards Paris – or rather the area known as this, including the Paris Hotel and the giant, fake Eiffel Tower that looked over the Strip, and Marlowe followed it past storage rooms and employee break areas, the sounds of the casino floor growing distant.

A swipe-card entrance marked the transition between properties. Marlowe shouldered through the fire escape next to it instead, setting off an alarm that would soon bring security running.

Let them come – by then this would be over, one way or another.

The Paris back corridors mirrored the Horseshoe's, but were wider, designed to handle the food service traffic from multiple restaurants. Marlowe cut through the loading dock area, past confused kitchen staff starting their morning prep, and into the Paris casino proper. The artificial sky ceiling was set to early morning blue, the replica Eiffel Tower visible through the faux windows.

The men were still following; having given up on any attempt at subtlety.

The main entrance to Paris beckoned ahead, and as Marlowe pushed through the morning gamblers and tourists, there to look through the high-end shops along the sides of the "mall", the three killers followed, their footsteps echoing on marble floors as morning light beckoned beyond the glass.

The Paris's main entrance opened onto Las Vegas Boulevard, where temporary walls had transformed the normally wide Strip into concrete and metal canyons. In a week's time, Formula One cars would scream past this very spot, but for now the morning light cast long shadows across fresh tarmac and bare metal framework.

Behind him, Marlowe heard the blond man and his companions spreading out, trying to cut off potential escape routes as they headed, like Marlowe had, into the busy morning crowds of tourists. They'd waited until now, avoiding the cameras and witnesses of the casino floor, and in a crowd there was still a problem. But Marlowe knew that for a million dollars, they could at any moment simply say, "screw it" and start firing. Or they could surround him, shank him quickly and then leave him to bleed out as they walked off.

Marlowe needed to get out of the crowd if he wanted to stop them permanently, but his only option was to leave the crowded Strip, where everybody could be another waiting assassin, and head into the still-being-built track area.

Track it is, then.

A narrow gap between barriers beckoned, barely wide enough for a person, probably used by the construction crews for access. Beyond it lay the foundation work for what would become the race control tower, steel beams reaching towards the Nevada sky like industrial ribs.

The chain felt cold in Marlowe's palm as he slipped through the space, hearing footsteps approach from behind as he did so. The blond man's voice carried in the morning air, confident now they were away from civilians.

'End of the line, Marlowe.'

The first attack came as Marlowe rounded a corner, away from the crowds. A whisper of movement, then steel flashing towards his throat. Marlowe flicked a length of chain and clasp, wrapping the attackers knife hand and jerking it violently down and away. His attacker recovered with a trained fighter's grace, but not quickly enough,

Marlowe let the chain flow like water, its dragon-headed

tip cracking across the man's face. Blood sprayed, and as his wounded assailant groped for his damaged face, Marlowe slide-stepped inside and behind him, the chain now biting painfully into the man's neck. Another violent twist sent him reeling face-first into a concrete barrier, and the would-be killer crumpled to the floor. Marlowe looked down to see the killer's blade protruding from the man's own chest, dark red blood now flowing freely.

Whoops.

The blond man appeared at the corridor's end now, his partner moving to flank through the construction site. Time was running out, so Marlowe moved deeper into the maze of barriers, forcing his hunters to follow. Every step took them further from witnesses, from cameras, from help.

Exactly what they wanted. Or so they thought.

The construction site was a skeleton of what it would become – raw metal framework waiting for grandstands, stacks of barriers ready to line the track. Marlowe counted footsteps behind him, measuring distances, calculating angles. The chain moved between his fingers, and the vase in his left pocket felt heavy and dangerous. He didn't want to use the CZ - that would lead to more trouble than he was willing to deal with right now. He weighed up his options and waited for the coming attack.

When it came, it was fast. The blond man's partner lunged from behind a barrier, what looked to be a KA-BAR combat knife leading – twelve inches overall, seven of which were razor sharp. At the last possible second, Marlowe side-stepped, his chain snapping out to wrap the man's knife hand. One sharp pull sunk the dragons head into the man's hand and sent the blade clattering away into the shadows. Marlowe counter-spun, the chain a blur of steel that slammed into his attacker's face and across the eyes, sending him staggering back blindly into a stack of framework poles. The resulting crash echoed off the barriers like thunder.

Marlowe spun once more, his off hand smashing the paper bag covered uranium vase into the side of the man's head. With a double crunch of bone and glass, the opponent slumped to the floor.

The blond man moved last, emerging from the concrete and steel gloom with cold professionalism. His scar twisted as he smiled.

'Hello, Marlowe. Been looking for you.'

'You and half the professionals in Europe, it seems.'

'A million dollars buys a lot of attention,' the blond man's hand moved towards his jacket. 'Nothing personal.'

The chain whistled through the air as Marlowe's response, catching his last attackers' wrist before he could draw, steel wrapping around expensive suit fabric. Marlowe yanked him forward and slammed his off balance opponent's face into the broken vase, still in his off hand, now jagged and razor sharp. However, while the blow sent some shards biting into the blond man's face, he had turned with the force of the blow, reducing the potentially lethal impact, and finished his movement by firing an elbow towards Marlowe's temple.

But Marlowe was spinning too, away from the elbow, while letting the chain run through his hand until he spun the heavy steel at his attacker. The weighted tip cracked across the blond man's knee, the scream he made echoing off the barriers, raw and animal – but even injured, the blond man was dangerous, as, dropping to one knee, he drew a Glock 42 from an ankle holster.

Marlowe dove for cover behind a stack of framework, as

bullets sparked off metal, the sound lost in the growing noise of late morning Vegas traffic.

Marlowe counted shots. *Four, five, six,* then the telltale sound of the sub-compact pistol's slide locking back on an empty chamber.

He was moving before the sound of the last round fired faded, chain flowing out in an whirling arc that caught the blond man's gun hand, whipping the wrist painfully to the side with a loud crack of bone, the pistol spinning away from his attacker. As his opponent howled in pain from his latest injury, Marlowe slid in behind the wounded attacker, his chain wrapping around the blond man's throat. Not to kill though – information was worth more than a bounty.

'Who's coordinating the contract?'

The blond man tried to laugh, blood staining his perfect teeth.

'You know how it works. Brokers. Cutouts. Dead drops.'

'*The* Broker?'

'Yeah.'

Marlowe knew he wouldn't get anything else from the man, but the accent was familiar. Chechen, maybe?

'The scar. Where do I know it from?'

'Cambridge.' The blond man's voice was wet with pain. 'You blew us up.'

Memory clicked. Marlowe had been trying to contact Raymond Sykes during the Rubicon mission. The Ukrainian, Stepan Chechik had been hunting him with his men, and Marlowe had used three hidden propane bottles under a tarpaulin to detonate, sending Chechik's men to the ground, screaming with rage as pieces of torn, burning tarpaulin and plastic rained down on them.

The blond man had been younger then, unscarred.

'Sorry,' Marlowe replied. 'Nothing personal.'

'And Stepan?'

'In my way. So this is personal for you, then?'

'Just business.' The blond man's eyes rolled towards the sky. 'But someone really wants you dead, Marlowe. Today was just the first attempt.'

Sirens wailed in the distance – casino security finally responding to the gunshots. Time to disappear.

Marlowe leant close.

'That's twice you've hunted me, and twice I've beaten you. If there's a third, you won't be around afterwards.'

Marlowe punctuated his threat by slamming the blond man's head against a barrier, knocking him out, ensuring he'd have a headache to match his broken bones. By the time anyone found him, Marlowe would be gone.

The defence chain slid back around his wrist as he moved through the construction site, the morning painting the Vegas sky in colours that had nothing to do with neon. If Marlowe was clever, he'd take this as a sign it was time to vanish, find somewhere quiet to think. After all, a million-dollar bounty attracted a lot of attention.

But Marlowe had never been clever when it came to his own personal safety.

And Marlowe had a job to do.

Pulling his phone, he dialled a number.

'Trix, move to a new location,' he said as she answered. 'We had visitors.'

'Gotcha,' Trix could be heard already packing her items up. 'Tom, Dick or Harry?'

'Make it Tom.' Marlowe hurried back across the road, now merging back into the Strip. 'I'll meet you there.'

'You okay?'

'Yeah, busy morning,' Marlowe replied, making sure if anyone was listening, all they had was banal chatter. 'Heard a friend is at a casino I used to frequent. Heading over to have a chat. Who knows, I might even strike it lucky.'

With that, Marlowe whistled for a cab, and headed away from the strip, and any potential killers waiting to be next in line.

15

REFURBISHMENT

A FEW MONTHS EARLIER, THE GOLD STRIKE CASINO HAD opened to one of the most infamous beginnings of a casino's career. Within a matter of hours, it had been closed down, having lost over fifty million dollars in a single evening, and within days, the logos, boardings, and adverts had been removed. If you'd gone away for a couple of weeks and returned shortly after this happened, you wouldn't even have known that the Gold Strike Casino existed.

Instead, there was the *Velvet Oasis* Casino; the same one as the Gold Strike in all but name, probably because it was cheaper to keep it that way.

Well, this was what Marlowe assumed, as he walked through the main entrance.

He hadn't bothered putting a disguise on. If people were going to come for him, they'd find him no matter what. But he was curious what would happen the moment Tom Marlowe, Orchid High Council member and apparently public enemy number one, entered.

Apparently nothing – which was interesting, considering

how advanced the cameras were here, something he knew from firsthand experience.

Deciding to push it further, he bought a hundred dollars' worth of chips at the cashier's desk and wandered around, examining tables as he did so. He'd had his moments here; he'd bet and lost against his brother, although that had been deliberate. He'd had an open hit placed on him in the middle of the casino, fighting for his life just to get out. He'd attended his father's memorial in their main room, had a fight in the middle of a cage, and had caused one of the biggest heists in casino history.

To look around, you wouldn't have believed it.

The casino was designed in a gold, green and burgundy colour swatch, with the carpets patterned and reminding him of a rather nasty tartan he'd seen years ago in Edinburgh; one that an American had claimed was his family's tartan, but had likely been just picked up from a costume shop and passed on to the unsuspecting victim. The main area was filled with slot machines, all with brightly coloured lights, licensed on a variety of random franchises; there was even a slot machine licensed on *Monty Python and the Holy Grail*, which came as a surprise to Marlowe. The film was almost fifty years old, after all.

As he walked along, snippets of songs and musicals would chirp from these machines, each one connected to the franchise it was now part of, while elderly women and short, bespectacled men pumped in more coins, hoping they'd win.

Past the slot machines were the poker tables. Marlowe remembered from the last time that poker was a far more popular pastime in Vegas than the crap tables or roulette. But again, nothing had really changed from the designs he'd seen when he was last here. He hadn't even been checked to see if he was wearing a gun. He guessed that Las Vegas was fine with it, and if they were fine with it, so was he.

It was on his third table that Marlowe noticed he was getting interest. A man in a suit had walked up, watching him from the side. Marlowe gathered his chips, walked to a different table to try some blackjack.

The man followed.

Marlowe wasn't winning; if anything, he was just about breaking even, so he knew he wasn't being targeted because they thought he was cheating. They had to know who he was, and Marlowe wondered what kind of crisis was now going on in the main ops room, as the guards realised the guy who'd stolen millions from them ... had *returned*.

Eventually, after the fourth occurrence of this, he got up, walked over to the man who was trying to look the other way, as if he hadn't even considered the man walking over, and stood in front of him.

'Problem?' he asked.

The man stared impassively at him. He was an inch or two taller, with a brown buzz-cut haircut. His suit was wide and well-tailored, expensive and made to measure, which was probably because no off-the-rack suit would actually fit the man. His chest looked like it was carved from granite, and his arms were both easily double the size of Marlowe's, even if there was only an inch or so in height difference. He looked in his thirties, maybe his forties, his chiselled jaw pock-marked with what looked to be possibly acid, or maybe a terrible razor burn. Marlowe wasn't sure.

Unintimidated by the guard's expression, he didn't back down.

'I'll ask again,' he said. 'Do we have a problem?'

'Why would we have a problem, Mister Marlowe?' the

man spoke, and Marlowe smiled. He wondered if the guard was supposed to have given it away, or whether this was the whole point. He looked up at one camera and gave a little wave.

'I'm guessing you're watching me,' he said. 'That's nice. Can you tell me who?'

'I have an invitation to take you to the manager's office.'

'That's lovely,' Marlowe replied. 'I'm not going. But thank him anyway.'

'It isn't a request.'

Marlowe leant in.

'I think you'll find it very much is a request,' he muttered. 'Because there's no goddamn way you're going to make me do anything I don't want to do right now.'

The guard, tiring of whatever this limey Brit was talking about, landed a meaty hand on elbow, intending to forcibly guide him. Before he could move again, Marlowe had trapped the hand with an old school *Hapkido Z Lock*, rolling the man's wrist inward while turning, his other forearm putting pressure on the guards trapped wrist. To anybody watching, it looked like the guard was in distress and Marlowe was still just leaning in to help. The reality was one of the most painful wrist locks imaginable, capable of shredding bone, ligaments and tendons with relative ease.

Marlowe leaned further and whispered in the bigger man's ear.

'Tell your boss,' he said, 'I'll meet him on the floor.'

'He can hear you,' the guard groaned.

'Good,' Marlowe replied. 'If he can hear me, then he'll hear what's in my voice. He can tell whether I'm genuine in what I say, or whether I'm just stringing you a line.'

Marlowe was deliberately talking, giving time for the

guard to yelp and mutter as he kept that wrist painfully locked.

'It's very simple, Mister Manager who can hear me,' he continued. 'If I don't see you by the time I count to ten, I'm going to break his wrist, and maybe his forearm, too.

One ... two ...'

He left a good few seconds in between each one; he remembered how close the manager's office was to the casino floor and had already turned to watch the doorway as he continued counting.

'*Six ... seven ...*'

'Please,' the guard said. 'I don't know how long—'

'*Nine.*' Marlowe stopped, smiling as through the door a familiar figure emerged.

Gabriel Rizzo. Black sheep of the West Coast Rizzo family.

He hadn't changed since the last time Marlowe had seen him; his hair was short and cropped at the sides while slicked back on the top, a side parting giving volume. He wore a pastel-blue shirt under a horrid burgundy suit, and on his feet were the usual Converse trainers. He now had a goatee beard, though; that was new. But if he'd grown it to add some kind of gravitas, the clothing threw that away. It actually looked however that the beard had been grown to hide a burn scar on his cheek; Marlowe had seen Gabriel burnt badly the last time they met, and wondered what else was covering burn scars.

Marlowe let go of the guard's wrist and the guard grabbed it with his other, cradling it, trying to force back tears while glaring at Marlowe, who had already started walking away, heading towards Gabriel.

'You know, I really didn't expect to see you back here,' he said. 'I thought if the CIA didn't stick you in some kind of black hole, Orchid would definitely have killed you for stealing their money.'

Gabriel Rizzo gave a slight bow.

'By the time Orchid had a chance to kill me, you'd broken them into tiny little pieces,' he said. 'So, in a way, I have you to thank for my continued success.'

'Continued success?' Marlowe looked around. 'Your glorious golden casino doesn't seem to be what it once was. If anything, I'd say you're running on half the budget that you had before. How's your sister doing? Angelica? I heard she was taking over and fixing your screw ups?'

If his words affected Gabriel, the man didn't show it, simply shrugging as he motioned for Marlowe to walk with him towards the bar.

'Let's just say I have a new employer,' he said. 'A benefactor that's willing to give me the money I need to keep this place in the style that people are accustomed to.'

'Enough to keep your family off your back, you mean.' Marlowe took another look around the casino. 'If you think grotty-green-and-red tartan is what people are accustomed to, then you have really been living out of the wrong place.'

Gabriel ignored the comment as they arrived at the bar. The barman had already made his drink and looked at Marlowe who waved that he was okay.

'Steele said to watch for you, to wait, but I knew you'd come. You're predictable that way.' He straightened his gaudy burgundy suit. 'Everyone else – CIA, Orchid, even Steele – they think small. Clinical. But Vegas? Vegas understands spectacle. Have a drink, Marlowe. It might be the last one you ever have.'

Marlowe shrugged, turned around, and smiled at the man.

'I'll have a Virgin Mary,' he said. 'Easy on the spice.'

'So, basically a tomato juice?'

'Sure,' Marlowe continued his smile.

'Whatever you want,' the barman walked off to make the drink.

'Thomas Marlowe, drinking tomato juice in a casino,' Gabriel tutted mockingly, shaking his head as he did so. 'My, how the spies of the British Secret Service have collapsed in my estimations.'

'That's all right, I'm not part of the Security Service anymore,' Marlowe replied. 'I'm here as a personal favour to somebody.'

'Frank Maguire.'

'Now how the hell would you know that?' Marlowe turned slowly to face Gabriel.

'I hear things,' Gabriel shrugged in response. 'I also know that you're looking for Lawrence Bassett. I know you've spoken to the CIA and your little group of gossips, so I'm guessing you're trying to get this done quickly. Sounds to me like you need a little help.'

'And why would you help me?' Marlowe asked. 'I destroyed everything for you. Gave your sister the opening she needed to take over.'

'Did you, though?' Gabriel asked, the hint of a smile on his lips. 'You gave me a connection to the CIA that I've used multiple times already to get away with things. That red-headed woman you aimed me at? Oh, she's like my personal fairy godmother – even fixed my family issues.'

Marlowe kept his face emotionless as he looked out across the casino, wondering if "fixing family issues" included removing his sister from the board. If so, Marlowe hoped it wasn't a permanent situation.

The barman passed him his tomato juice, or what was at least left of the Virgin Mary that wasn't spicy, and he took a sip as he contemplated his next question.

'Who are you working for?' he asked.

'I think we both know the answer to that,' Gabriel smiled.

'Are you part of the new Orchid?'

'Orchid is Orchid,' Gabriel replied. 'There is no new or old. It is just Orchid. Some of Orchid don't talk to the others in Orchid. Some of Orchid believe the others should be removed. But while they are Orchid, then—'

'Please ... shut up,' Marlowe sighed, noticing that the guards that had walked out with Gabriel when he had exited the door to the manager's office had moved away, still watching, but giving them distance. Marlowe felt his adrenaline spike.

Was this a set-up?

He placed the glass down. The last thing he wanted to do was drink anything more made in this place.

'Is there a problem with your drink?' Gabriel asked with a smile, picking it up and taking a deep sip of it. 'Nope. Tastes just like tomato juice.'

'Can't help to be too careful,' Marlowe shrugged as he replied. 'You never know what someone could have placed in it.'

'I agree,' Gabriel said. 'But don't worry, Marlowe. If you die today, it won't be because you were poisoned.'

'And why would I die?'

'I don't know,' Gabriel shrugged. 'Pick the wrong team, enter the wrong casino, stand out in public when there's a million dollar hit on you.'

'Is that what this is about?' Marlowe asked. 'You want your million dollars?'

'I don't need a million dollars anymore, and you owe me way more than that,' Gabriel grinned. 'Money isn't what I need. Power is where the game is played now. I didn't realise it before, but now I see.'

He leant closer, his voice now a whisper.

'I'm a gambling man, Mister Marlowe. You probably guessed that because I run a casino. But I'm always about the odds. St John Steele has big pockets funding him. He wants to bring Orchid into the future. But then there's you, a man with nothing to offer, yet who seems to always defeat the odds. And I know you're not counting cards. So my question is, who do I side with? The sure thing? Or the thousand to one?'

He gave a dark, humourless smile.

'And then I thought ... why not both? After all, the money I could lose from betting against a sure thing would be gained by betting against you. I'd even the books and still come out the winner, whoever won.'

'And what would Steele say if he heard you'd gone against him?' Marlowe asked politely.

'Steele thinks this is about algorithms and market control,' Gabriel replied. 'Clean. Clinical. The perfect operation.'

He laughed, but there was no humour in it.

'But he never understood Vegas. Never understood that sometimes you need to make things personal. You took everything from me. My casino. My reputation. My family's respect. Steele wants to change the world ... I just want to watch yours burn.'

'Sounds like you're not "Team Tom" after all,' Marlowe replied calmly, while weighing up the situation.

'Just letting you know where I stand.'

'As Steele's "Vegas lapdog"? I see that.'

'I'm no lapdog,' Gabriel hissed, tapping at his beard-hidden scar. 'Steele thinks he's in charge, but he's as guilty of this as you are.'

'How do you see that?'

'He underestimated you. But then you underestimated him, too, didn't you?'

'So what, you hate me and Steele? Whoever wins means the other loses, and this is win-win for you?'

Gabriel shrugged.

'Steele thinks I'm playing his game, but I've always played my own,' he said. 'You're not going to have a great time playing it, so I felt I need to give you an advantage.'

'Let me guess, you intend to take Steele's stolen money for yourself?'

'Why not?' Gabriel shrugged. 'I know what he needs in Vegas, and amusingly, I seem to be the one person who can sort it for him. He needs me, while I don't need him.'

'And what would you offer me for this?' Marlowe asked, still unsure where the conversation was going.

'I could get your hit removed for a start,' Gabriel replied. 'I could tell Steele that the wrong people were turning up into town, that he was making too much of a scene. I could even pay off the debt myself, show you Lawrence Bassett.'

'You know where Bassett is?'

'I do,' Gabriel nodded as he waved to his two guards to come closer. 'Devon, take Mister Marlowe here to see Mister Bassett.'

The guard, now named Devon, frowned.

'Are you sure, boss?'

'Did I stutter?'

'But Mister Steele—'

'Do I look like I take orders from Mister Steele?'

Devon sighed, nodding for Marlowe to follow him, but Marlowe paused, using the act of finishing the Virgin Mary to give himself a moment to consider his options.

Marlowe didn't like the way the conversation had gone, but he was more worried about the way the conversation was *likely* going.

More importantly, he had a feeling that he was about to see Lawrence Bassett on a slab...

And possibly *join* him.

16

COLD BODIES

Marlowe had been in the depths of the casino before, although this was a different time and apparently under a different regime. As they carried on down the rear stairs, concrete steps that seemed to lead ever downwards, Marlowe wondered if this was actually assistance of some kind from Gabriel Rizzo, or whether he was about to be taken somewhere out back and shot in the head.

He coughed twice, a signal for Trix, listening through the earpiece, to respond.

No answer.

This didn't worry him too much; he was deep enough into the building that the signal was either not getting through, or, more likely, Trix was busy.

If it was being jammed, however, that was an issue.

The guard, walking him down, looked back at him.

'I was here when you did your thing, you know,' he muttered. 'Almost cost me my life.'

'Sorry,' Marlowe replied. 'I hope you understand it wasn't personal.'

The guard, if he understood that, said nothing, just narrowing his eyes for a moment and then shrugging as if to say, 'Yeah, whatever,' as they got down to the bottom of the stairs and a basement corridor. Opening the door, Marlowe saw he was as deep as he could get underground; the corridor in front of them was wide, wide enough for some kind of golf cart to drive up and down, and was over a couple of metres high with black pipes running along the top. If anything ever screamed out “basement passage”, this was the one.

The guard, however, didn't seem to want to go down there, indicating to a door on the right.

'Go in there,' he instructed.

Marlowe paused. *This was not what he was hoping for.*

As if understanding Marlowe's reluctance, the guard held his hands up.

'I'm not going with you,' he said. 'Don't worry. That's where Bassett is.'

Sighing internally, Marlowe cautiously opened the door and entered the room.

The first thing he noticed was that his breath was visible as it left his mouth. The temperature was a lot lower here; not walk-in freezer level, but there'd definitely been some attempts to make sure that this was cooler than normal temperature. Entering the room, the lights automatically turned on as soon as movement occurred and, as they did so, Marlowe could see why it had been kept artificially cool.

On the counter in the middle of the room was a body under a sheet. Marlowe's concerns about finding Lawrence Bassett dead seemed to be true. Walking over, he stood beside the body for a moment, shrouded in mystery, and then took the corner and pulled it back.

The last face he expected to see looking up at him was that of David Kelly, his eyes closed in death, his face at peace.

He was wearing a suit and tie, and it looked like he'd just been placed here, rather than any kind of autopsy or examination being checked. Realising that something was amiss, Marlowe pulled the sheet off fully, staring down at the man who, only a few days earlier, had stood in a Canary Wharf Tower, given him a keycard and told him to run.

David Kelly didn't deserve any kind of death like this but, as Marlowe scanned the body, he could see there was nothing visible on it. No blood, no wounds to the face or hands, no defensive marks, as Marlowe quickly examined using the edge of the sheet as a makeshift pair of gloves. The last thing he wanted was to have any of his fingerprints or DNA on this body, after all. Gabriel Rizzo was holding it for a reason and Marlowe now wondered if he'd hoped Marlowe would leave something here, and therefore become the prime suspect.

The guard had entered the room, staring from the doorway, and Marlowe paused, looking back at him.

'What happened?' he asked.

'Heart attack,' the guard said.

'Bollocks,' Marlowe shook his head. 'I know this man. There was no way he would have a heart attack. He was fit as a horse.'

'Even people who are Olympic runners can have heart attacks,' the guard replied.

Marlowe returned to the body.

'Where did he have the heart attack?'

'In one of the private rooms downstairs,' the guard continued. 'He'd turned up a couple of days ago. The boss wanted to check into him properly before we released the body to the police.'

Marlowe looked back at the body. He'd been in Canary Wharf four nights earlier; he'd been held by the police overnight, spent the next day planning and then attempting the attack on Harrington House – where Katherine Saito had died – before spending the next day speaking to Maguire and planning for his trip to Vegas, of which the day after was the flight, and that all led to today.

Three days.

If David Kelly had left for Vegas the day after the attack on Durrant Capital, he could have been here two days ago. Durrant and Voss arrived a day later, and apparently brought Lawrence Bassett with them on the jet, so would have arrived yesterday.

Had they discovered Kelly and killed him?

The guard, bored by the conversation, nodded towards the door.

'Look, my boss said he wanted you to see this. You've seen it. Let's go.'

'You can wait a second,' Marlowe said, looking at the body. 'I need to check something.'

'Look, we don't have the time to screw around with Bassett's—'

Marlowe spun to face the guard.

'We'll have the time,' he said carefully, interrupting, 'because this isn't Lawrence Bassett. This is an MI6 agent known as David Kelly, who I last saw in London a few days ago. So forgive me if I'm taking my time here, but I've yet to work out *why the hell you thought he was Bassett.*'

The guard, as if expecting this answer, walked over to the side cabinet, opened the drawer, pulled out a billfold wallet, and tossed it over.

Marlowe caught the wallet; it was brown leather, expensive looking, and opening it up, the first thing he saw was a British driving licence in the name of Lawrence Bassett, with David Kelly's face next to it.

Marlowe shook his head. *This wasn't right.* Lawrence Bassett was supposed to be a good thirty years older than the man laying down in front of him. Maguire was absolutely convinced he'd already gone to Vegas.

So, what was going on here?

He examined the rest of the wallet and was actually surprised to see that the money, twenties and fifty-dollar bills, were still inside it, as were credit cards all in the name of Lawrence Bassett. Whether these were the real Bassett's cards or whether these had been just given to Kelly, Marlowe didn't know.

'As I said, he turned up a couple of days ago,' the guard said. 'Claimed Durrant had a room for him, but they weren't coming in until the following day.'

That was wrong. Kelly wouldn't have announced himself like that. Unless ... he wanted someone to know he was there.

But who?

Again, the guard motioned to the door.

'You can examine his body if you want,' he said. 'But we've already gone through the pockets, checked under the nails, in the ears, all the stuff you'd expect from an episode of CSI. And believe me, that show started in Vegas, because we know our shit.'

Marlowe nodded, and then, leaning closer, he sniffed at the mouth. There was a strange smell, something that seemed familiar. He also noticed that the fingernails were slightly bluer than they should have been.

Poison, perhaps. That would explain the collapse. Marlowe would have to check into this.

Rising, Marlowe held up the wallet.

'Do you mind if I keep this?' he asked. 'I need to check a few things.'

'Mister Rizzo will decide on that,' the guard waved back to the door leading to the corridor and the stairs. 'We'll take it to him, see what he says.'

Marlowe nodded, placing the wallet into his pocket.

'And what's next for me?' he asked.

'I don't know what you mean,' the guard said, but his eyes flickered, as if he was wary of the question.

Marlowe smiled.

'Rizzo said he was going to take on both sides,' he explained. 'He's helped me by showing Lawrence Bassett, which, now I know, just like he also knows, *isn't* Lawrence Bassett. So what's he gonna do now for Steele?'

Through the half-open door, he could hear movement, more men walking down the stairs.

'You require help?' Marlowe nodded through the wall, and the guard glanced back through the doorway, realising whatever was going on was something Marlowe had now worked out. Before he could react, Marlowe leapt across the room, slid behind the guard, and locked him in a sleeper hold, instantly cutting off the flow of oxygenated blood to his brain – in a couple of moments, the guard slid to the floor, unconscious.

Marlowe rummaged in the guard's pockets, pulled out the keycards to get through the various back-casino areas, and then quickly ran out into the corridor. He could still hear footsteps coming down the steps; guards, laughing, unconcerned about whether they needed to hurry or not. He reckoned he had maybe a minute at best before they'd realise he wasn't where he was supposed to be.

Was there space on the sideboard next to Kelly for him?

Marlowe decided it was easier to escape now and claim a misunderstanding than it was to take on whoever was coming. He ran down the corridor, realising as he did so that the familiarity he had had when he arrived was understandable.

This was the corridor in which St John Steele had shot and killed his half-brother, Ichabod.

He'd watched it from a security camera, and the utilitarian design, the walls, everything was the same. Suddenly Marlowe recalled that there was an exit to the left, around twenty feet further on down the corridor, and he ran for that now. Marlowe had no doubt that whoever was sent down to join the guard had arrived and found their friend unconscious, but he really didn't care – He'd already reached the external doors, using the guard's key card to emerge out the back of the casino, walk quickly and quietly into the car park, and then out to blend in with the lunchtime crowd.

AS MARLOWE WALKED AWAY FROM THE CASINO, KEEPING HIS head down and staying among the crowds of afternoon tourists, he realised that not having a car definitely wasn't the best idea right now if he truly intended to get away clean.

It only took another minute of walking for Marlowe to realise he was being followed again.

Whoever it was this time must have been waiting for him, and picked him up as he walked down the back roads of the casinos, the same routes that Ryan Gates had told him many locals now took while the Formula One race was blocking the main roads.

Strangely enough, being forced down these routes actually helped Marlowe's getaway, as tailing him by car was much more difficult, given the tangle of various walkways and ramps that had been created.

That didn't stop them following him by foot, however, and Marlowe knew he had to stop whoever it was as quickly as he could. If it was anyone following on behalf of Gabriel, he could bluff it out. If it was another bloody assassin, he'd have to end them quickly. The biggest problem he had though, was that he didn't know his destination. He hadn't expected to find David Kelly, and definitely didn't expect him to be dead, and with a full ID kit for Lawrence Bassett. This stunk of MI5 or MI6, likely the latter, given Kelly's past working for McKellan.

Did McKellan do this?

Marlowe quickly went over the conversation they'd had, remembering to the best of his abilities what'd been said, but nothing had seemed out of place. However, something Katherine Saito had said before her death rang alarm bells now.

'Kelly, by the way, had worked with Steele, when he was at MI6. I'd seen messages between him and McKellan, so I'm guessing he was sent in undercover, to see what he could find.'

If McKellan sent Kelly into Durrant, it made sense he sent him to Vegas. But why as Bassett?

There was too much to unpack here, and Marlowe had a more immediate problem. Sliding down an alley, he tucked in behind a large dumpster, drew his CZ and quietly threaded a CGS Mod-9SK suppressor onto the weapon. Under five inches in length and a little over six ounces in weight, this tool was a perfect balance of size and weight – and firing sub-sonic rounds, was plenty quiet. He didn't particularly want to shoot anybody, but if it was a case of his life or theirs? Well, then there wasn't an option here that didn't end with bloodshed.

After a minute, a figure cautiously entered the alley, paused while slowly panning their view all around them, and then continued in. As they walked slowly past the dumpster, Marlowe slipped silently out behind them, his CZ pointed squarely at their centre of mass.

'Freeze,' he said. 'Hands where I can see them, no fast moves, don't turn around.'

As his pursuer slowly raised their arms, Marlowe clearly saw a Glock 19 in their strong hand.

'Very, *very* slowly, drop that pistol – make one bad move and you're dead.'

With an audible sigh, the man did as he was told.

'Now turn towards me, slowly, if you want to stay alive.'

As his pursuer turned, Marlowe raised his eyebrow in surprise.

'Well, I have to admit, Colonel Voss,' he said, 'I really didn't expect to see you down here.'

Martin Voss, ex-Royal Marines Colonel, and as far as Marlowe was aware, still head of security for Diana Durrant, stared at Marlowe with a look that was anything but friendly.

'Marlowe,' he replied, his voice calm, emotionless. 'We need to talk.'

17

OLD BOSSES

Although Voss and Marlowe had both served at the same time in the Royal Marines, Marlowe wouldn't have considered Voss a friend, or even a companion in the services. When Marlowe was there Voss had been a higher rank and, no matter what military service you were in, officers and enlisted men rarely spent time together. In fact, outside of training sessions when he'd first arrived, Marlowe had only met Voss five or six times in the entire time that he was with the Corps.

He knew Voss had a memory for faces, and this had been a concern when he saw him at Canary Wharf. But, as far as Marlowe had been concerned, he didn't even know if Voss had considered him after he'd left for MI5. Bar maybe a comment of, "Oh, I didn't expect him to go that route" when he learned Marlowe was an ex-MI5 agent, perhaps.

Now, however, the Voss that stood in front of Marlowe in the alleyway seemed troubled, less assured of himself. The "Lympstone stance" that Marlowe always accredited to the man because of where he'd done his officer training, was now missing. Voss was almost dancing from foot to foot, nervous energy coursing through him, and looked out of place in the alley's half-light, his expensive suit a stark contrast to the graffiti-covered walls and overflowing dumpsters.

Marlowe's CZ remained pointed at Voss' broad chest.

'Did you kill him?' Marlowe asked.

'Who?' The question was genuine. Voss had no idea what Marlowe was talking about, or, perhaps too many people had been killed for the singular to be used without a name attached.

'Kelly,' Marlowe replied.

At the single word, the name, Voss's eyes darkened, and his shoulders slumped in resignation.

'No,' he muttered. 'I'm guessing Gabriel Rizzo showed you him?'

'He did, but I don't know what game Rizzo was playing,' Marlowe replied. 'He believed he was showing me Lawrence Bassett, and I can tell you now there was a good thirty or forty years' difference in age between the two of them.'

Voss nodded, and now Marlowe's gun moved down to a low ready, deciding that this was a conversation that no longer needed to be had at gun point. Voss seemed torn, looking around nervously.

'Perhaps we could have this conversation elsewhere?'

'I'm fine to have it right here,' Marlowe replied. 'I don't think people would be happy if they saw us like this in more civilian locations.'

Voss nodded.

'I didn't kill Kelly,' he said. 'Although I terminated him—'

He held up his free hand to stop Marlowe's CZ from rising again.

'Terminate is the wrong word,' he added quickly. 'I meant

I fired him, handed him his notice, kicked him out of the company as quickly as we could.'

Marlowe waited, knowing that Voss had just started, and there was more to come.

'We knew he'd helped you in Canary Wharf,' Voss continued. 'When we examined the location, we saw that he'd had a face-off with you. We couldn't tell from the CCTV whether he'd been for or against your entry, but the keycard that you dropped on the floor, well ... when we realised it was linked to Kelly, and we'd seen on the CCTV there'd been no fight, we knew he had to have given it to you willingly.'

'I could have coerced him,' Marlowe said, now concerned that his slight error in the Durrant Capital building could have caused Kelly's death. 'Blackmailed him with something that I knew about his past.'

'If that was the case, Marlowe, then we would have fired him for being corruptible,' Voss shrugged. 'Either way, once the noise stopped, the sprinklers ceased, the exploding servers were brought back under control and the fires put out, we knew it was time to have a conversation.'

'And let me guess,' Marlowe said. 'The conversation was about how Kelly had basically been helping the wrong people and was allowed to leave?'

'No,' Voss shook his head and his eyes had gone cold. 'I'm not going to treat you like an idiot, Marlowe. After the police left, Kelly was interrogated by me.'

Marlowe nodded. In the Royal Marines, Voss had been known as a man who would interrogate new recruits when they reached that section of training. He was also often used by the SAS on selection because of his abilities. Many of the traits that Marlowe learned over the years had been because of people like Voss passing them down.

'How well did he do?' Marlowe asked.

'He didn't even try,' Voss barked a bitter laugh. 'McKellan had told him the moment it all went wrong to simply admit the truth. MI6 had sent him into Durrant Capital, concerned that there were erroneous data transfers and financial dealings that needed to be looked at. He was given a legend that showed him leaving MI6 unhappily, giving him enough reasons to move across.'

He shook his head.

'It was a pity hire and the worst thing was, he knew that'd be the case. Relied on it. Once we realised McKellan was still his boss, and that he still had a connection to you, we knew there was no way we could keep him.'

Marlowe laughed. 'You realised there was no way you could keep him,' he mocked. 'It makes it sound like you almost tried.'

'He was a good man, until he wasn't,' Voss shrugged.

'So, how did he end up here, on a slab in a casino?' Marlowe asked bitterly.

At this, however, Voss seemed perturbed.

'I genuinely don't know,' he replied.

'Don't give me that,' Marlowe shook his head. 'I know you turned up on a jet with Bassett. And then Bassett just happens to be David Kelly, who was with you four days ago.'

'I never killed Kelly,' Voss repeated, and his eyes flashed angrily as he did so. 'The Bassett we travelled with was a different man.'

There was movement from the side, and the door in the alley opened; a kitchen staff member of one hotel popping out for a cheeky cigarette. As they saw the two men facing each other, bodies positioned to hide the weapons in their hands, they thought better of it, nodding and then returning to the building.

Marlowe looked, returned his attention to Voss.

'I'm all ears to hear how this one happened,' he said.

Voss took a deep breath and nodded as he did so.

'May I retrieve my gun now?'

Marlowe, seeing this as a moment of truce, nodded. Voss picked up his Glock and slid it back into a shoulder holster, while Marlowe removed the can from his CZ, and holstered it as well.

'We brought Bassett over,' he said. 'That's true. Steele had wanted him safe, but Gabriel Rizzo, who I believe you know? He told us Bassett was invaluable for a meeting here. Said Steele had heard it from an asset of his, an MI6 woman named Saito.'

Marlowe cocked his head at this.

'Katherine Saito said Bassett needed to be here. She's the one who effectively sent me here to get him back.'

'I don't know the full story. I'm just a soldier,' Voss replied. And as he said the word "soldier", he actually straightened, as if the word itself was enough to remind him of his glory days.

'I know, however, she'd been talking to St John Steele, and St John Steele had been talking to Diana Durrant. They were passing information back and forth, and at the time I wasn't aware that you were a topic of discussion.'

'You didn't know I was there?'

'Not until I saw you,' Voss replied. 'Honestly, nobody had informed me of anything to do with this. Even Kelly had kept quiet after you'd escaped, claiming that he'd seen you, but you'd left before he could gain full identity. He'd even pointed out the keycard didn't work for you, claiming he knew that, and *this* was how he proved himself. But we knew this only happened when your technical backup was locked out, as all the keys under a level five clearance were flashed and paused.'

Marlowe was impressed. He hadn't realised that Kelly would have tried to give him more time when Voss had arrived.

'But how does that affect America, and your visit here?'

At this, Voss shrugged.

'Diana Durrant didn't give a shit about London,' he replied. 'She didn't care about crappy little villains in their crappy little territories. Why waste time making pennies when you can make millions? London would never have given her the return ratio she wanted. But Frank Maguire hadn't just been a gangster. As well you know, he'd worked for MI5, even MI6, willing or unaware, a couple of times, and Durrant had been informed of this.'

Marlowe grimaced.

'Katherine Saito told her.'

'She told Steele, and Steele told her, yes. The problem was they didn't realise that the things that Maguire found out while working for Saito gave him advantages in building up and climbing the ladder to where he was.'

Marlowe nodded at that. He'd always wondered how someone like Frank Maguire could get such a chokehold on Essex, when there were other more vicious gangsters around. Learning he'd had the help of inside knowledge from the government itself made sense.

'The other problem, though, was that Bassett is dead,' Voss continued. 'And I don't mean Kelly, here.'

He shifted, uncomfortable now.

'Lawrence Bassett was a reliable accountant for Frank Maguire for almost twenty years, but almost a year back, he died. Nothing nefarious, just a stroke, in bed, in Essex. Well, that's what I was told.'

'And how did you get told this?'

'When I discovered we were working with Bassett, I looked into him,' Voss replied calmly. 'Due diligence. And you'll be surprised at the amount of ex-serving men who now work for people like Maguire. I had a few favours owed, played up the Corps loyalty ... eventually I gained the same story from several reliable sources.'

'That Bassett was dead.'

'More than that. I heard Bassett had retired from accounting five years back, was kept on retainer by Maguire, but a year ago was believed to have died ... then nine months ago apparently returned to life and applied for a passport,' Voss watched Marlowe as he spoke, as if trying to see if his words were believed or not. 'And then started travelling the world, attending conferences.'

'So, someone took his identity for themselves?' Marlowe considered this. To take the legend of someone legally dead took serious power to push through. MI5 or MI6 levels.

Or CIA levels. A line from Clarissa came back to him.

'Lawrence Bassett is a CIA asset. Has been for the last year.'

Voss had been quietly watching him, and now leant closer.

'Here's the kick, though,' he said. 'Bassett came back to life, but it was like he never died. Up to a month ago, he was still working for Maguire.'

Marlowe had expected this; now he understood what Frank Maguire had meant, when he became obtuse in Marlowe's home.

'... she was the one who told me I had to get Bassett back. Fact

of the matter is, I haven't seen Bassett in a while. I can't explain why.'

Was Katherine Saito in charge of the fake Bassett? Had the CIA inserted him, and Katherine was trying to warn Steele? That was a question for later.

'So, let me get this right,' Marlowe leant back, gaining some space as he considered this. 'Bassett is what, a good accountant—but then dies, is replaced by someone with an eidetic memory, who then starts using the identity to visit other places, who is believed to be a CIA asset, while working for Maguire, a now-known MI5 and MI6 asset ... and who now finds himself in Vegas, with you and Durrant?'

Voss gave the slightest of nods.

'Again, I'm just a soldier.'

Marlowe considered the conversation so far.

'Let me guess,' he replied. 'You flew over here with "Bassett" to do whatever Diana Durrant needed to do in Vegas, likely with Gabriel Rizzo, and when you arrive, they tell you that Lawrence Bassett is dead. What a shock, especially as you have the real one – well, at least the current one – in your hand.'

'Somebody, somewhere decided that it was time to remove him,' Voss nodded. 'All I can assume is MI6 had given Kelly orders to infiltrate the Vegas operation. He knew we were coming, he knew Bassett was a lie and was supposed to be here, and so he turned up a day early, maybe to find out what he could before he needed to retreat. Unfortunately, he was quickly discovered and had a terrible accident.'

'You genuinely think it was an accident?'

Voss shook his head.

'Oh no, Marlowe, I know for a fact it wasn't an accident.

They poisoned him, caused his heart to explode, claimed it was a heart attack, and that Bassett had died.'

'But they didn't make it public,' Marlowe said. 'No autopsy, no coroner, no police brought in.'

'Of course not,' Voss shook his head. 'Gabriel Rizzo isn't an idiot. And seven hours after Rizzo found "Mister Bassett" dead, we turned up with *another* "Mister Bassett". As far as the hotel systems were convinced, Mister Bassett wasn't dead. We just had a dead, anonymous body to decide what to do with.'

He looked back up the alley.

'And in Nevada, Marlowe, there's a lot of desert with graves in.'

Marlowe didn't want to consider that.

'Why are you working for Durrant?' he asked.

'Because I need the money,' Voss said. 'My pension is minuscule and, by the time I need it, the government will probably have got rid of it altogether. The work I did over the years gained nothing more than a pat on the back and a "thank you very much". Working for Diana Durrant? I'm making seven figures a year. That might not sound much to someone like you who runs around on *James Bond* expense budgets but, to me, it gives me the life that I've always wanted, that my family always wanted.'

'You have a family?'

'What, you thought I was a lifer?' Voss laughed. 'I've got a wife and child. They're in Singapore. I haven't seen them for three months now. But, by the time I finish this contract, I'll have enough to set us up so that we never have to work for someone again. I'll create my own agency.'

He chuckled.

'I probably would have invited you to join, if it wasn't for all the obvious issues ... and the million dollar hit on your head.'

Marlowe now wished he hadn't put away his gun, narrowing his eyes at the comment.

'It's a quicker way to make your million,' he said.

'It's not the way I want to make my millions,' Voss replied. 'And, if you remembered me at all from our time together, you would know that.'

'I'll be honest, Martin,' Marlowe said, deliberately using Voss's Christian name rather than rank or surname. 'The man *I* remember wouldn't stand beside someone like Diana Durrant.'

'Security jobs are security jobs, nothing more,' Voss replied. 'I don't get involved in any of her random shit, which is why I'm worried now that I'm in too deep.'

He glanced around again, and Marlowe wondered what, or who, he was looking for.

'There's a bar over the road,' he said. 'Can we please go somewhere to talk that isn't a bloody corridor, alleyway, or road?'

Marlowe nodded.

'I know just the place,' he said.

18

MOVING SUITES

WHEN MARLOWE HAD TOLD HER TO MOVE HOTELS, TRIX HAD known he wasn't suggesting it as a passing idea. From the moment they'd first arrived in Vegas, they knew there was a chance this would have to happen. Once somebody knew where Marlowe was, everyone would converge on him, especially with a one-million-dollar hit on his head.

With that in mind, they'd set up three backup locations, codenamed Tom, Dick and Harry, after the tunnels used in *The Great Escape*. The chosen spots were the Venetian, The Cosmopolitan and the Bellagio; each had a suite booked under a fake name and alias they'd prepared in advance. The bookings were flexible – able to be cancelled at the last minute if needed – but the cost of holding a suite paled compared to the cost of ending up dead.

If Trix was being honest while moving to the Venetian, the Horseshoe Casino, albeit nice if slightly dated, still gave her memories of the last time they'd been there, while this was an opportunity to try somewhere new. The only annoyance was that she'd already unpacked her tech equipment, and had already set up quite an excellent base of operations. One thing Trix had worked out, however, over the years working with Marlowe and being out in the field, was the ability to take down what she'd put up in less than ten minutes.

She hadn't brought the laptop that Katherine Saito had been using with her; she'd spent the day before they'd flown using the encrypted key that Marlowe had found, copying every file on it across, so she could work on it from her own system rather than bring more equipment than necessary.

Trix also had a hatred of Macs. It was harder to create your perfect system with a Mac OS. That said, she wasn't a massive fan of Windows either and preferred a hand-altered Linux configuration for her usual setup. But this was irrelevant, as she packed it all back into her large hard case.

The strap on top of it said *Handle with Care.* As far as customs had been informed, they'd been preparing a light show in Vegas, hence the need for such equipment cases. It wasn't too large though, no more than a luggage-sized four-wheeler that could be moved quickly when needed.

The monitor went into a second wheeled case, her clothes into a cabin bag. Marlowe had only brought his usual hand luggage; the life of a spy was too hard to break, even when flying business class. A holdall with his immediate needs and a Carl Frederik hard case cabin bag, which carried everything else.

Once she was packed – literally less than twenty minutes after Marlowe had made the call – Trix went to call down for the bellboy to come pick up the luggage, but then paused, realising this would draw attention. Instead, she walked out of the suite, heading down towards the elevator, picking up a luggage trolley en route. With this in hand and returning swiftly, she could now place her luggage onto it and—

She returned to the suite to find a man waiting for her.

He was young, Latino in looks, wearing an oversized black hoodie with the slightest hint of a moustache trying to grow. Trix cursed her eagerness to grab the trolley, because in doing so, she hadn't picked up any kind of weapon. She wasn't the kind of person to walk around with a gun, but she had a small hand taser she liked, one she'd bought online and had sent to the suite by courier, and her pepper spray was usually in her pocket.

However, as he saw her walking towards him, the young man raised both hands up to show that he was unarmed.

'Clarissa sent me,' he said. 'My name's Mason.'

At the name, Trix relaxed. Clarissa had helped her in the past, and Marlowe had gone over to speak to her earlier that day. He hadn't mentioned that he'd sent somebody to come pick her up, and she didn't know if this was an extraction team ... or anything else.

Walking back to the door, Mason stepped to the side as she dragged the trolley into the suite.

'Are you going somewhere?' he asked.

Trix looked at him, raising an eyebrow, and Mason, intelligent enough to not continue, smiled sheepishly.

'You know how it works,' Trix said, almost apologetically. The young man seemed eager, but she did also worry that he was a bit too young to be doing the job.

Don't be stupid, a voice in her head chided. *You were doing this as a teenager. Pearce Associates found you before you even left school.*

'What do you have?' she asked, already placing the first

case onto the trolley. Mason paused, went to reply, and then helped her with the second as he continued.

'I was told to find out about Bassett,' he said. 'We checked into him using sources we have—'

'You hacked into systems,' Trix smiled. 'Don't need to play the spy game here. Hackers know hackers.'

'Alright, so here's the thing,' Mason said, rocking back on his heels, hands stuffed deep into the pockets of his hoodie. He spoke fast, West Coast twang sharp on every word. 'Lawrence Bassett? Not his real name. Dude's running a mask. I can't tell you what it actually is – well, not yet – but I got a nibble. First name's probably Evan. Found it buried in some old training files linked to a dead ops database.'

'You were in a dead ops database?'

Mason reddened.

'Clarissa gave me the codes,' he admitted reluctantly. 'Wasn't obvious, had to backdoor through a dormant sub-domain, but it's there. Feels solid.'

He glanced around like he was expecting someone to be eavesdropping, then leant in a little closer, voice dropping a notch.

'Here's where it gets weirder. He's CIA-trained. No doubt on that one. Way too many pings connecting him to Agency certs; digital fingerprints on old instructor logs, comms protocols, a couple of obscure sandbox systems only The Company runs. But he ghosted a couple of years back. Whole trail just ... like, evaporates. Like, dude went dark. Off-grid, no network hits, no service metadata, nada. Could mean he's freelance now. Could mean he's back in, just moving quiet. Either way, spook vibes are high.'

Mason pulled his hands from his pockets, rubbed them together like he was hyping himself up for the next drop.

'Then we got Vegas. Get this – man scored a hundred grand at the Desert Orchid Casino last night. No trace of him buying in, though. No chip logs, no wire transfers, not even a swipe on a loyalty card. But boom, cash-out recorded, clean as a whistle. Hundred K, just like that. That's not luck, that's leverage. Could be he's washing cash, could be he's pulling some inside play with the pit boss. Either way, it stinks.'

Trix nodded as she considered this. A hundred grand sounded very much like an off-the-books payment. *But for what?*

Mason rocked back again, eyes still scanning the room like a motion sensor.

'But that ain't even the whole of it. He's been to Vegas twice in the last three months—'

'No, we saw his passport,' Trix shook her head. 'If he's using Basset's passport, he's not been here since he renewed it.'

'Sure, there's no passport stamps sayin' so, but I clocked his flight history,' Mason smiled now, proud of his achievement here. 'LHR to LAX once, LHR to Boulder City another time. Two trips, tight windows. Both times, he hires a car. And you know what's between LA and Vegas, yeah? About four hours of open desert road. No cameras, no logs, no nothing. Man's sliding under radar. Leaves Heathrow, "goes to LA", but nah – he's rolling into Vegas quiet. Drop the car back, hop the plane home, nobody's clocking him. If you ain't looking, you don't see it. Same with Boulder.'

Mason scratched his jaw, eyes flicking back to her.

'So, that's what I got. Evan-something, ex-CIA, plays ghost, wins big in Vegas without buying chips, and drives in like he's in Ocean's Eleven. Tell me that ain't a story.'

Trix smiled, reaching into her pocket. Mason winced, but relaxed when she pulled out a hundred-dollar bill.

'You never saw me, you never told me, you never looked into this,' she winked. 'Stay safe, Mason.'

Mason's eyes widened at the tip, but he had the sense to sniff, hold his emotions in check, give a tap of the fingers to the forehead and leave.

Trix was amused by the teenager. *Had she been like that?* Either way, she was still going to wait a few minutes before leaving, just to make sure he didn't see her.

As it was, her phone buzzed and, expecting it to be Marlowe – after all, few people had the number – she answered it without checking.

'You'd better be bringing back burgers—'

'*Please hold for Sir Walter McKellan.*'

Trix bit back an expletive. McKellan was the last person she needed to speak to. That said, he'd be able to help with some extra items she was short, as long as he was calling to be on their side.

Yeah. She'd deal with McKellan, and then she'd go to the cab rank and travel across to the Venetian.

Sighing, she looked at the remaining cases as she waited for the call to connect.

Next time, she'd use AR glasses. Way lighter.

THE *CABINET OF CURIOSITIES* WAS TUCKED AWAY IN THE LOWER levels of the Horseshoe Casino, far from the bustling chaos of the gaming floor. If Marlowe was being honest, it felt like stepping into a collector's private gallery: dimly lit, intimate, and steeped in mystery.

Shelves along the walls displayed an assortment of peculiar artefacts, including a tarnished sextant, a jar of marbles that glinted faintly under the soft amber lighting, and a faded map that seemed more decorative than functional. Each item hinted at a story but left the details to the imagination. And, if your imagination wanted more, there was a fake vault door that led to a small speakeasy.

Marlowe didn't care about tourist traps, however.

The air was heavy with the scent of aged wood and spiced whisky, and the quiet hum of conversation was punctuated by the occasional clink of glasses. It was the kind of place where people spoke in low tones, as if afraid to disturb the secrets the bar itself seemed to guard. The bar staff moved efficiently but unobtrusively, crafting cocktails as much for their visual flair as their taste, each drink a work of art. It claimed to have a happy hour that, for all intents and purposes, seemed to be the entire day.

Nobody paid a second glance to the two men talking. On a weekday, around one in the afternoon, there was every possibility that these two men were from the conference that was likely happening on the floor above, in the conference suites at the back of the Horseshoe.

Marlowe sipped at his sparkling water, still not wanting to drink anything alcoholic while facing off against someone like Voss. Voss, however, had opted for a vodka on the rocks, possibly even a double from the amount of liquid that had been in the glass when he came back from the bar.

He sipped at it, staring down at the table.

'If they can do what they did to David Kelly, knowing that he was a UK operative, or at least an asset, then they won't think twice before having an accident with me,' he said. 'You know the rule about masked kidnappers.'

'That they hide their identity?' Marlowe frowned.

'Yes,' Voss replied. 'Masked kidnappers, masked bank robbers, anyone wearing a mask doesn't want you knowing their identity, doesn't want you being able to give it away to the police. Hence the mask. But when a kidnapper or a bank robber turns up and they're *not* wearing a mask ...'

He trailed off, and Marlowe knew he didn't need to finish the sentence. If a kidnapper or a bank robber wasn't wearing a disguise, and had a gun in his hand? The chances were he wasn't worried about you seeing his identity because you weren't likely going to live.

'Are you trying to tell me you've been kidnapped?' Marlowe asked.

Voss leant back on the chair, looking up at the ceiling, exhaling a long, sad breath before looking back at Marlowe.

'No, but they've allowed me to see their faces,' he replied. 'I've seen too much, Marlowe. There will be a point where they'll realise that I can't be trusted to keep quiet. They already know that I'm only here for the money. Sure, they could offer to pay me off, but I'm not a lifer. They'd know that at any point I could change my mind, and ...'

He raised his glass.

'Bullets are cheaper than bonuses.'

'You think it'll be sooner rather than later?'

'I don't know,' Voss shook his head. 'I'd like to think that I'm mistaken, and nothing'll happen, but the callous way they killed David Kelly makes me think that there's more going on than even I know, more going on than probably *you* know, and you seem to know more about this than I do.'

He leant forward, placing his tumbler on the glass table, staring intently at Marlowe as he lowered his voice.

'I want out, Marlowe,' he said. 'The million would have

been nice, but I'd rather have my life. I can always make more money. I'm guessing you have an issue with Durrant and you're here to try to stop her. If you succeed in doing whatever you're doing, then there's every chance that I'm dead. If you fail, there's every chance that I'm dead as well. But if you succeed and take me with you, then perhaps I have a way out of this.'

Marlowe nodded.

'I can put you in front of people who can get you out,' he said, although, as he spoke the words, he actually realised he wasn't sure if he could. In the past, he would have just phoned up Sasha Bordeaux and asked if the CIA wanted a cool asset that could help. But now, having seen Gabriel Rizzo back in his old role, and knowing that Sasha wasn't the woman he thought she was, this option was no longer viable.

'The only person I trust to get me out, Marlowe, is you,' Voss replied. 'We served together. Regardless of whether I was higher, or you were lower, "rank hath no privileges" in this situation.'

'What's your offer?' Marlowe asked.

'I don't think things are as clear-cut as they seem,' Voss replied. 'Steele seems in charge, and Diana's listening to what he says, but then there's Gabriel Rizzo, and since we arrived he's been acting as if he's the power, and Steele's the observer. I'd say he's full of shit, but he seems to have the ear of powerful people, and he's calling the shots right now.'

He leant closer.

'Nobody's seen Steele for days,' he said conspiratorially. 'Like he's off the grid, hiding out. Almost like he's aware Gabriel's making a power play, and he's using him as a distraction. Which is fine, but not when we're there standing next to the prick.'

'I get that,' Marlowe nodded. 'So, you think Gabriel is actively making a play, or he's being set up?'

'No idea. I don't know the man well enough to gain a bead on what he'd do. All I know for sure is where Lawrence Bassett is,' Voss replied. 'Or at least whoever claims to be him is. He's in a suite at the Velvet Oasis, and he's giving some kind of presentation to a select group of influential people tonight.'

'He is?' Marlowe half rose, almost instinctively moving to return to the casino and hotel, before pausing. 'Do you know who they are?'

'People Steele is courting for some new think tank,' Voss shrugged. 'Money men.'

Marlowe forced himself to stay calm; money men that Steele was courting meant people he wanted in his new Orchid. Maybe these were people on the fence, who could be turned?

'Why Bassett?' Marlowe asked, but then paused. A man with an eidetic memory could read a list of figures and then rattle them off to someone else later. Bassett wasn't giving a presentation – he *was* the presentation. Everything he'd picked up over the last year of travelling, while keeping his head down, making Katherine Saito believe he was on their side, as per Steele's orders ... all together meant Lawrence Bassett, or whoever he was, could be the most vital, and dangerous person to Steele right now.

If Rizzo turned him into an ally, there was every chance he could come out of this on top.

'I can get you to him,' Voss continued. 'Once you're there, it's up to you what to do. I can find a reason to not be around when it happens, but the moment it happens you need to get me out, because they *will* be looking for scapegoats and I'll be damned if I'll be the one.'

'Could be dangerous.'

'Everything's dangerous, Marlowe,' Voss chuckled. 'But, right now, even sitting here having a drink is dangerous and I don't want to be in a world where that's the case. And please don't take this the wrong way, but once this is done, the only time I'd want to see you would be at a Corps Christmas piss-up.'

Marlowe nodded.

'Do you know how to contact me?'

'I know you're at the Horseshoe.'

'Not anymore,' Marlowe shook his head. 'We're at the Venetian.'

'Why the change?'

'The aforementioned million dollar hit on my head,' Marlowe sighed. 'I shouldn't even be here right now, but I thought it'd be best to come back, talk to you here, and if anybody sees me, they'll think I'm still connected to the hotel.'

Voss considered this and nodded.

'It needs to be tonight. St John Steele might be there too, perhaps, or whoever's funding him.'

'I thought he had government money he was using?'

Voss shook his head.

'That's something I do know,' he replied. 'Whatever money he thought he was getting, it hasn't turned up yet. It's why they were trying to move slush funds through the finance hubs.'

He finished his tumbler and rose.

'They're going to remove Kelly,' he said. 'The body, that is.

It'll be dumped somewhere, likely in a desert. Rizzo will have his people do it. I don't know if he had a family or anything, but I'll see if I can find out where the grave is. Perhaps MI6 can bring him home. Soldiers should always be brought home.'

With that, Martin Voss, onetime Colonel of the Royal Marines, gave a short but curt nod to Marlowe and left the bar. Marlowe sat alone for a moment, finishing the sparkling water. He didn't know if Voss was playing him or not and this was some kind of trap. But, if there was a way to gain Bassett out from underneath Diana Durrant's hands and find whatever information he had, information that seemed to connect to Steele's sudden possible financing, then this was the perfect opportunity.

He had to take the opportunity.

Rising, he slipped out of the Cabinet of Curiosities, heading back towards the main casino floor. He needed to get back to Trix and the Venetian as quickly as possible, and this time, hopefully, with no assassins – he'd had enough death for one day – but there was still a curiosity on whether anyone was still here watching for him.

It took less than three minutes before he found them, and, after taking photos, making sure he could see the faces in the images, he left the casino, leaving the watchers to wait for nothing.

19

PLANNING MEETING

'So, hold on a second. You're telling me the real Lawrence Bassett died a year ago?'

Trix frowned at her laptop screen, her fingers moving across the keyboard in that familiar blur of motion that Marlowe had seen a dozen times before. Around her, the suite of the Venetian, the first of their locations, was lit by the glow of multiple monitors, each displaying different aspects of the mystery they were trying to unravel.

The suite at the Venetian Hotel was large, almost too large. A sunken living room with a low couch and armchairs sat to the side, the gold trim on the furniture catching the light from a chandelier overhead. The bed was king-sized, raised on a platform, with heavy drapes that matched the deep-red and cream colour scheme, a similar one in the room next door. The floor was polished marble, cold underfoot. Floor-to-ceiling windows overlooked the Strip, the glow of neon spilling into the room. In the bathroom, Marlowe had seen a soaking tub and a glass shower taking up most of the space, with a double vanity stretching along one wall. Everything was clean, precise, and expensive, but impersonal. It felt more like a stage than a place to relax. Although Marlowe didn't think they'd be "relaxing" anytime soon.

'Apparently, it was a stroke while living in Essex,' Marlowe confirmed, examining Kelly's wallet again, the one passed to him by the security guard at the Velvet Oasis, looking for anything that could give a clue why he was there. Although, if he was being honest, he was probably given it as a distraction while the guard was waiting for *more* guards to come down. 'According to Voss, he's been retired for five years. Maguire had kept him on some kind of retainer, but that was probably more out of loyalty than need.'

'Then who's this?' Trix pulled up a passport photo on one of her screens. The image showed a man in his late fifties, dark-haired, unremarkable except for the intensity of his gaze. 'Because this is the guy that's been using Bassett's identity for months now.'

She sifted through images; the strange man in his fifties at financial conferences in Dubai, Tokyo, Los Angeles, always in the background, always watching and always remembering.

'These are from the social media sites of a dozen different conferences,' she said.

'How did you find them already?' Marlowe asked, frowning.

'Facial recognition from when Lawrence Bassett – *this* Lawrence Bassett, I suppose – applied for his passport,' Trix explained. 'Every time he's been somewhere, it's been stamped. All of these conferences are within a day or two of his arrival and departure. It wasn't that hard to work out which of these he'd go to. The first appearance was a global banking summit in Singapore. Then there's these private meetings with hedge fund managers.'

'If they're private, how do we have photos?'

'They're private in the respect that people don't know what happened during them, but the hedge fund managers are stupid and like social media,' Trix grinned. 'A couple of them have very large followings on their Instagram, and they do like to know what's happening. As you can see here, though, although Bassett isn't smiling for the camera, he's simply in the middle of a scene that they've taken a shot of. And then we have what Clarissa's little friend told me, that he's been to Vegas twice, driving in under the radar.'

'Maybe he's debriefing?' Marlowe frowned. 'But that would insinuate Gabriel Rizzo debriefing, and that doesn't feel very much like Steele.'

Trix tapped at her lip with her pen, staring at her monitor.

'From what I can work out, he's been gathering information. The kind that doesn't show up in any database.'

'Perfect cover, too. If he's got an eidetic memory, then everything that's in his head is everything he's seen,' Marlowe replied. 'It makes sense to do it this way. Lawrence Bassett, the accountant, was never known for such skills. Nobody would have expected the man walking into their room to be able to look at a single sheet and gather every number on it.'

'Right. He's like the Chinese girl in *Safe*,' Trix muttered to herself, noting that Marlowe was now confused. 'Jason Statham movie? He plays a guy who has to save a girl and she's like some kind of living computer for the Triad, has a list of numbers in her head. Similar kind of thing to this.'

'Apart from the fact that Lawrence Bassett isn't a small child and I'm not Jason Statham.'

'Don't put yourself down,' Trix patted him reassuringly on

the arm. 'You could be Jason Statham. Just shave your head and, well, spend a few days in the gym. Or weeks, maybe.'

Marlowe carried on examining the wallet, ignoring her comment. Kelly had followed the money trail from London to Vegas, probably believing Bassett was just another banker turned informant. But he'd found something bigger. Going through Kelly's wallet again, Marlowe noticed something he'd missed – a folded receipt, forced to the bottom of one of the credit card slots. The receipt was from the Velvet Oasis's high-stakes room, dated two days earlier.

Had Kelly seen something in that high-stakes room – something worth killing for?

'Voss gave the impression that Kelly had seen something connected to Stone Blind. Something worth killing for,' he said, looking back up.

'Probably more than that,' Trix's voice carried an edge of excitement as she brought up another image on a side monitor. Marlowe wasn't sure where the monitors all came from; they seemed to be portable ones that appeared out of nowhere. It did explain why Trix's checked luggage was quite heavy.

'Look at his travel pattern. Every conference he attended, every meeting, they all connect to banks that were, back in the day, involved with Operation Quicksilver. Even coming to Vegas helps with the funneling of it. Back in the nineties, Vegas was a goldmine for cleaning dirty money – mob or government, they weren't picky.'

'The missing millions,' Marlowe said, nodding to himself. 'He's mapping the money.'

As he spoke the words, the implications hit Marlowe almost like a physical force.

'If this new version of Lawrence Bassett has an eidetic

memory, and he's been gathering financial data for months, he's reconstructing the entire pipeline,' he intoned. 'Every account, every transfer, the entire network.'

'If he's able to do that, he's literally a human database,' Trix whistled, leaning back in her chair. 'And that means he's one that can't be hacked or copied, just extracted.'

Marlowe straightened. 'What do you have on the Oasis?'

Trix switched screens, bringing an architectural plan of the hotel-casino complex up. The original blueprints had been changed, showing security systems, camera placements, patrol routes, all that kind of thing. Red lines, drawn in what looked to be some kind of art program, marked automated systems, blue showing guard patrols, while the green showed potential blind spots.

'You have been busy,' Marlowe said.

'They might have painted it up a little, but it's still the same place we stole millions from a few months back,' Trix shrugged. 'I just dusted off the old blueprints, found new ways into the system and started looking for upgrades.'

'Any there?'

'Oh, loads,' Trix nodded. 'Almost as if they were caught with their pants down by an incredible hacker and her bearded sidekick, and were desperately trying – and failing, I'll add – to upgrade everything.'

Marlowe let the "sidekick" comment slide.

'When you mentioned this was where Durrant had been keeping Bassett, it was only a matter of time to work out how she'd do it.' She tapped the monitor. 'Bassett's in the chairman's suite. Fortieth floor, East Tower. Durrant's got a whole security team, probably somewhere near eight men on rotation. Plus, we've got the hotel's own security and there's the automated systems to think about as well. As you saw, they bloody hate you.'

'Do we have an approach yet?'

'Three ways in,' Trix highlighted routes in different colours. 'Main elevator's got a biometric control. Service elevator needs staff keys and passes. External's possible but exposed. They're taking no chances, his suite is basically a cage. Durrant's got eyes on him twenty-four-seven.'

'Again, you've got all this because ...'

Trix looked back with an almost hurt expression on her face.

'Dude, when we broke into the Gold Strike, I had four backup plans ready to go. Now I get to use them all in one. Don't crush a girl's dreams.'

Marlowe said nothing as Trix, poking her tongue out at him, pulled up security footage showing the corridors. On the screen, Marlowe saw guards patrolling in pairs, their movements precise and professional.

'Yeah, they didn't change the back door passwords, either,' she smiled.

Marlowe, however, didn't join her.

'Which feels off,' he said. 'Surely that'd be the first thing they'd do?'

'Don't look gift horses in mouths,' Trix waggled a finger at him.

'They're not casino security,' he muttered. 'Look at them. That's ex-military, maybe special forces.'

'You think Voss could have hired them?'

'Possibly,' Marlowe replied. 'He did make a comment to me about how many ex-regiment men and women seemed to move into private security. It would make sense that, if he was in such a prime position for hiring, he'd bring in people.'

'Are you thinking you might know them? Have a way past them?'

Marlowe shrugged.

'Voss has said he's on my side and he wants to get out. Maybe there's a chance here of using him,' he replied. 'But the guy I saw earlier wasn't British. And I can't see Rizzo being too happy about Voss changing his team. The guy thought he was *Gladiator*, remember? Fighting all comers in the octagon cage.'

'More Commodus, the wannabe emperor who lost everything in the arena, than Maximus Decimus Meridius, Commander of the Armies of the North, General of the Felix Legions, Loyal servant to the true emperor—'

'Apart from the fact that Rizzo doesn't seem to have lost anything,' Marlowe muttered quickly, stopping Trix from finishing the speech. 'Maybe Voss is our option.'

'That might not work,' Trix said slowly, looking back at Marlowe. 'I was checking into the system and it looks like Voss's security clearance was revoked two hours ago.'

'Two hours?' Marlowe considered the timing of this additional fact. This would have been shortly after Marlowe had left Gabriel Rizzo when Voss was following him.

Had Voss realised that he was being locked down? Isolated? Did he know he was compromised at that point?

He hadn't realised, but he'd spoken the words aloud, and Trix turned in her chair.

'He's either compromised or they're expecting you to use him,' she said. 'It could be a trap.'

'Oh, it's definitely a trap.' Marlowe continued to study the plans, rubbing at his chin as he did so. 'The question is, whose trap? Durrant's trap? Steele's? Or is it someone else entirely?'

'You're going to need some toys,' Trix reached down and pulled a metal case from underneath her desk. Grabbing it by the handle, she walked over to the sofa in the suite, placing it onto the cushion and opening it up. Inside, nestled in form-fitting foam padding, lay an array of specialised equipment: wireless bypasses, signal jammers, even custom keycards, the kind of gear that wouldn't trip conventional security, but could slice through it like butter under the right hands.

'Where the hell did you get this?' Marlowe exclaimed, impressed.

'Probably best not to ask,' Trix replied, lifting out a small black device. 'Latest counter-surveillance tech should get you past the biometrics. And this—' she held up what looked like a smartphone, '—custom firmware, lets me piggyback the security feeds.'

'You've been busy.'

'Well, someone has to keep you alive.' Trix started checking frequencies. 'The real problem isn't getting in, it's getting out with Bassett. If he really has reconstructed anything to do with Stone Blind's financial network, or even back when it was called Quicksilver ...'

'Then everybody wants what's in his head,' Marlowe finished. 'Someone placed him with Maguire, but lost control when Durrant grabbed him. Now Steele, probably through Rizzo, wants the information to reclaim the missing millions.'

'And Durrant?'

'Durrant just wants power,' Marlowe said as he examined one keycard. 'The money's just a means to an end.'

'Speaking of means,' Trix pulled up another screen. 'His phone wasn't on his body, but Kelly had been taking photos and uploading them to the cloud. I spoke to McKellan – I hope you don't mind – and he gave me the details to get onto it.'

Marlowe placed the keycard down and stared back at Trix.

'You spoke to McKellan?'

'Yes,' Trix replied. 'He still doesn't like me, possibly because I shot him in the foot that time, but ...'

Marlowe looked down at the tech that was in the case in front of him.

'This is MI6, isn't it?' he said. 'They've got someone over here, someone who could provide you with this while I was out.'

'Marlowe, don't look a gift horse in the mouth—'

Marlowe slammed the case down, staring back at Trix.

'We don't work for them anymore,' he said. 'We don't do their dirty jobs.'

'Then whose dirty jobs are we doing?' Trix snapped back. 'Ingrid's? Eva's? Sonia Shida's? Before that, it was bloody Sasha Bordeaux! We've always been doing someone's dirty jobs. And if you don't realise that, then you're a bigger bloody idiot than I thought you were.'

She calmed down, looking back at the case full of tech.

'A guy came by about half an hour ago, passed me this, no questions asked. McKellan had asked him to do it,' she continued, her voice tight with repressed anger. 'Chances are if McKellan's passing it on, then the CIA probably already knows. You'll be getting a door knocking from Reynard Massey or Sasha Bordeaux at any minute unless we get moving fast. Either way, when McKellan learned Kelly was dead, he sent us Kelly's cloud details, which gave us, in turn, the last few photos that David Kelly ever took.'

Looking back at her monitor, the screen now showed a

series of photos. They were surveillance shots of the Oasis's service areas, delivery schedules on the wall, staff rotations written upon them, guard changes.

Kelly had been building his own infiltration plan.

'He wasn't just investigating either,' Marlowe said. 'It looked like he was planning an extraction himself.'

Trix nodded as she swiped through them once more.

'I think he was brought in as Bassett to bring the real Bassett out. Came in a day early, let people know his fake identity, mainly so that when he was leaving, there wasn't that much of a confusion. But either way, if he was planning an extraction, you're now using his plan,' Trix's voice carried a warning note. 'The same plan that looks like it got him killed.'

Marlowe reopened the case and picked up one of the bypasses, testing its weight.

'Well then, we'll have to improvise,' he said.

'Your improvising usually involves explosions.'

'Only when necessary,' Marlowe checked his watch. 'We'll need to move fast if they're already looking at Voss. How long before we can be ready to go in?'

Trix's fingers flew across the keyboard of her mobile command centre. Multiple screens were now showing different angles of the Velvet Oasis, each one a potential advantage or threat.

'These are CCTV shots,' she said. 'I hacked in about three hours ago. I could be kicked out at any moment, and I don't have any of *my* cameras in there, so at any point you could go blind. But just remember, if Bassett really has seen Stone Blind's structure, he's not just a witness or an asset now. He's a walking fortune, the kind of fortune people kill for.'

Finally, she looked back at Marlowe with a smile.

'You know, like *you* are right now, too,' she finished.

20

INFILTRATION

'You're sure about this?' Marlowe muttered, adjusting his server's bow tie as he pushed the service cart through the Velvet Oasis's back corridors. 'If I'm walking around in the open, I'm risking everything.'

'Everyone's busy tonight,' Trix spoke through his earpiece. 'There's a Formula One event in the main ballroom, and the big spenders are all here.'

'Convenient.'

'It's put a few noses out of joint, too,' Trix continued. 'People on the Strip asking why they've moved out of town for the event.'

'It's not really out of town though, is it?'

'That's the excuse,' Trix could be heard tapping on the keyboard. 'They're claiming it's close enough for Vegas, but distant enough to not be affected by the racetrack. Relax, nobody will pick up on you until it's too late,' Trix's voice carried an amused lilt through his earpiece. 'Right now, you're James Morrison, called in from the Golden Nugget to cover.'

'Jim Morrison?'

'What can I say? I love *The Doors*.'

The cart's wheels squeaked slightly on polished floors, champagne bottles clinking as Marlowe guided it past security cameras. Each bottle contained vintage Dom Perignon; apparently, the billionaire banking class didn't drink anything else. But it was the specially designed base of the cart that impressed Marlowe, housing his equipment and weapons in a hidden compartment constructed an hour earlier.

The Velvet Oasis' upper service corridors had changed little since his last visit when it had still been the Gold Strike. Same beige walls, same utilitarian lighting, same maze of passages designed to keep staff invisible to the guests. But there were differences too; subtle security upgrades that suggested Gabriel Rizzo and his new paymasters had learned from past mistakes. Extra cameras. Key card readers on doors that used to swing free. Regular guard patrols.

All because of what he'd done to them last time.

A kitchen porter hurried past, head down, avoiding eye contact. That was new, too. The staff had been briefed about today's meeting, and told to stay invisible, efficient, unremarkable. Marlowe wondered how many here were actually Clarissa's people; in his experience, the best infiltrations were the ones where even the infiltrators didn't know who else was involved.

'Guard post coming up,' Trix warned. 'Three men, all Durrant's.'

Marlowe fished out the temporary staff card he'd picked up from Clarissa as he approached the checkpoint. She claimed it'd work for him and, having seen her work, that was good enough for his concerns; but there was always the chance something could screw this up.

Think small. Think unimportant.

All three guards wore identical black suits, earpieces marking them as private security rather than hotel staff. The leader, a thick-necked man with a scar running along his jaw, examined the card carefully. The scar tissue looked recent, probably from the same incident that had taken his left ear, an injury that suggested he was more soldier than security guard, and his eyes carried that thousand-yard stare Marlowe recognised far too well from old soldiers.

The other two flanked the corridor, their stance suggesting extensive close protection training.

'You're not on my list,' the scarred man said, tone suggesting this was a problem Marlowe wouldn't survive.

'Last-minute addition,' Marlowe kept his accent American, neutral. 'Party specifically requested the Dom seventy-one. Had to call five hotels to find it.'

He gestured to the cart.

'I can take it back, though. They'll be happy to have it returned, but I'm not explaining to them why this vintage champagne isn't available.'

'All right, calm down. We're just doing our job here. We'll verify that,' the guard's eyes narrowed, hand moving to his radio.

'Perhaps you could check with Ricardo in catering?' Marlowe suggested, noting the positions of the other two guards. Both carried concealed weapons; shoulder holsters were barely visible beneath their jackets. One had his hand already resting near his weapon, while the other maintained his position, blocking the corridor. 'He cleared it personally.'

The scarred man, obviously in control here, spoke quietly

into his radio, eyes never leaving Marlowe. After a moment, a crackled response came back, and Marlowe knew "Ricardo in catering", in actuality one of Clarissa's people, had confirmed the story. The scarred man's expression didn't change, but his hand moved away from his weapon.

As he shifted, his sleeve rode up slightly, revealing a tattoo on his wrist; 22 SAS, partially hidden by his watch.

That explained the missing ear and the professional stance. These weren't just security, they were ex-special forces, the muscle you hired when you were expecting serious trouble. And with Diana Durrant being British, it made sense Voss would stay local.

'Tenth floor,' the scarred man said finally. 'Pearl Room entrance only. Try any other doors, we'll know.'

'Of course, sir,' Marlowe pushed the cart forward, keeping his movements casual, measured, doing his best to give the kind of steady pace that didn't draw attention. As he passed between the guards, he glimpsed the second man's watch, noting an expensive Breitling that definitely didn't match a security guard's salary.

Durrant was paying well for this level of protection.

There was a corridor to walk along before the elevator ride to the relevant floor, and this walk gave him time to consider the implications. Ex-SAS didn't come cheap, and they didn't work for just anyone. Either Durrant had deep pockets, or someone was backing her play. Someone who understood the value of what Bassett carried in his head. Marlowe would have suggested Steele's sugar daddies if pressed, but there was something off here. Marlowe still wasn't sure what the gameplay was. The obvious answer was that Bassett, or whoever this cuckoo was who'd been playing him for the last year, would be there to give information. But there was every possibility he was there to take it; watching a meeting gave an advantage, maybe for Durrant, maybe for Steele ...

There was something wrong, and Marlowe couldn't work it out yet.

'Hey,' he said softly, now in an area he couldn't be observed. 'Can I ask something?'

'Sure,' Trix's voice came through the earpiece.

'The drive at Durrant Capital. Did we find anything on it?'

'No, I think the programmer was yet to use it,' Trix spoke, 'but I'm diving into the source, seeing if I can repurpose code.'

'How do you mean?'

'I mean the programmer had grabbed it to use as a backup, and he'd deleted the previous files to make space,' Trix explained. 'However, he didn't reformat the drive to completely clear it. All I can think is he was stressed and in a hurry, as even though he deleted the files, they've still got ghost images in the code. You know, in case someone needs to bring folders back in.'

'So, he didn't delete?'

'Oh no, he deleted, but I'm that good I can re-jigsaw the fractions together to bring the folders back to life,' Trix laughed. 'Problem is, it takes time.'

'Okay. And what about the laptop data?'

'What's the matter?' Trix's tone changed. 'Not like you to get diverted on a mission.'

'Something's not right,' Marlowe whispered, cricking his neck to release a kink in it. 'I feel it.'

'Okay, so we'll look into it,' Trix said, and Marlowe felt the voice was a little too soothing, as if she was worried that "the guy in the field" was getting the yips. 'As for the laptop data, the code key opened up the files, but also a forum. It feels like the Crime City virtual meeting area that Orchid had, but this one's way more complicated. Without the key, I'd be screwed, and I'm bloody brilliant.'

'Do you have an ETA on it?'

There was a pause.

'I, um, don't have it.'

'Please, tell me you didn't give it to McKellan.'

'I'm not that stupid,' Trix muttered. 'When we sorted the ID card you're now using with Clarissa, I ... I asked her to look into it. I hoped she might have tech that could work.'

Marlowe didn't know whether to curse or to laugh as he moved along the corridor and entered the service elevator. In one respect, it was refreshing to hear Trix so humble. But, on the other hand, there was the fact that Clarissa might gain more information here than Marlowe wanted.

Still, she probably knew it already. The woman was an Intelligence savant.

'Getting some interesting chatter,' Trix said, bringing Marlowe's attention back to the present as the elevator climbed. 'People are nervous about something. Lots of coded radio traffic.'

'Define nervous.'

'They've doubled the guard rotation on the upper floors. And they've got a helicopter on standby at McCarran.'

'Exit strategy,' Marlowe muttered. 'They're expecting trouble.'

'That's not all. I've been monitoring their communications – they keep referencing "Phase One". Whatever the money men are discussing in there, it's just the start.'

The elevator slowed as it approached the tenth floor. Marlowe adjusted his bow tie again, checked his reflection in the polished doors.

'Time check on Voss?'

'He's in position. But Marlowe ... something else. When I went through the data, I saw there were some global markets Durrant was interested in. As she was interested, *I* was interested, so I looked into it.'

'And?'

'They all align with major sporting events. Formula One races, championship fights, anywhere there's global coverage.'

'Using the events as cover,' Marlowe said. 'No one looks too closely at market fluctuations during major broadcasts.'

'Exactly. But here's the thing; one thing I did get from the code we pulled from Canary Wharf was that Hong Kong's market is predicted to crash next week. The day *after* the Vegas race.'

The elevator doors opened onto the tenth floor's plush carpet and wood-panelled walls. The difference between staff areas and guest spaces was dramatic, as here, there were no more utilitarian tiles and fluorescent lights.

This was old money territory.

'How many guards on this floor?'

'Four visible, probably more out of sight. Mix of Gabriel Rizzo's people and Durrant's. Plus hotel security doing random sweeps.' Trix paused. 'Watch the corners, they've got new motion sensors installed, probably because of you, and the last time you were here.'

'Shouldn't be a problem.' Marlowe guided his cart around the first corner, noting security camera positions. 'Unless someone knows we're coming. Any sign of Steele?'

'Not yet. Maybe he's not coming?'

Marlowe frowned. If there was a big money meeting, it felt odd that Steele would leave it to Gabriel Rizzo ...

'Any sign of Rizzo?'

'No,' again, Trix's voice was quiet, and Marlowe wondered if she too was feeling something off here. Was Durrant running the event? Was she higher up the food chain than Marlowe realised?

'Hey, just a thought,' Trix spoke up again. 'Rizzo. Could he be making his own play here? Going rogue?'

'I'm considering that,' Marlowe continued as he walked along the corridor, curving gracefully towards the Pearl Room's ornate double doors, the walls displaying expensive abstract art that probably cost more than most people's houses. 'I'm wondering if Steele and Rizzo are both courting money, which means there's a definite sibling rivalry going on.'

Marlowe passed a mirror, glimpsing movement behind him; a suited figure quickly stepping into a side room.

Hotel security, doing their job ... just a little too obvious.

'You've got a tail,' Trix confirmed. 'Two of them, trying to look casual.'

'Good thing we're not going anywhere suspicious, then,' Marlowe muttered.

Two more guards, wearing subtle blue ties that probably cost more than Marlowe's entire outfit, but were probably some kind of uniformed colour scheme, flanked the Pearl Room doors. They were younger, less experienced than Durrant's men downstairs, but they carried themselves with the arrogance of people used to guarding the wealthy. Private security firms; most likely ex-military, but without the hard edge of the SAS men below.

Through the doors, Marlowe could hear someone – British, their cultured tones carrying clearly; the kind of voice that expected to be listened to – explaining something about market forecasts and probability curves. It sounded like the sort of financial talk designed to bore listeners into submission while hiding its true meaning.

'Side entrance,' Trix directed. 'Service corridor to your left. Clarissa's got someone waiting with an update.'

Nodding to the guards, Marlowe continued on past them, wondering how long it'd be until someone walked up and asked where he was going with the bottles. It was a standard ploy in offices; if you walked purposely with a folder in hand, people never stopped you.

Servers with bottles, however, were a different matter.

As Marlowe approached the service door, it opened smoothly. A young woman in hotel blacks stood waiting, her name tag reading "Sarah".

'Two minutes,' she said quietly as Marlowe pushed the cart past, almost imperceptible to anyone close. 'They're finishing the Asian markets' analysis. Bassett's been leading the presentation, but there are no screens. I dunno how he's managing it.'

The Pearl Room's service area was a maze of prep stations and storage spaces. Staff moved efficiently, but Marlowe noted at least three who gave him subtle signals; more of Clarissa's people. The room itself was visible through serving hatches, giving him his first clear view of the players.

The man claiming to be Lawrence Bassett dominated the space physically and metaphorically, his hands moving with precise gestures as he indicated imaginary projected figures in the air, every movement calculated for maximum effect.

Eight other men and Diana Durrant sat around the conference table, all wearing the same expression of calculated boredom that masked careful attention. Each one most likely represented serious money; Marlowe didn't know who else Gabriel and Durrant had brought in on behalf of St John Steele, but from past knowledge he assumed these probably included hedge fund managers and banking executives, people who moved markets with a phone call. However, none of them had their phones out, and Marlowe noticed none of them were taking notes.

They were here to listen, not record.

The man using Bassett's identity looked exactly like the photos Trix had found of him; unremarkable except for intense eyes that missed nothing. Marlowe moved around the back of the service area, trying to gain a better view of the presentation, but he couldn't get around enough without giving himself away. Through the serving hatch, he could see Bassett had moved on to a new set of projections, while for the first time, images appeared on the screen behind him. These showed major sporting events; Formula One races, title fights, international tournaments, each one was accompanied by predicted market behaviours that looked suspiciously precise.

'Hong Kong's markets are particularly vulnerable,' Bassett was saying, his tone suggesting he was discussing the weather rather than economic devastation. 'The timing, as you can see, coincides perfectly with several major events. Natural fluctuations that no one will question.'

A younger man at the table – designer glasses, too-bright, obviously veneered smile – raised his hand.

'And the algorithms account for all variables?'

'The Formula One event provides perfect coverage,' Bassett replied calmly. 'Global attention focused elsewhere, trading patterns already disrupted by time zones. When the crash comes, it will seem entirely organic.'

Marlowe watched Bassett's reaction to the man asking the

question. Nothing showed on his face, but his eyes ... there was something there.

Recognition?

Satisfaction?

'More security arriving,' Trix reported. 'Two teams just came up the main elevator. And Marlowe? They're carrying heavy hardware in instrument cases.'

'Time to move?'

'Not yet. Wait for my signal. Voss is ...'

She paused.

'Hang on. Getting some weird chatter on Durrant's frequency. Something about a phone.'

Bassett was continuing, but there was something off. As he spoke, he was looking over at the door, and as he did so ...

'Earpiece,' Marlowe whispered. 'He's being fed information.'

'He's not eidetic?' Trix sounded surprised.

'Either that, or like me, he's got someone backing him up off site,' Marlowe said, looking around. Was it the CIA? Steele? Even Rizzo?

'Searching for the signal,' Trix said quietly as the service door opened, pausing Bassett's continuation as Martin Voss entered, face carefully neutral as he made his way to Diana Durrant. He looked composed, but Marlowe caught the tension in his stride.

'They've found Kelly's phone,' Trix said urgently. 'And it looks like they were able to open up his photos.'

Marlowe went to ask how, but then stopped himself. *David Kelly was probably still on a slab downstairs.* Retina scans, fingerprint scans, all were still valid in death. And now it was open, they'd see he'd cased the hotel for his own extraction. They'd lock down—

And Marlowe would be trapped.

'Tom, you need to get out,' Trix whispered urgently. 'Remember what happened in Canary Wharf? Where I found myself locked out of the system, and other people started to screw around with it?'

'What about it?'

'Well, it's happened again,' Trix said reluctantly as if on cue, fire alarms pulsed through the building. Not the standard evacuation tone; this was the alert for security staff only. Around the room, guards straightened, hands moving to weapons and earpieces. 'Whoever did this there ... they're here, and, oh no.'

'What?'

'I hacked the feed,' Trix said, and rather than explain, she connected Marlowe to what sounded like Gabriel Rizzo.

'Everything has to be perfect,' Gabriel's voice spoke, but it sounded off, like there was wind hitting the microphone, as Marlowe realised this was going directly into Bassett's ear. *Was he outside the hotel? Why wouldn't he be here?* 'I don't care what Steele's protocol says. This isn't London or Berlin. This is Vegas. We do things differently here. You're good to go. Just make sure Marlowe sees it happen. I want him to feel it.'

Shit. They knew he was there.

'It's Marlowe,' Diana Durrant said, rising, drawing Marlowe's attention back to the room. 'It has to be. Find him.'

Marlowe looked across the room to see the man she'd spoken to; one of the suited guards was already barking commands into a radio, telling his team to put up Marlowe's image everywhere, see if he was in the building ...

That was the point Marlowe knew he was in *big* trouble.

21

LOCKDOWN

'Ma'am,' the guard with the scarred face approached Durrant. 'We need to move you.'

But Diana Durrant waved him away irritably, focused on Bassett's presentation.

'I've not seen Marlowe around, and I'm not leaving until I see him sprawled out, dead, on that boardroom table. Continue with—'

'It's not a drill, Ma'am.' The scarred man's voice was cold, professional now. 'We have a new situation, and it isn't the primary target.'

Through the serving hatch, Marlowe saw Bassett's reaction; a slight narrowing of the eyes, a tension in his shoulders as he listened from the head of the table. The man was too controlled to show genuine emotion, but something had definitely registered.

Who was he?

'Getting reports of smoke on multiple floors,' Trix reported. 'Clarissa's people are keeping security busy, but they'll figure it out soon. Whatever you're going to do ...'

'Wait,' Marlowe murmured. The guard who Durrant had refused to follow was speaking urgently into his radio now, his expression darkening. Behind him, Voss had positioned himself near the main doors, one hand resting casually near his jacket.

Durrant finally seemed to register the situation's gravity.

'Perhaps a short recess would be—'

'Sir!' One of the guards listened to their radio, their voice cutting through the room as he looked over at Voss. 'We have confirmation of ...'

The lights went out.

In the sudden darkness, Marlowe heard the distinctive sound of weapons being drawn. Emergency lighting kicked in, bathing the room in a red glow that turned everyone's movements jerky and uncertain. Through the serving hatch, he watched the careful choreography of professional security trying to control chaos. He knew he needed to move, to fulfil his own mission, but he couldn't help but wonder who was doing the same thing.

Steele? McKellan? Rizzo? Was this Sasha Bordeaux or Reynard Massey, even?

'Phase Two is blown,' someone said. 'We need to abort.' But Marlowe's attention was now on Bassett. In the confusion, the man had moved, not towards the exits like everyone else, but towards the now confused audience for his talk. His movements were quick, practised.

Professional.

'He's copying files from their phones,' Trix said. 'He's using a locational cloner, connecting from a short distance. For the data he's pulling down, I've not seen this since ...'

'Since what?' Marlowe asked, but Trix wasn't replying. Marlowe wasn't sure if he actually wanted to know the answer, anyway. The last time he saw something like this, it was Fractal Destiny, in Whitehall, and it almost destroyed every UK-based agent under a fake name.

'Trix?'

No answer. Whatever she was doing, Marlowe hoped she was okay.

TRIX HAD HEARD THE KNOCK AS SHE SPOKE TO MARLOWE; IT always felt a little odd to be this close to the action, while being half a mile away in a penthouse suite. Almost as if she was playing some first-person e-gamer competition, or working through a *Crime City* game server.

She hadn't ordered any room service, so she didn't answer, simply staying silent a moment as she listened.

There was a door knock again.

'Miss Preston?' A young, male voice spoke through the door, and Trix froze. To know her real name meant whoever was on the other side definitely wasn't connected to the hotel. 'Miss Preston? It's Mason. Clarissa sent me. It's urgent.'

'I'm busy,' Trix shouted back.

'I know, and it's a trap,' the voice continued. 'That's why I'm here. I was told to tell you analogue beats digital when people listen in.'

Trix leant back. She'd been cut out of the system, so someone was definitely playing games. Quickly pulling off her headset, she ran to the door, looking through the peephole.

Mason, the nervous teenager, stood outside.

Sighing, Trix opened the door—

And fell to the floor as the door, once open a millimetre

smashed in with force, as the two burly men in suits used their combat boot on it. Rising quickly, she turned to grab the Sig on the side of the desk, only to be grabbed by the hair and slammed back onto the carpet of the suite.

Her head spinning, she looked up at the ceiling and groaned as a familiar figure moved into view, dangling what looked to be a pair of steel handcuffs in his grip.

'Hello, Miss Preston,' Gabriel Rizzo said with a smile. 'Fancy meeting you here.'

IN THE PEARL ROOM, DIANA DURRANT'S SECURITY WAS TRYING to evacuate her, but the banker was arguing, refusing to leave without her asset. Meanwhile, Bassett had stepped away, merging into the background like a ghost.

Chaos was building in carefully managed stages. Durrant's security had formed a protective circle around their principal, weapons drawn but not yet raised. The other bankers who'd been in the meeting were now being moved slowly towards the door, their calculated boredom replaced by genuine concern.

And through it all, Bassett moved like a shadow – every step precise, measured, professional.

This wasn't some accountant with an excellent memory. This was someone trained in covert operations.

Through the serving hatch, Marlowe watched the guard captain grab Voss's arm, speaking urgently. Voss's face remained carefully neutral, but his body language changed subtly; a fighter preparing for action.

'Trix?' Marlowe whispered; if ever he needed to know

what was going on it was now, but Trix still wasn't answering ... which was concerning him, now.

The emergency lighting chose that moment to fail, plunging the room into true darkness. In the confusion of shouted orders and running feet, Marlowe heard the unmistakable loud clack of an assault weapon being charged. What kind didn't really matter – if it was capable of three-round bursts or full auto, it was very, very bad indeed.

Multiple breaches. Ground floor, roof, service entrance. These guys weren't messing around.

Marlowe's night vision was adapting, picking out shapes in the darkness. Durrant's security could be heard more than seen, trying to hustle her towards the exit, Voss with his back to the wall, one hand inside his jacket. And Bassett ...

In the half-light, Bassett was smiling.

The service door burst open, and a small team in tactical gear entered, weapons raised. In the strobing light of their tactical torches, Marlowe saw the confusion on their faces, looking around the scene at the hired security, all with weapons aimed at them, as they realised they weren't alone. Communication was obviously not top of the list here, and all that did was help the chaos.

And in that moment of hesitation, Bassett made his move.

A flash-bang grenade rolled across the floor; Marlowe threw himself behind the service cart, covered his eyes, and turned his head away from the grenade. The flash-bang detonated, transforming the Pearl Room into a rage of noise and light, and dimly, through ringing ears, he heard the distinctive sounds of close-quarters combat; the thud of bodies, the crack of gunfire, the controlled shouts of professional operators trying to maintain discipline in chaos.

Another flash-bang followed the first, and again Marlowe

did all he could to limit the damage to his senses. In the strobing chaos, he caught glimpses of the scene through the serving hatch. Durrant's men were engaging the assault team; Marlowe wasn't sure who they were, still, but their kit looked like CIA or NSA stuff - so likely American.

Near the back wall, Marlowe could see Voss, using the confusion to work his way towards Bassett, who was also moving, but with lethal efficiency through the mayhem.

'Total system crash!' someone shouted through the chaos. 'Hotel security, cameras, elevators – everything's dead!'

The service area was a seething battlefield. Marlowe guessed that elsewhere Clarissa's people were creating deliberate confusion, with drinks servers running in panic, dropping trays, slamming doors, shouting - anything and everything that could help Marlowe get in and get out. It was perfect chaos to allow Marlowe to retrieve his weapon from the cart's hidden compartment, sitting with his back to it as he decided whether to risk entering the Pearl Room, or just wait until people left – or died. The CZ felt comfortably familiar in his hand, the TruGlow TFX Pro sights clearly visible through the smoke and chaos as he tracked Bassett's movement. The man wasn't running for the exits like the other civilians; instead, he was working his way methodically around the room's perimeter, using the confusion as cover to eliminate specific targets. Two of the eight men who'd been watching the presentation, both likely billionaires in their own right, were already down from precise head shots.

No wasted motion, no hesitation.

Deliberate.

Marlowe realised with horror that Bassett was cleaning house, taking out anyone who'd been here for the presentation. It'd been a honeytrap, to draw the big money types in and kill them. But why? Steele needed them—

It wasn't Steele. This was Gabriel, firing the first shot.

He rose subconsciously, following Bassett with his eyes, but a burst of automatic gunfire forced him back down. Half of the likely-CIA team had taken up position near the main doors, engaging Durrant's men across the room. The other half was trying to reach Bassett, but he was a ghost in the chaos.

Voss appeared through the smoke, taking cover beside Marlowe. Blood ran from a cut above his eye, but his voice was steady.

'Your boy's more than just a memory man.'

'Figured that out, thanks.' Marlowe checked his weapon. 'I'm told he's a ghost, but even ghosts have names.'

'If he does, it's above my pay grade. Whoever he is, he's been playing everyone. Durrant, Steele, probably even the CIA.'

'Are they CIA?' Marlowe waved at the units. If they were, this was confusing, as Bassett was supposed to be a CIA asset, too. *Were they here to exfil Bassett? Cause chaos to get him out with plausible deniability, keeping his legend clean? Or were they a kill squad bent on terminating the man?*

Voss risked a glance over the cart.

'Whoever he is, he's taken out most of the money in this room.'

Marlowe looked back at the bodies on the floor. Bassett had been cloning their phones as he killed them; *what was Gabriel Rizzo doing with that data right now?*

Another explosion rocked the room – not a flash-bang this time – more like some kind of breaching charge, and through the new hole in the wall more figures emerged.

These moved differently, suited and shouting in Vegas accents.

'I reckon hotel security just joined the party,' Voss confirmed.

The Desert Oasis' team's arrival had shifted the battle lines – now three separate groups fought for control of the room, while Bassett used the chaos to continue his methodical elimination of witnesses. Durrant's security team had got their principal into a defensible corner, but they were quickly running out of options.

Marlowe moved through the service area, using the industrial kitchen equipment as cover. Smoke from multiple flash-bangs and weapons fire filled the air, creating a choking fog of war that transformed the familiar into threatening shadows. Behind him, Voss matched his movements, the ex-Colonel's breath a controlled cadence.

The CIA – Marlowe still wasn't sure if they were or not, but it was easier than saying "group of unknown soldiers with CIA kit" – were trying to lock down the floor, but they were meeting heavy resistance. Marlowe watched the likely Desert Oasis crew with a frown. They were moving in a pattern he didn't like – they weren't trying to capture anyone; they were stopping people from leaving.

This was a cleanup operation, in the same vein as Bassett's - They were providing cover for his kill zone.

Gabriel Rizzo was definitely behind this.

'Dammit, Trix, where are you?' Marlowe muttered as, through the serving hatch, he continued to track Bassett. The man moved like a ghost through the battlefield, each action absolutely surgical.

Another burst of automatic fire forced Marlowe down again; one of Durrant's guards had apparently decided everyone was a threat, spraying bullets in a wide arc that shattered expensive artwork and punched holes in the smoke. Return fire from multiple positions answered, disciplined and accurate three-round bursts that spoke of professional training and experience.

'Keep eyes on Bassett,' Voss muttered. 'He's working towards the secondary exit.'

But Marlowe had noticed something more - Bassett's movement wasn't random – he was closing in on Durrant herself.

He's not just cleaning house, Marlowe realised. *He's following a plan. Everything that's happening – the CIA, the hotel security, all of it – he knew it was coming.*

Voss cursed softly.

'This whole thing was a setup. Get the players in one room, then eliminate all traces.'

'Including us,' Marlowe added.

The firing was dying down and the smoke was clearing somewhat, revealing the scale of the battlefield. Bodies lay scattered across expensive carpet – some security, some tactical operators. The survivors had created pockets of resistance throughout the room, each group trying to maintain control of their sector while figuring out who to trust.

Durrant's remaining security had backed into a corner, using overturned furniture as cover. The banker's aristocratic calm had finally cracked, and she was shouting into a phone that clearly wasn't connecting. The CIA team moved with cold purpose, eliminating anyone who presented a threat, their kit and tactics suggesting capabilities beyond normal tactical teams.

'Bassett's moving again,' Voss warned.

Through the clearing smoke, Marlowe tracked their

target's progress. Bassett had reached a position that gave him a clear line of sight to Durrant. His weapon was raised, the shot already lined up ...

Marlowe moved without thinking, his CZ already tracking. The shot caught Bassett's shoulder, throwing off his aim, but not enough. Marlowe saw Durrant's body jerk as the round struck her – he couldn't see whether or not she was badly hit, as her security team was already moving, bundling her towards a service exit.

The room erupted into fresh chaos. Bassett rolled with the impact, coming up firing. His shots were decent, despite the wound, forcing Marlowe back down behind the service counter. Voss returned fire, but Bassett was already moving, using the general confusion to mask his trajectory.

'He's heading for the main elevator shaft,' Voss reported as, through the smoke, Marlowe caught glimpses of the tactical ballet unfolding around them.

'We need to move,' Voss said, reloading.

Marlowe rolled under a burst of gunfire, coming up behind an overturned table. The CZ barked and two casino guards went down, though more were already moving to flank his position.

Bassett had reached the elevator doors, working hard to pry them open. But something in his movements had changed – less confident, more desperate. The shoulder wound was affecting him more than he showed.

'Marlowe!' Voss's voice carried real urgency now. 'The whole power grid is—'

And then things started to explode.

22

SNIPER ALLEY

In the red-tinted emergency lighting, Marlowe heard the CIA team reloading in a very choreographed manner – They'd obviously been waiting for this event.

They may have been ready for it - *But so was he.*

He ripped a flash-bang off his belt, pulled the pin and let fly. Taken by surprise, the explosion of light and sound caught them mid-advance and visibly upset their rhythm – Unsure who'd thrown the grenade or where it came from, they opted for a second of caution. Marlowe took full advantage, moving fast and low across the battlefield, heading once again for Bassett.

The elevator doors had finally yielded to Bassett's efforts. But, instead of an empty shaft, yellow light now spilled out. A maintenance platform waited, occupied by more operators. Their weapons tracked upward as Bassett raised his hands.

'Asset secured,' one of them reported into a radio. 'Moving to extraction point.'

'You really think you have me?' Bassett's laugh carried

clearly across the darkness, and there was the clink of a grenade pin being removed. This wasn't another flash bang, though – This was the recognisable clink of a U.S. military M67 fragmentation grenade. The blast from a flash bang would probably surprise most people, but while it was certainly loud, there was very little flame and quite a bit of smoke. The M67, however, boasted a kill zone of five metres, and the elevator Bassett had tossed this one into was significantly smaller than that.

Fortunately for Marlowe, Voss, and for that matter, Bassett, the elevator and shaft contained the lion's share of the thin metals fragments the explosion had unleashed. The unmistakable result was the immediate and horrific death of every operator in the elevator.

Marlowe and Voss had both dived low for cover as soon as they heard the pin pulled. Through ringing ears, Marlowe now heard screams, although he knew none of those were coming from the shaft.

As he took a quick peek around, he saw that Bassett was already moving, vaulting over debris, his movements precise despite the shoulder wound. Two operators tried to intercept him. His response was two precise head shots that dropped them instantly.

Metal shutters began descending over windows and exits. Emergency bulkheads – ones that had to have been installed after Marlowe's previous visit – slid into place with pneumatic hisses. The Pearl Room was being sealed, trapping everyone inside.

'Lockdown initiated,' a computerised voice announced. 'Please remain calm.'

'They're containing the situation,' Voss appeared beside Marlowe, blood still running from the cut above his eye.

'Making sure no one gets out with whatever was in that presentation.'

The original group of CIA operators – well, what was left of them anyway, had fallen back to defensive positions, trying to make sense of the changing battlefield. And through it all, Bassett moved with purpose away from the compromised elevator shaft, and towards what looked like a blank wall.

'He knows something we don't,' Marlowe realised, looking at Voss. 'We need to stop him.'

Voss raised his gun, but Marlowe paused him, holstering his CZ and unclipping his security defence bracelet.

'Alive,' he added.

Bassett reached the wall, his fingers finding invisible catches, and a panel slid aside, revealing a narrow passage beyond. The emergency lighting cast everything in bloody shades of red as he prepared to step through.

'Stop him!' The order came from multiple sources – CIA, Voss, even Durrant's people had the same plan. Every weapon in the room tracked towards Bassett's position.

But Marlowe was already moving. The security chain from his wrist unwrapped like liquid steel, its weighted end catching Bassett's injured shoulder. The man's cry of pain was swallowed by renewed gunfire as every faction tried to down him.

Bassett staggered but didn't fall. He turned the stagger into a spin, rolling with the chain's impact and bringing up his weapon. But Marlowe was uninjured and faster, already inside his guard, using the chain to close distance and keep his opponent off balance. They crashed together into the hidden passage, previous injuries forgotten in the desperate close-quarters battle.

Behind them, the battle for the Pearl Room reached new

intensity. The CIA operators continued their methodical sweep, but none of that mattered now. In the narrow confines of the passage, Marlowe fought for control against an opponent whose technical skill matched his own. Bassett's every move spoke of advanced training, likely CIA; each strike precise, each counter perfectly timed.

'You don't understand what you're interrupting,' Bassett grunted, blocking a strike that would have crushed his windpipe. His accent had changed, no longer the careful British tones of Lawrence Bassett, but something harder to place. Eastern European maybe, or possibly Israeli. 'This is bigger than Steele, bigger than Operation Stone Blind.'

'Enlighten me,' Marlowe drove a knee into Bassett's injured shoulder, earning a hiss of pain. 'Oh, and Frank Maguire says hi.'

Both had a grip on the chain now, neither willing to grant the other control of the weapon.

'The algorithms weren't just predictions,' Bassett's laugh held no humour. 'They were proof of concept. Show what can be done when you control the right pressure points. This wasn't about crashing markets, it was about proving they could be controlled. Guided. Weaponised.'

Behind them, someone had breached the panel. Tactical lights swept the passage as shooters converged on their position.

'Your friend Steele thinks he's playing a long game,' Bassett continued. 'Building his power base, accumulating resources. But he's just another piece on the board. The real players ...'

He smiled through bloodied teeth.

'Well, that's who I just removed. The names behind everything. The ones who funded Quicksilver. The ones who really control Stone Blind.'

Marlowe paused – was Bassett really an enemy here?

'If you're not a fan of Steele, why did you come over with Durrant?'

'Durrant was a pawn,' Basset hissed. 'And Steele a patsy—'

'Target located!' someone's voice echoed down the passage. 'we're gonna take him!"

'Too late,' Bassett's smile widened, and the floor beneath them shuddered. Hidden charges – placed before the meeting – detonated in sequence. The passage collapsed, debris raining down as support structures failed.

But retreat wasn't an option. The chain was tangled around both men, binding them together as the passage disintegrated. Bassett fought with renewed desperation, even as the ceiling came down around them.

And then the floor gave way completely.

They fell together into darkness, the chain their only connection as decades-old maintenance shafts collapsed around them. Somewhere above, multiple teams converged on their last known position.

THE SHAFT WASN'T DEEP, JUST A SERVICE AREA BETWEEN floors, but the impact still drove the air from Marlowe's lungs as they crashed through a maintenance platform. Water from ruptured sprinkler systems had flooded the level below, turning the service area into a shallow pool that helped break their fall.

Bassett recovered first, using the chain's momentum to

pull free. In the red emergency lighting, Marlowe saw him reach for something – not a weapon, but a small electronic device. Above them, tactical teams were already preparing to rappel down.

'Asset located!' one mercenary reported. 'Preparing to—'

Bassett thumbed the device. Every piece of electronic equipment died instantly, weapons, tactical gear, comms. Even Marlowe's earpiece went silent – although the squawk it made was the first sound he'd heard through it in minutes. In the sudden darkness, Bassett moved through the shallow flood, heading for a service exit.

'He's got an EMP disruptor,' Voss's voice echoed down. 'Russian tech – we used to see it in Ukraine.'

Marlowe struggled to his feet, the chain now a dead weight in his hands, resisting the urge to remind Voss that *he knew what a bloody EMP disruptor was, as he'd used one in Canary Wharf.* Through the darkness, he could barely make out Bassett's form, but the sound of splashing water gave away his position as he reached what looked to be a service door, while the chaos above intensified. With their enhanced equipment dead, the various teams resorted to basic tactics, filling the area with gunfire.

'The algorithms weren't random,' Bassett paused now, and called back to Marlowe, his voice echoing off the concrete walls. 'Every major sporting event creates market fluctuations. Formula One, World Cup, Olympics – perfect cover for controlled crashes.'

'Who are you?' Marlowe rose and moved forward carefully, aware that Bassett likely had more tricks ready.

'I told you, I'm just someone who recognised what Steele was planning,' Bassett replied.

He smiled through the darkness.

'They all think they're in control, but there's always someone higher up pulling the strings.'

Marlowe turned as an explosion took out a section of plasterboard, raising his hand in case another flash bang was head his way. Seeing no movement, Marlowe hurried to find his own exit through the hotel's back passages.

MARLOWE EMERGED ONTO A LOADING DOCK JUST AS POLICE sirens began converging on the building. The night air was thick with smoke as fire crews arrived, their lights painting the scene in strobing red LED light.

Bassett was nowhere in sight. Whatever his plan had been, he'd completed it.

As Marlowe clambered to his feet, a faint hiss of clicks reached his ear – the sound of a microphone coming back to life, a connection being made.

'Trix,' he said. 'About bloody time. I need you to—'

'Marlowe,' Trix's voice interrupted, calm but soft.

'Trix?'

'I'm sorry,' she murmured, her voice trembling. Marlowe caught the fear in her tone, but before he could ask what was wrong, a commotion crackled over the line, followed by another voice.

'I'm afraid Miss Preston can't come to the phone right now, Thomas,' Gabriel Rizzo's voice slithered through his earpiece.

Marlowe froze, horror gripping him.

'Gabriel,' he started.

'You know, when you left the hotel without saying goodbye, it was rather rude,' Gabriel continued. 'I know you Brits like to call it the Irish goodbye, but in Vegas, we call it being a prick. I had such plans for you, Thomas, and now they've all had to change.'

'Gabriel, whatever you're thinking, Trix isn't part of this.'

'Oh, but she is, Thomas,' Gabriel sneered, venom dripping from every syllable. 'You see, you didn't steal from me alone. You had help. One by one, I'll find and kill every single person involved. But right now, I get to start with your friends, your closest friend. She is your closest friend, isn't she, Thomas? She's not a lover, is she? That would be ... tragic.'

'Gabriel, I don't know what you're thinking of doing—'

'That's right,' Gabriel cut him off. 'You don't know what I'm thinking. But Miss Preston can tell you what I've already done. Go ahead, Miss Preston.'

'Tom,' Trix whispered, her voice shaking. 'He's handcuffed me to my bloody chair. I'm in front of my monitor. Gabriel, he ... he killed Mason, Clarissa's hacker, and he's placed C4 in the suite.'

'Gabriel, if you touch her – if you hurt her—'

'My dear friend, I've already touched her, and I've already hurt her,' Gabriel interrupted. 'And now I'm going to kill her. You cost me everything – everything I wanted, everything I loved was taken from me when you made me the fall guy for your heist. My sister took over my empire. My family and friends disowned me. Orchid turned their back on me. Now, Thomas, you get to feel what it's like to lose everything.'

'Gabriel, you don't have to do this,' Marlowe said, desperation creeping into his voice, before looking around, trying to gain a hold of what was going on here. 'What would Steele say if he knew what you were planning?'

'He'd probably give me a medal, but I don't really give a

crap,' Gabriel's sneer was almost audible down the line. 'Steele prefers clean kills. I want you to suffer.'

Marlowe remembered the snippet of audio they'd heard earlier that evening; Gabriel Rizzo speaking to someone.

'I don't care what Steele's protocol says. This isn't London or Berlin. This is Vegas. We do things differently here. You're good to go. Just make sure Marlowe sees it happen. I want him to feel it.'

Marlowe felt a chill slide down his spine.

Rizzo set everything up.

'This wasn't Steele's plan, was it?' he asked.

'No, Tom,' Gabriel was relishing this now. 'It was mine. Steele's allies? All dead. The only person who knows their input codes?'

'Lawrence Bassett,' Marlowe understood now. 'You turned him, made him your man.'

'Wasn't that difficult,' Gabriel boasted. 'Diana Durrant did the heavy work. But then they knew you were coming up behind them, sniffing their trail.'

'You were the one,' Marlowe looked around, trying to work out how to defuse the situation. 'You made Saito doubt Steele, knowing she'd bring me in.'

'It helped when I learnt Lawrence Bassett worked for one of your contacts,' Gabriel laughed.

'How did you even know where we were?' Marlowe was now running through the red-lit back corridors of the hotel.

'That's the problem, Thomas,' Gabriel said, his tone sharp with contempt. 'You've become so arrogant, thinking everyone you talk to is your friend. Have you ever heard of the term Sniper Alley?'

'Sniper Alley? No. What is it?'

'For normal people, it's the stage of life where random disaster can strike: a heart attack, a stroke, cancer. One moment, you're fine; the next, you're gone. The term refers to the idea that people need to "duck and dive" to avoid these conditions when you hit a particular age range. But for someone like you, and I suppose someone like me, it's the uncertainty of life. For *yay, though you walk through the valley of darkness,* Sniper Alley always looms. And in every shadowed window, there's someone new who wants you dead.'

'If you want me dead—'

'Oh, I *do* want you dead, Thomas,' Gabriel chuckled darkly. 'But you interrupted me. I could have asked a dozen people and gained your answer. Even the teenaged boy who we got to knock on the door. But the cold, hard fact of the matter is I've always known where you were, Marlowe. Ever since you arrived in Vegas.'

Marlowe paused.

'The laptop?'

'The drive you found in Canary Wharf, the one Miss Preston here used her incredible skills to bring back from the formatted dead,' Gabriel cooed. 'There was nothing on it, but once Miss Preston here realised that for herself, it instigated a tracker beacon, always pointing true.'

'Gabriel, please, your fight is with me. Let's meet, and you can do whatever—'

'As tempting as that sounds, I think not today. Today, I'm not killing you. I want you to experience everything that happens from the moment I disconnect this call. Today? I'm going to kill Miss Preston.'

'Rizzo, no!' Marlowe shouted, but a click silenced the connection. The line went dead.

Marlowe bolted, running for the hotel exit. Pushing through crowds, he knocked aside anyone in his way. Outside, he spotted a man handing his car keys to a valet;

without hesitation, Marlowe slammed into him, snatched the keys, and leapt into the car. Pressing the start button, he sped off, ignoring the man's shouts behind him.

He raced towards the Venetian, weaving through traffic, his heart pounding. Then, just as he approached, he saw it – the flash of light, milliseconds before the sound followed. A deafening explosion erupted as the entire fourteenth floor of the Venetian hotel was engulfed in a ball of flame and fury.

Marlowe skidded the car to a halt and climbed out, staring in stunned silence. Smoke billowed into the night sky, the flames burning so brightly they outshone the neon lights of Vegas itself.

It was the destruction only a suite filled with C4 could cause. There was no escape from that blast. Everything he'd brought with him to Vegas – his phone, his money, his belongings – had been in that suite with Trix. Now, all he had was a gun and an earpiece that no longer worked. The distant wail of sirens grew louder as Marlowe pulled the earpiece out and flung it to the ground.

Trix was gone. He'd been too late.

There was nothing left for him. And right now he was still a target, with a million-dollar hit on his head.

Abandoning the stolen car, he turned and sprinted away, leaving the strip, leaving Vegas...

Leaving the lights, the chaos, and the nightmare he'd just witnessed.

23

AFTERMATH

TRIX WAS GONE.

The explosion at the Venetian had taken everything: the hotel suite, their equipment, and most importantly, her. The flames had reached so high into the Vegas night sky that they'd outshone the neon below, the type of destruction that only military-grade explosives could cause.

The kind Gabriel Rizzo would have access to. Gabriel wanted revenge, and he didn't care who he'd killed to make Marlowe hurt.

He couldn't go back to the hotel. His IDs and various legends he'd brought with him were all in the suite and had now been destroyed – or taken by Gabriel Rizzo. He had no communication equipment apart from the knackered earpiece he'd thrown away.

The person on the other end was no longer speaking, anyway.

He hadn't brought a phone, and all he had with him was a wallet containing around a hundred bucks and a couple of credit cards. Even then, the cards were now useless if Gabriel

Rizzo had access to his identities. Marlowe didn't trust them, anyway; if everything had been destroyed in the fire, Gabriel could have still found out who Marlowe was using the identity of, and ensured the cards were flagged.

Marlowe, for all intents and purposes, was on his own.

It wasn't the first time Marlowe had been in this kind of situation. In Germany recently, he'd escaped a torture session with only fifty euros and the clothes on his back. But when that had happened, he'd had a destination, a way back to Trix.

Now she was gone.

No, she was alive.

He didn't know how, but she had to be alive.

He couldn't believe he'd lost her like this. She'd been his rock, his support, his friend. If Gabriel Rizzo had killed her, Marlowe would burn every single thread of his empire to the ground. And if it was connected to St John Steele, he'd do the same to him.

Marlowe would become vengeance incarnate.

However, right now he needed to go to ground. Regroup, work out his retaliation and, with Vegas now in lockdown, and with his location betrayed, he had no one he could call upon.

Clarissa had known Trix was at the Venetian. Mason had even knocked on the door. Could she have done this?

No. Mason had been killed. Clarissa wouldn't have allowed that.

Reynard Massey had been watching Marlowe. Could he have done this?

The CIA team could have been sent by him. Would he have gone full scorched earth, or was this someone higher, with a penchant for chasing their name?

Without allies right now, and without alternatives for the moment, he went for the next best option: the Horseshoe Casino.

ALTHOUGH THEY HAD LEFT AND GONE TO THE VENETIAN, THEY hadn't checked out officially - Trix had simply taken the cases and left. The last thing Marlowe wanted was for anybody to think they were deliberately not coming back; this way, Gabriel's people, and the various legions of hitmen hunting their million dollar target would waste time and effort watching the wrong hotel.

Arriving at the Horseshoe, Marlowe used one card still in his possession to access the automated machines and retrieve a secondary room key. Then, keeping his head down and using the keycard, he went back to the empty suite.

There was nothing there. Trix had taken everything she could see when they moved. But she wouldn't have taken what she *couldn't* see, and that was what Marlowe was counting on.

In the bedroom he'd claimed as his own, Marlowe knelt down beside the ornate King-sized bed he'd only slept in once. Under the bed, taped between two slats, was a small sling bag.

Even Trix hadn't known about this.

It wasn't that he didn't trust her; it was simply a habit he'd picked up years earlier. You never knew when you had to return somewhere quick, and it was always good to keep something there for backup. He actually wondered how many sling bags were still under beds across the globe, the hotel staff having not checked the slats themselves. Marlowe had planned to retrieve it the day they left, but things had moved too quickly.

Opening the bag, he found cash, as well as credit cards and a driving licence in a fresh name. No passport – he hadn't expected to need one – and if he was being honest, Gabriel's line about becoming arrogant rang true. Marlowe had genuinely thought he was invincible.

Not anymore.

There was also a burner phone with preloaded numbers. Quickly, he threw the sling bag over his shoulder, dropped the room key on the floor, and left the suite. Taking the fire stairs rather than the elevator, Marlowe headed back to the casino floor. In the hotel tourist shop, he bought a baseball cap and hoodie to change his appearance. The cap bore the famous "Welcome to Las Vegas" logo, and the hoodie featured Formula One branding. Dressed like a tourist, out for the night, Marlowe moved through the crowds, the weight of the CZ pistol in his concealed holster a reassurance.

Turning on the burner phone, he entered the passcode and made his first call.

'I heard there was an explosion,' Ryan Gates said as he answered, not even asking who this was. 'Are you guys okay?'

'No,' Marlowe replied curtly. 'Unsecure line. Need help.'

'Meet me where we first ever met,' Ryan said. 'Do you need it now?'

'No. Tomorrow at ten. Things need to die down first.'

'Got it. Want me to look into the explosion?'

'Yes,' Marlowe replied, then disconnected.

His second call was to a number he'd memorised recently, hoping he'd never need it.

'I'm guessing this was you,' Reynard Massey's voice was

laced with sarcasm. 'You can't just blow shit up when you visit Vegas, Marlowe.'

'I wasn't there,' Marlowe replied flatly.

'I know where you were,' Massey snapped. 'Back at the bloody Gold Strike or whatever it's called. You know we've got a body count there that's rivalling *John Wick* movies. I'm guessing you and your tech woman were—'

'Trix is dead,' Marlowe interrupted, his voice emotionless.

'Are you sure?' Massey asked, his tone shifting immediately. 'What happened?'

'The explosion at the Venetian,' Marlowe said. 'It was our suite.'

'Jesus,' Massey muttered. 'We're on site now. The fire's out, but the place ... it's bad. Tom, you'd better sit down.'

'What did they find?' Marlowe asked sharply.

'A body,' Massey admitted. 'Young, female, blonde hair. She was handcuffed to a chair by the computer.'

Marlowe clenched his fists as Trix's last words echoed in his mind.

'Tom, he's handcuffed me to my chair. I'm in front of my monitor. Gabriel, he ... he's placed C4 in the suite.'

'Do you know who did this?' Massey asked.

'Gabriel Rizzo,' Marlowe replied. 'But I'll guarantee you won't find him at his casino. Especially after your tactical team came in looking.'

There was a long pause, but no denial.

'Above my pay grade,' he eventually said. 'That's all I can tell you.'

'Were you after Bassett?' Marlowe couldn't help asking.

'I wasn't, but it seems there were people who were,' Massey admitted. 'This wasn't on me, I swear. But if you'd told me what you planned, I could have pre-warned you.'

'Yeah, well, hindsight's always twenty-twenty.'

There was a pause before Massey continued.

'Are you going after him?'

'Damn right,' Marlowe said. 'And I think I know where he is.'

'If you need anything, you know where I am,' Massey said. 'No tricks, no deals. Just tell me, and I'll help you take him down. It's the least I can do. Oh, and Marlowe? Your young friend wasn't the only one who died.'

Marlowe paused from answering, wondering where this was going. *Did Massey mean the teenager, Mason?*

Realising he wasn't going to get a reply, Massey continued.

'Diana Durrant was shot and killed in the meeting as well.'

Durrant was dead? Marlowe thought back to how Bassett was taking out anyone who'd been in the meeting, remembering how he'd deflected Bassett's kill shot... obviously not by enough, though; hollow point rounds would do that...

Looks like Durrant wasn't as in control as she claimed to be. But with her dead, and both Rizzo and Bassett off books, what was Steele going to do now?

'Thank you for the offer of help.' Marlowe replied before ending the call.

He felt no tears, no grief, only cold, hard hatred.

Someone was going to pay for Trix's death.

He didn't give a damn about Durrant. She'd made her bed the day she sided with Steele and his allies.

Once he had his credit cards and cash, Marlowe headed east. He didn't intend to go far; he knew he had to return the following morning to see Ryan Gates. But he needed a place that was out of the way, and far enough off the radar, that he wouldn't expect anyone there waiting to kill him.

He already knew tomorrow's news; if it *was* the CIA who had been in the Velvet Oasis Hotel, they would likely blame it on terrorists, and the explosion at the Venetian Hotel gave them a perfect opportunity to suggest there were multiple targets. Sure, Vegas would be worried, but they could pin it to the upcoming Formula One race; activist climate change protesters annoyed at the amount of fuel that was going to be used, or something along those lines.

Marlowe found a motel a couple of miles out of town. Paying cash – this was the kind of dive where names and ID weren't needed – he settled down in the grimiest motel bedroom he'd been in for a long time. The room stank of stale cigarettes and despair, but it was anonymous. *Safe, for now.* All he wanted was a bed to collapse into, but as he did so, lying in the darkness, all he could think of was Trix's last words.

She couldn't be dead; there had to be a way to save her.

But then Massey's line came back to his mind, talking of a blonde woman found handcuffed to a chair.

Marlowe bit back tears of anger, lying back on the bed, staring at the ceiling.

How had everything gone so incredibly wrong? That he couldn't understand. This was supposed to have been a simple mission; go to Vegas, retrieve some accountant for a gangland boss, look into Durrant, and work out what she was doing with Steele. That was it.

The accountant turned out to be some kind of CIA

special operative working with Gabriel Rizzo, and the extraction had turned into pretty much the most chaotic op he'd ever been in – and Marlowe had been in quite a few – with a higher body count than there had been in pretty much most of Marlowe's recent missions put together.

He couldn't sleep.

He rose from the bed, walking over to the side table, pulled out his CZ and field stripped it. He didn't have the tools to do a good cleaning job, but he would do what he could and make sure it was good to go. He'd found two loaded 17 round magazines in the sling bag, but that still didn't leave him much to work with. With luck, Ryan Gates could help him the following morning.

Help him do what?

Marlowe leant back on the chair.

There was nothing.

Even if Trix had survived, Gabriel would have the data Bassett had gathered. Marlowe couldn't get that back, and no matter how much he tried or how long he spent reading books and taking lessons, he couldn't become anywhere near the hacker that Trix was – and even she was finding it hard work.

No, he needed to go old school here.

He leant back, trying to think.

What did he know? What had already been decided?

Steele had resurrected Operation Quicksilver under a new name; Stone Blind. Something about it had spooked Katherine Saito enough to risk everything, but before she could tell him what, she'd been killed.

Bassett was no ordinary CIA asset. His skills, his knowledge – he'd been playing everyone. Even Diana Durrant hadn't known what she really had.

And now Gabriel Rizzo had taken and murdered Trix.

Trix.

Wait. What had Trix said about the laptop?

He tried to recall what she'd said back in the UK.

'From what it looks like, the laptop recently downloaded every single op Katherine had ever been involved in while at MI5 and MI6, from some kind of online resource folder, kept somewhere deep in Whitehall. There's a ton of Hong Kong operations here. There's a few UK ones that she wasn't even connected to, so God knows how she found those, or why she wanted them.'

It connected to an online forum in Whitehall. Could he find a way of getting into it?

Not without serious help.

And then there was Gabriel Rizzo. What was his plan here? *Was it just to get revenge on Marlowe?* No, the bloodbath upstairs in the Pearl Room showed that this was more than just an attempt on Marlowe. This was a coup, an attempt to take control for the first time.

Sleep wouldn't come.

Marlowe sat at the room's grimy desk, his reassembled CZ within easy reach. The Pearl Room's chaos played through his mind; Bassett's fluid movements, his presentation about market manipulation, the way everything had fallen apart exactly when it needed to.

It was too perfect. Too planned.

Marlowe needed help. Not just weapons and equipment – he needed resources beyond what Ryan Gates could provide. He needed someone who understood what was really happening.

A name surfaced in his memory: Sonia Shida. High Council member, one of the old guard who'd opposed Steele's power grab.

If anyone knew what Stone Blind really was, it would be her.

Finding her would be another matter entirely.

The mission had changed. Bassett, Steele, Stone Blind – they were all connected, but now they were secondary.

Gabriel Rizzo had made this personal.

And Marlowe was going to make him regret that decision.

24

REUNIONS

THE ATOMIC MUSEUM'S PARKING LOT WAS EMPTY AT TEN; although the museum was open, Marlowe assumed the usual crowds were either delayed by the roadworks, or simply hadn't woken up yet, its modern architecture a stark contrast against the desert backdrop. The building stood ominously under the bright Nevada sun; housing exhibits on the atomic testing era, it served as a reminder of the city's pivotal role in the Cold War's nuclear history.

Marlowe found Ryan Gates leaning against his red Corvette, looking more worried than usual.

'You look like shit,' Gates said, as Marlowe approached.

'Sleep wasn't high on my priorities,' Marlowe replied. 'And I walked here from the crappy motel I stayed in last night.'

'I looked into Trix,' Gates said, almost carefully. 'They've not identified the body, but—'

'Blonde, twenties, handcuffed to a chair,' Marlowe nodded. 'I was told.'

Gates said nothing, just stared past Marlowe at the museum's brutalist architecture. And for a moment, the ghost of Trix Preston hung between them.

'I can get you some hardware,' Gates eventually continued, 'but nothing like what you're probably looking for. Most of my contacts have gone dark since last night. Something's spooked them.'

'Steele? Or the CIA?'

Gates went to reply, but paused as a black SUV pulled into the car park, driving over to where they stood. Marlowe felt rather than saw Gates tense, and reach for a weapon.

'Hold,' he whispered. 'If it's who I think it is, I called her.'

Marlowe turned back to the SUV, now parked, and saw Sonia Shida emerge from the rear seats. She looked exactly as he remembered; elegant in her expensive clothes, her short black bob framing features that spoke of old money and older power. She always carried herself with that air of superiority that came from being part of something exclusive, something special, and although Marlowe had worked with her before, through Orchid, he still didn't trust her.

'You're a long way from your private clubs,' Marlowe said.

Shida's lips curled into a slight smile.

'When the High Council fractures, Thomas, we all must occasionally leave our comfort zones,' she said as she checked her nails. 'I got your message.'

'I wasn't sure you'd come,' Marlowe relaxed a little; there hadn't been any other guards appear from the SUV, so Shida obviously felt comfortable on her own. That said, the last time he'd been in a car with her, she'd ordered her driver to fire rocket launchers out of the window, so she wasn't the most rational of people.

Shida glanced at Gates, first as a concern as to who this newcomer was, and then warmer, as she smiled.

'I remember you! You played The Gravedigger!' she exclaimed. 'Brave man. Or stupid. Would you give us a moment?'

Gates looked to Marlowe, who nodded. As Gates reluctantly walked out of earshot, Shida's demeanour changed; the aristocratic facade dropped away to reveal something harder.

'You're over your head,' she said coldly, returning her attention to Marlowe once more. 'Grab a new fake name and piss off.'

'Not right now,' Marlowe replied, and his voice was soft, the anger held back. 'And ally or not, if you speak like that to me again, I will *end* you. I'm still High Council.'

'You'll end me?' Shida barked a laugh. 'Like you "ended" Steele and Rizzo? Tell me, how's that working out for you? Christ, he's nothing more than a wannabe mob casino boss, and he got one over you!'

Marlowe went to reply angrily, but then sighed. *She was right.*

Seeing his response, Shida continued.

'Stone Blind isn't just another of Steele's games,' she said. 'And the problems between him and Rizzo aren't over. What happened in Vegas was just the beginning.'

'You know about Stone Blind?'

'I know it was originally called Quicksilver,' Shida moved to stand beside him, both now looking at the museum.

'And now?'

'Now Steele's made it worse. Quicksilver was about taking slush funds from the UK and US, and using them to control markets. Stone Blind? It's about controlling everything,' she turned to face him. 'The Formula One race isn't just a test run. It's proof of concept.'

'For what?'

'Global economic warfare. Every major sporting event creates market fluctuations, based on consumer decisions made through adverts, or their favourite team making it to the finals—sponsors link to locations, items become "must have".'

'The boots that score the winning goal must be special so we all need to buy them?' Marlowe frowned.

'Exactly. The World Cup finals can shift billions. Olympics can affect entire economies. Look at Egypt; they've built, from scratch, a swanky new multi-billion dollar capital city in the desert. The New Administrative Capital's the size of Singapore, and this Olympic City, with a ninety-thousand capacity stadium is one of its crown jewels. It's cost over a hundred billion dollars so far, all to be the first African nation to host the Olympics. and they don't even have a slot yet to host the bloody thing! They haven't even placed a bid to hold the Olympics there yet! But... with things like that, if you could predict these shifts ...'

'You could manipulate them somehow,' Marlowe finished.

'Precisely. But Steele's gone further. He's found a way to weaponise them. Create artificial crashes, controlled collapses.'

She shook her head.

'The technology exists in a facility at Mount Rushmore, and he's using the money he found in these accounts from the nineties to grease enough wheels to give him control of it for the moment.'

'Rushmore? The tourist trap?'

'The perfect cover. Hidden in plain sight,' Shida reached into her bag, pulled out a thin file. 'The complex was built during the Cold War. They claimed it was building work that was cancelled when the whole thing stopped, but they carried on without people knowing.'

'Why?'

'Sneaky shit. Who knows.'

Marlowe took the file, opened it. Inside were architectural plans, security protocols, staff rotations ... everything he'd need to infiltrate the facility.

'And Bassett?' he asked. 'Where does he fit in?'

'From my sources, I'd say he was CIA originally. Name's not confirmed, but there was a guy who disappeared around the same time that Bassett reappeared, name of Evan Cross. Deep cover specialist with a particular talent of perfect recall. He could memorise entire networks, financial structures, command chains. Sound familiar?'

She looked back at Marlowe and continued before he could reply.

'He was flirting with Orchid, but whether he was doing this on his own cognisance or because he was told to, we don't know. But something happened during an operation with Steele, one where he went off books. He was burned by the CIA, disappeared.'

'Until he showed up working for Frank Maguire.'

Shida nodded.

'As far as MI6 were concerned, the CIA's loss was their gain. Steele, still technically their man, brought Cross in, and he kept to the shadows. Steele suggested Saito use him with some London gangster—'

'Frank Maguire.'

'Yes, as an unknowing asset. Perfect cover for Cross, now Bassett, to move in financial circles gathering intelligence.'

Marlowe frowned.

'But why use him there?' he frowned. 'That seems small time, not worth his effort.'

Shida watched Marlowe carefully.

'When did you have the issues with Rubicon?' she asked.

'Almost a year back ...' Marlowe said and then stopped. 'Are you telling me Katherine Saito, controlled by St John Steele, aimed him at Maguire *after I was kicked out of MI5?*'

Shida said nothing, still standing with an irritating smile on her face.

'Think about it,' she replied. 'A couple of months later, your father puts a hit out on your life to get you to visit him. Steele would have been working with him, realising he was dying, seeing him reach out to you as a potential threat. You were about to become a player. He knew, through Saito, that you had been working as Kieran Lachlan – hell, you used the legend during the Rubicon debacle, right?'

'To help the brother of an arms dealer.'

'Deacon Brodie. An arms dealer who'd worked with the CIA, and was working against Orchid,' Shida folded her arms. 'Steele saw you as a threat, wasn't sure if Maguire was part of things, learned that MI5 had been using him, assumed he was your asset. It's a simple mistake.'

Marlowe leant back against the Corvette as he tried to take this in. He hadn't met Steele until months after Rubicon, and only after his father, Taylor Coleman, had reconnected, much as it was. He'd considered him a potential ally at the time.

And all the while, Steele was planning his downfall.

'And now Cross – Bassett – he's working with Steele?'

'That's what's interesting.' Shida smiled that superior smile again. 'No one knows whose side he's really on. The

CIA thinks he's gone rogue. Steele thinks he's an ally. And Rizzo ...'

She shrugged.

'Rizzo just wants the power he thinks Cross, as Bassett, can give him.'

Gates was walking back now, phone in hand, and Marlowe didn't need to be trained in micro-expressions to see he looked worried.

'Local news is reporting the Venetian explosion as a terrorist attack,' he said. 'They're linking it to protests about the Formula One race.'

'Convenient,' Marlowe muttered. He wasn't surprised at this; he'd already assumed this would be the story.

'Everything about this is convenient,' Shida replied. 'The race provides perfect cover, increased security, restricted areas, communication blackouts. By the time anyone realises what's really happening, it'll be too late.'

As Gates took the hint from Shida's expression and returned to a safe distance, Marlowe studied the file in more detail. The Mount Rushmore facility wasn't just a bunker – it was a complete operations centre, built into the mountain itself. The tourist areas were just the surface; beneath them lay a maze of tunnels, control rooms, and what looked like a sophisticated database.

'How did you get these?' he asked.

'Orchid has always known about the facility,' Shida replied. 'We simply chose not to use it. The risk was too great.'

'But Steele didn't agree.'

'Steele never agrees with anything that limits power,' Shida took the file back, pulled out a specific page. 'This is what you need to focus on. The central processing hub. Everything Stone Blind does flows through here.'

The schematic showed a vast room filled with servers, not dissimilar to what he'd seen at Durrant Capital. But this was on another scale entirely.

'Bassett's presentation,' Marlowe said. 'The algorithms he talked of – they were just a fraction of what this place can do.'

'The Formula One race will be their first major test,' Shida confirmed. 'Use the event as cover to crash the Asian markets. Once they prove it works ...'

'They can target any event they want. And people will pay them whatever they want.'

'Security looks tight.'

'It's meant to be impenetrable,' Shida replied. 'But there are always ways in. Especially if you know the right people.'

Marlowe looked up from the file – *Clarissa would likely have contacts that could help.* And if not ... then he'd have to go begging to McKellan.

'I'm guessing this isn't just about stopping Steele and his pet,' Marlowe said.

'The High Council is fracturing, Thomas. You've seen it happening. Steele's faction grows stronger every day. If he succeeds with Operation Stone Blind, the money coming in will dwarf our war chest. There'll be no stopping him.'

'And you want to make sure that doesn't happen?'

'I want to make sure the right people keep control,' she smiled that superior smile again. 'The ones who understand the responsibility of power.'

'Like you.'

'Like your father,' the smile faded. 'He knew what Steele was capable of. Even tried to have him removed. And now ...'

'Now it's my job to finish what he started.'

Gates coughed politely from his position across the car

park, loud enough to gain their attention once more, nodding down the road.

'Not to interrupt whatever secret squirrel shite you're both spouting, but we've got movement. Three SUVs just turned onto East Flamingo.'

Shida nodded.

'That's my cue to leave. The rest of what you need is in the file.'

She turned to go, then paused.

'One more thing. Martin Voss has been asking questions, and it's been noticed.'

'About what?'

'About you. About Stone Blind. About a lot of things he shouldn't know about.'

'It's fine, he's been working with me.'

'Has he?' she gave him a meaningful look. 'Be careful who you trust, Thomas. Everyone has their own agenda in this.'

With that, she was gone, disappearing between the cars as silently as she'd arrived. The SUVs Gates had spotted cruised past without slowing, but Marlowe knew they were likely Massey's people, checking who either she, or Marlowe, were talking to.

Or they were the other CIA team, the one with the body count.

'Well,' Gates said after a moment, walking back over. 'That was interesting.'

'That was Sonia Shida being Sonia Shida,' Marlowe opened the file again. 'The question is, how much of what she told us is true?'

'You think she's playing her own game?'

'She's always playing her own game. The trick is figuring out how it aligns with ours,' he studied the facility plans again. 'Can you still get me hardware?'

'Some. Not enough for what you're planning.' Gates nodded at the file. 'That's a military-grade facility. You'll need more than a few guns and some spare mags.'

'Then we'll have to be creative,' Marlowe closed the file, and looked back at the Corvette he was still leaning against.

'Could you give me a lift to Charleston?' he asked.

THE CHARLESTON SWAP MEET WAS QUIETER THAN USUAL AS Marlowe walked down the familiar path between stalls. The usual buzz of haggling was muted, replaced by an undercurrent of tension that seemed to reflect Vegas itself; the terrorist bombings, as they were now being classed as, had placed a cloud over everyone.

Clarissa's stall was empty. No uranium glass glinting in the morning sun, peeking through the top windows, no elderly woman in her wheelchair dispensing wisdom and information. Just an empty space that somehow felt deliberate rather than abandoned.

The stall opposite was also vacant. Marlowe remembered seeing a young girl there last time, one of Clarissa's eyes on the ground. Now there was just another gap in the usual bustle.

'Not here,' a male voice said from the shadows between stalls. 'Keep walking. Exit's at the back.'

Marlowe followed the instruction, moving casually through the market and heading through the exit. In the loading area behind the stalls, he found Clarissa waiting. She'd positioned her wheelchair in a spot that gave her clear views of all approaches while keeping her in shadow.

'I'm guessing that was one of your people telling me to come here?' he asked.

'One of the few that remains, yeah,' Clarissa said without preamble. 'Half my people are gone, disappeared in the night. Some are dead. The ones that are left are scared.'

'Clarissa, I'm sorry,' Marlowe said, the shock on his face visible. 'If I'd known, I'd have kept you out of this. Was it Rizzo?'

'Someone bigger,' she wheeled closer, her face hard in the dim light. 'My contacts started going dark right after you visited the Oasis. Then the explosion at the Venetian ...'

She trailed off, but Marlowe caught the unspoken meaning. Trix had been one of her people too, in a way. Someone who understood the value of information. And Mason, the one she'd sent the girl to find, had also been killed by Gabriel Rizzo.

'I need transport,' he said. 'And hardware. I need to kill some vermin.'

Clarissa stared at him for a long, quiet moment.

'In that case, you need more than the basic package,' her voice carried an edge he'd never heard before. 'What do you know so far?'

Quickly, Marlowe explained what he'd been told by Sonia Shida. He didn't bother hiding identities; the chances were Clarissa knew about her already.

Probably even where she lived, and her favourite restaurant.

When he finished, Clarissa sat back in her wheelchair, ruminating.

'Her plans are good, but they're outdated. The facility's been upgraded. New security, new protocols.'

'How do you know about—'

'Because I helped design the original systems,' her smile was bitter. 'Back before I lost my leg.'

She looked around, checking to see if anyone was watching.

'You understand it's Mount Rushmore, right?'

'Yes.'

'You understand why?'

'Trix said something about a chamber.'

At this, Clarissa nodded.

'Back in '27, when Borglum first started on Rushmore, he had this vision that went far beyond just carving faces into a mountain ... he wanted to create this grand chamber behind them, the Hall of Records, where we'd keep all our greatest documents: the Constitution, the Declaration, everything that made America what it was.'

She paused, gathering her thoughts.

'When the war started, everything halted. And then Borglum died in '41, middle of the war, leaving this unfinished chamber behind Lincoln's head. By '46, when things with the Soviets started heating up, someone in intelligence realised what we had; a remote location, heavy tourist traffic for cover, and an unfinished cavern already carved into a mountain.'

Once more she looked around before leaning forward. Marlowe, unconsciously, did the same.

'But they couldn't use Borglum's chamber; too many people knew about it, there were too many surveys and photographs floating around. So they built it off to the left, behind Roosevelt's head, right behind his left eye. That's where your man likely gained his "Operation Stone Blind" name, you know. Roosevelt had lost the sight in that eye years before, back in 1908, boxing in the White House basement of all places.'

She shook her head with a small smile, as Marlowe sighed in frustration.

Steele was taunting with the op name. Leading people to the secret. Man couldn't help himself.

'They hid the entrance behind a maintenance staircase, made it look like just another access point for the park service, and that was that,' she continued. 'The facility operated throughout the Cold War, but by the nineties it was obsolete. They decommissioned it, sealed it up. Then, in '98, they put on this entire show about finally completing Borglum's original Hall of Records, filling it with all those historical documents in titanium vaults ... but they kept it closed to the public. Not because of anything in the Hall itself, mind you, they just couldn't risk anyone poking around and finding the other entrance.'

'And now Steele's gained it.'

'Yup. Probably through a shit ton of cash and one of his pet senators, or something. You do have pet senators in your swanky secret society, right?'

Before Marlowe could respond, she reached into her chair's side pocket, pulled out a thick envelope.

'Your girl sent me data before ... before last night,' she continued, hesitating as she spoke about Trix, but catching herself. 'The stuff she pulled from Durrant's servers? If the main servers are at Rushmore, then they've turned the entire complex into something else. Something worse.'

'Through sporting events?'

'That's just the start. Think bigger,' she handed him the envelope. 'Elections. Natural disasters. Anything that affects market stability. The Formula One race is their proof of concept. Show they can crash an economy without anyone realising it's deliberate.'

Marlowe opened the envelope. Inside were building plans and security protocols, showing modifications and upgrades.

'They've improved the old Cold War systems,' Clarissa explained. 'Connected them to modern networks. But that's not why you're really going, is it?'

'I need to stop Steele.'

'No.' Her eyes were hard. 'You want Gabriel Rizzo. You want revenge for what happened to Trix Preston.'

Marlowe said nothing.

Clarissa nodded, as if his silence confirmed something.

'Good. Revenge means you won't hesitate, won't second-guess yourself when the moment comes.'

She pulled out another envelope.

'I've got a contact at McCarran. Ex-CIA pilot who owes me more favours than he can count. He'll get you to South Dakota.'

'What about hardware?'

'My people might be scared, but they're not useless,' she handed him a key. 'Storage facility on Eastern Avenue. Unit 237. Everything you need is inside.'

Marlowe turned the key in his hand.

'Look, this is dangerous, even more so than ever for you. Why are you helping me?'

'Because Rizzo and Steele's people didn't just kill your friend last night. They killed Mason and took out three of my best operators. People who've worked for me for years,' Clarissa's voice hardened. 'And because I don't like people who think they can change the world with violence and fear.'

She wheeled forward again, close enough that Marlowe could see the steel in her eyes.

'They're using the race as cover for something bigger. My

pilot contact will be ready in three hours. That gives you time to get what you need from storage.'

With the conversation now over, Marlowe watched her disappear into the growing morning crowds at the Swap Meet. He had what he needed: transport, equipment, intelligence. Everything required to infiltrate Mount Rushmore and confront both Gabriel Rizzo and St John Steele.

Everything except answers.

But those, he'd take from them both himself.

25

TRAVEL ISSUES

The storage unit was larger than Marlowe expected. When he rolled up the door, Ryan Gates beside him in a borrowed red SUV – the Corvette deemed too small for the amount of firepower Marlowe was intending to take, but Gates had insisted on the colour – the smell of gun oil and cordite hit him immediately.

Inside was an arsenal that would have made MI5's quartermaster jealous, and having been stationed there as a punishment once, Marlowe knew that for a fact. Racks of weapons lined the walls; everything from compact submachine guns to long-range precision rifles. Cases of ammunition were stacked neatly, each calibre clearly marked. Tactical gear filled shelving units, including body armour, night vision equipment, communication systems.

'Jesus,' Gates muttered from behind him. 'Your friend doesn't mess around.'

'I think she's been planning this for a while,' Marlowe replied, examining a rack of CZ Scorpion variants - the latest models, not even available to military units yet.

'Think she knew this was coming?'

'I think she's been waiting for someone to do what she's been worried about since her CIA days,' Marlowe selected a range-finding monocular, peering down it. 'It turned her into someone with nothing left to lose.'

They spent the next hour loading gear into Gates' borrowed SUV. Weapons, ammunition, tactical equipment – everything they'd need for an assault on a fortified facility. Marlowe noticed Gates had picked up some hardware himself.

'Just in case,' Gates said when he caught Marlowe looking. 'You might need backup.'

'You don't have to—'

'Yeah, I do.' Gates checked a magazine before sliding it into a pocket. 'What happened at the Venetian? That wasn't right. Even in our world, there are lines you don't cross. And before you make some joke about "our" world being one of actors ... don't. I liked her too, Thomas.'

Marlowe said nothing, continuing to pack. His mind kept drifting to Trix, to that final conversation.

To Gabriel Rizzo's voice coming through the earpiece.

In a corner of the unit, he found more of Clarissa's preparations: medical supplies, emergency rations, even changes of clothing in various sizes. She'd thought of everything anyone might need.

'She's not just helping us,' Gates observed. 'She's definitely been planning this, waiting for the right moment.'

'Or the right person.' Marlowe picked up a small case of electronic countermeasures, the type of gear Trix would have loved. 'Someone desperate enough to take on the entire operation.'

'You really think Steele will be there?'

'He'll want to oversee it personally. The Formula One race, the market crash – it's his chance to prove Stone Blind works,' Marlowe closed the case. 'If he isn't? Then it'll be Gabriel, hiding and waiting for another moment to strike.'

'You think Steele knows there's a viper in his shoe?'

'If he doesn't, he's a bigger fool than I take him for,' Marlowe muttered as he did a last check of his equipment. He'd chosen to keep his old CZ, although "old" meant only a matter of days, but it was still custom-triggered, and felt right in his hands, like greeting an old friend. That didn't stop him from taking one of the factory-fresh ones as a backup, however. He noted Gates took a mix of CZs and Sigs, checking them with the speed and skill of someone well versed in their usage.

Body armour under his jacket, spare magazines distributed for easy access, a knife in his boot, the steel chain around his wrist, Marlowe finally started to feel better about the situation. He had everything he needed to kill St John Steele and Gabriel Rizzo.

'We've got one more stop first,' he said, as they walked back to the SUV. 'Need to see a man about some answers.'

'Voss?'

'He knows more than he's telling. About Steele, about Stone Blind.' Marlowe closed the back door. 'With Durrant dead, he needs a cause to fight for, and I need to confirm once and for all whether he's going to aid me, or stab me in the back.'

THROUGH SOME CONNECTIONS GATES PROVIDED, MAINLY A selection of bar staff and servers that probably rivalled

Clarissa in a small way, asking each if a man with a particular description was in their establishment, they eventually found Voss at a diner off Industrial Road. He sat alone in a corner booth, his back to the wall, a cup of coffee growing cold in front of him. His eyes tracked them as they entered, but he made no move to stand.

'You look terrible,' Marlowe said, sliding into the booth opposite.

He did. Voss's usual military bearing was gone, replaced by something more haunted. Dark circles under his eyes suggested he hadn't slept, and his clothes looked slept in.

'Been a long night,' Voss replied. 'I'm deemed a turned asset now, it seems. Durrant's people – the ones I didn't hire, or who haven't joined Gabriel Rizzo and Steele – have been hunting me since I left.'

He pulled back his jacket slightly, revealing a shoulder holster.

'I'm guessing professional hits are Gabriel's way of saying "you're fired" and all that.'

'But you're still here.'

'Royal Marines, remember?' A ghost of his old smile crossed his face. 'We're hard to kill.'

The server approached their table. Voss waited until she'd refilled his coffee and left before continuing, after he took a sip of his fresh coffee.

'So, you know they're at Rushmore, right? That Steele and Rizzo are carrying on with the plan?'

'The question is, what are you planning to do about it?' Through the diner's window, Marlowe watched a trio of black SUVs cruise past, and was pretty sure they were the same ones that had passed while they met Shida.

Had they been following her, or was this for him?

Voss had noticed it too, his hand moving imperceptibly closer to his weapon.

'They're not Durrant's people,' he whispered. 'Different approach pattern. These are government – CIA, maybe, or they're making it look like they are. Perhaps it's Steele after all.'

'Following you?'

'Following anyone connected to last night,' Voss's eyes tracked the vehicles until they disappeared. 'The Oasis incident got a lot of attention. *High-level* attention. Eight multi-millionaires, maybe even billionaires dead, their logins cloned, their accounts drained until they were stopped ... I know Diana's account lost about three million before they halted it. I can only guess what the others lost. Although they're not going to care, it's not like they need it.'

'I saw the same cars earlier—' Marlowe started, but paused as Voss hissed in anger.

'Christ, Marlowe. They're following *you?*'

Marlowe couldn't answer either way, as Gates shifted position at the counter, angling for a better view of the street. He caught Marlowe's eye, gave a subtle nod.

The three vehicles had returned, boxing in the diner.

Voss pushed his coffee aside.

'Whoever they are, they killed Durrant,' he growled. 'I intend to end them. Steele's got people everywhere. Deep cover operatives waiting to be activated. What happened to your friend? That was just the start.'

Marlowe's hand tightened on his CZ under the table.

'What do you know about that?'

'I know Gabriel Rizzo's involved in whatever Steele's planning.' Voss held his gaze. 'And I know the explosion at the Venetian wasn't what it seemed.'

'Meaning?'

'Meaning there are things about Stone Blind you don't understand yet. A fight for power that's spilling out into the real world,' he glanced at the window again. 'We've got seconds before they move.'

Through the window, Marlowe saw men in tactical gear emerging from the vehicles. Not making any effort to hide now; they wanted to be seen, wanted to pressure the targets inside into making mistakes.

'Time's up,' Gates called from the counter. 'Back exit's still clear, but not for long.'

Voss smiled that ghost of a smile again.

'You still remember your escape and evasion training, Marlowe?'

'I didn't sit on my arse after leaving the Royal Marines. I was MI5, remember?'

'Not exactly a glowing recommendation,' Voss replied as his hand moved to his weapon. 'Because we're about to need it.'

'Kitchen,' Marlowe said, already moving. 'Gates, create a diversion, please.'

'Way ahead of you,' Gates pulled something from his jacket – some kind of signal disruptor. But before he could use it, the kitchen staff scattered as Marlowe and Voss burst in through the swinging doors. Marlowe caught glimpses of the diner staff's startled faces as he moved past grills and prep stations; the back exit was exactly where he'd expected – all diners had the same basic layout.

'They'll have the alley behind covered,' Voss said, checking his weapon.

Knowing this, but also knowing they didn't really have a choice, Marlowe pushed through the exit into morning sunlight. The alley ran behind several buildings, connecting to larger streets at both ends.

'Split up,' he said. 'Gates, get to the airfield. Start prep. We'll meet you there.'

'What about our friends out front?'

'They're about to have bigger problems.' Marlowe pulled out his CZ 75, dropped and reseated the magazine, then quickly press checked the weapon.

Full and one in the pipe. Good. Just don't kill any of them until you know where they came from.

'You got a plan, or we just making it up as we go?' Voss asked, eyes flicking down the alley.

'Both,' Marlowe said, twisting the defence bracelet on his wrist, unlocking the clasp. A sharp click, and a metre of steel chain dropped loose, catching the light with a muted glint.

Voss tilted his head.

'I thought I saw that last night,' he said, pulling it up, checking it. 'Interesting.'

'No time for show and tell,' Marlowe replied, eyes scanning the alley. The SUV had pulled in at the far end, blocking it off.

Doors popped open. More tactical gear. Helmets. Balaclavas. No chatter on radios. Hand signals only. Definitely CIA, or similar. But how did they find him?

'Shit,' he muttered, pulling through his pockets. 'They've got to be tracking me.'

'Or they know your moves,' Voss suggested. 'Three coming from each end. They want us boxed in.'

'Then we break the box.' Marlowe nodded towards the

side of the building, quickly rewrapping his chain. His eyes were on the fire escape, the iron stairwell bolted to the wall above them.

'Up?' Voss asked.

'Up,' Marlowe nodded.

Voss stepped to the wall, lacing his fingers together without being told. Marlowe planted a foot in Voss's hands, and with a grunt of effort, he was hoisted upwards. It was strange, working hand-in-hand with a man who once was his superior officer's superior officer, but the private sector made strange bedfellows. His hands caught the bottom rung of the fire escape. Rust bit into his fingers as he hauled himself up, feet scrambling for purchase until he could swing a leg over the catwalk.

He glanced down; Voss was already moving, head low, back against the wall, shadowed behind a row of dumpsters, watching the incoming gunmen, waiting for them to make the first mistake.

Marlowe took a very cautious look below. The first two operators reached the middle of the alley. Their eyes were scanning everything, led by their weapons. The third lagged back, covering their six. Not by much, but just enough.

There was a screech of tyres – Ryan Gates was off towards the airstrip in his borrowed SUV, the noise enough to distract them for a second.

And that was all Marlowe needed.

A double tap into center of mass of one of the leading pair barked out; the agent stumbled forward, and hit the concrete hard, a muffled grunt of pain. Marlowe was already gone, moving higher, climbing with the CZ tight in his hand.

No sense staying in one spot. Movement was life.

The other two agents turned at the noise, eyes scanning for the source. Their gazes swept high but didn't linger as Voss moved as soon as they were distracted, his steps soft, deliberate. Marlowe caught sight of him circling wide, eyes locked on the second man.

It happened fast, a short, brutal exchange of weight and leverage. Voss's strong side arm wrapping around the agent's neck, his other hand locking the rifle against the man's chest. A quick twist and a vicious elbow strike to the side of the head, and the agent crumpled to the ground.

Marlowe was impressed. *Looked like Voss had kept at his training.*

The third agent covering the pair's tail was slower to react – too slow. Voss moved in behind him – a jerk of the back of the agent's collar spun him around to face him. Hand flat, fingers slightly curved, he struck with his palm just below the operator's Adam's apple, a shōtei. The operator folded, sucking desperately for air.

Marlowe stayed still, watching the other side of the alley. The first team from the SUV, clear of the diner, was now moving in quickly, more coordinated. Two of them saw the downed men, and their alert level snapped up. Voss muttered, flattening himself against the wall, eyes darting for options, but Marlowe spotted it first.

The stack of wooden pallets leaning against the fence halfway down the alley.

The agents were moving fast, rifles sweeping the alley; their trigger fingers were indexed, but it would take them only a fraction of a second to fire. Another ten steps and they'd see Voss.

Marlowe took a breath, and then jumped, a long arc that ended with his boots catching the edge of the top pallet. The pallets tipped forward with a slow, creaking lurch. Momentum did the rest, and they crashed down, one after the other, like dominos. The first hit the agent on the right square in the back, driving him face-first into the concrete. His partner spun, eyes up, searching for the source.

Too late.

Marlowe was already on him. Hands on the back of his vest, he rode the operator to the ground with raw force. The agent hit the ground hard, his head slamming into pavement. Marlowe snatched the man's assault rifle, dropped the magazine and kicked it across the alley, pulled the charging handle, clearing the round in the chamber, and tossed the weapon into the nearest dumpster.

With the agents down, Marlowe could hear the faint sounds of sirens in the distance. The chances were someone in the diner had called the police, and they were arriving shortly.

'Plan?' Voss was out of breath a little as Marlowe decocked and holstered his CZ.

'Airfield, then South Dakota,' Marlowe replied, already searching through the downed agents' pockets. 'From there? Well, I think you know where I'm going after that.'

He rose triumphantly, the key fob for the SUV the team had arrived in now held in his hand. Voss considered his statement.

'You're looking to infiltrate?' he asked as they ran to the vehicle. 'It's not going to be that easy to find a back way in.'

'I know,' Marlowe smiled as he climbed into the driver's seat, turning on the engine. 'That's why I intend to walk in through the front door. Don't worry, I have a plan.'

'Is that why you came to find me?' Voss snarled, climbing

into the passenger seat. 'To get me to help you take down my own men?'

'No, to take down the guy who killed your boss,' Marlowe replied. And, before Voss could say anything in return, Marlowe slammed the SUV into drive and sped off towards McCarran airport, and Clarissa's pilot friend.

26

RUSHMORE

THEY'D MOVED FAST THROUGH MCCARRAN AIRPORT. MARLOWE led, shoulders loose, head low, eyes tracking every movement at the edge of his vision. He'd headed to the FBO terminal, not the main concourse. Instead of the more familiar tourists, he was surrounded by corporate travelers in polo shirts and noise-cancelling headphones, execs in tailored suits talking too loud on Bluetooth headsets. Private flights didn't have queues or security checks. Just leather sofas, FBO reception desks, and a straight walk to the tarmac. No need for passports, no TSA, no metal detectors, just a glance at the manifest, if there was a manifest.

And as for that, Gates would have already sorted this, the contents of the SUV likely being loaded into the plane.

The woman at the desk glanced up, smile pre-loaded but thin. Early thirties, and bored eyes. She clocked Marlowe and Voss, but didn't ask for names. She'd seen their type before – men who didn't want to be remembered.

Her eyes flicked to her screen, tapped once on the keyboard.

'Party for Clarissa?'

'That's us,' Marlowe smiled. 'Our friend—'

'Already on the tarmac,' the woman replied. 'Pilatus, tail number November-One-Eight-Two-Lima, gate two. Pilots ready, and you're clear to board.'

Voss tapped twice on the counter as he passed, a quick show of acknowledgment, like tipping a bartender. Marlowe assumed Voss was more used to this form of private flying.

He kept walking.

Out on the tarmac, the air hit harder, the faint bite of jet fuel hanging in the back of the throat. The concrete shimmered in the distance. Planes lined up in neat rows – Learjets, Cessnas, Gulfstreams. All wealth. All corporate ambition.

Theirs was the one that didn't fit.

The Pilatus PC-12 sat near the edge of the lot. Sleek but unassuming, it had low wings, a single engine, and definitely had no flash. No one noticed it, and that was the point. The only person moving was the pilot, standing at the bottom of the airstair, one foot on the ground, one foot on the step, wearing sunglasses and a baseball cap pulled low. He gave them a small nod.

'All set, your friend's on board and the cargo's squared away,' he said, leaning back to let them board.

He didn't ask names. *Clarissa had likely paid him enough not to.*

Inside, the cabin was cramped but functional. Six passenger seats, three on each side. Voss slid into a rear-facing seat, and Marlowe noted Gates had taken the back nearest the luggage compartment. Marlowe sat closest to the cockpit, one row behind the pilot's seat. The pilot followed them up, pulled the hatch closed, spun the locking wheel until it clicked.

'Two hours, thirty minutes to Rapid City. You'll feel the climb, but it smooths out after ten thousand.'

'We're not going to Rapid,' Marlowe said, eyes still on the cockpit dials.

The pilot turned, one brow raised behind his sunglasses.

'Clarissa said—'

'Custer State Park,' Marlowe said. 'Drop us there.'

The pilot's jaw worked like he was thinking it over, but he nodded.

No questions. No pushback.

He tapped the seat next to him.

'Buckle up, then,' he said.

THE CLIMB WAS ROUGH.

Small planes always were; a shuddering push of gravity as the nose lifted, wheels leaving the ground. The air hit differently at low altitude, and pockets of turbulence made the frame groan, like an old ship in high seas. Gates leaned forward, head down, breathing slowly like he was pushing through nausea. Voss stayed still, head back, eyes half-closed like he was counting the bumps. Marlowe didn't move. He watched the pilot's hands, tracking every change on the controls.

At ten thousand feet, the turbulence eased. The hum of the propeller turned soft and steady, like a white-noise machine in the cabin. The desert stretched out below them in wide, sunburnt patches of tan and rust-red, as Marlowe checked his watch.

Time passed slowly. The cabin stayed quiet.

There was no conversation, no small talk; just the hum of flight and the faint creak of metal shifting under pressure. Gates leaned against the window, eyes closed. Voss flipped through a small notebook he kept in his coat pocket, scanning a page of rough sketches and short-hand notes. Marlowe sat back, eyes closed but not asleep, his fingers tapping on the armrest.

Waiting, but not resting.

After two hours, the pilot's voice crackled over the intercom.

'Five minutes to descent,' he said. 'No approach control. We're going in cold.'

Marlowe opened his eyes. Gates stirred in his seat, and Voss snapped his notebook shut as they dropped fast. It wasn't a gradual descent; this was a hard break, nose down. The pressure shift pressed them into their seats, ears popping as altitude dropped. Out the window, the Black Hills of South Dakota rose from below, filled with green forests, interrupted by the occasional jagged peaks of stone, and Marlowe craned his neck to see it. These weren't mountains exactly; they were something older.

Harder.

The descent was faster than it should have been – it wasn't about safety right now, after all. It was about being seen for as little time as possible.

'Landing in two,' the pilot said, his voice calm. 'Strip looks clear.'

The frame of the plane rattled hard as they touched down on the narrow strip at Custer State Park Airport. There was no paved taxiway, no flashing lights, even. Just gravel, dirt, and two tyre tracks worn into the ground.

Which, as far as Marlowe was concerned, was exactly how he wanted it.

The wheels bounced twice before holding, and the plane rolled to the end of the runway and stopped, dust swirling up from behind. The engine powered down slowly, its hum fading to silence, as the pilot flicked off switches overhead.

Voss hit the hatch wheel, spun it, and pulled the door down as the smell of forest air rushed in. It felt crisp, earthy and cool, filling the cabin in a single breath. Passing him, hand on his hip, likely ready to pull a weapon at the first sign of trouble, Gates swung down first, his boots crunching softly on the gravel. Voss followed. Marlowe stepped out last, eyes sweeping the treeline.

No SUVs. No movement. No one waiting.

Just trees and quiet.

The Dodge Durango was right where it was supposed to be, courtesy of a friend of Voss this time; a call made while in the air, while making some other calls, and setting the scene. Parked under the low canopy of pines, there were no fresh tracks, and the keys were right where they should be, in a magnetic box tucked inside the wheel well.

Voss slid into the passenger seat and, after helping Marlowe unload what they'd taken from the lockup, Gates took the back, tossing a last black duffel onto the seat beside him. No one said anything as the engine started, and with a last nod to the pilot, already prepping to return to Vegas, they drove out slow.

No one spoke.

They didn't take Highway 16A right away; Marlowe had felt it was a little too obvious, especially if Shida had played both sides and had somehow followed. Instead, Marlowe followed the old service road, winding through the forest like a trail worn by deer. They only joined Iron Mountain Road after they'd put enough distance between them and the airstrip.

The first tunnel swallowed them whole, with stone walls tight on both sides, the rumble of the Dodge's tyres echoing like distant thunder. When they emerged into daylight, Marlowe saw the sun cutting across the forest ridge. Surprisingly, there was no traffic behind them. Just light, shadow, and a road that kept bending.

Trix would have loved this.

Marlowe pushed the thought back.

He'd mourn after he killed everyone related to her death.

There were another three tunnels, two pigtail bridges and forty minutes of switchbacks, stone, and green shadow, until they saw it.

Mount Rushmore.

The faces stared down from the ridge; silent, immovable, and watching.

Judging.

MARLOWE STOOD AT THE EDGE OF THE VIEWING PLATFORM, hands in his coat pockets, eyes on the stone faces above. Washington, Jefferson, Roosevelt, Lincoln – four men carved into granite, immortalised as legends. The late afternoon sun cast long shadows over their features, chiselled brows deep in thought, gazes fixed on the horizon like they saw something the rest of the world missed.

Tourists milled around him, and the area was filled with people taking selfies, and the sound of laughter. To his right, he heard parents calling out to kids on the loose. The clatter of footsteps on stone echoed in short bursts as people clambered around the sides. An old man in a baseball cap explained the history of dynamite carving to a bored teenager scrolling on his phone. A woman in a red jacket leaned on the railing, staring up in quiet awe.

Marlowe stood apart. Not obvious, not hidden. Just another man taking in the view.

His gaze didn't shift, but his awareness stretched in every direction – the movement of shadows, the rhythm of people coming and going, the gaps in the crowd.

Escape routes, cover, faces that lingered too long.

A passing tourist nudged his shoulder. It was accidental, but Marlowe barely noticed. His eyes stayed on Washington's face, rough and unyielding. No mistakes. No hesitation. Stone didn't blink, and neither did Marlowe.

Next, he turned his attention to Roosevelt, and in particular his left eye, the one damaged, permanently blinding him in a White House basement boxing match.

Stone. Blind.

He breathed in the cool air, fresh with the sharp bite of mountain pine, and let the quiet weight of it settle. This was where people came to look, reflect, and feel like they were part of something bigger.

But Marlowe wasn't here to reflect.

He was here to finish things.

STANDING BESIDE THE SUV, VOSS AND GATES WERE WAITING for him as he returned.

'This is a stupid bloody idea,' Voss muttered. 'You're aware of that?'

'I am,' Marlowe replied, looking back up at Mount Rushmore. 'But we're not going to get in any other way. This place is a vault.'

He wasn't over-exaggerating either. To get to where they needed to go, a narrow pathway up the side of the mountain led behind the head of Abraham Lincoln. Even on a normal day, Marlowe expected Park Rangers galore. With what was likely going on now, there was no chance whatsoever of Marlowe being able to get there without being seen.

Instead, he knew he had to go a different way.

Gates passed him a shotgun, but Marlowe placed it back in the trunk of the SUV.

'There's absolutely no point me taking weapons in, as they'll be gone the moment I'm taken,' he said as he still wrapped the metal self-defence chain around his wrist, connecting the dragon-head clasp securely.

'Apart from that,' Gates noted.

Marlowe smiled.

'Apart from this. What I have on me will be enough.'

'It had better bloody be,' Gates replied irritably. 'I agree with Voss. This is a bloody stupid idea.'

'Hey,' Marlowe shrugged. 'I might be going in the front door, but you guys are the ones who are going to be doing the more dangerous work.'

At that, Voss and Gates looked at each other.

'I should go with you,' Voss replied. 'I know the people.'

'It's the fact that you know the people that I'm relying on,' Marlowe said. 'You know what to do.'

This stated, Marlowe shook hands with both men, turned and walked off towards the path that led up to the mountain.

After a minute or two of preparation, Ryan stared up the path after him.

'He's going to get killed,' he said. 'We should get out of here before—'

He hadn't realised that Voss had walked up behind him, and he didn't feel the arm slipping around his neck until the last moment. By then, though, it was too late. His eyes widened, his mouth opened to call after Marlowe, but Voss tightened the choke, locking it in under the jaw.

If anyone was watching, they would have seen the panic on Gate's face hit fast. He clawed at Voss's forearm, nails scraping uselessly against skin. His breaths came quick and shallow, sharp little gasps that went nowhere. He twisted, tried to plant his feet, but Voss had the leverage.

There was a pause – a heartbeat of stillness – and in that moment Voss shifted his grip. A slight movement, barely a change at all. His hand slid higher, his wrist pressing up against the base of the skull. Then, with a short, brutal twist of his hips, the jerk was quick and vicious, if surprisingly quiet in the car park, the movie lie of a loud, audible "crack" when a neck was snapped nothing more than something to show the viewers what was going on.

But there was nobody there to see what was going on.

Everything went loose. Gates' body went heavy all at once, dead weight dropping in Voss's grip. He crumpled against the back of the SUV, head slumping awkwardly to one side, mouth half-open, eyes still wide.

Voss didn't pause. He caught the body before it hit the ground, hooking an arm under the shoulders, dragging him upright with ease born from practice.

Dead weight always moved differently.

The hatchback swung open, and Voss hefted the body in one smooth movement, knees bending with the lift, his breath steady and measured like it was nothing at all. The weight settled awkwardly inside the cargo space, arms splayed like a broken doll. Voss adjusted them, one at a time, folding them in tight so nothing hung over the edge. He stood there for a moment, looking down at Gates.

There was no movement. No breath.

No mistakes.

He pulled the hatch down, heard the soft click of the latch as it locked into place, and now alone, Voss looked up the path where moments earlier Marlowe had walked.

Pulling out his cell phone, he looked up at a tree across the car park, where, nested into the branches was a security camera. Anyone watching on it could only see the left side of the car, but they would have seen the act of murder Voss had just performed, the body dumped professionally.

Quickly, Voss typed in a message.

It's done. He's on his way to you. I'm following. You'd better fulfil your side of the deal.

A moment later, he had a reply.

Come join my team. We have badges.

Voss read, looked up at the camera and nodded. Then, moving to the side of the SUV, he prepared for his own mission.

THE PATH UP TO THE BACK OF LINCOLN'S HEAD WAS A DIFFICULT one to find. In fact, if you looked on trail maps, you'd never find it. Even looking down on Google Maps, you would see where the "Hall of Records" was at the back of the heads, but halfway down the path, it disappeared into a wash of shingle. This was because the path itself had been disguised on all public maps, something that had been continued from its days as a Cold War base.

Marlowe, however, had a map given to him by Clarissa that had the original pathway, off the Presidential Trail near the start, and up through the forest to the right of the mountain. It was old, a piece of paper rather than an image on a phone, and Marlowe felt like he was back in his orienteering days as a child, maybe even when he was doing reconnaissance in the Royal Marines, checking his compass against the path, and carrying on up towards his destination.

He'd worn a Kevlar vest under his jacket, mainly in case Gabriel Rizzo thought it'd be funny to simply shoot at him, but apart from that, there were no other visible weapons on him. No night vision goggles, no webbing, no combats. If he'd been stopped, a man in jeans, sweater, and a brown leather collared jacket, he could have been a confused and lost tourist out for a stroll on a chilly November afternoon.

It certainly wasn't as hot as Vegas had been. Marlowe couldn't believe he was actually missing the Vegas weather.

After about half a mile of walking through the backwoods, a winding trail that often seemed to come back on itself, most likely to make sure that nobody randomly came this way, Marlowe eventually walked out onto the path that led to a long metal staircase, easily a hundred steps, that led between the two rock faces; to his left the rear of the Presidential Sculpture, to the right the black stone of what was once known as "Six Grandfathers" to the native Sioux.

This was where things could go wrong.

If, at the top of the steps, the base was being guarded,

there was every chance that someone trigger-happy might decide to take Marlowe out. Alternatively, Steele himself might have left the command to kill Marlowe.

Also, there was still a million-dollar hit on Marlowe's head.

It was a bold move, and one that Marlowe felt was worth trying. Steele would have expected some kind of infiltration, maybe abseiling down the face of George Washington and trying to sneak in through some secret cavity up the nose, but Marlowe had decided there was no point. He had the old layout from 1927, where Gutzon Borglum had begun building, and he had a vague idea of how the Cold War bunker would have looked. There was likely an exit that led out into the Black Hills woodlands, but there was no way you could enter through it. The only way in was the main entrance; likely fake-looking rocks underneath the walkway up to a guard-house where the Rangers could look out over the statue.

Marlowe wondered whether the Rangers even knew about this as well. The lack of them to stop him made him wonder if they'd been told to take the day off. There would have been, after all, a large amount of back and forth in this area right now, and the wrong kind of Ranger might have asked the wrong kind of questions.

At the top of the metal steps Marlowe entered the last part of the pathway. Thirty yards to his right, he could see the rectangular opening that led to the seventy-foot tunnel that was effectively the Hall of Records. Marlowe had seen this on YouTube; a couple of influencers had been allowed to visit. They hadn't filmed the route up, but the Park Rangers had allowed them to record where the plaque was, the vault underneath it holding various copies of historical items on thin enamel sheets, the idea being that thousands of years down the line, their descendants would find these, and even when the faces on the wall were unknown, they could still learn the histories.

Twenty yards ahead of that was a metal staircase heading upwards towards the gantry. This was where Marlowe was intending to go, but instead, he stopped at the gate to the Hall of Records, turning in a slow circle.

'Come out, come out, wherever you are,' he said. 'Fee-fi-fo-fum, I smell the blood of a dead man.'

He held his hands out, spinning in a constant, slow circle, allowing every inch of his body to be seen. He guessed that there were probably cameras watching him right now, probably with thermals attached, and so he opened his jacket out, to show that he had his gun in his holster.

'Come on, Steele,' he shouted. 'I'm here. Where are you?'

He stopped, waiting. There was nothing. The faint sounds of crowds far below the mountain were all he could hear.

Maybe he was wrong.

He paused, looking back down at the path. In the scuffed up earth, beneath his feet, he could see tracks and footprints that had been made recently, the rain of a couple of days earlier not washing them away. Following the tracks, he saw they headed straight for the staircase.

So, he made his way to the same stairs.

There was nothing at the base that could be seen to be any kind of entrance, and so he started up the metal staircase.

There was a middle point about fifty steps up where he could see a gantry that turned slightly, and as he started towards it, he saw the rock formation to the side looked a little *fake*. The rocks were real, but they seemed cut in such a way that natural wind and rain would not have created. Marlowe wondered if he needed to bang on the rocks, shout again, but he didn't need to, as five steps onto the staircase, he heard the shouts.

Looking around, he saw the armed guards in full combat gear, rifles up and aimed at him.

'Stand down!' they shouted. 'Stand down!'

'Can I convince any of you to discuss our Lord and Saviour?' Marlowe smiled.

On a monitor screen deep under where Marlowe was now standing, Gabriel Rizzo stared at the image of Marlowe, arms out, shaking his head as he laughed.

'You've got to admit, your man has balls,' he said, straightening, as he turned to the figure to the side. 'The question is, do you think he's here for you or for me?'

'Considering he thinks I'm dead, I would think he's here to kill you,' Trix Preston replied calmly. She was sitting on a chair, no more than six feet from Gabriel, relaxed, ignoring the man with the Glock aimed at her skull.

'And, if this prick wasn't here, I'd be doing the same,' she added.

27

WAR GAMES

MARLOWE HAD BEEN RIGHT ABOUT THE LOOK OF THE COLD War bunker – but even his grim expectations had undershot the mark. The walls weren't just concrete; they were brutalist slabs of reinforced grey, ribbed with steel seams like the plates of a battleship's hull. Every surface seemed to drink in the light from the narrow overhead strips, casting long, oppressive shadows that crawled like insects over the floor. The air changed too. Cooler, denser. It had the smell of damp concrete, metal, and old machine oil – a stale, recycled tang that clung to the back of his throat.

This wasn't some relic from World War Two; it felt newer, tighter, like it had been built with more precision than the rough, rushed fortifications of the early Cold War. Late fifties, early sixties, if he had to guess. The Cold War paranoia had been at its peak back then, and it showed. Every seam was clean, every bolt had purpose. This wasn't a place you built in a hurry – it was made to endure.

The stairs dragged him down in a slow, deliberate descent, each step the same rough concrete as the walls. He'd climbed metal steps earlier to reach the entrance, but now he was heading right back into the dirt, which was standard practice for bunkers like this. Go deep, stay hidden. Anything too close to the surface would be useless once the world up top started burning.

At the bottom of the stairs, the space opened up into a large chamber. Fifty metres across, roughly octagonal in shape, though not a clean octagon – the angles were just off enough to make it feel unnatural. The ceiling hung high overhead, crisscrossed with thick yellow I-beams and vent grates. It reminded him of an old industrial shipyard; functional, solid, but never pretty.

A few vehicles moved through the space – small, low-slung transport buggies with wide tyres and armoured frames. They drove in slow, purposeful routes towards narrow corridors leading deeper into the bunker. Marlowe watched one roll past, its driver wearing a dark-green coverall, his eyes straight ahead. No small talk, no nod of acknowledgement. Everyone down here seemed focused on their own lane.

The room wasn't crowded; he'd expected more people, maybe engineers or soldiers, but the place was running on minimum capacity, literally a skeleton crew – enough to keep it operational, but nowhere near the manpower it was built for. He glanced at the walls and noticed the signs posted next to the heavy metal doors.

Pressure Lock Procedures
Clearance Required Beyond This Point

Doors like that weren't there to keep people out. They were to keep something in.

The passageways leading away from the main room were narrow, only wide enough for a single vehicle to pass at a time. They stretched into the distance at sharp angles, creating a natural choke point. Marlowe had seen it before in underground facilities; the design was deliberate – if someone breached the bunker, they'd be funnelled into kill zones.

It wasn't subtle, but it was effective.

The whole place had the feel of something planned, calculated, controlled. Everything was where it needed to be, there was no wasted space, no clutter, no distractions. The hum of machinery was a constant undercurrent, low and steady, like a heartbeat you could only hear if you stopped and listened.

He took a slow breath, his eyes scanning the space. No obvious cameras, which was odd for a place like this. Either they'd been hidden in the walls, or the people running this place didn't want anyone watching.

At the push from one guard, Marlowe adjusted his pace and stepped towards one of the larger corridors, his boots making a faint echo on the concrete. The space ahead stretched long and straight, flanked by smooth walls and overhead lights spaced too far apart, each one creating a pool of brightness with long shadows in between; it felt like walking into a tunnel with breaks of daylight ahead. He kept moving, his pace steady. Places like this weren't meant for sightseeing, and you definitely didn't stop to admire the architecture. You got where you were going – and you got there fast.

The two men who had found him were acting as if they'd hunted him down in a vicious manhunt for the amount of hand-slapping and *hoo-rah* chants they made. Marlowe guessed they were ex-military, but what military, he wasn't sure. Private security was private security. They took from a lot of places. He'd even heard a couple of accents in the bunker that gave him the impression that there were French here, Albanian too.

French Foreign Legion perhaps? Marlowe wasn't sure. But the *hoo-rah* made him assume they were ex-US Marines. Which meant they were people he didn't want to piss off right now.

Eventually, he was led down a long corridor, emerging into what seemed to be some kind of control centre. Here, the decor looked way more familiar. Banks of servers whirring away, their green neon lights giving the room a strange ethereal look as it mixed with the more subdued fluorescent lighting above. Monitor screens were across the wall in a "mission control" kind of way, and Marlowe could see that anyone who had been here during the Cold War would have been able to get instant responses to everything that had happened outside. If anything, this looked very much like the control centre that had been used in the eighties movie *War Games* with Matthew Broderick, a film Marlowe had grown up on, and now he wondered just how much of *that* set design was based on fact.

At the far end, staring up at the screens, which at the moment seemed to show a variety of different sporting events, giving Marlowe the impression that the room was a mixture of sports bar and Cold War bunker, was ...

Gabriel Rizzo.

Marlowe paused, looking around the room. *Where was St John Steele?*

However, before he could ask, Gabriel turned to face Marlowe.

'I knew you would come,' he said. 'I knew nothing would stop you. Are you here to kill me for what I did?'

'I'm here to kill Steele first,' Marlowe replied. 'Is he here?'

'Christ, no,' Gabriel laughed. 'Why would he come here, of all places? He's doing the big work, the important stuff, while I get to sit in the underground bunker.'

Marlowe noted a slight twinge of bitterness in the voice and wondered if he could use this. Stepping closer, looking at the screens as he did so, he saw on two of them some CCTV footage. One of these showed the car park and a Dodge Durango that looked familiar.

'So, you've been watching me since I arrived,' he said, a sinking feeling now appearing in the pit of his stomach.

'We have,' Gabriel shrugged. 'Just me, and a small number of invited guests. Nothing major.' He looked off to the left and Marlowe followed his gaze, and his heart skipped as he saw the familiar blonde woman held between two guards.

'I knew you weren't dead,' he said, and the relief was palpable.

'Bullshit,' Trix mumbled. 'You believe anything. I bet you held a wake and everything. You should have. A kid died. These bastards need to pay for that. *This* bastard needs to pay for that.'

'Yeah, that's the plan here,' Marlowe smiled darkly, returning his attention back to Gabriel. 'The kid dying; was it part of your game?'

In response, Gabriel shrugged.

'Everything I do is part of a game,' he replied. 'Having you chase your tail, running around, thinking you're saving the world while you're doing nothing more but being a pain, helping me along.'

'Helping you? Or helping Steele?'

'I think you've realised by now we're the same thing.'

'Oh, I doubt that,' Marlowe laughed. 'He's always been the organ grinder to your monkey.'

'Well, I'm happy to be the monkey if I'm made incredibly rich, and others take the fall for my – our – actions.'

He waved at another image. It was a browser page showing a news story from the Washington Post.

Terrorist attacks Las Vegas hotels, Formula One race in doubt.

Underneath it were images of both the Venetian and the Desert Oasis, as well as an artist's impression of Marlowe.

'Let me guess,' Marlowe said. 'This was all aimed at making me some kind of public enemy number one while giving you what you wanted?'

'As much as your arrogance and attitude irritate me,' Gabriel replied, 'this time you're correct. This has all been for you.'

'And yet Steele placed a hit on my head,' Marlowe muttered.

'He learned from your father about that one.'

'What, that he was hiring shit assassins?'

'No,' Gabriel replied. 'We learned that just like a cockroach, you simply won't die.'

He waved around the control room.

'This is Operation Stone Blind. You know why it's called Stone Blind?'

'Because you're directly behind Roosevelt's left eye,' Marlowe said. 'All the official records say that the Hall of Records is behind Lincoln, but when you look at it on a map, Lincoln's facing the other way. The top of the staircase is behind Lincoln. The Hall of Records is behind the two of them. But this entrance, well, it fits a little more. Although Jefferson is probably a closer bet.'

He looked around the control centre, tutting as he did so.

'You know, for the amount of millions Steele gathered up from Operation Quicksilver, this seems to be a bit of a waste of money.'

'Not at all,' Gabriel said. 'What we have here is an impenetrable bunker which has been gifted to Steele's organisation for the next fifty years thanks to some zoning laws and a couple of friendly senators. We effectively control the park. That is, *Orchid* controls the park.'

'Really?' Marlowe raised an eyebrow. 'That's outstanding, thank you very much.'

'Not *your* Orchid,' Gabriel snapped. 'Not you traitors. The *real* Orchid. The ones that understand what needs to be done to get power.'

'Right, yes, the crazy ones,' Marlowe nodded, his face giving a very patronising expression as he did so.

Gabriel Rizzo, however, noted that Marlowe kept staring up at the CCTV.

'Are you worried that your friends aren't going to come and help you?' he asked.

Marlowe frowned.

'I came alone,' he replied cautiously.

'Yes, you did,' Gabriel said, and his voice was tinged with sadness as he spoke. 'Shall I show you how alone you are?'

He nodded to a technician standing to the side, and Marlowe recognised the man as the technician who had been at Durrant Capital.

'I'm guessing if he's here, Diana Durrant's other

employees are around,' Marlowe said as the technician started typing on the computer keyboard.

'They are,' Gabriel nodded. 'I felt so bad when she was killed last night in my casino, I owed it to her to at least keep all of her people in gainful employment, until, you know, Durrant Capital worked out who took over.'

'And do they know who'd be taking over?'

'Oh, that'd be me, of course,' Gabriel said. 'Diana signed it over right before she was murdered by you.'

'I didn't do any such thing,' Marlowe growled. 'That was likely Steele's pet, Evan Cross.'

'And yet you were there, and the police think you're a terrorist,' Gabriel replied calmly. 'Who do you think people will believe more? You're ... well, look at the shit show your CV has become of late. Steele? Well, he's kind of a big thing now. Presidential level. I don't know if you got the memo, but billionaires own politicians now. It's the way of the future. We understand technology. We understand business. The eight billionaires in my hotel yesterday? Shortly before they died, they all digitally signed a partnership agreement, giving me twenty percent in each company.'

'Digitally signed?' Marlowe asked, and as he did so he realised what Cross, as Bassett, had been really doing. 'Let me guess, they each connected when they arrived, didn't they? Maybe in front of "Lawrence Bassett?"'

'He had to confirm their identity,' Gabriel shrugged. 'Usually they'd have people to do this, but they wanted to be a little, well, discreet. "Mister Bassett" wasn't aligned with anyone. He was Switzerland, here.'

'Switzerland with a photographic memory,' Marlowe nodded. 'And when he cloned their phones, he could retroactively sign for them, before the news of their deaths came out.'

'The news of their deaths?' Gabriel looked around in mock surprise. 'They're dead? Surely the news channels would have said something?'

Of course they wouldn't, Marlowe realised. *The last thing the boards wanted was to reveal their CEOs or whatever had been killed at some kind of uber-secretive, "one-percent" meeting to screw over the world.* They'd likely allow the deaths to be announced quietly, slowly, and probably swallow anything done during the meetings – including any minor takeovers – until they fixed this. By which point, whatever the plan was, would have been completed, the shares likely sold on.

Marlowe held his hand up, the action pausing Gabriel.

'You don't have to hold your hand up to ask a question,' he snapped.

'I felt I really should at this point,' Marlowe replied. 'You see, you're sounding a little crazy.'

'You speak so casually for a man who is about to die,' Gabriel said icily as he nodded back to the technician. 'Play the video. Show this limey prick how alone he truly is.'

The car on the screen flickered, and now there were three men standing there. Marlowe recognised it as the moment he'd left Voss and Gates, and on the screen Marlowe shook hands with both men and walked off, out of sight.

'Okay, so you know I'm not alone,' Marlowe replied. 'That doesn't...'

He paused as, on the screen, Voss walked behind Gates, grabbing him, and after a second of struggling, snapped his neck, throwing the dead man into the back of the Dodge Durango.

After a moment, he came out of the back of the car,

looking up at the camera as he typed on his phone, texting or checking an app.

After completing whatever he did, he grabbed a duffel bag and walked off, following the route that Marlowe had gone, the Dodge now empty and lifeless.

'As you can see, there's been no movement since that,' Gabriel said. 'I'm sorry to tell you, Mister Marlowe, but Mister Voss has been working with us the entire time. In fact, you just witnessed him finalising the deal.'

He waved to the back of the command centre, where the doors opened, and Voss, *not* being led by guards, entered, duffel over his shoulder as he walked up to Gabriel.

Who, seeing this, looked at Marlowe again, noting his expression, and started to laugh.

'Now he gets it!' he crowed. 'Now he understands! All your plans turned to shit in an instant, Tommy-boy! This time, *the house wins!*'

28

VIDEO MESSAGES

THERE WAS A LONG SILENCE IN THE CONTROL ROOM AS VOSS, like Marlowe had before him, looked around, confused.

'I expected to see Mister Steele,' he said.

'Yeah, we're getting a lot of that today,' Gabriel winked at Marlowe.

Voss considered the statement, looked from Gabriel to Marlowe and then back to the man obviously in charge, and straightened.

'Mister Rizzo,' he continued. 'I understand my men's contracts, and also mine, have reverted to you, then, due to your acquisition of Durrant Capital.'

'Don't worry, I give good bonuses,' Gabriel gave a grin as he looked back at Marlowe. 'Especially for loyalty. Go speak to your men, tell them how rich they'll become under me. *My* guards will show you to them.'

'Under you, or under Steele?' Marlowe interrupted.

'As I've already said, it's the same thing.'

'Yeah, I wouldn't let Steele hear you say that to people,'

Marlowe grinned. 'He's a little thin-skinned where rivals are concerned.'

He looked back at Voss, who shuffled uncomfortably.

'Sorry, Tom,' he said, 'but I did tell you I needed retirement money.'

He looked back at Gabriel.

'Do you want us to begin work now?' he asked. 'I couldn't help but see your own security is a little ... lax.'

Gabriel raised an eyebrow.

'You think you can do better?'

'I know I can,' Voss sniffed. 'Yours seem to be taken from your casino; good for hotel security, but not for this. My men are all highly trained. I have what, ten, fifteen men here? I'd expect them to do double what your, what, thirty men can do.'

'Forty,' Gabriel smiled. 'And as much as I'd like to see that, I have other jobs for you, after I've finished here. Join your men, as I have another person for you to guard. Man by the name of Evan Cross. I think he's made a lot of enemies recently.'

'The man who killed Diana Durrant?'

'Is that a problem?'

'Not at all,' Voss shook his head. 'As I said to Marlowe here, I need my retirement fund. Diana Durrant was going to give me that. She can't if she's dead. I need to move on.'

'Awesome. Then do me a favour and move on,' Gabriel waved for the guards to lead Voss to his men. As Voss left, the two guards leading him to a door to the side of the control room, Marlowe lunged for Gabriel, but the remaining guards had been prepared for it, and in a scuffle, they threw him back to the floor.

Marlowe glared from his position on the ground as Gabriel looked down at him.

'I like this,' Gabriel smiled. 'Yes, you on your knees looking up at me as your world falls apart.'

Marlowe looked helplessly at Trix as Gabriel Rizzo stared up at the screens, one of which was showing a replay of a race from the weekend.

'You know what's fascinating about Formula One, Tom? It's not just about the cars or the speed. It's about precision. Control. The ability to calculate a thousand variables and turn them into perfect execution. Rather like the financial markets, wouldn't you say?'

'This isn't you, Gabriel. You're a gangster, a failed casino owner,' Marlowe snapped. 'Steele's using you as a tool, something that does a job for him, until like all the others, he tires of you.'

'When I was rising in the family, I learned that the best heists, the best moneymakers are the ones where your target does exactly what you want, while thinking they're working against you,' Gabriel continued, ignoring Marlowe. 'Take Diana Durrant, for example. She was ambitious, connected, but ultimately disposable. I needed someone obvious, someone who would draw attention while the real work happened here. So I worked on Steele, and after that he had Katherine Saito whisper in Durrant's ear about Maguire, his accountant Bassett, and about a chance to build her own empire.'

'You killed Saito?' Marlowe asked coldly, rising now to his feet.

'Now now, Tommy boy. Don't jump ahead of the narrator,' Gabriel waggled his finger mockingly. 'We needed you to jump when we called, and with Saito's help, you did exactly what I knew you would. Charging in to investigate Durrant, never seeing that every step took you further from what was really happening. Even that poor bitch Katherine played her part perfectly ... so desperate to prove her loyalty that she never realised she was just another piece on the board.'

He paused, leaning closer.

'Until yes, Steele killed her,' he said. 'And I don't think you're giving him credit for what he did there. Across a lake, at night, and with only a thermal scope? Come on. Give a sniper some love.'

'I'll give you both something else,' Marlowe held himself back. 'A nice, slow death.'

'Good man, stay on brand, that's why we love you so,' Gabriel laughed. 'You know, Steele was mortified when he heard Saito was distrusting him, going against him. He had a genuine tear in his eye when he flew off to end her personally. Shame he didn't check the source first, as I might have exaggerated a little, you know.'

'You're the reason she's dead?'

'Marlowe, haven't you been listening? I'm the reason for pretty much most of this,' Gabriel extorted as he waved around. 'He was already working on moving the Quicksilver funds when I first met you, back at the Gold Strike, in the octagon cage. There you were, thinking he was a buddy, while even then he was pushing your buttons. Operation Quicksilver was brilliant but crude – government funds manipulating markets through back channels, the CIA and MI6 both claiming it was their toy box until it was decided to hide it, so nobody got to play with it, and everyone forgot. But Steele didn't bloody forget, Tom. He remembered.'

Gabriel waved at the technician.

'Earn your money,' he shouted. 'Put that video up for Mister Marlowe to see.'

Marlowe stared at Gabriel, then slowly shook his head, a hint of sadness in his eyes.

'You know, you are by far one of the stupidest men I've ever met,' he said. 'The first time I met you, you were just middle management, and I get it – that was a job you probably felt you had to stay in for the moment. You were trying to climb higher in Orchid, trying to prove to your way-more-successful sister you weren't a screwup, and that's completely understandable. But Steele? He tried to steal AI drones, enough weaponry to take out a small country, and when that failed, he went after satellites that could fire EMP waves at his rivals. And, well, if I'm being honest, I've got no idea what he was really hoping to achieve there. Every time he tried something, he failed.'

He started to bitterly laugh now.

'I'd ask why you've hitched your wagon to him, but it's pretty obvious that screwups seek their own kind,' he smiled. 'So, now what, Steele started Stone Blind to funnel Quicksilver money and fix sporting events, and you said, "sign me up, buddy"? I genuinely thought you'd aim higher than that. Or did you decide to let him do that, while seeing a bigger picture, taking the billionaires he'd sourced, and stealing their companies – and lives?'

Gabriel said nothing, staring at Marlowe. On the screen, the beginning of a video message was being set up, and on it the blue screen turned to one of a library, where St John Steele stared down at the room. He was sitting in a familiar library; the one Marlowe had been in days earlier.

The one where Katherine Saito had died.

'Steele thinks this is about algorithms and market

control,' Gabriel replied, pacing now. 'Clean. Clinical. The perfect operation.'

He laughed, but there was no humour in it.

'But he never understood Vegas. Never understood that sometimes you need to make things personal.'

He turned to Marlowe.

'You took everything from me. My casino. My reputation. My family's respect. Steele wants to change the world, thinking money is power – I just want to watch yours burn.'

'Money is power, that's true enough,' Marlowe replied. 'And you've always suffered from both – a distinct lack of money and not that much power. So why is this different?'

Before Gabriel could reply, however, the video on the screen began, and St John Steele's voice echoed around the control room.

'Hello, Thomas,' he said. 'I'm guessing you're watching this, as I left orders to play this only when you were there to watch it. I do hope you're well.'

He waved around the library.

'Recognise it?' he asked. 'I ask because as I record this, Katherine Saito is on her way here, and I'm sure, after last night's debacle, you'll be on your way too. I won't be here, however, as I'll be somewhere out there—'

He punctuated the comment by pointing towards the window, off screen.

'—across the lake, most likely, with a sniper rifle. Don't worry though, I won't be killing you. I'll need you for later.'

He chuckled.

'Forgive me, this is a little odd,' he continued. 'Like I'm seeking my last words. I got the idea from your father at his memorial. You remember that? You pissed off a lot of people when you were given the coin.'

'Does he get to the point?' Marlowe asked Gabriel. 'I'm bored already. Swipe left.'

'By now, you're probably making some quippy line about this,' Steele smiled onscreen, and for a moment Marlowe wondered if this was another mind game, and that Steele was actually live, and watching. 'Or, you're restrained and muzzled like Hannibal Lecter in Silence of the Lambs. I haven't yet decided what to do with you. If you make it here, of course. You might be dead in a Las Vegas grave for all I know, and Gabriel's watching this with everyone at the Christmas party.'

He leant closer to the screen.

'I'm very sorry I can't be there today, wherever there is, and wherever on your personal journey you are, but honestly? I can't be bothered. 'I'm at capacity right now, and the small things – you know, irritants like you – have to be sorted by my underlings.'

'You hear that?' Marlowe mocked Gabriel. 'He called you an underling.'

'He meant people like Voss.'

'You sure?'

Unaware of the argument on the control room floor, Steele continued.

'Anyway, even though I'm super busy, I couldn't help making sure I was here for this, your last moments alive. I wanted you to know exactly how deep I went here.'

He frowned.

'Or am going,' he added. 'Because for me it's future tense, but for you it's past tense.'

He settled back into the chair, picked up a tumbler of what looked to be whisky or brandy, and toasted Marlowe.

'I should thank you,' he continued. 'Because of you and

your various actions over the last year, I'm no longer handcuffed by Orchid. You see, when I was the Arbitrator, Orchid had their hands positioned over mine. They stopped me from doing the things I wanted to do, from making the plays I wanted to make. They didn't believe in me the way I knew I could succeed.'

Marlowe considered this for a moment, his eyes narrowing as he looked at Gabriel.

'So what, he felt he wasn't getting enough love from Mummy and Daddy?' he shook his head, disgust clear in his face. 'What happened to Max Schen? Wasn't he Steele's sugar daddy? And now he's collecting new billionaires to fill that void?'

'Max turned out to be a gutless coward,' Gabriel said flatly, nodding for the video to pause. 'He didn't have the fire we believed he would provide; what I needed.'

'Colour me shocked,' Marlowe replied with a slow clap of mock applause. 'And what exactly did *you* need, Gabriel?'

'I needed to have Bassett take out everybody else in that meeting, and use his eidetic memory to remember things, before you turned up and, as ever, brought chaos with you.'

'I can't claim all the credit,' Marlowe said, offering a sly smile. 'The CIA did a lot of the heavy lifting. It was CIA, right? Trying to take back their British accountant asset?'

He stared long and hard at Gabriel, eyes locked like a predator eyeing its prey.

'Or rather Evan Cross, their rogue CIA agent. They seemed to really want him. But you didn't know that, did you? Steele hadn't let you into the entire plan.'

He laughed with realisation now, looking at the other people watching him as he turned a slow circle.

'All this? You've gone off script!' he exclaimed. 'Bassett –

Cross – whatever his bloody name is, he was brought in by Steele and sent to you, making you think you'd poached him. And what, you decided you could do better? Was the whole thing with Durrant's death your plan, or did you crib it from Steele?'

Gabriel glared daggers at Marlowe.

'I heard about Bassett's skills,' he intoned. 'Diana vouched for him, Steele knew him. I realised there was a way to make more money than Steele was planning.'

'And so you went against Steele, possibly for the first time,' Marlowe replied. He paused as a thought came.

'Wait, are you *hiding* here?' he asked incredulously. 'Is this you, hiding from Steele, knowing he's going to be pissed you broke his toys? All of this to keep everyone from looking too close at what you were doing ... fixing sporting events?'

'It's not just fixing bloody events!' Gabriel screamed out now. 'Every major sporting event creates market fluctuations: billions in trades, currency shifts, market adjustments. Natural movements that nobody questions. Patterns that a man with Bassett's skills could map, could predict, could control! The Formula One race isn't just a test. It's a demonstration. The "terrorist attacks" have added a volatile element to the market – so, when the race is targeted again, and the markets in Hong Kong crash next week, no one will question it. They'll blame it on normal trading patterns, on the excitement of a global sporting event, on the "terrible terrorists doing terrible things". They won't see the algorithms working beneath the surface.'

This stated, Gabriel turned to look at Trix.

'And Miss Preston? Well, I needed something to keep you distracted, emotional, reckless. What better way than to make you think your closest ally was dead?'

Marlowe waited for Gabriel to finish, and Gabriel hadn't noticed yet, but Marlowe was calmer, more assured.

'I don't think you understand what an eidetic memory is,' he replied calmly. 'He's got a good memory. He's not psychic.'

'I think you should shut the hell up—'

'I think you should keep playing the recording,' Marlowe interrupted. 'The person who's actually in charge should speak.'

Before Gabriel could reply, the technician restarted the recording, and on the screen, Steele jerked back into life.

'Yes, I've had to make sacrifices and alliances I didn't want to consider,' Steele continued. 'That prick Rizzo, for a start. I'm guessing you've tried to repeatedly kill him by now? Maybe you've sided with him against Durrant. Or perhaps they're all dead? I know Gabriel Rizzo has such a flair for the dramatic. I suppose by now, Gabriel's made a mess of things. He was supposed to be an asset – local knowledge, nothing more. But he always had delusions of grandeur. The problem with casino men, Thomas, is they think everything needs to be a show. They don't understand subtlety.'

He paused, considering something.

'You know, I don't think I need him anymore. His family absolutely hate him, so there's no love lost ... maybe I'll let you kill him before I run out of uses for you. Would you like that? Maybe I'll put you in one of those octagon rings he loves so much, throw you a blade each and let you have at it against each other.'

'I'm good with that,' Marlowe shrugged as he looked back at the horrified Gabriel, hearing words he'd never expected.

The man he thought he was playing turned out to have zero respect for him. And, more likely, was playing him.

But on the screen, Steele hadn't finished.

'But then what, though? Say you do succeed again ... would you run back to Daddy McKellan or Mummy Wintergreen? Perhaps you could beg Orchid to take you back? No, Tom. The old powers – governments, intelligence agencies, secret societies who stopped being secret years ago, even our former employers – they'll be obsolete. The world will belong to those who control the flow of money. And we'll rewrite the rules of global finance. I wish I could see your face. I'll have someone take a photo for me. Goodbye, Thomas.'

Steele stood tall now, turning off the recorder, and Marlowe could see that all the years of being the go-to black bag man for Whitehall, all the years arbitrating for billionaires at Orchid, all of this had led to the man on the screen in front of him, as it faded to black.

As origin stories went, it was worthwhile.

Shame he had to kill it, now.

'Cool story,' he said to Gabriel as he cricked his neck, subtly stretching, aware he was about to fight. 'And Bassett?'

'He's provided me with what I needed, and now I'll pay him handsomely to disappear,' Gabriel replied. 'He'll go back to Steele, or he'll do something else. Not my problem.'

'Maguire?'

'Christ, Marlowe, weren't you listening? Steele couldn't give a shit about him. He was a means to an end.'

'Voss and the other men that Durrant controlled?'

'Meat suits, nothing more. I'll use them here until I tire of them. And then I'll probably fire them. Or something more permanent.'

'Voss won't be happy with that,' Marlowe shook his head. 'But it's irrelevant anyway – you won't last long enough to do it.'

He glanced over at Trix, aware that all of this hadn't been

discussed with her around, and that she might be caught as unaware as Gabriel was. However, he saw Trix's eyes never left the screens, fingers twitching slightly at her side, unconsciously "typing" on her thigh as she analysed the setup. The tech might have been Cold War era, but she could see the newer systems layered on top – and their weaknesses.

She caught Marlowe's eye briefly, a slight nod telling him she had a plan, and Marlowe hoped it meshed, rather than contradicted, his own.

'Why? Are you seriously saying you'll stop me?' Gabriel laughed now.

Marlowe straightened, smiled, and nodded. As he did so, one of the servers at the back of the room ... *stopped.*

Not exploded, or anything violent, just simply stopped working, one screen on the wall dying instantly as whatever feed was heading into the now dead server also stopped.

'Yeah, Gabriel, I think I will,' Marlowe smiled as the lights turned red, the sirens started and all hell broke loose.

29

BACKUP FEEDS

Before he'd been an actor, Ryan Gates had worked in security services on a variety of dodgy jobs. In fact, if he was being honest, he'd admit he enjoyed the "secret squirrel sneaking around and shooting people" stuff far more than *pretending* to sneak around and shoot people. He'd also been lucky enough to never be shot during his time in the service. In fact, the only time he'd ever received a violent wound was when his wife shot him with a spear gun at a *Robin Hood* convention in Milton Keynes.

Weirdly, he'd later learned it was Thomas Marlowe's uncle who had helped solve the case.

So, when he was given the opportunity to do both – act and do some "real" sneaking and shooting – Ryan Gates was over the moon.

The plan had been simple. They knew there was a camera; they guessed it was watching for intruders, with a direct feed into the bunker. So, they performed a little play for whoever was watching. They'd arranged a car to park in such a way that one door on the passenger side couldn't be seen. Marlowe had made a point of shaking hands heroically and marching off to "defeat the villains", while Martin Voss and Ryan Gates watched him go. A moment later, Voss would pretend to snap Gates's neck and dump him in the back of the SUV. The seats were down, which meant that once he was inside and out of the camera's sight, Gates could roll across the car and slide out of the passenger side without anyone being the wiser, while Voss, who'd made the call on the flight, asking to come in, let his new bosses know he was there and ready to start.

It would have worked perfectly if it hadn't been for the fact that Martin Voss had been a little too *eager* with his strangling. Ryan Gates wasn't a spring chicken after all, and he'd spent a good five minutes trying to regain his breath, convinced at one point his neck had actually been broken. The jerking motion Voss had made was incredibly realistic – mostly because it was exactly how you would break someone's neck. That he *hadn't* broken Gates's neck was only a testament to the skill of the man doing it.

The angle of the camera on the Dodge Durango meant that while Gates was in the back, nothing could be seen and, after catching his breath, Gates had spent the next ten minutes gathering up as many items as he could from the bag of tricks and toys they'd been provided with, without rocking the Dodge, and giving away that someone was alive in the vehicle. Some of these were even items that Gates himself had donated to the cause.

There was one toy that worked nicely – a laptop that sent a relay back to Vegas, where one of Clarissa's experts sat at a computer, recorded the footage of the Durango, and looped it to the camera's server. How they'd got into the camera's server, Gates didn't really want to know. He assumed it was one of Voss's friends – one of the operatives inside the company, inside Steele's organisation – who, like Voss, had been equally annoyed at the death of their boss, Diana Durrant. In fact, it had been several of Voss's friends who had provided them with the best "unofficial" way into the bunker, a small shaft that led from the rear of the base, a half mile trek through the woods and mountainside.

Sliding out slowly and crawling on his hands and knees away from the Dodge Durango, Gates had got out of the view of the camera before continuing on. He moved silently through the dense forest, keeping low as he approached the maintenance shaft he'd been aimed at. The entrance was exactly where Voss's people had marked it – a rusted metal door set into the mountain's base, almost invisible beneath decades of creeping vines.

He was about to approach when movement caught his eye. A figure emerged from the doorway; male, mid-fifties, dressed expensively but practically. Gates recognised him instantly from Marlowe's description earlier that day; it was Lawrence Bassett. Or rather, the man currently using that name.

Keeping absolutely still, Gates watched as Bassett pulled out a phone, his movements sharp with frustration.

'It's falling apart,' Bassett spoke quietly, but in the mountain silence, his words carried. 'Rizzo's gone off-script. The entire operation's compromised.'

A pause.

'No, you listen to me, Steele. I didn't spend a year building this cover to watch it implode because your pet casino owner can't control himself. I need extraction. Now.'

Another pause. Bassett's face darkened.

'That wasn't our agreement. I mapped the entire financial network for you! Every account, every transfer, every shell company, all funnelling from Quicksilver to Stone Blind. My part's done.'

His voice hardened.

'You want what's in my head? Then get me out.'

Gates held his breath as Bassett ended the call, watching the man check his surroundings before heading up one of the maintenance paths. Only when he was certain Bassett was gone did Gates move, approaching the door with practised caution.

Should he follow? No. Marlowe was likely up to his neck in shit right now.

That said, Gates made a mental note to check up that path later on.

The lock was old; standard Cold War era mechanical stuff. No electronic security, which made sense; this was a forgotten exit, probably not even on modern blueprints. With the tools he'd been given thanks to Clarissa's knowledge of the site, Gates had the door open in under a minute, slipping inside like a shadow.

The passage beyond was narrow, carved straight into the mountain. Emergency lights cast everything in a sickly green glow, and the air tasted stale, metallic. Gates moved carefully, checking corners, marking his path. The tech in his bag felt reassuringly heavy; a mix of old-school explosives and modern electronic disruptors. He wasn't here to destroy the facility; that would draw too much attention. But a few carefully placed charges in the right systems? That would create enough chaos for Marlowe to work with.

Finding the first junction box, Gates smiled.

Sometimes the old ways were best.

'Time to go to work,' he muttered, reaching for his bag.

MARLOWE HAD TO ADMIT – EVEN IF IT WASN'T TO GABRIEL Rizzo's face – that he was impressed with what Steele had managed. In essence, he'd created a complex shell game. While everyone, including Marlowe, had focused on Durrant and London, Steele was actually setting up a system to control global markets. Market fluctuations because of major sporting events were normal and expected; no one would question them. By the time anyone realised these natural fluctuations were actually controlled manipulation, Steele would have already showed his power to whoever he was trying to impress.

But then Gabriel decided he had to be involved too, and with Gabriel came contradictions and reversals. No wonder everything seemed complicated and convoluted – it was thanks to Gabriel sticking his nose into things, thinking, as ever, that he was the true power here, all while Marlowe was being led down another path by the unsuspecting Steele. Every step Marlowe took investigating Durrant pulled him further from discovering Steele's true operation. Each piece: Bassett, Durrant, Saito, Rizzo, they were all positioned precisely to keep attention focused anywhere but on Steele's actual operation. Layers of conspiracy created that, when investigated, only led from his true purpose.

Although Gabriel didn't seem to get the memo. Even now, staring at the man, Marlowe wasn't sure if *he* even knew what the true purpose was.

Gabriel, meanwhile, was reaching the shouting stage as the alarms shrieked and the lights flashed.

'What did you do?' he shouted at Marlowe. '*What did you do?* We planned for everything. There's no way—'

'There's every way,' Marlowe interrupted, holding a hand up. 'You looked at the numbers. You looked at the data. Just like you did at the casino you brought to the ground, you didn't think about the emotions. The *human* factor.'

As he spoke, the door opened and Martin Voss and the rest of his security detail entered the main hall, very armed, and very obviously angry.

'Take him down!' Gabriel shouted, pointing at Marlowe. 'Take him down!'

But Trix was already moving. As the guards, distracted by the chaos looked towards Voss and his men, she ran to a console, her fingers flying across the keyboard, muscle memory taking over. The guards holding her hadn't bothered restraining her hands – after all, what damage could one person do to a hardened military system?

A lot, as it turned out.

'What are you doing?' Gabriel looked over at her in confusion.

'You updated the security,' she said, not looking up from the screen, 'but you didn't change the base code. Rookie mistake.'

The first system fell in seconds. Then the second. More warning lights began flashing as she triggered cascading failures throughout the bunker. On the monitors above, security cameras clicked off one by one, emergency bulkheads began cycling randomly, and communication systems dissolved into static.

'What are you doing?' Gabriel's voice rose with panic as

he reached for his gun, only to find he didn't have one, probably because he'd felt safe in the bunker, surrounded by his own men. He looked back at Voss. 'Stop her!'

'Too late,' Trix smiled, executing her final command. 'I've locked everyone out. The system's mine now.'

The screens above them flashed red as system after system went into lockdown, and Trix caught Marlowe's eye again.

'You're not the only one who can make an entrance,' she said.

Voss stopped beside Marlowe, turned to face Trix, cycled his pistol ...

And then pointed it at Gabriel.

'Perhaps when I mentioned the human factor, you should have considered this,' Marlowe replied, relaxing a little, as he saw from his expression that Gabriel Rizzo was finally realising that everything he had planned on his own was going *very* wrong. As Voss aimed the weapon at him, his team – people that Voss had hired over the months since he had started working with Diana Durrant – fanned out. Some aimed raised assault rifles, shouting at the one-time casino guards to drop their weapons and get on the floor, while others were moving off in pairs, deeper into the base to do the same. With the element of surprise, this could become an incredibly bloodless coup.

Gabriel hadn't even realised he was beaten.

'I don't understand,' he said, looking over at Voss. 'You called me. You asked for a job.'

'I played you,' Voss replied, his voice cold. 'Because you killed my boss. What did you think - I'd happily change my allegiance? Diana Durrant might have had her faults, but she gave me a solid wage and a reason for being after I left the military. And you had her killed purely to give yourself some kind of tiny advance when dealing with St John Steele?'

'Oh, don't be so bloody-minded,' Gabriel snapped. 'People get killed for tiny advances all the time. I took her entire company.'

He glanced back at Marlowe.

'Well played,' he muttered. 'So what, you convinced Voss to side with you?'

'I didn't do much convincing,' Marlowe nodded. 'You did that when you had Cross kill Durrant. And once we had a scenario, it was quite simple to work it through. You see, I might not have had the full plan, but I'd seen enough to realise what Steele had done to me. I was so desperate to see the conspiracy that he was organising, the world-ending threat that he was likely to become – you know, playing to form and all that – I wasn't realising that *he* wasn't playing *me*, giving me the pathway he wanted me to travel down, but that it was *you*, countering his orders, playing your own game. Telling me what I needed to do. Guiding me every step of the way. And like an idiot, I followed.'

'Oh, I forgot,' Voss pulled the duffle off his shoulder, passing it over. 'Yours, I believe.'

'Ah, thanks,' Marlowe pulled out the CZ, sliding it into his holster, while slipping his Fairbairn-Sykes knife into his jacket. Now armed, he walked over to Gabriel, standing only a couple of feet away.

'If he'd continued alone, I'd likely have failed. But then you had plans. "Kill" Trix to throw me off balance, when all it did was sharpen my edge. Destroy your own casino, again, just so your sister couldn't have it. Blow up Vegas, just because they didn't bow to you. Kill Diana Durrant, all so Steele had fewer allies, all while claiming it wasn't you – and gaining a company with the latter. Sneaky shit – you know, playing to form and all that – which all backfired in your face. Again, playing to form. So, when I realised, and this was thanks to all the people you'd managed to piss off along the way, I decided it was time to do what you did to me. But back at you.'

He pointed over at the screen, showing the Dodge Durango.

'Isn't it surprising that nothing's happened there? All this time we've been talking and not one person has passed.'

Gabriel stared, realising as Marlowe spoke.

'That's right,' Marlowe grinned. 'If Voss is working for me, why would he kill Gates?'

Gabriel turned back to the technician.

'Update, now!'

The technician was already typing, frowning as he did so.

'He's right,' he said. 'This isn't live, it's a loop.'

'Damn right it's a loop,' Marlowe smiled. 'A loop just long enough to hide the fact that Ryan Gates isn't dead.'

He checked his watch.

'By now, he's probably somewhere up above us. Or maybe down below us. Who knows how this place works.'

'What, you told him to come in and help you?'

'Oh God no,' Marlowe replied. 'I told him to come in and pull as many wires as he could out of sockets until eventually something turned off.'

'The server?'

'No, that was Voss and a small, timed EMP device,' Marlowe smiled, pointing at the ceiling, still strobing red lights. '*That* was Gates.'

Gabriel looked as if he was about to puke.

'You control these people, Gabriel, but only while you can

pay them,' Marlowe continued. 'And your trust fund is collapsing by the second, and I really can't see Steele being happy when he learns what you've done. Trix?'

He didn't need to ask anything else, as Trix was already working on the station, tapping in code faster than Marlowe could physically see.

'Who was the fake Trix?' Marlowe asked, turning his attention back to Gabriel.

'The what?'

'The blonde woman you killed to make me believe Trix was dead.'

'Oh, that,' Gabriel shrugged. 'I think she was connected to the bitch in the wheelchair.'

Marlowe bit back the urge to shoot Gabriel Rizzo in the face for the dismissive way he spoke.

The blonde girl who sat at the table opposite Clarissa, who'd passed a message from her – she was the right size and build.

'Give me one good reason not to kill you now,' he hissed, as beside him, Voss held his gun ready to join in.

'The hit!' Gabriel said, as if grasping at straws right now. 'The one Steele put on you! I did it for him, I dealt with The Broker. I can sort it out! If I die, it stays on forever. The money's already in an account, and Steele's already washed his hands of it. The Broker will see it through, even if either, or both of us are dead. Only I can take the hit off you. Kill me and live your life looking over your shoulder.'

'You think I don't do that already?' Marlowe shook his head. 'Where's Bassett, or Cross, whatever you call him?'

'Gone,' the technician, still at his console, whispered. 'He's just called for an extraction outside.'

If Gabriel had expected this answer, he made a good job of faking his surprise.

‘He what?' Gabriel's voice cracked with disbelief. 'That wasn't the plan. He was supposed to ...’

'Stay?' Marlowe offered. 'Help you take over from Steele? From what it sounds like, he's already made his own deal.'

'All systems are locked down,' Trix called from the console. 'I've created a cascading encryption that'll take weeks to break – and that's assuming they have someone as good as me.'

She glanced up at the sheepish technician, a fierce grin on her face.

'Which they don't. Even their backups are useless now.'

Voss stepped forward, his weapon still trained on Gabriel.

'Cross killed Diana,' he said, his voice cold. 'Shot her in the middle of that meeting while everyone was distracted. I'm not letting him walk away from that.'

'Martin—’ Marlowe started, but Voss was already moving.

'Take care of Rizzo,' Voss called over his shoulder. 'Cross is mine. Men? Shoot any guard that moves.'

The moment's distraction was all Gabriel needed. He lunged for the emergency exit, shoulder-barging past two of Voss's men. The guards raised their weapons, but in the cramped control room, with systems sparking and alarms still blaring, they couldn't risk shooting.

'Trix?' Marlowe was already moving.

'Go!' She didn't look up from the console. 'I've got this. He won't get far, anyway, I've locked down most of the exits.'

Gabriel had a head start, but Marlowe knew the man was running on pure desperation now. Everything he'd built, every plan he'd made, was collapsing around him. Even his bargaining chip – control of the hit on Marlowe – felt hollow now.

Marlowe ran after him, into the tunnels that led deeper

into the mountain. Behind him, he could hear Trix coordinating with the guards, securing the facility. But his focus was ahead, where Gabriel's footsteps echoed off stone walls that had kept America's secrets for nearly a century.

And now would keep one more.

30

WASHINGTON'S FOREHEAD

MARLOWE FOLLOWED GABRIEL THROUGH THE NARROW maintenance tunnels that smelled of old metal and damp stone. Ahead, he heard the clang of boots on steel grating, then the grinding of ancient machinery. Unsure what this was, he emerged into a vast vertical shaft, dimly lit by emergency lights that cast everything in strange, blood-red shadows. A mining elevator, probably dating back to when they first carved it, was already rising, Gabriel visible through its rusted cage. Without hesitation, Marlowe leapt, catching the elevator's outer frame as it ascended. The metal was slick with decades of moisture, and his fingers burned as he pulled himself up.

Through the cage, he could see Gabriel's face twist in fury. He hadn't realised that Marlowe had made it onto the elevator and was staring upwards towards their destination. Marlowe usually believed he had a good sense of direction, but inside this cavernous bunker, even he had found himself twisted. He believed he had been heading southeast, which would bring him back underneath the President's monument. The elevator shaft gave credence to the fact that this had been some way for the carvers to get up there, but he wasn't sure. There was every chance he could find himself coming out on another path to the Black Hills or the Six Grandfathers, as it was known, maybe even in a car park.

Perhaps he was trying to cadge a ride on whatever was coming to pick up Bassett?

However, his thoughts didn't take long as the elevator ground to a halt with a shriek of metal. Gabriel kicked open the gate and disappeared into another dark tunnel while Marlowe hauled himself onto the landing and followed.

The passage twisted upwards, carved directly into the mountain's heart. These weren't maintenance tunnels; they were part of the original sculpting work, channels cut by the men who had shaped the president's faces almost a hundred years earlier.

The wind howled across Washington's granite brow as Marlowe emerged from the tunnel. Dusk was painting the Black Hills a deep red; the shadows stretching for miles.

Gabriel Rizzo stood at the edge, but there was nothing of the composed Vegas casino owner left in him. His suit had been torn in the escape, and his carefully styled hair was wild in the wind.

Marlowe moved carefully across the granite. The drop was thousands of feet, the tourist viewing area below empty in the evening light. One wrong step meant death.

'It's over, Gabriel.'

'Over?' Gabriel laughed now, a sound with no humour in it. 'This is never over.'

Marlowe stopped walking.

'I know for Steele, this wasn't about money or power,' he said. 'It was about proving what he could do that the High

Council couldn't, what Wintergreen couldn't, McKellan, Whitehall, what all of them couldn't. You? I'm guessing Steele threw you a lifeline, but like always, you couldn't help but to nibble at the hand that fed you.'

'He treated me like an employee,' Gabriel snarled. 'Me! He was a shitty little Arbitrator when he came to my casino! *My* casino! Not his!'

He raised a finger, pointing at Marlowe.

'And then you turned up and spoiled everything!'

'It doesn't have to end this way, Gabriel,' Marlowe offered. 'Help me take down Steele.'

'And then what? Are you going to let him go again?' Gabriel barked out a laugh. 'Are you going to let him walk away and try to kill you again and again? Be serious, Marlowe.'

He pulled something from his jacket, and Marlowe stepped back as he realised it was a detonator.

'The whole mountain's rigged,' Gabriel said. 'Old mining charges, left over from the original construction. One press, and Mount Rushmore becomes a pile of rubble, faces wiped from the side. How's that for market disruption?'

Marlowe wasn't sure if Gabriel was bluffing yet again. But he couldn't risk it. It was like the man to throw everything away on the roll of a dice. He'd seen Gabriel do the same in his casino, walking into the custom-built MMA ring in his underground club to fight all comers.

But never had Gabriel Rizzo expected to lose when he did so. Now, Marlowe could see genuine fear in his eyes.

'You'd die too.'

'Would I?' Gabriel's smile was terrible. 'After everything, you still don't understand. I'm Gabriel goddamned Rizzo! I grew up in blood and death, and the goddamned Grim

Reaper, complete with hood and scythe? He's my godfather!'

'You don't understand what you've done,' Marlowe said, advancing carefully across the granite. 'Steele's plan could have worked. Clean. Simple. But you had to make it personal.'

'Personal?' Gabriel's laugh echoed across the mountain. 'Of course it's personal! Steele thinks he can control the world with algorithms and market predictions. But actual power? Actual power is watching someone lose everything. Just like I did. Just like *you're* going to—'

He lunged suddenly; the detonator forgotten as he struck at Marlowe with lethal precision, yet another of the MMA moves Marlowe had seen when attending his father's memorial months earlier. Marlowe blocked, but Gabriel's next blow caught him in the ribs, Marlowe's CZ sliding from his hand, skittering across the granite head and sliding off into the abyss beneath.

Marlowe knew he had to keep his distance from Gabriel. The last time they'd fought, it'd been in a vault under the Gold Strike, and he'd almost lost. The only reason he hadn't was that Gabriel had been more interested in a burning vault at the time, one that seconds later exploded, burning his face and clothes, giving him the faint pink scar under the new beard.

For Marlowe, this was a lesson he needed to remember; *Gabriel Rizzo was a stone-cold threat.*

'Did you kill Kelly?' he asked.

'Kelly appeared as Bassett and started poking around early. Found our setup for the Formula One operation.'

'He was undercover.'

'MI6,' Gabriel spat. 'He discovered what we were building

here – the whole operation. Steele told me to wait, to let Durrant handle it, but I couldn't risk it. So I took care of him myself.'

'Made it look like a heart attack.'

'Clean. Professional.' Gabriel's face twisted with pride. 'Even found a way to use his death – letting people think he was Bassett. Another layer of confusion while we prepared. Steele didn't like that part – said it was messy, drew attention. But that's what he never understood about Vegas. Sometimes you need a little showmanship. And the prick *did* tell everyone he was Bassett, what could I do?'

Marlowe moved to pull his self-defence chain, but didn't get the chance. Once more, Gabriel closed in, grappling with Marlowe at the edge, each strike echoing off the stone face. Below, the last tourists of the day were leaving, unaware of the battle happening hundreds of feet above.

Gabriel fought with everything he had. He knew this was his last option and was throwing in MMA training, street brawling, moves that came from a place of desperation. Each time Marlowe thought he had an advantage, Gabriel countered. They were too evenly matched, and the granite was still slick with rain from earlier that day. Marlowe's foot slipped, and Gabriel pressed his advantage, driving him towards Washington's hairline, the edge, and the sudden drop behind him.

'I made you,' Gabriel growled, his hands locked around Marlowe's throat. 'Everything you have in Orchid, every opportunity, every contact, it came from me and my casino. I turned them to you. I made sure they followed you.'

Marlowe drove his head forward, catching Gabriel's nose with a wet crunch, painting both their faces crimson. As Gabriel screamed in pain, the grip loosened just enough for

Marlowe to twist, using a move he had learned not from MI6 or MI5, but from his days in the Royal Marines. Weirdly, he realised as he did it, that it was something Voss had taught him back when he'd first started.

Gabriel, overbalanced, stumbled back, but caught himself at the edge.

'That's the difference,' Marlowe said. 'You think everything's about you, and what you get from it. But sometimes—'

He didn't continue, and instead, swept Gabriel's legs from him. But instead of falling, Gabriel grabbed Marlowe's arm, pulling them both towards the edge. They teetered there, locked together, on Washington's forehead, the abyss waiting below.

'If I go,' Gabriel snarled, 'you're coming with me.'

'No,' Marlowe tried to free an elbow or knee to break Gabriel's grip, but had no luck. Gabriel clenched all the harder - And that is when Marlowe realised that what Gabriel had a hold on was on his self-defence bracelet.

'You don't survive,' Marlowe grimaced as he reached down painfully with his free arm, unsnapping the dragon-headed clasp. 'Not this time.'

Gabriel's eyes widened as the metre-long length of steel chain unwound from Marlowe's hand, the friction tearing at Marlowe's wrist, opening up vicious welts, and tearing skin. But whatever Marlowe had, Gabriel Rizzo had worse.

His eyes widened, stunned, as he fell. But even then, he didn't scream. His eyes stayed locked on Marlowe's, that same cold intelligence burning, until he fell out of sight.

The detonator lay forgotten on the stone.

Crawling over to it, Marlowe picked it up, laughed as he realised it was nothing more than a plastic grip, a last bluff by a desperate man, and then threw it out into the void. Whatever Gabriel's final plan had been, it would stay buried in the mountain with him.

The sun hadn't set and was still over the horizon, catching the granite faces in the evening light. Somewhere below, a tour guide was probably telling the last visitors of the day about the mountain's secrets, but they'd never know about this one, the one that happened right above their heads. Gabriel Rizzo was gone, but somewhere out there St John Steele was still alive, and the hit? Well, the hit would stay on Marlowe's head until he could find another way of stopping it.

The wind whipped around Marlowe as he stared down at where Gabriel had fallen.

Then slowly, carefully, he began making his way back inside, back to the rickety mining elevator and the bunker.

VOSS CAUGHT UP WITH BASSETT NEAR ONE OF THE maintenance exits, a narrow tunnel that emerged onto the mountain's eastern face. Wind howled through the opening, carrying the smell of pine and rain, while Bassett stood silhouetted against the grey sky, phone in hand, still trying to contact Steele.

'Come on!' he cried into the phone. 'Pick up, you bastard!'

Voss levelled his SIG, arms steady.

'That's far enough.'

Bassett turned slowly. Nothing in his stance suggested surprise or fear, just the calm assessment of a trained operative. His eyes flicked to the gun, measuring distance, calculating odds.

'Colonel Voss. I wondered if you'd follow. If it means anything, I spared you last night because I respected you.'

'You still killed Diana Durrant.'

'Business,' Bassett replied with a shrug. 'Nothing personal.'

The attack came before the last word finished, a diagonal sprint from Bassett that ate up the space between them in less than a second. Bassett's left hand knocked the SIG up and away while his right drove straight for Voss's throat. It was standard CIA close-quarters technique, effective against most opponents.

But Voss had trained men like Bassett.

He stepped inside Bassett's strike, using Bassett's own momentum to unbalance him, finishing with an elbow strike to the neck – or where the man's neck would have been if Bassett hadn't continued the move further yet. His counter-strike caught Voss in the floating ribs; precise, clinical. The kind of hit that came from thousands of hours of practice.

The SIG clattered somewhere in the approaching evening's gloom. Didn't matter, though, as hands were just as lethal.

Bassett was fast – seriously fast and fought mathematically, each move exact, calculated, building on the last. Three strikes came in rapid succession: throat, solar plexus, knee. Voss blocked two, caught the third hard enough to numb his leg. He countered with an old Royal Marines combination – nothing fancy, just brutal efficiency designed to incapacitate.

They circled one another, trading blows, blocks and parries in the narrow space, the hard stone walls adding their own damage. Bassett's CIA training showed in every move: modern, advanced, lethal. But Voss had spent decades teaching men how to kill, and stay alive, in very unpleasant conditions. If Voss had an edge, that was it - Experience, especially in unexpected situations, counted.

Blood began to make the stone slick. Some his, some Bassett's. *Hard to tell in the dim light.*

'You know what your problem is?' Bassett's breath was measured. 'You're still playing soldier. Following a code that doesn't exist anymore.'

Voss drove a knee up into Bassett's liver. It wasn't precise, nor clinical – just raw fighting that produced instant sharp pain and impaired breathing. The strike gave him time to draw a surgically sharp Fairbairn-Sykes Commando Dagger, third pattern from a leg sheath; jet-black and lethal.

'Better than being a turncoat,' he said, slashing with it as Bassett moved back. 'How many sides are you playing?'

The fight moved closer to the exit. Below, the mountain dropped away into nothing, and Voss saw the SIG laying three feet away, near the edge.

Bassett saw it too.

They moved together; Bassett diving for the weapon, Voss tackling him mid-stride. The impact drove them both onto the stone. Bassett's hand closed around the SIG, but Voss stabbed Bassett's wrist with the Fairbairn-Sykes - once, twice.

Blood spurted and the gun spun free.

Both men lunged for the pistol again.

Both locked a hand around the weapon.

'This is for Diana,' Voss said.

The SIG barked once; the sound echoing off stone walls.

Both men stiffened.

Voss felt the warmth spreading across his chest, realising as the pain hit, that the round had hit him, not his enemy.

Bassett, seeing this, smiled.

'Sorry, Brit,' he croaked. 'You get to join your boss.'

'Least ... I took you with me,' Voss managed, and wincing as the adrenaline faded and the pain began, Bassett stared down at his own chest, where jutting out of his side was the Fairbairn-Sykes blade.

'Well played,' he whispered, raising the SIG up at Voss to finish the job, but Voss, expecting this grabbed Bassett close, and threw himself backwards. They hit the edge of the drop together, momentum carrying them into empty air, Bassett scrabbling for anything to stop this, but failing as he did so.

Voss's last thought, as the mountain rushed past, was that *at least he'd died following his code.*

And then, like with Gabriel Rizzo's own death on the top of the mountain beside them, there was nothing but silence.

IT TOOK MARLOWE A WHILE TO GET BACK DOWN THE ELEVATOR shaft.

The elevator itself seemed to have burned out from its one trip upwards, most likely not looked after in the intervening years since the bunker had closed. Marlowe eventually had to climb down a rickety ladder that had been embedded into the rock itself.

He no longer had his weapon, but he needn't have worried; when he arrived back in the control room, he saw that all of Gabriel Rizzo's men had been rounded up and disarmed by Voss' crew. They now sat dejectedly on the floor, hands on their heads. One of them, a man he recognised from the casino, looked behind Marlowe to see if he was alone, and upon realising he was, simply raised his eyebrows in silent question.

Marlowe nodded.

'He took the quick way down,' he muttered.

The guard slumped back, looking at the others. Voss's men, however, didn't seem as happy as they might have been. Marlowe glanced over at Trix, who at this point was standing beside the monitor banks, talking to Ryan Gates.

As he saw him approach, Gates shook his head.

'Voss killed Bassett,' he said. 'We just heard it over the radio. But in the process ...'

He didn't need to say the rest. Marlowe knew.

'He died as a soldier,' Gates continued. 'It's what he would have wanted.'

'No,' Marlowe snapped, unable to stop himself. 'What he wanted was money to keep his family safe. A million dollars. That's not going to happen anymore, is it?'

He forced himself to stop. He knew he was acting out in anger, but he couldn't help himself. *How much of this had been because of his own errors? How many deaths had been because he hadn't realised he was being played?*

'We can make it right,' Trix said. 'I've locked down their entire network. Even if Steele has backups, he won't be able to implement them without triggering every financial regulator in the world. But, as they originated here, we have a little time.'

She looked at the technician and smiled.

'Were you there when Durrant signed over the company?'

The technician shook his head.

'Was Voss?'

This time, the technician nodded.

'It was before the event at the casino,' he said. 'I was already here, setting up, but I was getting updates from the team. I don't think Durrant realised what was happening; I think she thought Steele was making a play to get her more money, but it was Rizzo making sure digitally the company belonged to him.'

'Did she have anybody else?' Trix asked. 'Husband? Children?'

'No, she was a loner.'

'Who would have gained the company if she died?' Marlowe asked.

'The board, most likely. But we know Steele had shell accounts that were syphoning power. So maybe it's Steele.'

Marlowe looked back at Trix.

'Find a way to take the money that Rizzo stole before Steele can get hold of it,' he instructed. 'Place it into a trust fund. Find everybody he hurt, or caused pain to, and give them it.'

He turned back to the technician.

'The only reason you live now is because I want you to spend your life finding every single person who Gabriel Rizzo screwed over and making sure that their families are covered. You understand?'

The technician nodded nervously, and Marlowe leant closer.

'If you don't, I will find you,' he finished. 'And my friend here, as you've seen, is very good with a computer. She'll destroy your life far more than I ever could.'

'You don't need to worry,' the technician said. 'I worked for Diana for five years, and I didn't want this to happen. I sure as hell didn't want that man to take the company. I'll do what's right.'

Trix nodded.

'You'd better,' she said. 'I want to see money taken from these accounts and passed to the people who need it.'

Marlowe looked off in a thousand-yard stare.

'And I want Voss's family to receive a million dollars,' he said. 'Tell them it's a life insurance policy made good, or a bonus. Because as God is my witness—'

And as if God himself was listening, the room shook.

Marlowe glanced in horror at Trix.

'Earthquake?'

They quickly realised it wasn't, as seconds after they felt the first rumble, they heard the noises. Trix ran to the console bank, flicking on switches, and on the screens they saw armed troops storming the base.

Finally, Mount Rushmore was being liberated.

Apparently, the senators who had spent the money allowing Steele to live there had decided that perhaps this was becoming a little too hot to touch. Or maybe Steele himself had given the base up. Either way, as the armed soldiers stormed into the control centre, screaming out to *put their weapons down*, rifles up, aiming them at Voss's men, the technician, Gates, Trix, and Marlowe – holding his own unarmed hands up – he knew that this was either going to go incredibly well or incredibly badly.

The first soldier, in full tactical gear, prodded Marlowe backwards with his rifle.

'On your knees,' he demanded. 'Who's in charge?'

'You'll find him at the base of the mountain,' Marlowe said, complying with the order. 'He had an accident.'

'Shut your mouth, terrorist,' the soldier barked. 'Yeah, we know who you are, and what you did to Vegas.'

And Marlowe suddenly realised this wasn't the cavalry, after all.

This wasn't the end ... by a long shot.

EPILOGUE

As Marlowe flexed his wrists, feeling the tightness of the surrounding cuffs, he sat forward on his chair, elbows on the table in front of him. He couldn't move much further if he'd tried, as the cuffs themselves were connected via a second pair to a metal bar that had been welded into the middle of the equally metal table. The moment he'd been arrested, or rather extracted – did the CIA even arrest? – Marlowe and Trix had been kept from each other.

It was standard practice, if he was being honest, to stop the suspects from being able to talk to each other and create a story that matched. But if Marlowe was *also* being honest, he knew that this was pretty much because someone in the CIA was pissed at what Marlowe had done, and they wanted him to suffer a little. The black site they were now in had been an hour's drive, give or take, from Mount Rushmore. Marlowe, with a bag over his head, had tried to listen to the surrounding noises, but the agents who had been tasked with bringing him in were clever enough not to speak, and the windows of the vehicle gave it an almost double-glazed, airtight, soundproofed journey.

There was a point half an hour in where it felt like the road had been forgotten and that they'd gone off onto some side tracks, but that had stopped shortly afterwards.

A base perhaps?

Maybe.

A warehouse built in the middle of nowhere with only a dusty gravel track to take him there?

More likely.

From there, he'd been roughly pulled out of the car, been forced down a variety of twisting left-and-right turns – likely to disorientate him – and dumped in this interrogation room.

It could have been worse, Marlowe thought to himself. The last time he'd been in such a situation, it had been a police interview room; he'd been given coffees, and the police had been friendlier. The time before that, however, he'd been stuck in a dog cage and forced to listen to screaming babies and barking dog sound effects while being soaked with a fire hose.

This, compared to that, was a vacation.

After a while, the door opened, and Marlowe looked up to see an unfamiliar man walk into the room. He didn't know why, but he almost expected to see Sacha Bordeaux walk in, her face arrogant and superior, as she mocked him for failing in whatever he was doing.

There was, of course, every chance she *was* here. Perhaps she was talking to Trix.

Marlowe hoped Trix was okay. He'd been trained for this. She hadn't.

The man sat opposite Marlowe, opening up a Folio iPad.

He was in his fifties, with slim, horn-rimmed glasses over a chiselled, shaven jaw.

'Marlowe,' he said. 'Thomas, ex-MI5, ex-Royal Marines Commandos, High Council member of Orchid ...'

'Look,' Marlowe muttered, 'I'm more than happy to bypass all this. You know who I am. That's great.'

The horn-rimmed man looked up at Marlowe in surprise, almost as if he hadn't expected Marlowe to want to jump to the more important part.

'Do you know why you're here?'

'Because I threw someone off the top of Mount Rushmore?'

'You were found on government property.'

Marlowe nodded.

'I was,' he admitted. 'I can't deny that.'

Horn-rimmed glasses swiped on the iPad.

'You're accused of causing terrorist attacks *in* the aforementioned government property. And on a national monument of historical importance.'

Marlowe shook his head.

'I wasn't the one causing the terrorist attacks,' he muttered. 'That, I think you'll find, was a man named Gabriel Rizzo.'

'And where is Mister Rizzo now?'

'You tell me,' Marlowe gave a smile. 'Last I saw, he was falling off the forehead of George Washington.'

There was a long, awkward moment of quiet at this statement. Marlowe knew that the horn-rimmed glasses agent was aware of this, and for the moment, he was happy to leave that as an uncomfortable point between them.

'Where's my friend?' he asked.

'Trixibelle Preston?' Horn-rimmed looked up. 'She's talking to another agent in a different room.'

'Fine,' Marlowe said coldly. 'I want my lawyer.'

'You don't get lawyers here, and you know that,' Horn-rimmed replied.

'Then I want to talk to your superiors,' Marlowe leant forward again, jangling his cuffs. 'I took down a terrorist organisation today and you bloody well know it. The only reason I'm here is because one of your higher-ups – redhead, likes fake names from comics – is being a dick and trying to give me some kind of object lesson in following the rules, and if I'm being honest, I'd much rather get out of here.'

Horn-rimmed said nothing, simply scrolling through some pages again.

'There's many people out there who want to kill you, Mister Marlowe,' he said. 'You have a very large hit on your head.'

'Ah, so I'm definitely with the CIA,' Marlowe tried to lean back but found that the chains held him in a middle ground, unable to fully relax.

'What do you mean?'

'I mean you're telling me stuff I already know,' Marlowe grinned. 'You're so far behind the pack, we're literally lapping you.'

Horn-rimmed didn't take the bait.

'We'd like you to work for us, Mister Marlowe,' he said simply, turning the iPad to show there was a document on it. 'If you sign here, we'll look after you – more than Wintergreen and MI5, or even McKellan and MI6 ever did.'

'Wait, is this what this is?' Marlowe raised his eyebrows in surprise. 'You're literally trying to *turn* me?'

Marlowe wasn't sure, but he thought Horn-rimmed seemed acutely embarrassed by this.

'I follow my orders,' he said. 'If it was up to me, I'd have you dumped in a black site so far away from light that you'd think you were a mole man.'

Marlowe considered the comment.

'I bet you would,' he replied. 'But let me guess, somebody somewhere likes me.'

He pushed the iPad away as far as he could with his chained hands.

'You don't get me,' he said, 'and I'm pretty much guessing that Trix will have said the same. I've worked with you in the past and I've seen what tricks you guys do. You've got nothing on me. If anything, I've helped you enough for at least a "get out of jail free" card here, so get on with it. I'm tired, I hurt, and I'm now bored.'

Horn-rimmed sighed audibly, looking up at a camera in the room's corner.

'You called it,' he said as he rose, closed the folio, and without another word to Marlowe, left the interrogation room.

Marlowe chuckled. *They had nothing on him.* If anything, they'd probably been pressured by someone higher to "get the Brit out of the country", knowing that he'd caused a small affray on Mount Rushmore, but in the process had probably saved a lot of American billionaires some money. Added to that, there were a lot of dead people in Vegas, and Marlowe had now managed to answer the question of who had likely funded the senators and governors who were now calling out, demanding answers.

Marlowe sat on his own, wondering how long they'd leave him this time, but it was only a matter of minutes before the door opened again and a familiar-looking woman walked in.

Sasha Bordeaux was in her mid-to-late thirties, red hair in an overgrown bob style and a charcoal suit over a crisp, white shirt. She sat facing Marlowe, pulled out a handcuff key and tossed it across, allowing him to uncuff himself.

'Last time I saw you, you were nasty to me,' she said, and Marlowe could sense the mocking hurt in her voice.

'The last time I saw you,' Marlowe replied calmly, 'you were trying to take a device and turn it to evil.'

'Every device the CIA takes turns it to evil,' Sasha grinned. 'I thought you were aware of that, Tom.'

She shook her head as Marlowe rubbed at his wrists, bringing life back into them.

'So, what do we do with you? It sounds like you don't want to join us and you don't do well when you go against us,' she waved around the room. 'I mean, how often do you want this place to turn up again in your future?'

Marlowe laughed.

'The only reason you have me here, Sasha,' he said, 'is because I allowed it.'

He nodded at the door.

'Who was the guy?'

'Just an analyst. I wanted somebody who had no idea who you were,' Sasha said. 'You'd be surprised how many people here think you're a goddamn hero. Brad Haynes wants to bash in the door and bring you out. Says it's an absolute crime that we've got you here. For once, I agree with him.'

Marlowe grinned.

'Trix?'

'She's with him. They're having a coffee in the cafe down the street.'

Marlowe raised an eyebrow.

'Okay, so it's not exactly a cafe down the street, but there is a cafe on site, and they're there.' Sasha shrugged, holding her hands up in an apologetic gesture. 'I had to try.'

'Ryan Gates?'

'Taken back to Vegas, allowed to continue with his life. We're aware of his actions, and we're grateful for his help.'

'Clarissa?'

'Rebuilding.' It was one word, simple but bleak, explaining the loss Clarissa had suffered in three syllables.

'So, what's the situation?' Marlowe asked, relaxing back into his chair for the first time since he'd arrived.

Sasha mimicked him, leaning back as she observed the bearded man in front of her.

'Gabriel Rizzo is dead, and whatever he was planning is over,' she said. 'From what we can work out, it looks like he'd decided that he didn't want to work for St John Steele, which seems to be more common than you'd think, and had decided his pet millionaires would be the ones to take over Orchid. He'd used connections he had in the CIA to contact and then turn Evan Cross, who you know as Lawrence Bassett.'

Marlowe nodded.

'I'm guessing his plan was to help Rizzo take the money Steele thought he was getting, these hundreds of millions from nineties black ops.'

'It wouldn't have worked,' Sasha nodded. 'There's no money to take. We funnelled it away years ago, back when Bush was in charge. And I'm talking junior, not the competent one.'

Marlowe nodded. He'd guessed as much.

'Steele?'

'Still out there somewhere,' Sasha cricked her neck, stretching her shoulder muscles, the simple act of which felt so sensual, Marlowe had to look away. She was a stunning woman, and Marlowe more than once had had *thoughts* about her. He'd even believed once, in Vegas, that she'd wanted to sleep with him.

She hadn't.

'We'll send you home,' Sasha continued, smiling as she watched Marlowe.

She knew damn well what she was doing, a cat playing with her food.

'I can find my own way home.' Marlowe shook his head. 'All I need is my go-bag.'

'I thought you had that?'

'No, that was my backup go-bag,' Marlowe smiled. 'The bare essentials, hidden in case. I mean the holdall Gabriel took from my hotel before it blew up, and that I'm guessing you found in Rushmore?'

'The bag full of money, credit cards, and a couple of passports?' Sasha smiled. 'Yeah, we brought it with us. We can provide you with better ones, though. And believe me, we *know* we can. We've looked over the ones you had thoroughly.'

'I'd like the ones I have.'

'As you wish,' Sasha's smile didn't waver. 'Be aware though, that we've catalogued every single one of them. We'll be watching you, no matter what you do.'

'I'm fine with that,' Marlowe grinned. 'It's always nice to know that my favourite people are watching, keeping an eye on me.'

Sasha couldn't help herself. She actually laughed at this.

'You know, Marlowe, if you'd have come to me at the start, this would have been a lot easier.'

'You know, Sasha, if you hadn't played super spy in Germany, this would have been a lot quicker.'

There was a moment of mutual silence and then Sasha rose from the chair.

'We've got a car waiting,' she said. 'It'll drive you wherever you want, or if you prefer, you can tell the driver to take the day off and you can take it for yourself. I don't care where you go or what you do, but your time in America is over.'

'Are you banning me?'

'Of course not,' Sasha smiled. 'How else would I have such fun adventures with you if you weren't here? No, what I mean is that the man you're looking for isn't here, and I think you're going to need to go home to find him.'

She rapped on the door, and as it opened, she looked back.

'Fly home domestic,' she said. 'No CIA planes for you, you bad boy.'

The agent who'd opened the door flushed, coming into the conversation late, but Marlowe just waved him off. The agent, however, passed across a black duffel bag. Marlowe checked it quickly, nodded, and followed Sasha out of the room.

In the time between leaving and gaining the bag, however, Sasha had disappeared.

Marlowe grinned.

No change there, then.

MARLOWE HAD BEEN ALLOWED OUT OF THE BUILDING, AND pointed to where the cafe-stroke-mess was on the base, and in there he found Trix and Brad, already arguing over some sporting event – or, rather, which was the better version. Marlowe didn't really want to give it oxygen, and so he grabbed a flat white, allowed it to eventually end, and then spent a pleasant hour catching up with Brad. Ever the gossip, Brad explained several senators had lost their seats over the "Rushmore Debacle" as they called it, and that the two bodies found at the base were still unknown.

Marlowe had reacted to this, wondering if Bassett, or Cross as he was rightly known was still alive, but Brad closed down the comment, pointing out it was only two, because Cross's body had been spirited away – too many questions for committees to ask if he was found.

Eventually, Marlowe and Trix walked from the cafe to the car Marlowe had been promised; he guessed it would be tracked somehow, but that was fine. He only intended to use it to get to Rapid City, and then he'd leave it, keys in the ignition, in a back road, and the CIA could have fun tracking whoever was next to drive it.

Brad promised to visit, grumbled as a text from Sasha arrived, telling him to get back to work, and Marlowe and Trix climbed into the car. As they did so, Marlowe closing the driver's side door, he leant back against the chair, holdall now on his lap.

'Okay,' Trix said, 'how exactly are we getting out of here? You know they've logged bloody everything in there, so we're under a microscope.'

Marlowe opened up the holdall and, pulling out his Fairbairn-Sykes blade, he cut at the side's interior.

'I know they would have checked through this,' he

replied. 'Every ID we've got in here is absolutely burned and they've probably checked the numbers of all the dollar bills we have, making sure that if any turn up, they'll know exactly where we've been. I can't blame them, I would have done the same thing.'

Trix noticed Marlowe wasn't cutting up the duffel bag at all. Instead, he was picking at the stitching along one of the seams. Slowly, he pulled aside enough material to reach into the skin of the duffel, pulling out a roll of hundred-dollar bills, an American Express Platinum credit card, and two passports.

He smiled, passing Trix one of them.

'Helen Bonneville's best,' he said. 'Secured them in here the day I got them. Always knew there'd be a point I'd probably need one.'

Trix took the passport, checking it, and then frowned as she looked back at Marlowe.

'I get you had a passport, cash, and a credit card ready,' she said, 'but why in God's name do you have mine as well?'

Marlowe looked up at Trix and shrugged.

'Because you're my partner,' he replied. 'Of course I'm going to have your passport. We're a team, right?'

Trix smiled, leant forward, and kissed him on the cheek.

'You know, I always knew you'd come and find me,' she said. 'You have that Don Quixote white knight thing going for you. It's actually quite sexy.'

Marlowe didn't quite know what to say to that, and surprisingly, actually reddened.

Trix, seeing this, laughed.

'So can I call you *daddy* yet?' she asked, mischievously.

Marlowe groaned and leant back against the chair.

It was going to be a very long journey to Rapid City.

In a Hong Kong hotel, St John Steele leant back on his chair, staring at the message that had been sent through a secure forum. Once more, Tom Marlowe had pretty much shit over everything.

He could have shouted, thrown things, found an underling and punched or even shot them, but St John Steele wasn't that kind of man. In a way, he'd almost expected this from Marlowe. The man was, after all, trained by the best, and from the looks of things, eight trusted one-percenters, including Diana Durrant herself, had been killed during Gabriel Rizzo's idiotic play for power, and the Mount Rushmore base, a location he'd had plans for, was now gone, the senators he'd made agreements with now distancing themselves before the pitchforks came for them.

Bugger.

Steele chuckled as he considered this, looking down at his laptop and the list of donors to his new organisation. To the side, written on a notepad was a list of people who had disagreed, or who had said they didn't want to be involved, or who had wanted more. It hadn't been a coincidence that *these* people had been the ones that Steele had sent to Gabriel Rizzo. In a way, Rizzo had done exactly what Steele wanted; he'd thrown one of his many plans under the bus, that was true, but his new Orchid had more than that. He'd realised the money in Operation Quicksilver was long gone very early on, but knew that the *story* of the money, the legend of hundreds of millions, in untraceable funds with sexy sounding algorithms controlling the world would be too tasty for most financiers to ignore. And while Evan Cross – now dead, rest his soul – had been there on behalf of Rizzo, giving him twenty percent of every company that he'd been able to gain the information of, with Rizzo's death, it continued on to Steele, through a few small shell companies created in the last month. When the authorities looked, all they would see was the paperwork in Gabriel Rizzo's name.

Steele laughed. *Maybe he should double the bounty on Marlowe.* No, if he did that, people might take it more seriously. Marlowe might actually be killed. He knew the tech girl, Preston would be trying to recover money for the victims, but she could just deal with the fact he was immensely superior here, and live with the loss. And currently, Thomas Marlowe was proving far more beneficial to St John Steele alive.

He picked up the phone, making a call.

'It's me,' he said. 'Pass the word. The New World Order is about to begin, and it's time to settle the scores.'

The message passed, Steele typed a similar message into the forum, sat back and smiled. It felt weird, but in less than a month, Thomas Marlowe would become one of St John Steele's closest assets. He just didn't know it.

Steele couldn't wait to tell him, but more than that, he couldn't wait to see Marlowe's face when he did.

'Welcome back to London, Tom,' he said, almost to himself. 'You won't be leaving there for a while, now. But don't worry, I'll be over to visit you real soon. I'm bring my friends... and oh, what a *game* we're going to play.'

Want the next Tom Marlowe Thriller? CLICK HERE on digital, or turn the page...

Tom Marlowe will return in his next thriller

SHADOW THREAT

Order Now at Amazon:

mybook.to/shadowthreat

Released 16th June, 2025

Gain up-to-the-moment information on the release by signing up to the Jack Gatland VIP Reader's Club!

Join at http://bit.ly/jackgatlandVIP

ACKNOWLEDGEMENTS

When you write books, you find that there are a ton of people out there who help you, and so I wanted to say thanks.

There are people I need to thank, and they know who they are, including my brother Chris Lee, Jacqueline Beard MBE, who has copyedited all my books since the very beginning, editor Sian Phillips and weapon specialist Eben Atwater, all of whom have made my books way better than they have every right to be, and my late father-in-law, Alan Farrow, who was an early supporter of these before he passed too soon - and he liked Clive Cussler books, so I had to be doing something right.

Also, I couldn't have done this without my growing army of ARC and beta readers, who not only show me where I falter, but also raise awareness of me in the social media world, ensuring that other people learn of my books.

But mainly, I tip my hat and thank you. *The reader.* Who once took a chance on an unknown author in a pile of Kindle books, and thought you'd give them a go, and who has carried on this far with them, as well as the spin off books I now release.

I write these books for you. And with luck, I'll keep on writing them for a very long time.

Jack Gatland / Tony Lee,
London, January 2025

ABOUT THE AUTHOR

Jack Gatland is the pen name of *#1 New York Times Bestselling Author* Tony Lee, who has been writing in all media for thirty-five years, including comics, graphic novels, middle grade books, audio drama, TV and film for *DC Comics, Marvel, BBC, ITV, Random House, Penguin USA, Hachette* and a ton of other publishers and broadcasters.

These have included licenses such as ***Doctor Who, Spider Man, X-Men, Star Trek, Battlestar Galactica, MacGyver,*** BBC's ***Doctors, Wallace and Gromit*** and ***Shrek***, as well as work created with musicians such as ***Iron Maiden, Bruce Dickinson, Ozzy Osbourne, Joe Satriani*** and ***Megadeth.***

His recent novels include the urban fantasy comedy ***Twelve Tasks,*** and the *Playing Card War* series.

As Tony, he's toured the world talking to reluctant readers with his 'Change The Channel' school tours, and lectures on screenwriting and comic scripting for *Raindance* in London.

As Jack, he's written several book series now - a police procedural featuring *DI Declan Walsh and the officers of the Temple Inn Crime Unit*, a spinoff featuring "cop for criminals" *Ellie Reckless and her team,* a third espionage spinoff series featuring burnt MI5 agent *Tom Marlowe*, an action adventure series featuring conman-turned-treasure hunter *Damian Lucas*, a series of thriller books following ex-UKSP operative *Liam Harper* and a standalone novel set in a New York boardroom.

An introvert West Londoner by heart, he lives with his wife Tracy and dog Fosco, just outside London.

Feel free to follow Jack on all his social media by clicking on the links below. Over time these can be places where we can engage, discuss Declan, Ellie, Tom and others, and put the world to rights.

www.jackgatland.com
www.hoodemanmedia.com

Visit Jack's Reader's Group Page
(Mainly for fans to discuss his books):
https://www.facebook.com/groups/jackgatland

Subscribe to Jack's Readers List:
https://bit.ly/jackgatlandVIP

www.facebook.com/jackgatlandbooks
www.twitter.com/jackgatlandbook
ww.instagram.com/jackgatland

Want more books by Jack Gatland? Turn the page...

MEDIA

Printed in Great Britain
by Amazon

58505998R00223